AMBER EYES

by

Peter Karl

TELEMACHUS PRESS

Cover designed by DiDonato and Associates, Chicago, Illinois

Publishing Services by:
Telemachus Press, LLC
7652 Sawmill Road
Suite 304
Dublin, Ohio 43016
http://www.telemachuspress.com

Visit the author website:
http://www.AuthorPeterKarl.com

ISBN: 978-1-956867-71-8 (eBook)
ISBN: 978-1-956867-72-5 (Paperback)
ISBN: 978-1-956867-73-2 (Hard Cover)

Category: FIC050000 FICTION / Crime

Version 2023.08.05

This book is dedicated to Kathleen D. Cenicola.
Her encouraging words prompted me to continue writing.
Rest in Peace, Kathy.

The Foundation Fighting Blindness is the world's leading organization committed to finding treatments and cures for blinding retinal diseases. I pledge that 20% of the profits from "Amber Eyes" will go directly to the Foundation Fighting Blindness to further its mission. To learn more or to connect with the Foundation, visit FightingBlindness.org.

ACKNOWLEDGEMENTS

My daughters and family have been a source of pride and inspiration for me and I want to thank them for their encouragement and support throughout this writing process.

Special thanks to: Foundation Fighting Blindness.

David Beedy my business partner and dear friend for his unending support to keep me focused and on track both in the writing and audio production of Amber Eyes.

Marie Remhoff and Tom Parker for their constant monitoring and work to keep this manuscript focused.

Pharmaceutical engineer Gary Allmaier for his review and critiques of DNA analysis and the carbon dating processes depicted in this book.

Retired Cook County Circuit Court Judge Frank De Boni and Cook County State's Attorney Kevin De Boni for their support and guidance through the judicial, legal proceedings and investigative techniques used in the law enforcement process.

Deborah Shaw for her intellectual input in keeping the chapters focused and consistent.

Attorney Samuel Fifer for his constant input, discourse, support, and encouragement through the months of writing this manuscript.

Forensic Psychologist Doctor Bruce Chambers for providing insight into the criminal mind and why serial killers act the way they do.

Peter DiDonato and DiDonato Associates Incorporated for their design of the cover for "Bug Man."

AMBER EYES

CHAPTER 1

A mber colored eyes are very, very rare. They occur in approximately five percent of the world's population. Amber eyes are commonly called "cat eyes." This reptilian eye color occurs because the reflective light from the iris casts off a near translucent, golden color. Chances are if you have amber eyes you would be from Asia, Spain, South America, or South Africa. The Ryan O'Toole family tree started in Ireland.

Ryan O'Toole, the fifth's, great, great grandfather, who was born in 1875, had "cat eyes," so did his great grandfather, and his grandfather, and his father. Number Five was born prematurely and didn't open his eyes for weeks but when he did that atavistic trait had been passed down through five generations.

The O'Toole's migrated to America in the fall of 1910 from County Cork, in the South of Ireland. They lived in New York City for nine years barely surviving; jobs were scarce and low paying, particularly for Irish immigrants. Ryan O'Toole, the first's, oldest son Riley got involved with an Irish street gang and was ultimately murdered by a rival gang. No one understood the message or the warning that the murderer left at the scene of the crime; Riley's right thumb was severed to his wrist at the trapezium, trapezoid and scaphoid joints.

It became part of a message that would be left behind more than a hundred times by an O'Toole.

~~~~

The city of Chicago was destined to become an international hub for finance, culture, commerce, industry, education, technology, telecommunications, and transportation. It was incorporated as a city in 1837 after its population reached a mere 4,000. A few short years later, in 1848, Chicago's railroad system began to flourish and the city's first telegraph service was installed. Expansion was inevitable. It soon became the second most populated city in the United States which lasted for more than 150 years. Immigrants from around the world began to migrate to Chicago because it offered them opportunities that could make the American Dream...a reality. The city occupied 36 times the amount of space as New York City.

The Chicago Board of Trade developed the wheat grading standard coupled with the innovation of grain elevators; the way crops were sold was transformed, and this further attracted more people to the city and its embryonic, but exploding systems of commerce, transportation, and industry.

The Western Illinois Light Company was rapidly expanding its services to become one of the nation's leading energy providers in the early 1920s throughout the Midwest. The Chicago Electric Company was a subsidiary that offered lineman jobs as the company began to develop and increase its ability to provide electricity to the growing area of Chicago's downtown business district known as "The Loop."

Chicago soon became a major hub of transportation and industry, every railroad company passed through the city hauling every form of merchandise known to mankind from the developing auto industry to household goods to perishable foods. The railroad companies also offered transportation job opportunities from fixing tracks to conductors collecting tickets.

Meat packing and livestock plants in an area called the "Back of the Yards" became a major industry and offered hundreds of butchering jobs. Other cottage industries surrounding food also began to flourish, offering employment to the ever-increasing population of the city.

~ ~ ~ ~

Ryan O'Toole put his family and all of their meager belongings on a train and moved to Chicago after his application for a lineman's job was accepted, and he was deemed physically fit for the work. He arrived with his wife Maureen and their two remaining children Margaret and Ryan Jr. on June 29, 1919. It was the day after the Treaty of Versailles was signed officially ending World War I.

Soldiers, sailors, and marines were returning home from the great war. As Immigrants from around the world continued to flood into America; large numbers of blacks from the south traveled north; all looking for better lives for their families. The city of Chicago was growing faster than city planners had imagined.

The demand for housing was multiplying daily but homes continued to be in short supply. Tenement housing and row houses soon became overcrowded. Limited educational opportunities and cultural and social indifference forced people to stick together by race and/or nationality in order to survive in a competitive urban environment.

A new era known as the "Roaring Twenties" was on the horizon. Chicagoans wanted to make merry and enjoy their lives after the great war. Freedom was forged with a heavy price. It was time to celebrate and people were entering into a period of prosperity and changing social mores and norms. Fashions were also changing. Music was louder and more upbeat. Parties and Speakeasys were flourishing as alcohol flowed in unprecedented amounts.

The city of Chicago was thriving even though it was filled with death, violence, discrimination, segregation, and apathy from corrupt city politicians and ruthless gangsters. Police commanders and police officers, who were on the take, turned their heads at criminal acts.

The La Cosa Nostra prospered in every major city in America, but in Chicago the rise of Al Capone and his organized crime activities offered the O'Toole clan the golden opportunities to kill their unsuspecting victims without being discovered and the era known as prohibition provided them the cover to hide their kills for almost ten years. The murders were not even noticed until decades later because almost all police actions and law enforcement activity was devoted to stopping the illegal manufacturing, distribution, and the sale of alcohol. It was a time of murder, bootlegging, prostitution, gambling, and racketeering. Gangland killings certainly captured headlines. The term serial killer would not be conceived until 30 years later.

Prohibition lasted approximately 10 years. It survived challenges from the Anti-Saloon League, the Women's Christian Temperance Union and federal agents who did not trust local law enforcement to stop any organized criminal activity.

The Great Stock Market Crash of 1929 finally brought the good times to an end, but by then O'Toole and his son had killed nine people since they first arrived in the second city.

~~~~

Ryan O'Toole, the first, was forty-two and six-feet tall. His hair that had a slight red tinge sat on top of a square face, his nose had experienced a blow or two, his thick bushy eyebrows shielded his amber eyes that defied his Irish heritage. His shoulders were square and broad and powerful. His legs and arms were muscular. Climbing up and down telephone poles had that effect on one's body. His grip was strong and firm. Pulling and clipping miles of electrical wire produced that certainty on one's hands.

His anger, narcissism, sociopathic and psychopathic tendencies twisted his evil, dark soul, and memory, leaving him with absolutely no feelings for his victims. No empathy. No remorse. No second thoughts. He was the perfect serial killer at a time when nobody even knew what that specific criminal behavior was.

Ryan O'Toole's first kill was on September 20th, 1921. It was anything but pedantic. It was spur-of-the-moment. Hasty and sloppy and bloody, but mostly satisfying. He was working alone pulling wire while spiked into a telephone pole in an isolated wooded area on Chicago's Southside. The day's gray sky cast a gloomy sense of doom over his dark and perverted psyche that was challenging his increasing desire to take some strong cathartic action. When he noticed a lone walker with red curly hair, five-foot-ten inches tall, ambling casually down a secluded path so narrow it almost seemed not to exist, a rictus smile creased his lips and his heart began to race in anticipation, as if the devil was whispering into his ear, "It's time."

The walker matched the only description, an eyewitness to his son's murder gave to the police more than ten years before: The killer was a white man about five-ten, medium build with curly hair that sprouted out from under his cap.

Ryan O'Toole gripped the handle of his sharp utility knife that he used to trim wire as he greeted the 18-year-old with a big grin and a nervous stomach. The boy immediately became alarmed when he noticed those amber eyes that seemed to come alive with some sort of distorted expectancy of great gratification. The blade went into the boy's stomach with smooth precision. Its sharp edge was upright and when O'Toole lifted the victim off his feet, the knife continued to easily cut upwards. The boy's scared, unsuspecting, questioning eyes began to water from the sudden sharp pain, but within seconds they turned lifeless and everything went black. The grunt of agony was muffled by the gurgling effect of blood filling his mouth, gagging him into a silent abyss.

O'Toole looked around for witnesses that he knew were not there. He then dragged the body through a field of tall weeds and dumped it into a deep drainage ditch, 30 yards away from the road, but before he covered it with gravel, he crudely chopped off his first trophy; the victim's right thumb up to the wrist. He took off the boy's new boots and decided to cut off his left big toe and left ear. It became the distinctive new O'Toole family's signature of death.

~~~~

Vincent was one of five children in the Carey family. He was also the youngest. He was reported missing two days later, but the police showed very little interest in his disappearance, they just assumed the missing teenager probably moved into the heart of the city, looking for a job, a new life, and the American Dream.

Vincent Carey became just another name in a police blotter of wasted lives.

CHAPTER 2

P eter Michaels was sitting low in the driver's seat of his black Ford Edge trying to conceal his presence, waiting to meet with the leader of the deadly, notorious Renegade Disciples street gang when his phone vibrated.

"News Michaels." He said in almost a whisper, just peeking up over the windshield.

"Hey it's me. Where are you?" Detective Jack Warren asked.

Michaels smiled when he heard Warren's voice. They were neighbors, beer drinking buddies and great sources of information to each other. They got to know one another when they were investigating a mentally deranged revenge serial killer known as "The Bug Man," who used microorganisms to kill his victims. Michaels was also a target of the sick, unhinged killer multiple times.

Over the years Michaels developed sources in every city and state agency, he also cultivated some really bad people like Shamir Halstead, who had a rap sheet that spanned 30 years of prison time with nine pages of criminal charges ranging from murder to criminal sexual assault to shoplifting.

"I'm waiting for Shamir Halstead. He's got some great information for me," Michaels said in a low voice as if protecting himself from someone in the neighborhood listening to his conversation.

"Are you nuts? Are you in Englewood, you moron? You know Shamir is ruthless. He survived a shiv attack in Statesville that left him with eleven stab wounds and a patch over his left eye?"

"Yeah. Of course, I know that, and I know since he was paroled 18 months ago, he quickly regained control of his old gang, leaving four unfaithful renegade generals with eleven stab wounds each and no left eyes. He's not going to hurt me. He likes me," Michaels tried to reassure his friend.

Everyone who knew Michaels thought that he was absolutely out of his mind for meeting up with gangsters like Halstead at any time of the day or night. Two things intrigued him enough to take the risk and set up this clandestine meeting in Englewood, considered to be the most dangerous neighborhood in the city of Chicago.

On average five people a day are shot in the seventh police district. It was a bloody, deadly place to live. Residents hardly leave their stoops when sitting outside on warm summer nights looking for relief from the heat and stray bullets. Drive by shootings were a fact of daily life in this once proud community that was beaten down and stripped of its dignity by deadly, horrific, and vicious crimes.

"Halstead said he had irrefutable proof that Commander James Burger beats confessions out of the people his detectives arrest for violent crimes. Burger's ability to close cases that no one else could solve was staggering by any law enforcement standards." Michaels said and continued, "his conviction rate is the highest in the city, but then there were all the rumors that floated around courthouses, prison yards and in defense lawyers' offices for years about the beatings."

"Yeah, I don't trust that guy. He's not my kind of cop. His confessions are infamous," Warren offered with a grimace.

It was a story that Michaels had been working on for years, but it always eluded him because nobody had the courage to step forward with any form of proof until now.

"Did you ever hear anything about a Latino copper, they call "The Closer?" Michaels asked.

"Yeah, Garcia I think. A lot of rumors are starting to pop up in all three area headquarters about him. Why? What do you know about him?" Warren responded.

"Halstead also told me that he had a connection in a Latino street gang who had information on a detective who had an incredible clearance rate on the criminal investigations that involved Latino gangbangers. He said this detective Lorenzo Garcia was legendary in the Latino community. He threatens bad guys and their families with deportation. He was known as 'The Closer' both on the street and in the Pilsen police district for his tactics to obtain confessions for the last 15 years," Michaels offered.

"That sort of shit can affect a lot of old cases. There are some very nervous commanders and prosecutors. I think Internal Affairs was looking at him," Warren said.

"Jose is trying to convince some clients to talk to me, but they are reluctant to, because of the deportation issue."

Jose Aguilar, a defense attorney, was a source of Michaels for 20 years. He took on tough pro bono cases and he was very successful in numerous wrongful conviction cases. Aguilar first tipped Michaels off to "The Closer" seven months prior to the phone call from Shamir Halstead.

"Hey, I gotta run, some shit is starting to happen," Michaels said looking out his side window sliding down out of sight.

"You be careful, Peter. I don't want to be investigating any shooting you are involved in."

~~~~

A man with striking yellowish eyes was following a student who just left the Northeastern University cafeteria. The night was hot and humid, the air was heavy like a thick curtain of suffocating smog. The student's long sleeve tee-shirt was wet with sweat and his hair was curling up and out from under his Chicago Cubs baseball cap, perspiration trickled down his cheeks, his eyes were irritated. The moon was trying to peek out of the dark gray clouds that shrouded it, but it was a futile battle. The student turned down First street that miraculously still had huge elm trees that survived the destructive beetle attacks decades before. The elms that lined the street formed a perfect tunnel of natural beauty offering shade from the sun during hot summer days and pleasant breezes and peaceful solitude at night. It was an old upscale, affluent neighborhood on Chicago's Northside. On this particular evening, the century old trees cast sinister shadows that provided camouflage for the man with amber eyes, who was silently and quickly moving closer behind the student.

"Hey, sorry to bother you but I'm lost. Can you tell me how I get to Sheridan?"

The approaching killer asked in a pleading, non-threatening voice not to raise suspicion by his seeking help.

The five foot-nine, Good Samaritan student stopped and turned around, his squinting brown eyes searched for the person asking for his help but the man blended into the dark environment like a shadow until the moon finally revealed itself offering a sliver of light.

"Yes, go back one block and turn left. It's two streets north," he said innocently.

The Good Samaritan then cursed himself inwardly. There had been an increasing number of attacks on white men lately because of all the negative publicity of white supremacy on the news. Large cities were particularly hard hit. There was something about the man's eyes that filled the Samaritan with angst immediately. *Were they dead? Were they evil? Were they really yellowish?*

Ryan O'Toole, the fifth, stopped in his tracks momentarily, this man was much older than eighteen. He couldn't see the color of the man's eyes, but he noticed his graying full beard. The man did not fit the typical O'Toole profile. Number Five dropped the knife and it fell silently onto the grass. He nonchalantly placed his foot on top of it, not wanting to alarm the student as he reconsidered his attack.

"Okay, thanks. I just realized I turned on the wrong street. Thanks again. Sorry to bother you," O'Toole droned.

"No problem," the Good Samaritan said letting out a heavy sigh of relief, feeling that he just avoided something very ominous that was about to happen to him then he turned and continued his walk home.

O'Toole's change of heart was instantaneous. He had been seen and that unnerved him. So, he reached down, picked up the knife and with two quick steps, he lunged forward, grabbed the student by the forehead, and pulled his head back to expose his neck upwardly. The knife's blade was so sharp, the student never felt the swift slice from one ear to the other before any pain could register in his brain. His limp body fell silently down on the sidewalk, his lifeless eyes were wide open, expressing horror and disbelief. It was the tragic end to a fulfilling life of a successful cardiovascular surgeon.

A dog's barked interrupted the silence and O'Toole's train of thought. He looked up and noticed a couple turning the corner casually walking their golden retriever bending over to pick up its poop. He crudely sliced off the right thumb and left ear. He tried to unlace the victim's left shoe, but decided time was critical, and he could not take his third trophy, the left big toe, and escape was the only thing that mattered at that moment. He walked away at a natural pace and at an angle to cross the street silhouetting his body into the dark safety that the elm trees fulfilled.

Less than a minute later he heard the dog again, barking louder and more frequently, a malicious smile widened on his thin lips as he slithered into an all-night diner on Sheridan Road. He ordered a cup of black coffee and apple pie a la mode before he went to the restroom to wash the blood off his hands.

It was his seventh kill in five years. The 51-year-old still felt that same surge of excitement and satisfaction, but no remorse. He knew that his mentor, his father taught him well over the years and now he thought about, how he was going to eat the student's thumb. He looked into the mirror and noticed for the first time that he was starting to show his age. He ran his wet fingers through his short graying hair and leaned in closer to examine his eyes. A ghoulish smile inched into the corner of his lips and thoughts of his father pierced his memory. "Thank you, daddy," he whispered.

~~~~

Shamir Halstead set up the meeting near the most notorious heroin and crack cocaine drug corner in Englewood. One in every nine residents who lived here would become the victim of a violent crime. It was known for its high crime rate; 9,386 reported crimes occurred in a population of 25,000 people every year. FBI figures reveal that this district alone has a seven times higher violent crime rate than other cities in the entire country.

The intersection of 57th Street and Racine was tired, worn out from years of neglect, only twenty barely livable houses remained on the four streets that formed the intersection, and one corner included Moran Park. The amount of drugs sold there was mind boggling and rumored to be a thirty million dollar a year revenue machine for the Renegade Disciples' criminal enterprises. It didn't matter that selling drugs near a park automatically increased the criminal penalties, the renegades operated with impunity knowing the drug operation would never be shut down for more than 24 hours. All of the streetlights have been shot out for security reasons, not for the police but for the drug dealers protection.

The dealers know the police have infrared cameras whenever they took evidence pictures, but it didn't faze them one iota. They all wear white tee shirts, blue jeans, and red bandanas not to conceal their identities but to promote them. Every gangbanger looks the same. It's a defense attorney's perfect strategy to challenge the veracity of any description and it worked incredibly well because positive identifications were almost impossible to prove beyond a reasonable doubt at trial when everyone looked the same. If the corner was closed down by the police, the gang could have it up and running again before the arrested dealers were processed.

The only source of light on this overcast evening came from the moon that was being curtained by on and off again dark, slow moving threatening storm clouds. A secondary form of illumination came from the flashlights used by the dealers conducting their business as customer's came by car and foot to the pickup points. A drug transaction took less than three seconds.

There was an unwritten code amongst the dealers and their customers and rival gangs. The buyers/users would be safe and protected. No one interfered with a drug sale. No one bothered a customer driving up to the point of sale and away from it. If any unfortunate incident occurred to a buyer/user, the perpetrators were hunted down and killed within 24 hours.

Michaels was thinking *holy shit* after he witnessed about 40 transactions in just under 30 minutes before he saw Halstead's huge frame emerge from the eerie dark tunnel between two boarded up buildings. The clouds started to clear and the moon came to life along with a new southerly wind pushing the humidity higher, creating a heavy haze and the beginning of what looked like a thick fog. Beads of sweat glistened off of the big man's shaved head. His once muscular physique that was carved by hundreds of pushups and pullups a day and the use of free weights in the prison's rec yard was now the victim of age, steaks, fried chicken, barbequed ribs, lots of fries and lazy apathy. His breathing was labored and challenging. His tropical silk, light green shirt was opened down to his navel. Two 24 carat gold roped chains hung around his thick neck; one chain with a five inch circular medallion, infused with diamonds stuck to his dark shining skin like it was attached with glue, the other one was longer and swung freely around his neck. A smile creased his lips and exposed perfectly white straight teeth when he noticed Michaels. With the slight wave of his right hand, Halstead summoned the information seeker to come to him.

Michaels opened his car door but turned off the interior light as a precaution, that's when the night air was violated by the eruption of what seemed to be dozens of AK 47 rounds, changing the peaceful night of tree leaves wisping in the wind into the sounds of a battlefield filled with rapid gunfire, despair, and carnage. Michaels dove headfirst to the cover of his rear wheel just as bullets shattered his driver side window. He dialed 911 and when he heard the screeching of tires fleeing the scene he burst to the protection of a nearby green garbage dumpster and prayed the shooters would not be coming back.

CHAPTER 3

"We just took fire. I think Shamir is down and two of his lieutenants were also hit. I am not sure if they're dead but they are covered with blood. I called 911 and you. Shit man that was close." Michaels said in a shaky, rushed, nervous voice. He was sitting in a CFD ambulance with a blood pressure cup attached to his right arm as a sexy, hazel eyed, blonde EMT monitored his condition.

"You're 140 over 82, not too bad considering what you just went through," the EMT reported.

"What's your name?" Michaels asked as he stared into her deep hazel eyes and grinned from ear to ear.

"Christine. Just relax. You need to calm down. Flirt with me later," Christine suggested with a mischievous smile. She was five-seven, lithe but muscular. Her smile was disarming but flirtatious. She was used to having patients hit on her.

Warren rolled his eyes in disbelief. His friend just barely escaped death and was now flirting with a woman. "You're unfucking believable, you know that?" Warren said as he squeezed the bridge of his nose and shut his eyes. "Is patrol there yet? Are you okay?" Warren asked anxiously, thankful his friend survived the drive by shooting, unscathed other than maybe pissing his pants.

"Yeah, I'm fine. My car has a few bullet holes and some shot out windows," Michaels said glancing around as several patrol cars arrived at the scene. "I think I see Sergeant Brian Alexander. He's coming my way. You coming here?"

"I'm on the way. I'll be there in a few," Warren reassured.

Michaels was trying to collect his thoughts without erasing anything that would be significant to the police investigation and his own. His hands were still shaking as he greeted Sgt. Alexander, who shared a lot of information with Michaels a few years back when he worked undercover as a narc in the Organized Crime Unit.

Alexander had a commanding presence. He was six feet, three inches tall, an athletic build with perfectly squared shoulders that gave him an air of confidence. His hair was thick and graying at the temples, blending into the stubble of his neatly trimmed beard. His blue eyes were working, searching the crime scene as he walked up to Michaels. His smile was calming, but his look was uncompromising. He wasn't happy.

"What the fuck were you thinking about, hanging out in this shithole drug dealing neighborhood?" Alexander asked upset but relieved that his friend was still alive.

"I was working a source on a story that I have spent more than half a year on," Michaels tried to explain.

Alexander was shaking his head with that "you dumb shit" look on his face.

Crime Scene Investigators had already identified 45 shell casings, four dead bodies including Shamir Halstead, two of his lieutenants and an innocent 13-year-old girl, who was studying in the front room of her house sitting by a window. Six others were wounded and being treated for non-life-threatening gunshot wounds by fire department paramedics.

"We think there are more victims that were dealing drugs but they fled the area leaving a trail of blood. We'll try to track them down," Alexander offered, and then he said to himself *shit* after realizing that he already gave out too much information, knowing Michaels would use it in his news story.

"Yeah, there were at least 20 people around when the shooting began," Michaels said as detective Jack Warren arrived in his beat up, filthy, dented blue Crown Vic.

Their eyes greeted each other with a sigh of relief and a ghost of a smile appeared on both of their lips simultaneously.

"Did you see the shooters?" Warren asked.

"Not their faces...AK 47s for sure, sticking out of the tinted windows of a big black SUV. GMC I think...I couldn't see inside. Of course, I took cover when I sensed what was about to happen. They pulled up and then the shooting started and I dove for cover behind my rear tire," Michaels said as got off the EMT gurney and steadied himself. "It seemed to last longer than it really was but maybe thirty seconds max. Shamir was the main target in my opinion. He came out from between those two buildings," Michaels said as he pointed over to the abandoned three flats. "He was smiling when he beckoned me over. I don't think he was expecting any of this," Michaels reported.

"You know if you would have left one second earlier to meet him, you would be dead right now. You know that, right? What were you thinking?" Alexander inquired with a sigh of relief, then added. "Do you remember anything else?"

"When I looked up they were racing away and I ran over to those trees and that dumpster hoping that they wouldn't come back. That's all I remember now."

"You taking this over Jack?" Alexander asked knowing this was personal, and he had no doubt Warren would not stop until he found out who tried to kill his friend.

~~~~

Detective Tony Quagliaroli was the first homicide detective to arrive at the northside neighborhood crime scene. He wiped sweat off of his forehead with a folded white handkerchief. The summer storm clouds had past, leaving a thick blanket of humidity smothering the fully grown elm trees, suffocating the air. The body was covered with a blue tarp, moisture was collecting on its top, unmistakable runnels of blood were filtering down the sidewalk into the grass from under the tarp.

Crime Scene investigator Thomas Vander Aarde was kneeling over the body looking at the slash that almost severed the victim's head from his body. He was identified as Phillip Kaley, an up-and-coming surgeon at the University of Chicago Hospital. He was 39 years old. Vander Aarde only worked signature homicide investigations. He specialized in cases that involved victims that were mutilated in some way. He had forensic serial killer training with the FBI at Quantico.

Serial killers fascinated him. He often worked cases for three days without sleep. His six foot, two sinew frame was surrounded with 192 pounds of muscle. His thinning white hair confronted his 45 years. When you shook his hand you were drawn into his hypnotic light blue eyes and his infectious, warm smile. You also felt his gnarly fingers that were filled with broken knuckles from years of playing 16-inch softball on every field in Chicago that had a baseball diamond. He walked with a swagger but slightly bent forward. His abs were tight but defied the theory that a strong core helped prevent back pain, a constant reminder of a baseball career ending collision at home plate in his junior year at South Dakota State. His friends called him Vando. A moniker he was proud of and that made him smile...boyishly.

"Hey, Vando, whatta we got? Detective Tony Quagliaroli asked looking down at the CSI who was moving his flashlight from the neck wound to the victim's severed ear."

"Hey Quag, good to see you. Long time. My guess...serial killer. Right thumb severed to the wrist. Left ear cut off. Probably trophies of some sort. He peeled back the rest of the tarp. I bet there was something more." Vando explained.

"Whatta you mean? More?" Detective Quag asked. Almost everyone called Tony Quagliaroli...Quag because they had a hard time pronouncing his real name. Quag worked with Vando on a number of complicated cases. He appreciated and respected Vando's tenacity and his thoroughness.

"Well look at his left shoe. It appeared that the killer was trying to take it off but was probably scared off or rushed away because the Hayworths noticed someone moving away when they came upon the murder scene while walking their dog," Vando said pointing his mag-light's beam at the victim's left foot. "The shoe was slightly off his foot stopping at the heel."

"Yeah, that is a little odd." Quag agreed staring at the victim's left heel.

"The ME is on his way. We'll know a little more once he does his autopsy," Vando surmised.

"Here we go again. We're living in a sick world," Quag said.

"Yaa think," Vando said shaking his head, frowning.

~~~~

The Cook County Forest Preserve is the oldest forest preserve system in the United States. Civic leaders more than 100 years ago had the wisdom and vision to create these natural recreational areas for Chicago's growing population. There are 27 natural preserves in the county, 22 of them are in Chicago. They offer more than 69,000 acres of rare habitats; open spaces, unusual natural forests, woodlands, savannahs, prairies, wetlands, streams, and lakes.

In November of 1914, Cook County voters approved the forest preserve system and in 1916 the first lands were obtained and the park now known as Deer Grove became the first park in the system. By the time, Ryan O'Toole, the first, died in 1930, the county already owned and was developing 33,000 acres of park land.

Number One was in a fetal position on his hospital bed when he took his last breath in November. He was 55. Two packs a day of unfiltered, hand rolled cigarettes ate away at his throat and lungs and left his once muscular body shriveled, decimated, and shrunken to 87 pounds. It was a painful death. He was a respected member of the Irish community. His family lived in an area known as Canaryville near the Back of the Yards meat packing plants. Everyone knew him as a hard-working, dedicated man. Not a single person ever suspected that he was a cold-blooded killer, except his son.

Ryan II knew his father as his mentor and a killer. Son number two worked for the Cook County Forest Preserve as a laborer, and he knew every inch of the land that was going to be created into parks, but more importantly he knew what portions of that land would not be touched for perhaps decades if ever. He was present for three of his father's kills and helped bury the victims in an isolated area of the Deer Grove preserve. Ryan II also buried five of his first seven victims in the same secluded area.

The O'Tooles used a number of these nature parks as burial grounds for five generations. By 1950, Thirty bodies were decomposing just a hundred yards from where millions of people visited each year celebrating birthdays, weddings, and softball championships. Those celebrating were singing, drinking, dancing, and cooking hamburgers, totally unaware that perhaps someone they knew would never make it to their twenty-first year. They would never hear the merriment, the music and the laughter of life and sadly may never be discovered.

CHAPTER 4

Peter Michaels and Ron Magers were walking off the six o'clock news set after Michaels reported on his horrific near-death experience of being caught in the crossfire of the drive-by shooting. The police were now calling it, the beginnings of a drug turf war and that the murder of Shamir Halstead was intentional. They called the tragic death of an innocent 13-year-old girl, just another senseless victim of street violence in Englewood.

"Are you crazy, Peter? Why in the world would you agree to meet with Halstead in the middle of the night, and of all places, Englewood?" Magers asked with a look of exasperation.

"Look Mage, that's where he lived and he was going to give me a great lead to get to the bottom of the Commander Burger story. I have been working on that for more than a year and nobody wants to talk about it. He had good intel. Now, that son of bitch will get away with all those illegal confessions. What can I tell you?"

"Well, I am just glad you're alive. You can't be doing stuff like that man," Magers said in a reprimanding tone.

"Yeah. Yeah. I know," Michaels said half smiling, half grimacing when his phone vibrated. He looked at the caller ID and smiled when he saw Jack Warren's name and motioned to Magers *let me take this.*

"Hey what's up?" Michaels said. "Want to get some beers after the ten?"

"Listen, I am just giving you a heads up. We just discovered a massive burial site at the Edgebrook golf course on North Central." Warren informed.

Michaels smile instantly morphed into a look of concern. "How many bodies are we talking about here?"

"Four so far. We stopped the digging. This could be a major burial site. We have to do everything by hand so we don't disturb the area."

"How did It happen? What led to the discovery?"

"The park district started digging to build some bocce ball courts and all of a sudden these bones were turned over," Warren said.

An official bocce ball court is 91 feet long and 13 feet wide. The Preserve had been inundated with requests to form bocce ball leagues. The county commissioners viewed the idea as an instant big money maker. There were even thoughts of building some courts with winter enclosures to keep the leagues going all year around and the money coming in.

"The skeletons were discovered after the plow moved closer to the tree line behind the pro shop. Workers didn't notice the bones until a supervisor came out to make sure the tree root system was not disturbed damaging the trees. He saw a head just sitting on top of a mound of upended dirt and called us," Warren said. "The CSI guys are on their way here now. We have no idea how big this thing could be."

~~~~

Dr. Robert Crine had his magnifying optics down, studying the body of Phillip Kaley on his operating table. The corpse had not yet been washed. The ME often talked to the corpses he worked on. It helped him think. "What can you tell me young man? You are a fine specimen. What do we have here?" He murmured. Both carotid arteries were severed, death was almost instant. "He must have been strong. This cut was deep and straight across your neck. Hum...deep enough to cut through your fourth cervical disk that offered no resistance at all."

The splenius capitis and splenius cervicis, the strap-like muscles in the back of the neck that help you extend and rotate your head were the only things that kept the head attached to the body. Crine gently laid the skull back down and redirected his light to the left ear. The incision where the ear was removed was exact, clean, and precise. "It took a very, very sharp knife to do this. Or did you use a scalpel?" He asked the body and then thought *this must have been a trophy.*

Dr. Crine was fascinated by the missing right thumb. It was removed with surgical like accuracy through three joints. Not hacked. Not sawed. He was rotating the hand around in a shallow circle and concluded that the thumb and the ear were indeed trophies.

Then he noticed some blood on Kaley's elbow. His instincts immediately kicked in and told him to save the sample. If the blood types matched Kaley's it was nothing, but if it didn't, it may provide an unexpected clue. He held the swab up to the light and it hit him like a lightning bolt, he shuttered as if he had the chills and he said out loud, "Oh my God, I wonder if your killer is a cannibal, and eats his trophies."

~~~~

Ryan O'Toole, the second, was washing the blood and dirt off his hands. He was 31 years-old and strong. He worked as a laborer for the forest preserve and he was in charge of a work crew that cut down trees and leveled the earth in parks that were being created throughout Cook County. The county's 33,000 acres of land provided him plenty of opportunities to dispose of his victims and his father's. He just returned home from burying the twelfth body along the tree line of the Edgebrook golf course that was just completed. *Golf, what a waste of time, only rich, stupid, people play that game or sport or whatever the fuck it is,* he was thinking and getting himself angry.

"Oh, No. No." Juliana, his wife, screamed out from their bedroom.

He ran into the room, his amber eyes, wide open with anticipation of another letdown, his hands were shaking when he saw his wife laying on the floor. "What's wrong?" He cried out.

It was her third pregnancy. The first two ended with miscarriages and this one had her in bed half the time. O'Toole was hoping for a boy.

"My water broke. It's time to go to the hospital," she said.

Number Two picked her up with ease and carried her out to his truck, a 1922 Ford. He couldn't believe how nervous he was. He had already killed seven people in his young life. His father wasted no time mentoring him and taking him down that evil path of revenge and murder. They were both bitter men but hid their anger and psychopathic behaviors well.

O'Toole ran into the emergency room with his wife already in labor. She was crying loudly as her contractions increased. The doctors and nurses on duty had little time to prep Juliana and she gave birth on the gurney. It was a boy with amber eyes.

Ryan O'Toole, the second, smiled vituperatively knowing it was his turn to become a mentor to his son Ryan O'Toole, the third. It was April 1, 1924.

CHAPTER 5

P aul Nagaro, Peter Michaels' cameraman, had his drone airborne shooting video of the Edgebrook golf course gravesite, trying to take advantage of what daylight was left on this hot summer night. The scattered skeletal remains on the surface looked eerie, seemingly reaching upwards out of the earth, and pointing to the half-moon forming in the crimson sky as if announcing their pleasure that they were finally discovered. The area revealed a path 20 feet wide that ended bluntly at the tree line, one hundred yards from the golf course's pro-shop. Darkness arrived quickly, like someone just blew out the candles and everything faded to black.

Nagaro had been flying drones as a hobby for a couple of years and he finally convinced the powers to be at the television station to invest in a high definition drone camera. He obtained his 107 FAA drone certification and enjoyed navigating the drone over the trees and the outline of what could possibly be a massive gravesite.

"I got all the shots that I can get until tomorrow," he said to Peter Michaels, who was on his way to the scene, but tied up in late afternoon traffic.

"I'm turning around and going back to the station for the ten. Is there anyone there you can get a quick sound bite from? Who is in-charge?" Michaels asked anxiously looking for an opportunity to do a 180.

"I think I see lieutenant Jimmy Vitas. Should I grab him?"

"Yeah. He's a great guy. Just ask him to explain the situation. He loves the camera and he'll do a great job," Michaels said knowingly.

Lieutenant James Vitas was a handsome man with premature thick, curly, gray hair. His five foot ten inch frame was muscular from working out at least four times a week. His blue eyes sparkled in a friendly manner. He smiles and laughs a lot. He had the sobriquet "The Greek." He was a strong leader with a modest style. His officers loved him.

"A forest preserve excavating team was leveling the ground to build some bocce ball courts and unbeknownst to them they uncovered what looks like a massive burial site. We have no idea how big this thing is. We are waiting for the medical examiner and the FBI's evidence guys to develop a plan on how we are going to proceed. That's all I got for you at this point," the lieutenant announced in the makeshift presser.

With a friendly smile, showing his perfectly straight, white teeth, Lt. James Vitas turned and walked away from the cameras. He knew his sound bite would lead all the nights' newscast.

~~~~

A small command post was set up hastily, close to the area where the first skeleton was unearthed. There wasn't much activity yet because the crime scene investigators just arrived and they were debating whether it was worth it to position field lights and start working through the night or wait until morning. No official decision could be made, however, until the medical examiner arrived to get a clear picture of what they were dealing with.

CSI Tom Vander Aarde (Vando) was chomping at the bit to get started. Patience wasn't a virtue he possessed, plus he was totally intrigued by this incredible find. He knew it was going to be an arduous task no matter how many bodies were buried there and he didn't want to wait for the FBI's Evidence Response Team to get started and give up CPD jurisdiction. Vando knew from experience that the bodies already exposed had been contaminated. The only thing they could do was gather those remains and try to piece the skeletons together one bone at a time, and that's what Vando decided to do…ME or no ME.

Once he got that look of determination, it was full speed ahead…no stopping him. He collected the gear he needed which was basically a two inch wide natural fiber dry paint brush, a small gardening trowel and several blue plastic tarps. He went back to the burial site, fired up the thousand-watt field lights and aimed the beams at what appeared to be a left forearm and said, "Fuck it! I'm going to start on these exposed bones. The scene is already contaminated. It's not going to change a thing."

He knelt next to the bone fragment and discovered that it was broken in half at the radius and ulna midway from the wrist to the elbow. He gently brushed the dirt off the bone and delicately placed it on a tarp.

"What do we have here?" He said in a voice a little louder than a whisper, after he noticed the knuckles of a right hand slightly protruding beneath the dirt's surface. He moved the light's beam directly at it, knelt and cautiously started brushing away the dirt. He was in his element. He was doing what he loved to do, find clues, and solve crimes. It took forty-five minutes to clear the dirt and grass off the arm that appeared to be broken at the humerus. Vando's left knee and lower back were aching so bad, he was gritting his teeth, hoping that it would relieve the pain, then in an instant the pain was gone and his mind was racing. His eyes widened in total surprise, "What the fuck," he exclaimed, as he raised the arm up to examine it and discovered that there was no right thumb. "I know I have seen something like this before, but where?" His expression was questioning, his eyes were studious and his brain was poking and prodding his memory for answers.

~~~~

Peter Michaels' phone rang but he didn't recognize the number on his dashboard screen. "News, Michaels."

"Hey, Mr. Michaels this is detective Lorenzo Garcia. I heard you want to talk to me. Is that right?"

"Yeah. I'd like to talk to you about your incredible clearance rate for violent crimes," Michaels said as a look of disgust etched his face.

"What's this all about?" Garcia asked with concern in his voice.

"Are you aware that you are being investigated by Internal Affairs?"

"You're kidding, right?" The concerned voice now seemed mixed with nervousness.

"I am not. I'd like to talk to you about your tactics," Michaels responded, his look of disgust mutated into one of anticipation.

"When? I got nuttin to hide. I'm an open book."

"How about tomorrow morning around ten?"

"Call me in the morning, you have my cell now," he said, then immediately hung up.

An expression of satisfaction spread across Michaels' lips only to be interrupted by another phone call and a number he also didn't recognize.

"News, Michaels."

There was no response on the other end. Michaels could hear breathing. "Hello, who is this?" He asked, but again there was no response. The breathing got a little heavier and then the person on the other end hung up the phone.

Michaels' expression of curiosity morphed into one of indignation. This had never happened to him before; it unnerved him and he didn't know why. He had been shot at, spit at, banged up against walls by bodyguards, but when people called him they always talked. He picked up his phone and dialed Jack Warren.

"Hey what's up? I thought you'd be out here at Edgebrook. This is going to be something huge," Warren said.

"I just got a very strange call, and now I have a strange feeling in the pit of my stomach."

"Talk to me," Warren said with concern.

"Could you see if your FBI buddy, Donna Blake, can run a number for me? I'm sure it's a burner phone."

"Sure, give me the number."

Michaels gave it to him but the strange, irritating feeling remained in the pit of his stomach.

CHAPTER 6

Medical Examiner, Dr. Robert Crine arrived at the burial site after nine and he was irritated when he saw Vando on his knees brushing dirt off the bones of those already unearthed. "What the fuck are you doing, Vando?" He asked in a grumpy voice.

Vando looked up with that look of "What the fuck do you think I'm doing," and answered, "This crime scene was already contaminated and I wanted to get a jump on things before the feds come in and try to take over."

Crine surveyed the bones on the blue tarps, took a deep breath and calmed down, he knew Vando was right. There were now three CSIs brushing away dirt and piecing together some of the skeleton remains. Four skulls were laid out on separate tarps but the fragments of all the bones already cleaned didn't add up to one full body.

Vando was sweating profusely in the white hazmat suit he was wearing. He grunted when he got up and brought the right arm with the thumb cut off of its hand to show Crine. "I think this might be significant, don't you?" He asked, a curious expression on his face.

Crine was stunned and put on his red, dollar store, reading glasses that were hanging on a lanyard around his neck on the tip of his nose.

"I just did an autopsy today, and the victim had his right thumb cut off his hand just like this, with surgical precision," Crine said as he took the arm and put it under the field light to examine it. "Son of a bitch, Hmmm. I'll be damned," he said as he rotated the arm over and over again. "I can't wait to look at this back at the office."

"When will the FBI's first response guys get here?" Vando asked sarcastically, wiping the beads of sweat off of his forehead with the back of his sleeve.

"Not until morning. I'll be back first thing to look at the undisturbed area to see what we have here."

"You want us to keep going?" Vando asked knowing what the answer would be. He smiled when Crine affirmed his efforts and that he was not in any trouble for taking the lead on this investigation.

"Yeah. Let's see what we can piece together tonight. It'll give us a better picture in the morning. Do not disturb anything else. Keep working this area only," Crine said looking over his glasses and pointing to the area that was already plowed up. "I have a feeling we are going to be here for a long time."

~~~~

By the time Peter Michaels got back to the station he settled down and he had expunged that feeling of angst from the voiceless, heavy breathing phone call. His producer David Beedy was in the editing room with Ed Land, their favorite editor, cutting the two stories that Michaels thought he would be reporting on the ten o'clock news.

Land was six feet, six inches tall with a handlebar mustache. His once brown hair was thinning on top and graying at the temples, his hazel eyes looked out through gold horned rimmed glasses giving him the look of a legal scholar. His deep voice and his loud laughter rounded out his gregarious personality. Everyone enjoyed being around Ed Land. He had a quick wit and a sharp mind, but more importantly he was very good at his job.

"Why are they cutting our time on the drive-by shooting that almost cost you your life?" Land asked as Michaels walked into the editing suite.

"It's old news. I don't know if anyone cares anymore. I think this gravesite at Edgebrook is going to be a huge story. I talked with Jack on the drive back after I calmed down. Did you get all the notes I recorded for you?"

"Yeah, I did. I already wrote the piece. How many bodies are they talking about?" Beedy asked.

"Not sure. Dr. Crine got there late, so they're going to reevaluate in the morning, but it looks as if the bulldozer plowed out at least four."

"I think Ron should do that story. It might be confusing if you do both," Beedy said authoritatively, looking upwards at his partner from his editing notes.

"Did you talk to him?" Michaels asked although he knew that Beedy already did. His producer was also a longtime friend. He was very meticulous about keeping records and he was a stickler for order. Television viewers don't like complicated stories.

~~~~

Magers was in the green room getting makeup when Michaels walked in. "What was that weird call you got…all about?" Magers asked with a look of apprehension.

"I don't know but I will tell you it freaked me out for a while," Michaels answered and then continued, "Probably some goof ball I offended with a story, who knows when."

"What are you going to do about it?"

"I gave the number to that FBI agent that I worked with on the 'Bug Man' stories. She is going to try to find out if it was a burner phone or not and where it was purchased. We'll get to the bottom of it…if there is something to it."

"Don't let it bother you. Let's go do these stories," Magers said as he got out of the chair.

~~~~

Ryan O'Toole, the fifth, shot out of his recliner when he saw Ron Magers on the news reporting about what could be a massive gravesite. "Fuck. Fuck. Fuck." He shouted. He knew that his great, great grandfather and great grandfather buried 12 of their kills at Edgebrook decades ago. His first kills were buried at Deer Grove. He learned about the county park system from the stories his father shared with him.

Number Five violated the O'Toole family's rules. He killed because he liked it. He loved the taste of the thumbs and toes he ate. He actually craved it.

Now that authorities discovered the burial ground, his mind was racing. He was killing so much that he was beginning to wonder if he left any trace evidence that could connect any of the murders to him, and the band aid on his right thumb was a constant reminder that he fucked up the other night when he killed that doctor. He should have let him go but he couldn't. He cut his thumb when he took the ear. He was rushed.

His father died of prostate cancer 20 years ago. It seemed that all the O'Tooles died of that cursed disease. His father had 17 ears in the jars they kept hidden in their cellars. Number Five already had 32. He smiled at the thought. He stopped pacing, turned off the TV and went to bed. He had to be at the hospital early. He had the first shift for the month of July.

CHAPTER 7

T he sun was burning bright orange as it rose over Lake Michigan announcing another hot, smoldering July day in Chicago. The lake's water appeared to be a deep Mediterranean blue and looked like glass, not a ripple on its surface from the windless morning. It would not be a good day for sailing and the irritating, biting, black flies would be out in mass.

Dr. Crine's blue oxford shirt stuck to his back. His sleeves were rolled up. His red and gray striped tie hung loosely around his neck, along with his red reading glasses attached to his Chicago Bears lanyard. The warm air that brushed his face did nothing to cool his temperature or his temperament as he ambled up to the burial site.

Vando's hair was wet and matted to his scalp. His white hazmat suit was opened to his belt buckle. More than a case of empty water bottles were scattered around the area. He and two other CSIs worked through the night and unearthed almost four full skeletons. They were slowly and delicately probing the ground with their trowels searching for a foot, a tibia, an arm, and a portion of a rib cage to complete their work.

"I am not sure if all these bones go together but it looks like they match," Vando offered as the ME approached. "Just a few more fragments."

"I'll be able to tell when I get them on the table. I think this is going to be a long arduous task, Vando," Crine said with a heavy sigh.

"Yeah. No doubt. When will the feds be here?"

"They're on the way. They are bringing some hotshot bone expert from D.C. That's why they decided not to come until this morning. Let's take a look at what we got to work with here," Dr. Crine said as he stooped down to examine the earth where the bulldozer stopped and the grass covered ground continued into the tree line.

"These graves are just deep enough to cover the body. The grass offers the rest of the camouflage," Vando opined.

"Let's find out," Crine said and pointed to an area for Vando to start his exploration.

Vando walked over to the spot that the ME designated, knelt down and began to outline a two foot square in the grassy area. He slowly and methodically pushed his trowel into the earth. At about a foot and a half he felt the trowel find a hard spot. "I think I found another one."

He then used his fingertips to move the earth and in a short time, he discovered another skull, the visage of its hollow eye sockets staring back at him penitently.

"This is number five," both Dr. Crine and Vando exclaimed at the same moment, both with remorseful expressions.

~~~~

Ryan O'Toole was with his second patient of the morning when the authorities found the fifth body at the burial ground site. O'Toole was an interventional radiologist technician for the last eight years, before that he was an ultrasound tech. Even though he had 20/20 vision, whenever he was at work he wore tinted glasses to conceal his amber eyes because when he first started working with patients they seemed to be startled by his unusual feature.

Ryan, the fifth, was the only O'Toole to ever attend college. His IQ was borderline genius. His ambition was borderline lackadaisical, unlike his constant urge to kill. The pay scale for an IR tech was double that of an x-ray technician, that's what motivated him to go back to school. It took him three years to complete the education and training for his new career.

IR techs are very important in the health care industry. Interventional radiology services are increasing in medicine as the use of non-invasive techniques are being utilized more and more in outpatient care. IR techs perform diagnostic imaging examinations of organs and body scans. They work closely with radiologists and physicians involved in the diagnosis and treatment of many maladies and diseases, including cancer.

During the time, he studied, he didn't kill, but this hiatus inspired him to start ignoring the O'Toole family rule to just kill young men who looked like his great, great uncle's killer. Gender no longer mattered to him either. He killed three women for no particular reason other than they ignored him in a bar.

O'Toole was moving the C-arm low pulse x-ray machine away from a patient on the operating table, when one of the doctors asked, "Hey Ryan. You okay? You seem a little distracted this morning."

O'Toole quickly thought and lied, "Yeah. Sorry. That patient reminded me of my dad who died twenty years ago. I don't know why."

O'Toole could not stop thinking about the burial site that was discovered the day before, he knew that it contained 12 bodies, and they could not be connected to him in any way but it still bothered him that they were discovered. He knew forensic sciences had come a long way from his medical studies.

O'Toole was 51-years old. His six-foot frame housed a chiseled, muscular body from working out four times a week both lifting weights and aerobics. His thick hair was cut Marine style close to his head with a flat top. He was proud that his amber eyes put him in a small class of people from around the world, but he mostly covered them with sunglasses whenever possible because they drew attention to his presence.

O'Toole killed an average of one person a year for the last 30 years. His father started desensitizing him when he was eight years old by taking a sick robin that fell out of its nest and snapping the bird's neck. He pulled the head off its body and smiled, assuring the child that it was okay to kill. Most serial killers are misfits from all fringes of society. The greatest percentage of all serial killers start their evil, hateful, sadistic lives by killing animals. The O'Toole family had been killing for more than a hundred years, and not a single one of them ever got caught or were ever connected to a murder.

The O'Tooles always hid in plain sight. They all had jobs and worked hard. They took part in some local community activities through their wives, but they never got too involved. The wives never suspected anything out of the ordinary because their husbands never talked work or complained about their work at home.

With the exception of Ryan, the fifth, they all had jobs that gave them access to various burial sites. He, however, had other methods to dispose of bodies: science, medicine, funeral homes, and body farms.

Number Five did not have a son or a daughter at least that he knew of. He was not licentious because he never had a serious relationship with a woman or a man. He was basically asexual. He did have several sexual encounters with women, but it never lasted more than a few weeks. He just did not have a huge sexual drive. The only drive he had was to kill, he liked it, that is what excited him; emotionally and sexually.

He made what he thought was the biggest mistake of his life a few nights ago when he left the body of that Kaley guy on the ground. He was trying to convince himself that it didn't matter and that the police would never make any connection to him because he didn't take the toe. The body wouldn't be the same as the others.

He leaned over the sink to rinse his face with cold water and looked into the mirror and saw a man not as he imagined himself to be, but to one of what he had become; a serial killer with wicked amber eyes and then a malicious smile ghosted across his face.

CHAPTER 8

T he mere thought of decaying and rotting human bodies would be repugnant to most people, but to anthropologist William M. Bass, it was the beginning of a new form of forensic research. Dr. Bass's concept is called a "Body Farm." He started the first research facility in the 1980s at the University of Tennessee. The intent of these body farms is to study the decomposition of a body from the time of death to the time of dry decay in all sorts of different environments, elements, and climates.

Law enforcement agencies along with scientists have a great deal of interest in this decomposition process because not only does it provide clues in death, but these body farms also provide teaching opportunities; like training cadaver dogs how to find bodies, search, and recovery maneuvers and how to process a massive burial site.

There are eight body farms in the United States and no shortage of bodies. Most corpses are donated to science in a will with specific instructions. Family members and next-of-kin can also donate the remains of a loved one with written authorization. Some body farms have been known to accept unknown or unclaimed bodies, however some object to this as unethical. The farms will not accept any bodies that have been infected with the human immunodeficiency virus (HIV), hepatitis, or antibiotic-resistant bacteria.

Each body farm provides different indigenous environments that can affect the decomposition process. Human remains are placed in areas around trees, covered with leaves, under concrete slabs or simply buried in the ground. Some bodies are also placed in the trunks of cars, others are submerged under water both fresh and salty.

In Florida, for example, there is a sub-tropical climate and sandy soil. The University of Southeastern Illinois at Vendee provides a very unique environment. It has the lowest average temperature, the highest average wind speed, the second lowest elevation, the most acidic soil, and the worst soil drainage of any of the other body farms.

Students studying forensic science take meticulous notes detailing the four stages of decomposition: the fresh stage, the bloat stage, the decay stage and finally the dry stage. Each of these stages occur over different rates of time which is affected by other conditions outside of the natural environments, like insect penetration and scavenging animals.

Once a corpse is totally decomposed, its bones are then cleaned and stored in evidence containers where they can be further studied. That is what was gnawing away at CSI Tom Vander Aarde, he knew he had seen something familiar when he first noticed the cut off thumb of one of the victims they had unearthed. It all came back to him when FBI agent Thomas Britten arrived at the Edgebrook grave site.

Britten dreamed of becoming an orthopedic surgeon but a rare neurological disease known as myasthenia gravis left him with no feeling in the forefinger and middle finger of his left hand. He became a forensic anthropologist instead and then he joined the FBI, and convinced his superiors there was a need for agents to specialize in the study of bones.

Britten was five feet, six inches tall. The mask of time was generous to him. His brown hair was prematurely turning gray, and his stylishly trimmed beard, gave him a scholarly presence. His blue eyes were hidden behind very expensive reflective blue sunglasses. His father was a retired Chicago homicide detective. A smile expressed itself when he saw his student, Vando, talking to Dr. Robert Crine near a newly dug gravesite. They both had broad grins when they shook hands.

"You look great agent Britten or do you prefer Dr. Britten?" Vando offered.

"It's just Britten. You look great too. It's been awhile Vando. How yah doing?"

"I'm doing fine. Back still hurts. Knee still hurts, but what can I tell you?" Vando responded as his smile morphed into a serious look when the agent asked.

"What do we have here?" As he pointed down towards the grave.

"I think we have a serial killer," Vando opined.

~~~~

Clinton City, Illinois was the home of the Benjamin Franklin Institute of Technology. It kissed the border of Indiana where I-65 and I-94 meet. Clinton City offered a rich history that dates back to 1822. Its unique downtown square not only housed the Institute of Technology with its brick colonial style façade, red tiled roof and two tall clock towers, but it also contained traditional main street shops, restaurants, coffeehouses, boutiques, and antique stores.

Beautiful, multicolored Victorian homes lined the streets surrounding the entire area. A creek flowed peacefully through the center of town. The sounds of its waters slowly somersaulting over rocks and boulders was soothing to everyone sitting on green park benches strategically placed along its serpentine route. Walking paths provided the opportunity for a quiet stroll or a scenic run.

Although Clinton City appeared calm and peaceful, its accessibility to downtown Chicago and its pro-business attitude made it a very successful enterprise. Its location attracted a number of global companies that called it home.

Its school system was ranked in the top five percentile in the United States and its low tax rate separated it from many other cities its size in the state of Illinois.

On the outskirts of town, the Institute's department of anthropology had a seven acre body farm that began in 1990. There was some opposition to the facility at first, but after a five foot high, red brick fence was built around the entrance, it gave the impression of just another colonial building on campus. There were 45 bodies going through various stages of decomposition. Seven of those corpses belonged to Ryan O'Toole, the fourth, and six to Ryan O'Toole, the fifth.

They created fraudulent wills for their victims stating that they wanted their bodies left for medical and scientific research and their jobs with funeral homes provided them storage space and a delivery system to bring the remains to the body farm. They also had nine bodies at the body farm at the University of Southeastern Illinois at Vendee which opened in 1993.

Number Four never hesitated to use any means possible to dispose of his victims. He even cut them into pieces and buried their parts in the caskets with the remains of mostly elderly people who had little or no family to suspect any wrongdoing. Number Four was an embalmer connected with five different funeral homes.

~~~~

Bones can tell law enforcement authorities a lot about death. The first two things a forensic anthropologist tries to determine is who the victim was and how was he or she killed. They Identify a victim as male or female by examining their pelvic bone structure. They create a biological profile of a victim to establish their racial ancestry, height, and age. Bones can reflect a victim's diet, how he or she lived, past surgeries and other trauma or fractures that were inflicted over a person's lifetime.

They search for any signs of trauma on the bones that can define the cause of death. They can conclude if a bone was cut by a handsaw, power saw, hunting knife or scalpel. They can determine if the killer was right or left-handed, and they can often estimate the height of the killer by the angle of the trauma that was inflicted.

All skulls have 22 bones but human skulls look different depending on whether or not it is male or female, and also what part of the world the person comes from. If a skull, for example, was bludgeoned with a baseball bat the fracture would look the same regardless of the shape of the weapon. An egg-shaped depression is typically formed because of the way the two layers of skull bone collapse and buckle. This is called blunt force trauma, and closer examination can determine the size and shape of the weapon used.

~~~~

The medical examiner was bent over a skeleton gently probing its bones and talking to himself and the victim. He asked, "What have we here?" as he examined the missing right thumb area. He was intrigued by the angle of the dismemberment. "Left-handed, I would guess," he murmured half expecting the remains to affirm his inquiry.

"Hey, doc...weird stuff, right?" Peter Michaels said as a way to notify Dr. Robert Crine that he just bypassed the morgue's security system and slipped into the autopsy room.

"How the fuck do you manage to get by security?" Dr. Crine asked shaking his head, pursing his lips, because Michaels acted as if he belonged there and everyone knew him.

Michaels started riddling the ME with questions about what he discovered from the autopsy of Edgebrook victim number one. "Can you tell how he died, doc?"

"I am fairly certain that he had his throat cut. I found some knicks between the fifth and sixth cervical disks."

"Can you tell how old the victim was? Is it male or female?"

"I'd say the victim was a six foot male, between 20 and 30 years of age. He's been buried a long, long time." Crine said rubbing his chin and squinching his nose and lips.

Michaels started recording the conversation as soon as he walked into the operating room. He didn't tell the ME though, but he knew that Crine knew. It was a cat and mouse game both of them played over the years. They have been acquaintances for a long time and he would never use the recording on the air without permission. He just wanted to make sure he didn't miss anything.

"How do you determine how old or how long ago a person was murdered?"

"That's where the FBI comes in. They can do some great things with Carbon-14 testing."

"What about DNA?"

"DNA testing has also come a long way. It is a very delicate procedure to get DNA from old, dried bones but it is now possible to extract total genomic DNA. These new and improved extraction buffers allow us to provide complete demineralization of the osseous materials resulting in an appropriate DNA sample for analysis."

"What does that mean?" Michaels asked with an inquisitive look.

"It means, yes we can get good samples and we can determine a DNA profile but it doesn't mean that we will find a match." Dr. Crine said rubbing his nose with the back of his right hand.

"Do you know how many bodies there are at the gravesite?"

"All I know right now is six. They unearthed another one just as I started this autopsy. It's actually the third one that I have done."

"Do you think these victims will ever be identified?" Michaels asked with a questioning look and then continued, "This could be a Sisyphean task."

Dr. Crine was bending over the remains, he stood up, flipped up his optical magnifiers, pushed his lower back with his left hand, winced at the pain and looked at his friend, "There is no doubt we will identify some of these victims whether or not we identify all of them is indeed the million-dollar Sisyphean question, isn't it?"

CHAPTER 9

D etectives Jack Warren and Tony Quag were meeting at the Office of Emergency Management and Communications with the highly trained police tech team that was investigating the murder of the renegade disciple's leader, Shamir Halstead, the unfortunate death of a 13-year-old girl and the attempted murder of Peter Michaels. Chicago's OEMC is one of the most advanced high tech and sophisticated law enforcement command centers in the world. It controls over 50,000 cameras that are strategically placed around the city. The OEMC also houses the city's 911 and 311 emergency calls center and, it coordinates the responses to all emergency and disaster situations within Chicago's city limits. Twenty-four hours a day, the command center is manned by 65 law enforcement officers and federal agents from every US Justice Department agency. When the police recover a phone they can use a geo-tracking system and can determine where that phone has been and how often it's been there. They can also ping phones in a very large area when tracking a suspect.

In the last few years, this network of cameras has been updated with high-definition units that operate around the clock, 365 days a year. They are basically indestructible but gang bangers still constantly try to disable them by shooting them. All the traffic light cameras that are used to issue drivers; speeding tickets, illegal turn tickets and running red light tickets, have been converted into surveillance units They also have tracking devices like LPRs, license plate readers, to look for suspects and cars thought to be used in felony crimes such as murder. The police also have cutting-edge cameras that respond to the sounds of gun shots and immediately track, focus, and record the area where the shots were fired in high quality video: day or night.

In the last three years, criminal leniency in prosecuting felony cases in Cook County has been so prolific, the state's attorneys and CPD detectives have a hard time convincing one criminal to be a witness against another one, so they have turned to a highly sophisticated computer program to help them collect evidence that can be used at trial. It has become a very effective way to record evidence, build cases and make arrests. A picture is worth a thousand words. Criminals can be caught on camera with dates and times stamped on the video, providing undeniable proof of their presence at crime scenes. In essence, they can create a video timeline of the crime.

Once the police knew that the getaway car in the Halstead murder was a black GMC model, SUV, investigators started searching for similar vehicles racing eastbound on 55th Street, and immediately spotted the suspects, parking at the corner of Garfield Boulevard and Ryan Expressway apparently to plan their getaway. Three suspects exited the car, one of them was wearing three ankle monitoring devices. After a short discussion the two vehicles entered the Ryan Expressway and sped off. All of the bad guys know the police would not give chase because it was against CPD general orders.

But that doesn't mean that they lost contact, using their sophisticated video technology program, detectives discovered that one of the suspects, Antonio Cornwell, who was out of jail on an I-bond (meaning he paid no bond money for his release from custody), was within ten feet of the Halstead murder at the exact time that the shots were fired.

~~~~

Cook County State's Attorney James Bertelsmeyer was a no nonsense, dyed-in-the-wool prosecutor who lived to put criminals behind bars. Bertelsmeyer's five foot nine body was lithe and defined. He was a runner and a swimmer, and every day he did one or the other. His brown hair was thinning and turning white. His blue eyes expressed confidence and knowledge. His grin relaxed everyone, who experienced it. His determination to get to the truth was incontrovertible and unstoppable. He was the only prosecutor in the entire office who never lost a murder case.

"That was fast. The video looks great. Good work." Bertelsmeyer said looking down at Cornwell's three page rap sheet. "This guy is a gift. He's wearing three ankle monitors. Do you believe that shit? He's 30-years old and has spent half his life in prison."

"Yep. The ankle monitors put Cornwell right in the middle of the murder scene at the exact time of the shootings. The facial recognition is undisputable. The video even picked up the skin imperfections on his right shoulder. It's Antonio, all right," detective Warren said with a grin that widened as he pointed to the computer monitor.

"The second guy is Mohammed Brown. He is in the hierarchy of the rival disciple lords. The gang unit is working on identifying the third guy," detective Quag interjected then continued. "We only got a partial of his face. A profile really, but the computers will be able to rotate the image and we'll get him, Bert."

"His clothes also stand out and look at those rings on his fingers. Dumb bastard. It shouldn't take long," Warren opined.

"What's going on out at Edgebrook golf course. I got assigned that one this morning," Bertelsmeyer said.

"I talked to Vando just before we came here. He says, 'no doubt. It's a serial killer.'" Warren's smile disappeared and an expression of apprehension took its place as he informed the prosecutor.

~~~~

Peter Michaels was doing what's called an "ambush" interview with newly retired and disgraced detective Lorenzo Garcia. Michaels had done a number of stories about convicted felons that spent decades in prison for crimes they didn't commit. They contended that Garcia planted evidence, beat them, and threatened them or their families with deportation if they didn't confess to the murders they were ultimately convicted of. The states attorney's office was reviewing dozens of cases involving the disgraced Garcia.

Garcia had retired from the department several weeks before Michaels informed him that he was being investigated by CPD's Internal Affairs. Michaels was chasing the disparaged detective down the street. "Why is it, in every legal issue involving you, you take the fifth amendment?"

Garcia was jogging towards his car. "Fuck you," he hollered back in a panted breath.

"Did you threaten Phillipe Torres? Did you promise you would deport his sister if he didn't confess to the murder of Jose Gonzalez?" Michaels right knee was throbbing as he caught up to Garcia who jumped into his car and locked the door.

"Did you threaten Torres?" Michaels asked defiantly.

Garcia behind the safety of his driver side window and locked door, looked out at Michaels with a malignant sneer, and gave him the middle finger as he put his car into gear and screeched off leaving tire marks on the asphalt street.

Michaels turned to his cameraman Paul Nagaro and asked with a grin, "Did you get all of that?"

Nagaro smiled back, "Every frame."

CHAPTER 10

R yan O'Toole, the third, was a prolific killer. He craved it. He was a butcher by trade. His shoulders were broad and his neck was thick. His biceps were rock hard from lifting sides of beef. His fingers were long and strong and durable. His amber eyes were vile and close together, the right one slightly crossed giving him the appearance of a wild cat ready to pounce. He always wore rose tinted glasses to shield his eyes, and perhaps his desires. He worked the midnight shift at the Wilson and Wilson Meat Packing Company in Chicago's "Back of the Yards." He killed 31 people, all males, all white, all matching the description of his great uncle's killer with the exception of one. He only buried 11 of his victims, the rest he cut into pieces at Wilson and Wilson. He worked by himself in an isolated area of the warehouse, and that gave him the perfect opportunities to carve his victims into pieces and mixed their fleshy remains into the ground beef that he produced every shift. He cut up their bones into small pieces and hid them with the legs of the cattle that he slaughtered. The bones were discarded into containers after every shift and shipped to factories that produced dog food. He volunteered to do the heavy lifting and all the dirty work giving the handful of other midnight shift employees nothing to object about, but more importantly they never interfered with his quirky activities. No one ever gave him a second thought. He did his work, kept to himself, and never took a sick day. He was the perfect employee.

The bodies he did bury were placed in two different park districts in isolated spaces near a tree line, away from the activity of park users. His father taught him well.

Six of the bodies were buried at Schiller Woods where trees provided cover when he dug the three foot deep graves. He never placed a body near the fishing ponds that attracted a lot of attention. The other five were hidden in Miller Meadows South which also offered dense forested areas, along with undulating, grassy fields. It was a favorite place for Northshore picnickers and hikers.

Whenever he accumulated four thumbs and four toes, he made the family soup with carrots, celery, onions, potatoes, beef broth and lots of pepper. He and his son, Number Four, were the only ones to partake in their special celebratory meals.

One night his wife Elizabeth came home unexpectedly from a neighborhood card party and discovered the two eating the soup. She went berserk and started screaming when she saw the jar of ears in the center of the table. She hollered, "What the fuck is this...a satanic cult meeting? What are you a cannibal?"

A trace of a worthless smile crept across the face of Number Three as he covered her mouth with one hand and slit her throat with the other. His knives were always sharp and always at the ready. The amber eyes of his son presented a look of satisfaction and gratitude. He hated his mother. They hardly ever spoke after he started killing at the age of nineteen.

Number Three went to work to dispose of her body without a single ounce of remorse. They wrapped her in a carpet, stuffed her in the trunk of his car and then they finished their soup and cleaned the dishes as if nothing else mattered. He told his son to put the ears in the cellar and then call the neighbor's house and ask for his mother in a half hour. They needed an alibi. It was Number Three's last kill. He took her thumb and toe, wrapped them in aluminum foil and told his son to savor them the next time he prepared the family soup.

CPD homicide detectives made O'Toole Number Three their prime suspect in the disappearance, but no charges ever surfaced because they never found the body. He died a horrible death of colon cancer 18 months later. It was 1974. Ryan O'Toole the third was 50 years old.

The disappearance and presumed death of Elizabeth Burke O'Toole remains one of thousands of cold cases in the archives of the Chicago Police Department.

~~~~

Dr. Robert Crine had the decayed, dry bones of five right arms and hands along with five left feet and legs under an intense beam of light on his operating table. He had a very strong magnifying glass up to his right eye as he examined the specific fragments of the bones where the thumbs and toes were severed.

His headache intensified and his hand felt an intense sharp piercing pain as his mind drifted back to his high school days when he broke his thumb during a soccer game. His mother called him a sissy, grabbed his thumb, and pulled it back with a sneer on her face. He was unconsciously rubbing his right thumb transfixed back to 1975 in his mind as if he was in a state of suspended animation looking down at himself in the present time. He was startled back to reality when his cell phone blared out the ring tone from the theme of "Mission Impossible." He was sweating profusely when his right thumb slid over the acceptance bar icon on his iPhone. *Shit*, he thought as he looked at the caller ID and regained his composure.

"I don't know why I take your calls Peter. You always seem to reach me at the most inopportune times," Dr. Crine said with anxiety in his voice.

Peter Michaels was a little taken aback at the curtness of Dr. Crine's voice. "Sorry, doc, but I just got off the phone with detective Warren. He says that Vando thinks this is the work of a serial killer. You agree?" He asked, anticipation seeping into his voice.

Dr. Crine started walking towards his office and slid his soaking wet Harley Davidson surgical cap off of his head. His hand was trembling as he fell into his chair; a deep sigh released from his mouth. "I don't think it's a serial killer," he said with another deep groan.

Michaels couldn't believe his ears, "Seriously?"

"Yes, seriously. I think it's the work of at least two serial killers. One is right-handed and the other is left-handed." Crine opined. "The left-handed killer was very strong. Very strong. The evidence doesn't lie."

"How can you say that he was very strong?" Michaels asked quizzically.

"The incisions were very smooth. Almost effortless with the left-handed killer. There was some hesitation or jerkiness in the pattern of the right-handed killer. He had to work much harder."

"Well, how many autopsies have you done on the Edgebrook victims?" Michaels asked curiously.

"Five so far. I've got another one that's being prepped right now."

"Any idea how long ago these murders took place, doc, and how many more bodies are out there?"

"There are certainly more remains out there. It's a slow tedious process to get these bodies out of the ground and onto my table. We'll find out eventually the time of their deaths."

"Your voice sounds questioning for some reason to me, doc. You alright?"

"Not sure. I am very disturbed right now."

"Why?" Michaels asked with snooping interest.

"Remember that young doctor who was killed a few days ago up by Northeastern?"

"Yeah. Dr. Kaley. Philip Kaley. Right? What about him?"

"He had his right thumb severed almost, if not exactly, like these victims." Crine said thoughtfully, looking up at the fluorescent lights that were humming a hypnotic tune before they accepted their last wattage of power.

"Doc that just happened a few days ago. You said these skeletons could be fifty, sixty, seventy years old or older. That doesn't make any sense. Does it?" Michaels asked expectantly.

"No. It doesn't make any sense at all right now, but remember Peter, the evidence doesn't lie."

CHAPTER 11

David Beedy was standing in front of his desk on the phone and he sounded incredulous when Peter Michaels walked into the I-unit's office. "Hell, yes we will do the story. Are you kidding me Denny? Can you get me some of the body cam footage?" Beedy inquired, now walking in small circles, rubbing his irritated eyes. The beads of sweat that formed on his forehead were trickling down his nose and causing his eyes to sting. Beedy, known for his exactness and meticulous record keeping, has been Peter Michaels producer for the last ten years. Not only were they work associates they were best of friends. He wasn't smiling.

"What's that all about? Were you talking to Denny Verbance?" Michaels asked as he handed a cup of coffee to his partner.

"Yeah. That was Denny. I can't believe what he just told me. The states attorney's office does not want to bring charges in a case where the suspect confessed to killing a guy. The prick was covered in blood from beating the shit out of the victim. It's getting crazier and crazier over there."

"So, Denny approved the charges himself?" Michaels asked incredulously.

Denny Verbance was the Area-2 Detective Commander. He was an imposing man. His two hundred pound, six foot body was lean and muscular. He literally glides when he walks into a room with an air of confidence. His piercing brown eyes penetrate any suspect he interviews, and he immediately knows if the guy is lying. He is normally mild mannered but today he was infuriated.

"The suspect is a guy named Gary Samples. The victim was a Daniel Fort. They met at the Inquest. You know the place, it's a LGBTQ friendly bar on the 1200 block of East 73rd Street. They hooked up and went to Samples' place where they must have had a horrible argument of some kind because he beat him with a hammer. Get this, he hit Fort twenty-five or thirty times, and the guy was still alive when the police found him in the alley," Beedy mourned.

"And prosecutors…don't want to bring charges? That's crazy," Michaels exclaimed.

"It's unbelievable. The tact team guys that ran across Samples in the alley have his confession on their body cams. He told the police he killed the guy; then dragged his naked body down three flights of stairs leaving a trail of blood, and he dumped him in the alley. He goes back upstairs got Fort's clothes and threw them in a nearby dumpster." Beedy was shaking his head, a disgusted look overshadowed his face.

"And they are not going to press charges. What the fuck is going on over there?" Michaels asked in disbelief.

"There's more. Not only was he was covered in blood: on his hands, on his clothes, and on his shoes, he had Fort's wallet in his pocket. The police found the bloody hammer in his apartment along with a blood-soaked mattress and blood stains and brains all over the bedroom walls. It's all on body cam video."

"There has to be a reasonable explanation, right?" Michaels asked putting his palms out. Shrugging his shoulders. "Does this Samples guy have a record?"

"He's on parole for attempted murder. Out on an I-Bond. His own recognizance. Do you believe that shit?" Beedy implored with a quizzical look shrouding his face.

"What did felony review say? There has to be something. It seems so cut and dry," Michaels responded impatiently.

"Prosecutors are refusing charges because Samples, get this, originally said that he fell into a puddle of blood and that Fort tried to rape him."

"Well, where did the puddle of blood come from? It just happened to appear out of thin air, and Samples has no injuries. No way," Michaels opined.

"He did the same thing just six weeks ago after he stabbed another guy that he just met at a gay bar in Boystown. He said it was self-defense then too, but they ended up charging him with attempted murder and a misdemeanor for assault and battery after he punched a bouncer at the club in the face," Beedy said.

"Didn't this override thing happen a few months ago in Area One? Commander Mike Schwab overrode the prosecutors and he approved murder charges for that asshole who shot that innocent seven-year-old girl, and wounded her older sister as I recall, right?"

"Yep. Schwab was in their face and they finally relented and brought charges. I think, they wanted to avoid public embarrassment. Man, they are messed up," Beedy said.

"Did Crine do the autopsy?" Michaels asked.

"Yep." Beedy said nodding affirmatively.

"I'll call him and get a comment. When are you getting the body cam footage?"

"I'm waiting to hear from Verbance," Beedy offered, "but I should get it by three or four. We should do this one on the ten just in case."

"Yeah. This will cause a shit storm. Only in Crook County. Only in Chicago." Michaels lamented.

~~~~

FBI agent/forensic anthropologist Tom Britten and CSI Tom Vander Aarde were both on their knees working next to each other unearthing Edgebrook graves number seven and eight. They were both sweating abundantly in the 92 degree weather. It was so hot you could fry an egg on the concrete sidewalk. The unrelenting humidity was so profound it felt like a sweltering, wet blanket was suffocating the city for the last week.

"Fuck...it's hot," Vando complained. His shirt was soaking wet and sticking to his body making movement heavy, strained, and exhausting. His white hazmat protective suit was opened to the navel and his knees were covered with mud. He was delicately probing the ground when he hit a hard surface predictably three feet down. "Got another one...I think."

Britten was cleaning dirt off the face of his victim. "What have we here? Shit, this may be a child or a small woman," he muttered to himself loud enough for Vando to hear. The other two CSIs working on other grave sites perked up to attention with Britten's proclamation.

"Well, that's different," Vando said.

Britten was now very deliberate and methodical. He slowly cleared the dry earth off the remains with delicate strokes of his two-inch brush. It took him five hours to clear the total surface of the skeleton. He was having some problems because the earth around and in the chest cavity was like hardened clay. He did not want to make any kind of postmortem marks on the bones, so he dug a four inch perimeter around and under the remains. Vando helped him put six, four inch wide canvas straps under the skeleton at various spots and then all the other CSIs came over to help.

"On my count, one, two, three," Britten ordered and they lifted the remains out of the shallow grave in harmony. Britten then brushed the remaining dirt off and said, "Well this is very different from the rest."

"What do you mean, different?" Vando inquired.

"Look at the pelvic region," Britten said. The three other CSIs immediately focused their attention on that area. "This is a young woman or an older child. Its thumb is still intact and the left toe has not been cut off...strange." Britten pondered out loud.

They slid the corpse onto a gurney and loaded it into the coroners' refrigerated transport van. Narrow runnels of water were inching their way into low spots and cracks in the pavement under the vehicle that had been running uninterruptedly for hours while the investigators continued their excavation work.

"After Dr. Crine finishes with these skeletons, I'm going to take them to Quantico," Britten said with authority. "We have some very sophisticated analysis equipment and we have a hell of a lot of unanswered questions."

"I've got a funny feeling about this," Vando offered. "I think we are just getting started. My gut tells me there are more graves and more bodies to be discovered."

CHAPTER 12

R yan O'Toole the fourth started working part time at Killeen and Calloway funeral home on Archer, two blocks west of Harlem after he graduated from high school, and after his first kill. He was fascinated with dead bodies and asked the owners to teach him the business. Their funeral home had six substantial viewing rooms and they were always busy because they were within a few miles of fifty churches of all denominations in the area.

Number Four was enthusiastic to study embalming. He enrolled at the City College of Chicago and began his classes in mortuary science which included subjects like; pathology, anatomy, embalming and restorative techniques, physiology, and funeral service law.

George Killeen, the principal owner, was thrilled when O'Toole finished first in his class with a straight A average and suggested that he take his skills to other funeral homes because there was good money for an exceptional embalmer. By the time Number Four was 24 years-old he had two kills. He stopped while he studied and he worked hard to develop some unique skills and techniques to help make his victims disappear.

Killeen and Calloway gave him raving reviews and great recommendations which led him to gainful employment at five different funeral homes. He chose his workplaces geographically, not because they would be closer to his home, but because they were closer to isolated areas where he could bury his victims' bodies that he couldn't dispose of through the funeral homes.

He learned how to sharpen knives from his father, the butcher. Number Three was very proud of his only son because he was the first one in the family tree that went to college. The father never encouraged his son to kill large numbers of men even though he desensitized him at a very young age. He once suggested that he was disappointed that Number Four had not told him any good stories lately that excited him.

The son replied, "Don't worry dad. I have developed new ways to dispose of our friends in an almost foolproof manner. The urge is there and its building."

The father smiled a sinful smile and rubbed his hands together saying, "That's my boy."

~~~~

"News, Michaels," he answered on the second ring.

"Hey buddy how ya doin," was the reply that brought a big grin to his face.

"Hey D-2 how you doin." Saying the word "doin" in a Chicago accent was a special greeting that they developed when they first met a couple of years ago.

Donna Blake was an FBI special agent. Blake was on loan to the Joint Terrorism Task Force when she used her technical skills to help identify Cyril Dobonovich better known in the Chicago area as "The Bug Man." A revenge serial killer who terrorized the city by killing people with deadly genetically manufactured microbiological organisms and pathogens. He tried to kill Michaels on three different occasions before he accidently stabbed himself with a syringe filled with TC-24, a deadly animal tranquillizer that was meant for Michaels.

"You sitting down, Peter?" D-2 asked, the smile no longer on her face.

"I am now. What's going on?" Michaels asked anxiously. His eyes revealing a deep sense of concern.

"That phone number you asked me to trace in my spare time."

"Yeah."

"Guess where it came from?"

"No clue."

"It's an EXEL-TELL, and it's one of the six phones the 'Bug Man' bought from Collardy's BEST DEALS."

Michaels felt like he wanted to vomit. An unfathomable feeling of angst instantly flushed through his entire being. His hands began to shake. "What the fuck!" he blurted out. "Are you sure?"

"That young gangbanger that Dobonovich killed bought six phones that day at BEST DEALS. We could only account for three of them," Blake said worriedly, running her fingers through her long, thick, curly, premature gray hair.

"You think there are more of those insane bastards running around out there?" Michaels inquired in almost a whisper.

"We don't know if the gangbanger turned all the phones over to the prick before he killed the kid. It could be that other gangbangers found them, and they wouldn't hesitate a second to steal them." Blake tried to reassure her friend. "We just don't know."

"Let me think about this for a while. Stay in touch and if you hear anything don't hesitate to call me," Michaels said, feeling helpless at the moment.

"You better alert your buddy Jack Warren."

"Yeah. I will. Hey, thanks," Michaels said sadly. The rosy character of his face was exchanged with a snowy, colorless, waxen tone like that of a bleached, unpainted canvas waiting for the artist's brush to bring it back to life. Michaels felt feverish, balmy, and anxious when he suddenly bolted from his chair, covered his mouth, and dashed to the bathroom.

~~~~

Everyday humans and animals alive begin to accumulate carbon-14 through carbon dioxide in the atmosphere. It's just part of life's cycle. When we are born we start to assimilate it and when we die we stop assimilating. It's that simple. Carbon-14 is a weak, unstable radioactive isotope of carbon. It can be used to date organic and some inorganic material, but it cannot be used on metals.

It is generally measured with three different principal radiocarbon dating methods. The most advanced method is Accelerator Mass Spectrometer. AMS is preferred because it is more accurate and precise, sample sizes are smaller and the analysis takes less time. The other two radiocarbon dating methods available are liquid scintillation counting and gas proportional counting.

Scientists can estimate the exact age of a person from the amount of carbon-14 in a sample and compare it against an internationally used reference standard. The impact of Radiocarbon dating is considered to be one of the most significant discoveries of the 20th century. One of its only limitations; If the sample is more than 60,000 years old it would be ineffective.

~~~~

FBI Agent and Forensic Anthropologist, Tom Britten, had no doubt that the FBI's technology and expertise could pinpoint with great precision the time of deaths of all the skeletons that were found at the Edgebrook Golf Course burial site.

Britten was in the office of Dr. Robert Crine to explain that he wanted to ship all the bodies to Quantico for AMS radiocarbon dating. He also said that the bureau's capability to extract DNA were second to none in the world.

"I have no objections whatsoever. As a matter of fact, I'm glad you can do it. It will save my department a lot of money." Crine said exhaling a deep breath then continued, "I would have to call in an expert anyway. We are not equipped to do this sort of thing. They're all yours."

"My guess doc…is…these bodies were buried around the turn of the century," Britten opined while looking at the small female on the ME's operating table. "What do you make of this?" Britten asked leaning in for a closer look of the right hand.

"I have just started working on her. So far I find no signs of murder or assault, but of course I need to be a little more thorough. My guess, she died of normal causes."

"It's the only female as well. The killers took no trophies from her. The others all appear on the surface anyway…to be around six feet tall," Britten stopped and once again leaned in and touched the girls hand and continued, "My gut tells me, these were ritual killings of some sort, you know what I am saying?"

The ME was nodding affirmatively, pursing his lips, and rubbing his recently trimmed goatee, "Ahh…hummm, yes, I have been thinking that since the fifth autopsy," Dr. Crine offered.

"If that's the case these two serial killers may have known each other. I'll talk with our profiling guys," Britten assured.

Dr. Crine shifted his weight from one side to the other, flipped up his magnifying optics and said, "I am convinced the stronger one is left-handed and the other was right-handed."

"We can determine if the female was poisoned if she wasn't stabbed like you're suggesting. She's just an anomaly in all of this. Just making it a more interesting mystery." Britten offered and then stated, "There is a lot of work ahead of us on this case doc."

"I know. Believe me, I know without a doubt. When I finish the autopsy on the young one, you can take them away. I have no objection if you want to take the other eleven today, I'll start making the arrangements. I've done all that I can right now. The rest is going to be up to science," Crine acknowledged.

"The bureau would like to get started as soon as possible. I'll start the paperwork on my end," Britten said with an affirmative nod. A smile inched in at the corners of his mouth. "Very anxious to get started."

CHAPTER 13

Michaels was exhausted after another long day that ended in some anxious moments. He flipped on the light switch in the hallway and turned into his bedroom. The pain felt like a bullet to the brain. His breathing became heavy, his mouth dry, his throat suffocating. He tried to yell for help but nothing came out. He grasped his neck and fell to his knees trying desperately to inhale oxygen, but nothing was there except the darkness of death. No air. No light. Only emptiness. He closed his eyes as his head hit the hardwood floor, fear filled his brown eyes along with tears and he screamed out, "Oh No!"

That's when he had awakened to sounds of another day starting early; a Streets and Sanitation garbage truck beeping while backing up to a dumpster in the parking lot below his tenth floor window, a police car running hot down Michigan Avenue, angry horns were already piercing the hot morning air. Another typical Chicago summer day was beginning. It was 6:45. The temperature was already 83 degrees. Humidity was hanging heavy in the air like an asphyxiating California smog.

Michaels was panting heavily. He was sweating profusely. His throat was sore and hoarse. His nightmare was back after a pleasant year of peaceful sleep and not a single thought of microorganisms and pathogens, or Cyril Dobonovich, "The Bug Man."

"Fuck," he said getting up from his wet sheets and pillowcase. His Harley Davidson tee shirt felt cold, clinging to his back and chest. He drained the bottle of water on his bedside table, brushed his teeth, gargled, and went to brew a cup of Dunkin Donuts coffee. It was too early to call anyone so he dialed his young buddy Jack Warren. "You sleeping?"

"Not anymore. What's wrong?" Warren asked, becoming fully awake, sensing that his friend sounded worried.

"That nightmare returned. It kinda unnerved me," he said.

"The Bug Man nightmare? You haven't had that for over a year," Warren responded now fully awake, rubbing the sleep out of his eyes.

"Remember I got that strange call a week ago?"

"Yeah."

"Well D-2 says the call came from one of Dobonovich's burner phones."

"Peter, that doesn't mean it's connected to Dobonovich. Some gangbangers probably stole them from the kid."

"Let's hope so," Michaels said, shaking his head wanting to believe that analysis, but not fully accepting it at all.

~~~~

Ryan O'Toole the fifth had his hearse on cruise control at 65 mph driving south on Illinois Route 127. It was a sweltering, hot, sunny day. The trip was boring and depressing with the air conditioner struggling to keep the interior of the old vehicle comfortable. This was his third and last trip to Southern Illinois.

It had been eleven months since he dropped off a body at the University of Southeastern Illinois at Vendee's body farm. His father transported a total of six corpses to the forensic facility since it opened in 1993. Two of those bodies were Number Five's kills. The body

Number Five was now transporting was his latest victim, number 31 of his iniquitous history. The victim was an older man who upset him in a bar after work two days before, because he incessantly stared and tried to talk to woman who apparently wanted nothing to do with him.

The fraudulent will donating the body to forensic science identified him as Walter Sullivan. His real name was Alex Birchman. He was a commercial real estate agent. Immediately after Number Five slit his throat, he transported him to the Logan and Logan Funeral home. He expertly cut off his trophies, except for the left ear, instead he took a piece skin the size of an ear from the scrotum sack for his collection. He cleaned up the body and stored it in the corner of an old freezer that was seldom used for current inventory. When he was ready to transport it to southern Illinois body farm early that morning, no one saw him come or go.

The death of Birchman was not reported on the news because as of today nobody even realized he was missing. He was scheduled to start his vacation on the night Number Five decided it was time for him to start killing again, and besides he thought Birchman was a pain in the ass.

The young college student who had intake duty that day was not pedantic about his work. His sleepy eyes seemed nonattentive. His breath reeked of stale beer from a fraternity party the night before. The killer was not worried about any type of interrogation from the disheveled intern. He noted that the remains of Walter Sullivan (Alex Birchman) were willed to the university by himself and that the body was delivered at two o'clock in the afternoon by the Logan and Logan Funeral Home. The student did not ask for O'Toole's identification when he signed the intake form. Number Five turned the victim's right hand slightly inward so that the young man would not notice the missing thumb and he propped the left toe inward as well.

The intern, however, did notice O'Toole's amber eyes when he took off his rose-tinted glasses to sign the receipt with his left hand. The student seemed to be a little shy and fortunately for Number Five so very inexperienced and better yet non-caring. O'Toole signed his name as Stuart Blakely, accepted the receipt, and didn't look back.

It was never disclosed how the facility would prepare and/or bury the body for decomposition. The O'Tooles didn't give a shit. Their only concern was that one more corpse was disposed of, and that they were never going to be questioned by law enforcement. It was the ninth and final body that an O'Toole would deliver to this body farm. Like father like son.

~~~~

Detective Tony Quag was listening intently to Dr. Robert Crine theorize about the remains of Dr. Phillip Kaley and how they coincidently matched those of all the victims, except that of the young woman, that were unearthed at the Edgebrook golf course.

"All of them appeared to be the same size, which is interesting in and of itself. Don't you think? All of them had evidence of knife inflicted wounds. Dr. Kaley had his right thumb cut off just like all the others. Don't you think that is too coincidental?" Dr. Crine summarized leaning back in his chair, looking up at the detective over his red dollar store reading glasses that were perched on the end of his nose.

"What about the clothes?" Quag asked.

"The clothes that they were buried in had deteriorated beyond any form of recognition but they could still possibly be used to help identify the time of death."

Dr. Crine opined but then said, "Back to Dr. Kaley."

"Yeah wasn't there something else?"

"Yes his left ear was cut off. With precision I might add by a left-handed killer." The ME offered rubbing his chin thoughtfully and pursing his lips.

"Well, these other bodies didn't have their ears cut off," Quag volunteered.

"We don't know that. All of these bodies were so badly decomposed to determine that fact, and that doesn't mean that they weren't cut off. We just don't have evidence of that right now."

"What about the toe? It wasn't cut off either, right?" asked Quag.

Dr. Crine opened his desk drawer and took out several crime scene photos and grunted as he handed them to the detective, "Look at these," he commanded mildly.

Detective Quag took the photos and started shuffling through them, staring at them intently. "Yeah. So?"

"Look at the left shoe. See it?" Dr. Crine said absent mindedly pointing his finger in the air at nothing in particular.

Detective Quag brought the picture closer, under a brighter light and mumbled, "I'll be damned."

"Yeah. Doesn't it look like the killer was attempting to take off the shoe," Dr. Crine asked with a new curiosity and eagerness in his voice as he stood and walked over to where Quag was examining the photos.

"Some people were walking their dog and surprised the killer in the middle of the murder. He had to get out of there for fear of getting caught. That's what I think," Crine offered.

"You might be onto something, doc."

"You know something Tony. Fact sometimes is stranger than fiction."

CHAPTER 14

G ary Swink was walking his golden retriever Wren on a freshly cut grassy area that suggested a natural pathway along a tree line in Schiller Woods Park on Chicago's near northside. The park district started expanding the park's picnic areas and walking trails. Landscape crews began leveling and cutting new grassy fields further away from the popular fishing ponds that attracted anglers of all ages every day the park was open.

Wren was an extraordinary two-year-old dog with an extremely mild temperament that made anyone who met her want to become a dog owner at that very moment. It was that pleasant characteristic that allowed her to be enrolled into a therapy dog training program designed to help sick people in hospitals, rehab centers and nursing homes find comfort and support for their emotional and physical ailments.

She had been in specialized training for over a year. That's why when Wren broke away from Swink abruptly and started barking loudly it was alarming. Then she began to dig a hole, over enthusiastically into the ground, something she had also never done before, he became unnerved.

"Wren...stop that," he commanded.

Wren obediently stopped digging and barking and sat down panting, Swink became even more unnerved because he was staring down at the rib cage of something that looked very human, like the skeleton he saw on display every time he walked into his chiropractor's office.

Swink's hands were shaking when he took out his cellphone and dialed 911.

"I think my dog just found a skeleton…just like the ones we have been watching on TV all last week," he told the 911 operator on the other end of his phone call.

"What's your location?" He was asked.

~~~~

Detective Jack Warren was on the phone with Peter Michaels, making sure his friend was all right from earlier that morning when the call came over his police radio that a new gravesite may have been discovered in Schiller Woods Park.

"What the…Hey I gotta go. A new gravesite may have been found," he informed Michaels.

"Where?" Michaels inquired before his friend hung up the phone.

"Schiller Woods. Along the north tree line." Warren said hanging up his phone and keying his mic, "This is 1432 responding in plain clothes to the call in Schiller Woods."

Warren turned on his siren and lights and pressed his foot all the way down on the accelerator and a twitch of a grin inched in the corners of his lips. He loved being the police, and he loved running hot. Most of all he loved the adrenalin rush that was pulsating through his body like water flowing over a dam, producing energy.

Michaels called his producer David Beedy and told him what happened and to get a cameraman out there as soon as possible. Just as he was ready to start up his black Harley Davidson Street Bob, his phone began to vibrate. He looked at the number that identified the caller as Gary Swink, a softball buddy. *Odd,* he thought, and then that ever present sign that read ANSWER THE PHONE in bold red letters that hung on the wall in the middle of his old newsroom in Detroit, instantly appeared in his memory. He answered the phone.

"Hey Gary, what's up?"

"Hey, sorry to bother you but you always said never hesitate to call if something happens that you think is important."

"Yeah, no problem. Whatta you got? I'm on my way north to Schiller Woods."

"That's where I am," he said in total surprise and then he smiled, "and that's what I am calling about. I was walking Wren and I think we discovered a grave, just like the ones you have been reporting about on TV last week."

"What are you doing?"

"Waiting to be interviewed by some detective, named Warren," he said nervously.

"He's a great guy, but do not tell him you know me. He'll tell you not to talk to me. I'll be there in a few."

Michaels started up his Street Bob, revved up his screaming eagles that displayed a roar that only a Harley possesses, then he gunned it and started weaving in and out of the heavy afternoon traffic on Chicago's beautiful Lake Shore Drive, with a grin from ear to ear that he could not contain.

~~~~

Ironically on this day, July 22,1975, some twenty-four years ago, Ryan O'Toole the fourth killed two people and buried them both in Schiller Woods. His father had died the year before and told him exactly where he had buried six bodies at the same site. It was a hot, sticky, humid night. Number Four worked tirelessly digging the graves in the isolated area hundreds of yards from the fishing ponds.

A waning crescent moon that lingered high in the dark sky afforded very little light, but it lived up to its reputation of bringing a sense of surrender and reflection. The moon provided dim cover and protection to the grave digger because dense summer storm clouds curtained the slit, making it nearly pitch black, as Number Four went about his business.

He parked his green Crown Vic in a lot next to several other cars that were stolen and could not be traced back to anyone. He then took the bodies one at a time to the burial site. O'Toole was forced to bury his latest kills because the unusually hot summer temperatures caused equipment problems and inventory issues at all five of the funeral homes where he worked as an embalmer. It was a predicament that had never occurred to him before and one that he had never even contemplated. The sweat that ran furiously down his back not only came from the weather conditions, but also from the anxiety that was exploding through his being. He swore at himself for not knowing he would be forced to hurriedly bury his new victims.

By the time he started digging the second grave, he was exhausted and dehydrated. He was looking over his shoulder more frequently than he did for the first one. Therefore, the grave was shallower than it should have been to offer the protection of time and detection.

The O'Tooles were sticklers about following family traditions, but over the years only Number One and Two never violated a single rule. As time passed, they got a little laxer but relished in the satisfaction that no one was ever connected to a crime until Number Three in a spiteful fit of rage killed his wife. He became the main suspect in the disappearance, but he rationalized the incident as no big deal because the police always looked at the husband first in those types of cases. He never realized though that his outrage would be the catalyst to the genesis of the next two generations of the O'Tooles' breakdown of strictly sticking to the basics.

Great, great grampa, the first, would be turning over in his grave if he knew that Number Four was trying to do too much at one time and that Number Five had already violated almost all of the rules he had established eleven decades ago.

CHAPTER 15

P eter Michaels pulled into the parking lot and when he saw all the flashing lights parked closer to the crime scene he naturally did the same and headed straight for all the police activity at the northern end of the park. He slid off his bike in one easy motion, dropped a square piece of wood on the ground so he could put his side stand on it to prevent his bike from toppling over. He took out his I-Phone 12 and started taking video as he quietly walked up to the cordoned off area like he belonged there.

The yellow plastic crime scene tape that marked the gravesite responded to the slight southerly breeze in the air, snapping, stiffening, and then slackening.

"How the fuck did you get here so fast?" Detective Jack Warren asked shaking his head.

Michaels threw his head in the direction of his Street Bob and grinned, "What's happening?" he asked but he already knew.

"We are waiting for a cadaver dog," Warren informed. "I can't let you go up there. You know that right? This is an active crime scene."

"I understand," Michaels said with a fake scowl and turned around to walk away, with no intention of leaving. He was thinking of a way to be at least allowed near the perimeter. Then he noticed that two K-

9 units arrived. He didn't recognize the first handler, a female officer with a great body and a regal looking German Shepard, but he grinned when Sergeant Mike Garofalo emerged from the second vehicle with his black Lab, Nosey.

It takes at least two years and some 1,000 hours of intense training to become a cadaver dog. Most dogs utilized by law enforcement for this assignment are either German Shepherds or Labrador Retrievers. Training a cadaver dog requires the use of human blood, decaying flesh, and bones. Canines have keenly acute senses of smell and dead bodies produce unique volatile compounds like cadaverine and putrescine. Once properly trained they are 95 percent accurate and that includes finding bones that have been buried for long periods of time.

Michaels first met Sergeant Garofalo at the Benjamin Franklin Institute of Technology's bone farm when he produced a series of reports about the importance of cadaver dogs for not only finding the remains of dead bodies but also for their incredible ability to find humans alive in catastrophes like tornado ravaged areas or collapsed buildings.

Michaels was holding up his camera phone as he approached his old friend, "How's Nosey?"

"Hey, you remembered his name," Garofalo said, grinning from ear to ear displaying his perfectly white teeth that seemed to glow even more brilliantly because of his dark tanned face. Garofalo was five seven. His muscular frame was tone. He was a college wrestler and his hands were strong, his knuckles were gnarly, his fist could still deliver a TKO punch on the first attempt. He was very competitive.

"Whose your partner? She looks hot," Michaels said looking over his shoulder as she approached them.

"Oh, that's Clare Claxton. She just finished her training with Bullet. This is their first encounter with the real thing. I'll be with her for a few months," the sergeant said.

"Lucky you. You still married?" Michaels asked with a coquettish grin.

"Yep, still married and still very much in love with Marg for 27 years and counting. Let me introduce you." His grin widening with a happy expression. His partner was not the first woman that he introduced to his friend.

Clare Claxton was five feet, three inches tall with a willowy, muscular body. Her blonde hair and tanned face made her blue eyes even bluer. Her smile was killer and her voice was soft and raspy and sexy. She spoke with a slight European accent. Swedish maybe.

Michaels all of sudden became very nervous. Like a shy schoolboy who just met the first love of his life.

"Hi," she said extending her slim, soft hand that offered a firm handshake, "I'm Clare Claxton."

Michaels caught himself in an awkward moment holding onto her hand a little longer than normal. He was literally tongue tied, but then managed to blurt out, "Peter Michaels…great to meet you," he said in a formal way that he regretted immediately.

Her eyes flirted with a smile. She turned to Garofalo and asked professionally, "What's the game plan, boss?"

Garofalo looked at his friend and said, "Let's talk later. I've got to get to work." They both turned around, summoned their dogs, who were sniffing each other, and walked toward the yellow tape that announced a crime scene.

Clare Claxton knew Michaels was eyeing her. She couldn't help smiling.

Michaels looked at his hands and they were trembling.

~~~~

FBI Agent/Forensic Anthropologist Tom Britten had the remains of the 12 victims sent to the FBI's state-of-the-art forensic lab in Quantico, Virginia. The lab was created in 1932 and has grown over the years into one of the most comprehensive crime labs in the world. It houses CODIS, the combined DNA Index systems. If a person commits a felony and a DNA sample is taken, the results are entered into CODIS and will remain there forever. Law enforcement from every jurisdiction can compare and exchange DNA profiles because of this data bank.

FBI scientists take a DNA sample, combine computer technology and forensic sciences into a tool that can link violent crimes. It can provide leads from any biological and bone evidence left at crime scenes. Those leads have helped authorities solve thousands of cases including those that have involved serial killers.

After agent Britten signed for the skeletal remains recovered from the Edgebrook golf course, he started giving orders to his forensic team to start conducting their specialty research.

"Okay, you all know the drill. I want DNA samples taken from the selected areas of the bones that will do the least amount damage, and then I want the bones that have been marked as the best possibilities of success for carbon dating to be entered into the Accelerator Mass Spectrometer (AMS). We need to find out exactly when these people were killed."

The team of scientists went to work without question when agent Britten's phone rang. He looked at the number and knew it was Dr. Robert Crine. "Hey, what's going on Bob?" he asked somewhat puzzled because he just talked to the ME less than two hours before. "We're good but we're not that good. I just got the team working on everything."

"Yeah. Yeah. I know that. You are not going to believe this?" Crine said anxiously.

"Believe what?"

"We found another skeleton. Same M.O."

"You're shitting me, right?" Britten said, scratching the stubble of his neatly trimmed white beard.

"No. Some guy was walking his dog in Schiller Woods and this dog is normally very calm and peaceful. She's like in special training to help really sick people. Anyway, it somehow picked up a cadaver scent and it went crazy and started digging frantically. Her nails did some damage to the rib cage but it will not be hard to separate the post traumatic injuries."

"Is it as big as Edgebrook?" he asked eagerly.

"We just got on the scene. We know of one body. I'm getting ready to go over there. CSI guys are out there and so are the cadaver dogs."

"Okay. Thanks. Keep me up to speed. I'll let you know when I know something from this end."

CHAPTER 16

C SI Tom Vander Aarde was kneeling on his one good knee, bending over the newly discovered site trying to determine the depth of the grave. He leaned forward with his trowel, gently prodding the earth around the shallow grave. He already removed the grass from the waist to above the head when his phone rang. He stood up and winced in pain from both his knee and back. "What's up doc?" he asked with a serious look as he backed away slowly, not to disturb anything. "So, you are on your way?" He nodded agreeingly and then noticed the cadaver dogs approaching. "Yeah. I was clearing the grave. The dogs are approaching as we speak. Yeah. See you soon."

Sgt. Mike Garofalo couldn't help but notice his buddy dressed in a white hazmat suit when he stood up with a phone to his ear. Garofalo, Vando and detective Jack Warren played together on the same 16 inch police softball team for the last four years. "What do you got Vando?" Garofalo inquired as his dog Nosey pulled him hard slightly past Vando and barked knowing he just identified another grave and sat down.

Before Vando could answer, Garofalo answered for him, "Whatever you got there, you have another one right here, next to it," he responded positively. "Good boy," he said to his dog, giving Nosey a little treat.

Clare Claxton's dog, Bullet, was pulling her further up the tree line, nose to the ground, tail swinging back and forth rapidly until he barked loudly and excitedly than sat down. Cadaver dogs sit once they make a discovery. They are trained not to dig at any site because it could destroy or damage potential evidence. Bullet was sitting and panting heavily. "Good boy. Good boy. We have another one up here," she yelled back and gave Bullet an enthusiastic rub on his ears. Bullet then moved slightly forward again, barked, and sat down looking up at his handler with very happy eyes. She leaned over and fed him a treat this time before giving him another enthusiastic ear rub.

Garofalo brought Nosey over to the new site and his dog started barking again and sat down. He yelled back, "Get some markers and more tape. We have another burial ground."

They both worked their dogs up the tree line and discovered three more graves. A total of eight.

~~~~

Deoxyribonucleic acid. DNA. The molecule of heredity. We all have it. We can all be identified because of it. It is our genetic fingerprint. It makes us who we are. DNA carries the instructions for development, growth, reproduction, and the functioning of all life. Each DNA codes a specific protein called a gene. It is estimated that the human body has 20,000 – 30,000 genes. Only one tenth of one percent of human DNA differs from one individual to another.

A trace amount of DNA can be left at crime scenes a thousand different ways; on a cigarette butt, on a bottle of water, blood, semen, fingernails, plucked and/or shed hair, sweat, teeth, and of course, bones. Once DNA samples are obtained they can be analyzed. Forensic scientists generally use two types of test: RFLP and PCR.

Restriction Fragment Length Polymorphism is the old fashion method of DNA testing. It was used in the trial of O. J. Simpson. It is a very time-consuming test but it can tell with a very high degree of certainty…999,999 chances in a million…that two samples are from the same person. About 50 nanograms of blood are required for this accurate of a reading. One millimeter of blood, about the size of a small pea, contains 20,000 nanograms. A RFLP test could take up to six weeks to produce accurate results.

Polymerase Chain Reaction on the other hand is a biochemical process that has basically replaced the RFLP method. PCR testing has come a long way over the years, and as more information about the structure of DNA was developed and how it replicates and copies itself, new PCR testing methods were developed along with it. The home COVID test for example is a PCR test and you get accurate results within minutes.

In forensic science, PCR tests are 95% accurate. This fast test requires only a minimum amount of DNA. A sample the size of the tip of a pin is all that is needed to conduct the test with a quick turnaround. The only thing that slows it down is the backlog of crimes that is overpowering law enforcement across the nation.

~~~~

Deborah Duke was five feet, four inches tall. She was slender and toned. Her hair was short and thick and naturally curly. Her skin was slightly tanned and smooth from walks on the beach. Her smile was gracious and soothing. Her eyes were brown and offered friendship. Her voice was soft and gentle, and she never raised it. Not in anger. Not in frustration. She was brilliant.

You would never know that she was blind unless you saw her sitting at a dinner table exploring the exact position of her water glass and silverware with that knowing touch of confidence. She was one of the best genetic detectives in the world and she was a good friend of Peter Michaels.

Retinitis pigmentosa started stealing her eyesight 30 years ago. She noticed it at first while driving at night and then gradually her vision began to blur. After she found out that she was adopted she became very curious about how she inherited this disease. Deborah Duke wasn't bitter. She would not let this set back stop her from living her life to the fullest. She became very inquisitive so, she started studying DNA testing, looking for her roots.

It began as a hobby. She was so intrigued by her research that she turned it into a successful business. Duke had a long history of helping people find distant relatives. Peter Michaels asked her to find a source's son years ago, and shortly after that it led to a career in law enforcement. She has contributed in solving numerous cases from murders to missing persons around the country. Deborah Duke was very, very good.

She was absolutely fascinated by the reports about all the bodies being discovered in Chicago. She wanted to be part of the action so, she picked up the phone and dialed her old friend.

~~~~

Peter Michaels had at least an hour's worth of very good video on his cellphone at the newest crime scene before his cameraman Kevin Reardon arrived. Kevin was six foot, seven with a lanky frame. His eyes were hazel and expressive. His smile was genuine and friendly. His Irish skin did not like the torture it received from sunny, hot summer days. Sunscreen was discoloring the eyepiece of his camera.

"Whose that blonde over there with the Shepard?" He asked knowing that Michaels had been eyeing her as he walked up to him. "When are you taking her out?" Reardon asked with a grin that immediately turned into a smile from ear to ear.

"Soon as I can," Michaels responded and winked.

"Good for you...Why do they have us so far away? This sucks," Reardon said while taking in the entire scene he was about to shoot.

"They just found more bodies. See if you can get some high shots. I got a bunch of stuff on my cell. It's good shit from earlier but they just found a few more gravesites and I can't get any more shots with this," he said holding up his cellphone, and just then it rang. He looked at the number, surprise widened his eyes, and a friendly smile appeared on his lips, "Funny you should call. How are you Deborah?"

"I am just fine. How about you?" She asked in a happy note.

"Very busy. Lot's going on here in old Shit-cago."

"I've been watching," she responded and that made Michaels' smile even wider.

"I was just thinking about you this morning and was going to give you a call. You interested in getting involved with this DNA identification?" He already knew the answer by the phone call.

"I would love too. Just tell me what I have to do," She responded.

"I am sure I can get the station to cover your hotel and some expenses but I am not sure what they will be willing to pay."

"I tell you what. You get me on the case. I won't charge you a thing. I am totally fascinated by all of this...Deal?"

"Deal. But you got to promise me one thing."

"What's that?" she said knowing what was coming next.

"Information."

"No problem," she said with a grin.

"Let me try to set some things up. I'll get back to you, soon," Michaels said with a new smile as he hung up the phone.

CHAPTER 17

N umber Five was on the hunt. His new victim was a patient
that he despised the moment they first met on the operating
table a week earlier. He did not fit the O'Toole family profile
in any way. Terry Peterson was 60 years old, fat, bald and obnoxious.
It didn't matter. He pissed off Ryan O'Toole because of his constant
complaining and haranguing.

Peterson lived in Garfield Park on the first floor of a newly
renovated three flat. Number Five followed him for four days. He was
a creature of habit. His routine was always the same; he left the house
through the backdoor, walked down the alley to his favorite
neighborhood tavern, watched sports that involved women only, drank
cheap bar well gin, and stumbled home around ten o'clock.

Every day of his recon, Five would get angrier and angrier as he
thought about the fat fuck's complaining; this room is too cold, this
table is too hard, can you get me a bigger pillow for my neck. *FUCK
YOU*, Five thought, and tonight was the night Peterson was going to
die. Once O'Toole made up his mind that was it.

The alley had a lot of potholes. The asphalt was bleached by the
sun. Ribbons of black tar that filled in its cracks, tattooed the crumbling
surface. Blue and black city garbage cans were scattered and tipped

over. A few crabgrass type weeds were trying to survive in the snaking runnels, reaching for the sun to give life to their roots.

O'Toole's dark blue van was pulled right next to a garage door. The headlights were out but the side door was wide open, the indoor light was covered with a cloth allowing a slight glow of light to make any passerby curious enough to look inside.

Peterson was staggering home and humming to himself, to what tune O'Toole couldn't tell nor did he care. As soon as the fat man stopped humming, Number Five knew he was poking his tumid face into the van. Peterson saw that the inside of the van was covered with a plastic sheet of some sort. *What the fuck* he thought. *This is strange.*

Five was on him in two quick steps, "You like what you see bitch?" He said softly as he plunged his sharp twelve inch knife into Peterson's fleshy stomach and pulled up severing his left anterior descending artery (LAD).

"It's Yo…" was the last thing Terry Peterson said with his eyes bulging out in total surprise recognizing his killer immediately. It was those amber eyes that revealed his identity in that instant before death. The pain may have registered in his mind for a split second. Death was almost instant.

Number Five had the knife's blade through a towel which was over his hand and as he pulled the knife out, he automatically covered the wound with it, trying to absorb as much blood as possible to leave no trace evidence in the alley. Peterson's lifeless body began to fall, O'Toole flexed his knees and rolled him into the van and shut the door. He looked around and a demonic grin creased his lips. No witnesses. No sound. No problem. He got into his van and drove away, looking back at his 32nd victim, he hollered, "Fuck you. You Fat Fuck."

Ryan O'Toole never noticed the elderly insomniac who sat by her rear bedroom window every single sleepless night waiting for her son to come home from his midnight shift at the 13th police district. She didn't see the whole thing but she saw enough to tell her Frankie that she witnessed a murder.

~~~~

Dr. Robert Crine arrived at Schiller Woods at midafternoon. It was muggy and hot. The blue sky was draped with a foggy cloud of humidity that almost sucked the air out of your lungs. Crine started to assess the situation and develop a plan to excavate the eight new graves. CSI Tom Vander Aarde was in the preliminary stages of removing the earth from the first grave, when Crine said, "Hey Vando before you totally clear that site try to find the right hand and see if we have the same hitchhiker killer."

Crine had no idea why he came up with the moniker "hitchhiker killer," other than he had just finished reading a Lee Childs' "Reacher" novel. Most hitchhikers use their right thumbs walking backwards to hitch a ride.

Vando conveyed a surprised expression and then smiled at the ME's choice of epithet for the killer or killers. It took him twenty minutes to get to the right hand as he gingerly cleared the area and carefully whisked away enough dirt to just raise it slightly. *Son of a bitch!* He thought and then yelled, "Hey Doc. You're right on. Come over and take a look. It's the hitchhiker."

Crine became contemplative, rubbing his white goatee, pursing his lips. *I'll be damned!* Everything was beginning to add up. After 35 years of doing this stuff he thought nothing could surprise him anymore, but he realized he was wrong.

~~~~

Peter Michaels finished his live shot for the six o'clock news and walked over to Clare Claxton who was congratulating her dog Bullet with ear rubs and doggie treats.

"Nice looking dog you have there," Michaels said with a coquettish grin.

"Thanks. He is a good boy," she said as Bullet was licking her face accepting her praise graciously. "You like dogs?" She asked with a flirtatious grin of her own.

"Oh yeah, I love dogs but I'm afraid I would be a bad dog daddy because I work such crazy hours," Michaels responded, his lips now trying to convey a disappointing look.

"Yeah, I get it and appreciate it as well," she said. "I hate it when people get a dog and then basically abandon it."

"I know. I could never do that. Say, would you like...like....to...to get a drink sometime?" Michaels stammered nervously.

"Sure. When are you thinking?" she responded still smiling.

"I don't know, soon as possible," he muttered and then felt stupid as his face flushed crimson.

"Tonight?" she suggested, still smiling.

"I'd love to, but I've got to be live on the ten, but after that we can go for a quick one," he suggested with a grin.

"Hey, I have never seen a live newscast. Why don't I come to your studio around 9:30 and we can go out after that," Clare said almost shyly. Her blue eyes smiling.

Michaels was surprised and happy at the same time, "Yeah I'll set it up," he said and handed her his card. "My cell is the best number to use. What's your number?"

"I'll call you and you'll have it. I'm going home to take care of Bullet and take a shower. I'll see you around 9:30," she said and led her dog to the police K-9 unit, SUV.

Michaels turned around with a smile that he could not contain and almost bumped into Dr. Crine. "Hey doc, what do you think?"

"I think you should be very careful. That's one good looking woman," Crine responded with a grin teasing his friend.

"No. Come on doc. You know what I mean. The graves. The bodies."

"I think we have a serial killer or killers. We have only cleared a portion of one of these graves but the evidence is suggesting that it's the same guy or guys."

"The thumb and toes?" Michaels asked his smile disappearing.

"Don't know about the toes yet but by God, the first body didn't have a right thumb."

CHAPTER 18

P eter Michaels was walking off the set with anchorman Ron
Magers after finishing his story on the new gravesites. "Hey
Ron let me introduce you to officer Clare Claxton. She and her
dog Bullet found some of those graves today."

Clare was in a flowery summer dress revealing a tanned, well-
toned body. Her smile was infectious as she shook the anchorman's
hand. "This is the first time I have seen a live newscast. It's pretty
impressive to see how it all comes together technically and
professionally with all the people behind the scenes."

"Sometimes it goes very smooth and other times there can be some
confusion, but we have a very good team," Magers responded.

Producer Dave Beedy came up to them with an anxious look on
his face, "You have to see this video. I just got it sent to me by a source.
It happened last night. Chicago is losing control. Look."

Beedy hit the play button and all eyes shifted to his I-phone. The
black and white video included sound showing a man being robbed at
gunpoint of his groceries and then his cellphone. Beedy began to
narrate, "Watch, a struggle ensues and the robber then shoots the man
in the chest...twice. He's asking for the password to the phone. Can
you hear him? The victim's moaning in pain and he gave the password

to his assailant and then the son of a bitch shoots him in the head anyway. The shooter doesn't even look back and gets in a car and drives away."

"Probably never solve that one," Clare offered. "These robberies and carjackings are happening every single day in the city. If we catch the bad guy, we are not sure if they will prosecute the crime."

"Yeah, I was involved in a drive by shooting and one of the shooters was wearing three ankle monitors. It put him at the scene of the crime and the police don't know if the bad guys will be prosecuted. The State's Attorney calls them mutual combatants. Is that crazy or what?"

"We see it all the time. It's demoralizing. I am so glad I work with Bullet and don't have to put up with a lot of that bullshit," Claxton said now blushing, then added. "Excuse me."

"Let's get out of here. It's been a long day. How about Blackie's? It's right around the corner. We can walk there," Michaels said.

"You sure you want to walk? I can park my car anywhere. I have a police tag."

"Sounds good. Anyone want to join us?"

Magers and Beedy looked at each other and then at Michaels and Claxton. "Naw," they both said in unison and then winked at Michaels shaking their heads, both with grins creasing their lips."

~~~~

Number Five was struggling with the dead weight of Terry Peterson's body. He was bigger in death than he was in life. Five was exhausted by the time he was able to get the body into the embalming room and onto the operating table. After he drained all the blood, he was getting ready to severe his limbs to hide them in a casket, but the casket was not there. He discovered that the family of the deceased changed their minds and decided to cremate the remains of the elderly person instead of burying them.

"Son of a bitch," Five screamed. He was working at McMurry and Macintosh's Funeral Home. Business was surprisingly slow but the owners were not concerned, they were headed to their Michigan summer home for a week. Five was debating if he should embalm Peterson or not, then it occurred to him that the Zoo Woods and McCormick Woods off of First Avenue offered him an answer to his dilemma. He noticed the woods the other day while driving by them and he thought to himself *These would be great burial places*. The trees were dense and overgrown. The area provided great cover. With less work than digging a grave, he could hide the limbs in various spots and the environment would do the rest.

He took his trophies and more. He had broken the O'Toole family rules so often, one more wouldn't matter and it might throw off the police, so for the first time he severed both thumbs and big toes. It had been a while since he had a feast. He carved up Terry Peterson into seven pieces; the arms, the legs, the torso he split in half and the head. He put the head in a box and shoved it under a shelf in the left corner of the old refrigerator. No one would ever notice it and the next time he took a body for cremation he would dispose of it.

The part time job at McMurry and MacIntosh's had helped him out of many troubling spots over the last fifteen years. He carried out Peterson's body two pieces at a time and placed them in the funeral home's blue van. Nothing could be traced back to him.

~~~~

Peter Michaels and Clare Claxton were the only two patrons left in Blackie's at 11:45pm. They were talking freely and endlessly when Michaels heard a cough and looked up to see Mel, the owner, with a grimace on his face. When he nodded towards the door with his head and a tired look, Michaels took the hint, that it was time to go.

"We better get out of here. I didn't realize what time it was," Michaels said with a continuous smile that was on his face all night when he wasn't talking. He was smitten and he knew it. "I don't want to be too forward on our first date but do you mind driving me home. My Harley is down in the garage and it'll be a bitch trying to get it out this late."

"No problem, but I've got an early call in the morning. I have to get home."

She said pouting with her lower lip.

That made Michaels stir. He liked where this might go. "What's up in the morning?"

"Garofalo and I are hitting some of the parks. The ME asked the superintendent if we could be put on a special assignment to look for more gravesites." She responded and continued, "I like this, but let's start slow. I don't want to ruin it. I think we could have a lot of fun."

Michaels nodded and said, "I agree. I think we could have a lot of fun."

"Where do you live?" She asked getting into the car.

"Turn left on Michigan Avenue. It's 880." Michaels said sliding into his seat, smiling.

~~~~

At two in the morning, Ryan O'Toole, the fifth, parked the van in an off the road clearing, deep in the Zoo Woods that offered camouflage from what little traffic there was at this time in the morning. The moon was high and full, illuminating his way as he penetrated the forest searching for copious areas to hide his kill. Even though it was hot and muggy, he had his pant legs tucked into his hunting boots and he was wearing a thick canvas jacket with a hood to protect him from being poked, pierced, or punctured from thick hanging limbs and branches. His shirt was saturated in sweat and his eyes were burning from the perspiration tumbling down his forehead over his eyebrows, around his nose and into his eyes.

He found a trench like area under some fallen trees. The green leaves high overhead were waving in the wind at the moonlight, casting eerie, moving shadows but it also offered Number Five some minimal relief from the heat. He unwrapped the six body parts with assiduity and wedged each of the exposed remains into the natural cervices under the branches and roots. He knew that exposure to the sun and rain and other elements, along with the insects and maggots, not to mention the animal predators looking for food, would expedite the decomposition process.

Satisfied his work was complete, as he stood to leave a short sharp branch sliced his cheek under his right amber eye producing a three inch jagged gash. He instinctively put his filthy gloved hand on the wound to stop the bleeding. He held his head back slightly and felt the warm blood seeping down his neck and onto his chest. He slowly retreated out of the woods to his van. It took forty-five minutes to complete the task. He shed the canvas coat, unbuttoned his shirt, took a deep breath, got in the van, put it in gear and returned to McMurry and Macintosh Funeral Home.

He had three days off. He needed the time to think, repair his cheek, and plan his next kill. His urges were increasing.

CHAPTER 19

Peter Michaels was glad that Clare Claxton wanted to get home for two reasons; one he was exhausted, and two he didn't want to move too fast and ruin the relationship before it even got started. It had been a long grueling week. When he got off the elevator on the tenth floor a chill ran up his spine. Even though he took just three steps he stopped and looked over his shoulder feeling as if someone was there, watching him. All he saw was the elevator doors closing. He slowly walked down the hall; the eerie feeling was persistent. He couldn't shake the thought of Cyril Dobonovich, the Bug Man, who tried to kill him three times, twice in his own building. He put the key in the door with his right hand then reached into his back pocket, pulled out his handkerchief, wrapped it around the doorknob as a precaution, twisted the knob and opened the door. "Hello," he said announcing his presence to the empty condo, flipping on the lights.

He took a long deep breath, exhaled through his nose trying to settle his nerves. It didn't work. He didn't know why. He went to the liquor cabinet, poured himself two fingers of bourbon and drank it down in one swallow. Sleep could not come fast enough. He prayed his nightmare would not return this night. He fell into a deep sleep instantly, but that only lasted for a couple of hours, restlessness and tossing and turning and sweat followed for the next five hours.

~~~~

Frank Tedesco was a tactical team leader. He worked in plain clothes chasing gangbangers and drug dealers. He had a busy night responding to another five shootings in his 13th district alone. Two died. His 87-year-old mother was waiting for him at the kitchen table when he walked into the house. Her small, soft, veiny hands were wrapped around a cup of steaming hot black coffee. It was one of the only warm feelings that gave her comfort in her old age. She was always tired. She hardly ever slept at night. Hopefully she would be able to cat nap during the day after she told her son what she saw at 10:30 last night.

"Hey momma, how ya doin?" Tedesco asked with a loving, reassuring smile. Tedesco had been on the job for 17 years. He loved being the police until the last two years. Morale on the department was at an all-time low. People they arrested were out of jail and back on the streets before they got their paperwork completed that put them in jail in the first place.

Tedesco's six foot two inch frame housed a muscular 200 pounds. A weight he has maintained since high school. He projected a tough ass veneer, but deep down he was a momma's boy. Though he always seemed to be smiling, his dark brown eyes revealed a sadness at times. The block lettered tattoo of J2D on his right calf revealed why. It meant: Just Today. It was a reminder of the day his late wife was diagnosed with pancreatic cancer. It was also a reminder to live everyday with joy and satisfaction and accomplishment. It was why he agreed to take care of his mother for the rest of her life.

"I saw something terrible last night, Frankie." She said with melancholy, tired eyes.

A cosseted look curtained Frank's face and he reached for his mother's hands. He could see she was trembling. "Momma, what are you talking about? What did you see?" He asked in a reassuring way holding her hands tenderly.

"I only saw a little bit out the back window. There was a van parked over there by the Corbett's garage. The side door was opened. That's why I noticed it. Why leave it open like that. You know what I am saying, Frankie?"

Frank nodded affirmatively. His eyes started to well with tears, feeling his mother's sadness and concern.

"This man comes walking down the alley and then another man like jumps him and pushes him into the van."

"You saw this last night. Momma?"

"Yes. Yes. I saw this white rag or something that was covered in what I think was blood," she recalled now turning pale.

Tedesco stood up and took his mother by the hand and led her to her favorite reclining chair and raised her feet, "Momma, you rest. I'm gonna go look out back."

He covered her with an Afghan, settled her down and walked out to investigate in the alley. The first thing he noticed was a dark wet spot in front of the Corbett's garage door of what appeared to be blood. He went back to the house, grabbed some latex gloves, some plastic baggies, and a few tools.

Tedesco grabbed his cellphone and dialed his buddy detective Jack Warren.

"Hey, Frankie, what's up? Haven't heard from you in a while." Warren said with a smile.

"Yeah, we've been crazy busy. Somebody is getting shot every night. Hey, listen, you are not going to believe this, but my Ma thinks she saw a murder last night."

"What the hell, you're serious." Warren exclaimed.

"Serious as a heart attack. I was just going to go out there to scrape a sample of what I believe to be blood off the ground." Tedesco said.

"Just go out there and protect the scene. I am just a few minutes away from you. I'll be right there."

~~~~

On this very weekend two decades before, Ryan O'Toole, the fourth, killed his 32nd and last victim, but he needed help from his son. Number Four had lung cancer and was getting very weak. It was the only time Four killed a woman. It was the start of Number Five's attitude about killing anyone he wanted to...disobeying the long-standing O'Toole family rules.

Number Four did all the planning and recon work. Mildred Wesinovich was a small, grumpy woman who looked much older than her fifty years. She cleaned three of the five funeral homes where Four worked. For more than five years, Number Four told himself *that woman has to die.* He could not stand her constant bitching about everything in her life; her husband left her, her kids don't talk to her, she's not being paid enough for all that she does, my life has no meaning. *No shit bitch that's why you are going to die.*

On that early Saturday morning more than twenty years ago, Number Four met Mildred Wesinovich as she was getting out of her car. She was startled at first but when she recognized him, she relaxed. He smiled at her and asked if she needed any help, to disarm her, but before she could answer his 12 inch knife was in her throat and her spinal column was severed. She was dead before she felt any pain. Four immediately pushed her back into her car.

Number Five just watched from the shadows, smiling at his father's agility even though he was getting frail. "I got her. I'll meet you at the funeral home. Go," Number Five said without a single ounce of emotion, he moved the corpse over to the passenger seat, pushed her head down so she was out of sight and started talking to her. "You ain't gonna bitch anymore, you old bitch," he said with an evil sneer and drove to Logan and Logan Funeral Home and Crematorium on Lincoln Avenue.

Five carried the body into the embalming room. No one else was there besides his father. The security camera was off. They cut her into seven pieces, stuffed her limbs and torso into an old, wooded casket with the remains of a 93-year-old woman who was scheduled to be cremated that weekend.

Five stoked the furnace and when it was at the desired temperature they rolled the casket into the flames. It took an hour and fifteen minutes to dispose of the bodies, total weight was less the 200 pounds.

There was very little blood in the car, all of it basically flowed downwards and away from the deadly wound. Five took a few Lysol wipes just in case he needed them. He drove her old beat up car to a busy mall off of Clybourne. He wasn't worried about his prints, he wore gloves the entire time but, he wiped the steering wheel as an extra precaution. He also wiped down the center portion of the seat where a stain appeared. The old car would blend into its new environment. Hiding in plain sight. It wasn't discovered until November and by then Ryan O'Toole the fourth had been dead for over a month.

By the time he died, the O'Toole family had killed 86 people and Number Five was looking for his 13th victim, and he was just getting started. It was 2000.

CHAPTER 20

The cold water that he splashed on his face did little to wake up Peter Michaels. He felt like he drank too much red wine. His head was pounding. His ass was dragging. He started rolling his shoulders to loosen the tension he was feeling in his neck and upper back. He plugged in a K-cup of Dunkin Donuts coffee and hit the strong button. His cellphone rang loud to the tune of the "William Tell Overture," Michaels smiled, he knew it was Jack Warren. "Hey, what's up buddy?" Michaels asked yawning.

"Did I wake your sorry ass up? Why are you yawning? Was Clare too much for you last night?" Warren asked smiling.

"How did you know about Clare?" Michaels asked surprised.

"Everyone is talking about it, man. A lot of the guys would love to take her out. She's hot," he said pulling to a stop for a red light.

"I am not sure when we will go out again. It went well. I don't want to push it too hard. She's working today with Garofalo. They're looking for more gravesites. Speaking of which, what do we know?"

"Agent Tom Britten called late last night. We should have some carbon dating answers very soon. They are also putting some DNA profiles together."

"Is he working this weekend?"

"I think everything is running at the labs and the new FBI candidates are on shifts over the weekend with specific instructions to notify him if any samples meet the profile parameters they established," Warren responded, then said, "Hey, It's Frankie; let me take this. I'll call you later."

Michaels hit the end button and started debating with himself if he should call Clare. Patience was something he lacked, and it always played havoc with his love life because he tended to move too fast. He decided to wait and as if ESP kicked in, Clare called him. He answered with a smile veiling his face. "Hey what's up? How'd you sleep?"

"I slept great but the time flew by. How are you?" she asked with a grin.

"I'm tired. Tough night sleeping. You interested in listening to some blues tonight at Buddy Guy's. It's right out my back door."

"Let me see how the day goes. I am not sure how long I will be working. Mike is calling the shots and he mentioned we might just try two or three parks today and pick it up again on Monday."

"Sounds good. I'll probably work the phones today. I'm dragging my butt. I tossed and turned a lot last night," he said trying to stymie yet another yawn.

"How about I text you when I am done with work. How's that?"

"Perfect. I won't bug you until I hear from you later," he said as they both hung up, smiling.

~~~~

Frank Tedesco was talking to his neighbor Billy Corbett when Warren pulled up. Tedesco had a scarred, dirty yellow traffic pylon next to the spot he thought was blood.

He didn't notice Jack Warren approaching until he heard his voice.

"Hey buddy, what's up?" Warren asked with a smile and then he looked down on the pavement and said, "That does look like blood."

Tedesco told his neighbor, "See you later," and turned around, smiling, and giving his buddy a fist bump.

"Looks like blood to me. I've got a fast blood test kit in my trunk. We'll know shortly," he said and they both walked down the driveway to Warren's car.

"How's Angelina?" Warren asked.

"I'm a little worried about mom. She isn't sleeping well and she is starting to forget things," Tedesco responded.

"She was sharp enough to see something last night," Warren said looking at his friend with concern.

A Rapid Stain Identification Blood Field Kit is designed for fast, easy, and reliable detection of human blood from evidence found in the field. They fetched the test kit, returned to the crime scene and Warren went to work swabbing the suspected blood. The kit has all the materials needed to gather an accurate sample in such a way to enable a proper DNA analysis. The test takes a full hour for a complete, positive result but within minutes it will reveal some indication of blood. Warren scraped some of the asphalt, bagged it and recorded it. He looked at the swab and said, "It looks like it is positive for blood."

"Should we call Vando? He's just around the corner," Tedesco said.

"That's a good idea. I think we have a crime scene that we have to preserve," Warren said looking at the sample.

~~~~

Tom Vander Aarde lived nearby in Garfield Ridge on Chicago's Southwest side, fifteen minutes from Midway airport. It's an area of two and three bedroom cape cods, Georgians, ranches and bungalows with neatly trimmed yards and colorful flower gardens. Every other house seemed to be occupied by a cop, firefighter, or city worker. Vando and his wife Coni were having their second cup of coffee reading the news on their computers when his phone rang.

"Shit, I hope this isn't work. It's been a long, long week," he muttered to Coni. A smile creased his lips when he saw Jack Warren's name appear on his caller ID. "Hey buddy, what's up? We gonna play some ball today?" he asked, the smile on his face deteriorating with Warren's response.

"Frank's mom, Angelina saw something last night in their alley. I just did a blood test and I think we have human blood here. I hate to bother you on your day off, but I think we have to make this official. It's a crime scene."

"I'll be right over, but you better call it in to the district to preserve the chain of evidence." Vando replied then lipped to Coni, "It's work. Gotta go."

~~~~

Ryan O'Toole, the fifth, woke up angry. His body didn't crave a lot of sleep but sleep evaded him last night. It didn't bother him in the slightest that he broke every O'Toole family rule, but he regretted that he disposed of Terry Peterson's body without much thought and that is what aggravated him.

Serial killers don't want to get caught but in their minds they actually like the fact that someone is thinking about them, the police, the media, their victims' families. The O'Tooles have been killing for decades and have never been discovered, not because they were brilliant but because they planned their kills and making mistakes can change all of that.

The more he stewed, the more he wanted to kill and the less he felt guilty about his disposal method of that fat fuck Terry Peterson. As a matter of fact, the more he thought about it he was considering to dispose of more bodies in similar ways. He was also starting to feel uncomfortable about how he was being treated at the funeral homes where he worked part time. More and more people were being cremated and his workload had been cut back considerably. He decided to install a stainless steel table in his basement to finish his work. He didn't need anybody else.

I have killed 32 people in the last 32 years. They'll never catch me. He thought as an opprobrium grin ghosted his face.

CHAPTER 21

D etective Jack Warren, CSI Tom Vander Aarde and Frank Tedesco were watching the crime scene investigators wrapping up their investigation in the alley behind Tedesco's house. There was not much more evidence that could be bagged and tagged, other than several more swabs of blood and some asphalt chunks. The crime scene was guesstimated to be a 20 by 20 foot square area in front of the Corbett's garage. It did not take long to photograph and process it.

"This is going to be like finding a needle in a haystack," CSI Tom Vander Aarde opined.

"Unless whoever this blood belongs to is in the system, I agree," said Jack Warren.

"You guys want to grab a big baby at Nicky's?" Vando asked.

"I need to spend some time with mom. She's very rattled with all of this. Another time," suggested Frank Tedesco. "I am going to have to go over to the district and write this up. That's all I need for the weekend...more work."

"Yeah, I could eat something. I'm starving and haven't been to Nicky's in a long time." Warren said.

Nicky's Hot Dogs is a 20 foot square single story faded yellow brick structure on the Northeast corner of Austin and Archer. It's mainly a takeout joint, but it offers six short stools lining the westside of the building looking down Archer Avenue and five stools with a view of the three fast order cooks preparing the best gyros in Chicago, hot dogs, and big babies. A big baby is a double cheeseburger with sautéed caramelized onions that melt in your mouth. With the exception of a new video menu board above the order station, Nicky's hasn't changed in 55 years. The old white subway tiles on the walls have faded to a yellowish brown and they're covered with signs; welcoming first responders, an autographed picture of Peter Michaels, a recognition poster from the Chamber of Commerce and sun-bleached photos of customers from over the years.

"Yeah, Coni would love a big baby. I'm starving," Vando said.

"Vando you should spend as much time as you can with your bride. I have a feeling we are going to be very busy. I think there are more bodies out there waiting to be found," Warren warned.

Vando pursed his lips and shook his head in agreement, "I think you're right about that my friend."

~~~~

Mike Garofalo and Clare Claxton walked the tree lines of three parks on the Northside with their dogs and did not find any more gravesites. The temperature was in the 90s and the air was humid and sticky and the dogs were panting and slobbering.

"Let's call it a day," Garofalo said. "We can pick this up again on Monday."

"That's good by me. What are you going to do with the rest of your day?" Clare asked.

"Probably barbeque something. You?" He asked.

"Not sure. What do you know about this Peter Michaels?"

"Good guy. He works hard. Jack loves him, says he's great. They live in the same building and Jack was there when that crazy scientist tried to kill him last year. Why?" Garofalo inquired with a smile knowing she was fishing for information.

"Well, I went out with him last night. I went to the studio and saw the newscast. It was interesting how they do all that stuff behind the scenes. Then we went to Blackies for a beer and burger. He seems sincere and he's very passionate about his job," Claxton said.

"He knows a lot of people. I don't know how he comes up with all the shit he does, but you are right, he is passionate about what he does. Are you going out with him again?" Garofalo asked with a smile.

"Yeah, probably. He's interesting," she said returning a smile and a wink.

~~~~

"Don't you ever stop working?" Dr. Robert Crine asked Peter Michaels.

"I love what I do. It's not like work to me." Michaels responded. "So, what can you tell me about the bodies?"

"We should have some news from the feds by Monday, but what I do know for sure is, all of the bodies are about the same size and height, five-ten to six-one. My guess is that they are all about the same age when they died. They were all killed with a knife or some other sharp instrument," Crine said.

"You can tell they are the same age?"

"Carbon dating will tell us for sure. DNA will also help ID them."

"Do you remember Deborah Duke? The genetic detective. I asked her if she wanted to be in on this. I think she can help. What do you think?"

"We will need all the help we can get. This could take a long, long time."

"She'll be here this week. So, what else?"

"I believe there are at least two killers. I told you that before, but now I am convinced of it."

"Why?" Michaels asked now getting out his reporter's notebook.

"I have no doubt they took trophies. I have analyzed the bones where they were severed. The cuts are very similar. I am puzzled by the body that I autopsied yesterday that was found at Schiller Woods."

"Why?" Michaels asked writing with keen interest.

"I think there may be a third killer."

"What?" Michaels exclaimed now totally enthralled.

"I am going to ask agent Britten to do a further analysis but I think the area where the thumbs were cut off had a different angle than the other two."

"What about the toes?" Michaels asked.

"There is a longer cutting area with the thumb, but with the toes that is not so easy to tell because those were basically cut off in a downward motion at the joint. Hopefully the FBI can find out more about that with their highly sophisticated equipment."

"Can they tell if different knives were used as well?" Michaels inquired.

"The FBI has some incredible equipment in their lab. So, I hope so."

"How many bodies so far?"

"Twenty; eight at Schiller Woods and twelve at Edgebrook golf course, but one of those was a young woman and I don't think she was murdered. I have no idea how she got there."

"There could be a lot more?" Michaels opined.

"I'm afraid so," Dr. Crine agreed stroking his goatee as if he was solving a puzzle.

~~~~

When Clare Claxton and Peter Michaels entered Buddy Guy's House of Blues they were greeted by the classic sound of Stevie Ray Vaughan's "Pride and Joy" and a smiling, six-foot-six, 350 pound bouncer. The name Big Eddie didn't do him justice. His 21 inch biceps and his ripped abs were restrained by a bright yellow, XXXL, tee shirt that clung to his body like a pair of latex gloves. His blue sweatpants hid his 28 inch thighs. His shaved head glistened from the overhead lights and his smile revealed a gold crown on his front tooth.

"Hey Peter, where ya'll been my man? Haven't seen you in a while," he said reaching out his large hand that probably couldn't fit into a pair of boxing gloves. "Who's your lady?"

"Eddie meet Clare," Michaels said watching Big Eddie eyeing her, his smile widening. His eyes taking in her beauty and body.

Clare's hand disappeared in Big Eddie's, "Glad to meet you. You take care of my man, here."

"I'll try," she said with a smile that brightened up her entire face.

"Hey Peter, take those two seats at the bar that I have reserved," the big man said.

Michaels led Clare to the bar, looking back at Eddie winking and lipping *thank you.*

"You come here a lot?" Clare asked looking up at Michaels, her blue eyes expressing delight as they settled into their seats.

"A few times a month. I love Blues. It's great when Buddy plays. How was your day?"

"Tiring and hot. We didn't find anything but I am sure we will. We are going to every park in the county starting Monday."

"I have a gut feeling this is going to be massive," he said and ordered an IPA for himself and a glass of New Zealand Sauvignon Blanc for Clare.

Buddy Guy's is a famous blues bar on Wabash Avenue. The stage is in the middle of the east wall and it is lit up with soft blue and white lights revealing a romantic, moody atmosphere. Tables were packed together making as much room as possible to accommodate the patrons and pressing Chicago's capacity codes to the limit. Talent from around the country often graced Buddy's on any given night.

Two hours later, a local group was playing the classic "The Thrill is Gone," by B.B. King. Clare was leaning back into Michaels' chest, slowly dancing in her mind to the music. It was one of those moments that only blues music can make you feel. She turned, looked up at him, her eyes penetrating his and said, "Ready?"

CHAPTER 22

P roducer David Beedy eyed Peter Michaels suspiciously as he
walked into the office with a smile so wide it seemed to leave
his face.

"You either won the lottery or you got laid all weekend," Beedy
said returning the smile as he took the cup of coffee that Michaels
handed to him.

"Without a doubt it was the best weekend I have had in a long,
long time," Michaels responded, his smile getting broader, if that were
possible. "I had a great time with Clare."

"Yeah, she's pretty hot," Beedy agreed.

"What's happening?" Michaels inquired, changing the subject of
his weekend.

"Did you hear about the copper who got run over with his own
patrol car?" Beedy asked. "I just got a copy of his bodycam video. It's
incredible."

"Come on."

"You know the guy. Eddie O'Halloran."

Eddie O had been a source of Michaels for years when he was
assigned to the Gang Crimes South unit. "Is he alright?"

"He's in the hospital. Big laceration on the head and bad gash on his leg," Beedy said as he plugged a thumb drive into his computer. "Here, look at this."

The video showed officer O'Halloran walking up to a woman who was lying on the street at the corner of Jackson Blvd and Kostner Avenue in West Garfield Park. He attempted to check on her, not expecting her to be fully conscious. She jumped up. Her well-endowed bare breasts were totally exposed. Her panties were down around her knees.

Officer O'Halloran asked, "Hey, are you alright? What happened?"

Suddenly she went berserk, pushed him and literally man handled herself around him and inserted herself into his squad car. She knocked him down, put the car into reverse and dragged him under the opened door, running him over and raced away.

"Did they get the woman?"

"After she got on the Ike (Eisenhower Expressway) and exited off Damen, she crashed into five other parked cars before she got out and tried to run away. The first guy she hit got out of his vehicle and tackled her. Police took her into custody."

"That's not like Eddie O. That would have never happened in the old days. Eddie O worked the toughest neighborhoods in the city," Michaels said.

"Peter, you know as well as I do. In the last three years things have changed so dramatically. Who in the fuck would want to be the police today? You're second guessed on every move you make," Beedy stated rhetorically.

"Yep. It's all different, alright. The police are scrutinized over everything they do. The State's Attorney doesn't even want to prosecute murder cases anymore. Like that one guy who allegedly beat his friend to death with a hammer. Hit him 30 times. It's crazy."

"Cops are hesitant to act and that only leads to injury or worse yet...death," Beedy added.

"Anyway, I am sure she's got to get a psych evaluation. Man, only in Chicago." Michaels said shaking his head.

"Hey Peter, line two," a young college summer intern yelled out.

"News, Michaels."

"I'm coming for you, you son-of-bitch," a startling low sinister threatening metallic voice warned.

Michaels froze and a worried look morphed his face. Beedy immediately saw his buddy drop into a chair. The color completely drained from his face like a blank, white artist canvas. His eyes expressed shock?

Michaels hit the record and speaker button so everyone in the office could hear the alarming conversation. The room went dead silent…an eerie atmosphere suffocated the air.

"Who is this? What do you want?" Michaels asked, now regaining his composure.

"What the fuck is this?"

"I'm coming for all three of you. You killed my best friend." The metallic voice emphasized.

"Three of us. What three are you talking about? Who did we kill? Who are you?" Michaels asked looking around the room making sure everyone was listening and taking notes.

"I'm Bing Lin An's…BFF. You bastard. I've already started. You'd better check on your buddies." The metallic voice warned again and then vanished as the phone went dead.

"Bing Lin An," Michaels whispered as nervous beads of sweat blanketed his forehead. "I haven't heard or mentioned that name in at least a year," he said standing up, looking at his producer/partner with a questioning expression.

The college intern asked, "Who is that?"

"The lover and partner of Cyril Dobonovich. 'The Bug Man.' A sociopathic killer," Beedy responded automatically not taking his eyes off his friend. "He tried to kill Peter, a year ago, near Soldier Field."

Michaels gathered his composure, grabbed his cellphone, and dialed Jack Warren.

~~~~

Clare Claxton's blue CPD baseball cap was soaking wet and scared with a thin salty sweat stain. Her protective vest only added to the perspiration that was funneling down her thin, sexy spine. It was already 87 degrees and the air was getting thicker and more suffocating by the minute. It was a typical smoldering summer day in Chicago.

Bullet was pulling Claxton forward hard; his nose was sniffing the uncut grass and his tail looked like a metronome on steroids whipping back and forth in a blur. They were working the northern edge of the tree line of Miller Meadows Park on the Northside. Suddenly his sharp bark pierced the hot morning air, forty-five minutes into their first scheduled search of the day.

Sgt. Michael Garofalo's ears perked up at the familiar sound, "This is 3024. Sounds like you have a hit," he said into his handheld mic.

"Northern edge about 300 yards from you. There's more than one," Clare Claxton responded.

By the time Garofalo and Nosey reached Claxton, she had placed red flags at four suspected gravesites. Uncharacteristically Nosey was in a very aggressive mood, he pulled his master past Claxton and Bullet and let out a piercing bark of his own and sat down.

Claxton looked over to her sergeant perplexed and said, "What the hell! Another mass burial ground?"

Garofalo stuck a flag into the ground and Nosey went to work again. Bullet also pulled Claxton a little further up the tree line, barked and sat.

They had discovered nine more suspected graves when Garofalo finally called his supervisor.

~~~~

Peter Michaels played the audio of the metallic voice to Jack Warren. "How many serial killers live in Chicago, Jack? What the fuck!"

"This is crazy man. Is this guy going to shoot us? Or poison us?" Warren asked unnerved.

"I know. I couldn't tell if it's a man or woman. I even asked the intern if she could tell if it was male or female?"

"Yeah, what did she say?"

"She said, she couldn't tell. It never occurred to her," Michaels said dejectedly.

"We need to meet up. Figure something out. I'll set something up. I'll call Quag and warn him. Send me an audio file of the warning."

"I'll see if we can find out who this could possibly be. This is nuts. Fifteen people a day are shooting each every day in Chicago and we're looking for two, three, maybe four serial killers. Now this?"

"Great place to live, right?" Warren asked sarcastically.

"Great news town. Every time you reach into the sewer you find another story. One better than the other," Michaels said shaking his head, the color finally coming back to his face whispering to himself, "Only in Chicago."

CHAPTER 23

Detective Tony Quagliaroli's empty coffee cup was sitting on the right side of his desk when detective Jack Warren entered the homicide unit at Area One. "Where's Quag?" he asked.

"Hasn't showed up yet," Lieutenant Tom Parker responded.

"He hasn't been answering his phone either," Warren said as he punched redial. It was the fourth time that Warren tried to call his partner. "Strange, he's usually the first one in."

"What's the matter?" Lt. Parker asked noticing the look of concern that shadowed Warren's face.

"Send a patrol car to his house. This is not good. Peter Michaels got a death threat call this morning that also included me and Quag. I'm going over to his place."

"What the fuck do you mean; death threat?" Parker asked, running his fingers through his thick combed back stylish black hair.

Lt. Tom Parker was the commander of Area One's homicide unit. His detectives had the best clearance rate in the department. Parker had been on the job for 22 years. He surrounded himself with what he called "the best of the best" and he seldom ever micro-managed their work. He just let them do their thing.

"Listen to this," Warren said as he pushed the audio button on his cellphone. The recorded metallic voice replayed the threat, he laid the phone on the desk and all the detectives in the squad room came over and listened in awe. Warren slipped away and dialed Quag's home number. No Answer.

~~~~

FBI agent/forensic anthropologist, Tom Britten flew into Chicago first thing Monday morning on the bureau's private jet and summoned Cook County Medical Examiner Dr. Robert Crine and the Chief of Detectives, Jeff Kaczka to FBI headquarters on Roosevelt Road. Thirteen files, stacked three high, were placed in a straight line in the middle of a four by twelve foot table that was centered in the bland beige colored conference room on the third floor. He vaguely recognized the willowy, tanned, blonde, curly haired woman who was holding onto Dr. Crine's elbow as they entered.

"Tom...this is Deborah Duke," Crine said guiding her to the chair next to his.

Britten recognized the name immediately and smiled, "The forensic detective. I have heard a lot about you," he said.

"I hope all good things," she replied with a hint of a smile.

"She volunteered her skills to assist us in identifying the remains. I think we need all the help we can get at the moment. Wouldn't you agree?" Crine opined.

"No problem. When did you get to town, Ms. Duke?" Britten asked.

"Just an hour ago. Dr. Crine was kind enough to pick me up at O'Hare," she said in her soft voice.

"Great, let's get started," Britten said and began to pass out the files. "If I had known Ms. Duke was coming I would have had a copy ready for her." He motioned to another agent in the room and asked him to make another copy. The agent nodded and left the room and Britten began the meeting.

"Eleven of the victims were murdered. The twelfth victim apparently died of cancer. We also have two killers. One was left-handed. He killed seven of them."

Dr. Crine held up his hand interrupting the FBI agent. "That is what I suspected and I think he was probably stronger."

"Lefty was stronger and probably taller than righty according to our 3-D imaging re-creation analysis."

"When were they killed?" Asked Chief Kazcka.

"Carbon 14 dating places the time of death about a hundred years ago," Britten said authoritatively.

"What about the girl?" asked Deborah Duke.

"She probably died in that time frame but we can't pinpoint exactly the time of death. Cancer fully metastasized throughout her spine," Britten expressed positively.

"The males all seemed to be about the same size. Correct?" Dr. Crine asked rhetorically knowing his theory would prove to be true; fully expecting a scientifically confirmed positive result.

"Amazingly they were all five-ten to six-one."

"How old were they?" Duke asked.

"Again, I am pretty sure they were all between 18 to 22 years of age. We have at least two serial killers on our hands. These victims were killed very methodically. Almost ritualistically, really. The killers took at least two trophies."

Dr. Crine finished the thought, "Right thumb. Left big toe."

They all sat quietly for a long moment in silence only to be interrupted by the agent who fetched a new copy of the findings for Deborah Duke. He handed her the files which she later would convert into braille, and then asked, "What does the DNA tells us?"

"We ran the results through CODIS and we only had one really positive hit. A distant familial connection really," Britten responded.

"How distant?" asked Duke.

"A rapist named Robert Burke. Arrested in 2016. Died in prison. He was shived in the mess hall. Stabbed numerous times," Britten informed.

"It's a very good lead. I can run that down. Maybe we can locate some relatives who will talk about someone from their past, who went missing," Duke said almost like thinking out loud.

"How do you find them?" Britten asked absorbed by her sincerity.

"I work with an ancestry firm that has an office here in suburban Elmhurst," she stated. "I talked to them and they love the publicity this case offers them so; they have provided us with all of their resources."

Crine smiled to himself and thought, *Where does Peter Michaels find all these people.*

~~~~

Peter Michaels and David Beedy were sitting in the general manager's conference room with news director Phil Rivers, GM Larry Voss, and station attorney Sam Phieffer. The walls were covered with journalism awards all of which were won by the investigative unit. It was a comfortable room that generally made anyone taking part of any conversation very relaxed. Today however, everyone sitting around the highly polished cherry wood table was anything but relaxed. There was tension thicker than the suffocating curtain of humidity hanging over Lake Michigan causing all the sailboats to luff and stall.

Sam Phieffer's brown eyes were surrounded by brown horn-rimmed glasses. His thick curly brown hair was graying at the temples. His expression was always calming and concerning, but sometimes it was dismissive. He was choosing his words carefully, "Peter, you should take a month-long vacation in some fucking cave. How do you get yourself in these predicaments?"

A smile twitched on Michaels' lips, "Sam you know I am not going to hide from anyone."

"You have to take this seriously, Peter. We need to set up some parameters for your safety," Phil Rivers said with a scowl on his face. "This is no time to be cute and trivial."

"I take all of this seriously, but I am not going to stop reporting on these stories," Michaels said.

"Look at the very minimum, we need to set you up with at least two security guards at all times. No ands, ifs or buts. Period. You also need to wear a Kevlar vest."

"I don't have a problem with that but I also need my space," Michaels stated.

"We should also consider putting him in a safe house for a couple of weeks. To see if security can spot anything suspicious," Phieffer suggested.

"I don't need a safe house. Put a guard at my door, fine, but no safe house." Michaels argued.

"Let's start making these arrangements, right away," Larry Voss the general manager suggested.

Michaels phone began to vibrate in his pocket. He took it out, looked at the caller ID and said, "I should take this. It's the police," Michaels said then answered the call.

"What's up Jack?" Michaels asked.

"Tony Quag is on his way to the hospital. We don't know if he's going to make it. It doesn't look good," Warren reported.

The color totally drained from Michaels' face. He put a shaky hand to his forehead and caressed it. Everyone in the room just stared at him, knowing it was bad news.

"I'll call you when I know more. We have to figure out what the department is going to do." Warren said and hung up.

"What is it?" David Beedy asked.

"It's Tony Quag. He's on his way to Rush Medical Center. They don't know if he is going to make it."

CHAPTER 24

T ony Quag had a migraine for several hours; he would not wish
this kind of pain on anyone; even an enemy. The hot humid
air played havoc with his sinuses all day. The temperature of
his house was set at 75 degrees. The cool air surrounded him and
immediately refreshed him, relieving some of the pain as soon as he
walked in the door. The sun had set nearly an hour before, it was still
muggy and storm clouds were gathering in the night's sky smothering
the stars and the moon creating a gloomy atmosphere of despair.

Quag took off his suitcoat, held it by the shoulders, hung it on top
of a dining room chair, walked over to the liquor cabinet and poured
himself two fingers of Basil Hayden bourbon, neat. He inhaled deeply
as the smooth dark liquid eased down his throat causing a smile to
crease his lips. The doorbell interrupted the pleasant moment. Tony
Quag looked at the door suspiciously when he saw no one standing
outside. *Peculiar*, he thought as he approached the door with his right
hand instinctively reaching for his Glock. He then realized that he took
off his weapon and set it on the dining room table. He sided up to the
wall and ever so slightly opened the storm door, cautiously inching to
his right to get a peek; that's when he heard the hissing sound coming
from a spray can type of device by his feet. His throat immediately

began to close. A paralyzing burning sensation ran down his throat like a rash.

"What the fuck. Oh God! What's happening?" he muttered as he staggered into the living room, went down on two knees, and keeled over on his right side. His mind painted a picture of pain and agony and nausea. His eyes were wide, red, and filling with tears. He tried to reach for his throat but his hands wouldn't move. He was gasping, heaving, inhaling desperately trying to fill his lungs with fresh air, to no avail. His brain told him something had just hit him in his forehead but he didn't feel any pain from the first kick, certainly not from the second nor the third. Everything went into another realm of consciousness and Tony Quag didn't seem to care. A smile emerged on his face. He was experiencing an out of body moment suspended in a tunnel of bright white light looking down at his killer wondering who was this stranger.

~~~~

The executioner was amazed that his victim was so graceful and smiling. "You motherfucker," he said out loud and then kicked Tony Quag again for the fourth time. This blow, however, was to the stomach. The murderer picked up Quag's suitcoat, searched it and found his badge, wallet, and an epi-pen; then he pocketed all the items. He slid the Glock into his waist band. Poured himself a glass of bourbon, took off his gas mask, drank the smooth liquid with satisfaction and took the glass with him.

He checked to make sure he didn't leave anything behind. He turned off all the lights, exited through the front door, pulling it shut. He picked up his backpack, pulled off the blonde wig with a ponytail he was wearing, stuffed it into the backpack along with the Glock and the drinking glass. He stripped himself of his nylon running pants in one smooth motion and casually walked away now dressed in navy blue shorts.

The assassin looked over his shoulder and waved goodbye to the dead man. Hiding in plain sight but nobody was outside on the hot, muggy night to notice him and his iniquitous smile.

The first of his targets had been eliminated. Two more to go.

~~~~

CSI Tom Vander Aarde and his team were on their way to Miller Meadows South when he heard over his police radio officers responding to a wellness check at detective Tony Quagliaroli's residence found him unresponsive on the living room floor.

"Shit," he shouted and reached for his cellphone and dialed detective Jack Warren.

"I don't know anything yet," Warren said without saying hello. "I am a minute out and I don't like what I am hearing."

"My team is just getting to the new site. You have to keep me up to date. Quag and I go back a long way," Vando said listening to the rest of Warren's conversation.

Vando got out of his beat up Crown Vic, grabbed his gear from the trunk and walked up to Sgt. Michael Garofalo and officer Clare Claxton. They both put their dogs into their air-conditioned vehicles and gave them some water.

"Did you hear anything?" Clare Claxton asked as Vando approached.

"Jack's there now. Quag has been rushed to the hospital, unresponsive. That's all I know right now," Vando informed his friends and colleagues.

"This is messed up," Garofalo added.

"Well apparently Peter Michaels got some sort of death threat this morning involving him, Warren, and Quag," Vando said.

Claxton went pale and her eyes turned concerned. She reached for her cellphone.

Vando told them the story that Warren shared with him just moments before.

"Does anybody know who this person is? Who threatened them?" Garofalo inquired.

"Nobody knows anything that I am aware of. Yet," Vando said.

"Do you think it is related to any of this?" Garofalo asked pointing to the nine new suspected grave sites.

"No Clue," Vando said.

~~~~

Clare Claxton walked away from the group and dialed Peter Michaels cellphone. He picked it up on the second ring, smiling at the ringtone, "Are you okay?" she asked anxiously.

"I just left a meeting with my bosses and Sam, our attorney. The station is setting up some security for me. Not sure yet how it will play out. I am waiting to hear from Jack. Apparently the department is calling an emergency meeting to plan some sort of security detail for him too and..." Michaels answer dropped off as a lump formed in his throat and tears started to well in his eyes. "I'm not sure what's going on with Tony, but it doesn't look good."

"Promise me you'll be okay. I'll call you later. I am at Miller Meadows South and the CSI team just got here. I am not sure if they are going to send us to look for more gravesites, or if we are staying here."

"I'll be fine. I just need to sort some of this out. I think it is connected to Cyril Dobonovich, the 'Bug Man.' Let's talk in a while," Michaels said, hanging up the phone and walking over to his partner's desk.

"What do you think?" David Beedy asked.

"I think you should get in touch with your brother-in-law and see if he can check if there was another person involved with Dobonovich and Lin An at Madison Mental Health Center."

"I can do that."

"I can't believe this is happening. I thought the 'Bug Man' was dead and the evil that encompassed him was dead along with him, but I am starting to get a feeling that something bad is looming out there. Something that is very evil and pernicious."

CHAPTER 25

Deborah Duke gathered the reports of the twelve DNA samples that agent Tom Britten had given her. Her driver was waiting to take the evidence to Certified Global Genetics in the western suburbs. She was anxious to get started with the analysis. She liked to work from home, but home in Chicago was a hotel room filled with her computers and specialized braille charts that she uses to outline family lineages.

She had one clue or connection in the first 12 cases, a rapist with a rap sheet. Duke liked to familiarize herself with each victim with as much information that was available. She tried to get a feel for every one of them. Because of her blindness, Duke had to focus intently; basically, memorizing every piece of information that she charts. Brutal, ritualistic murders create some anxiety, but they also create a deep motivation to get to the bottom of these cases.

Duke had acquired certain passwords that allowed her access to the CPD's computerized systems, including fingerprints, criminal histories and known DNA data banks for more than just criminals. She could access DNA histories from certain military records, medical personnel records, and federal and state government employees' records.

"I have identified two family members of Robert Burke," Duke told Peter Michaels.

"That was fast," Michaels exclaimed.

"That was because the FBI gave us the first lead. That rapist guy, Burke," she said and continued. "This is going to be a long, long process to establish these DNA profiles."

"What do you need?" Michaels asked.

"Help in finding Brendan Burke. He might be in his late seventies. He was a postal carrier. Last known address was in Bridgeport. The next person is Margaret O'Brien. She might be in her sixties. She is a retired naval nurse. Last known address was Michigan City, Indiana."

"Let me see what I can do," Michaels said. "Are you turning these names over to CPD?"

"Yes. Tomorrow. You've got a 24-hour head start, then I've got to turn the names over. Good Luck."

~~~~

Michaels' producer David Beedy got started with the names immediately. In fifteen minutes, he found an obit in the Chicago Herald for a Brendan Burke, a postal worker, who died of cancer in 2019. A half hour later he found Margaret O'Brien, a highly decorated retired navy nurse. She ran a successful home nursing care business in northwest Indiana and southeast Michigan.

Margaret O'Brien froze in her chair when Peter Michaels announced himself on the phone, wondering whether or not he had found something sinister in her business. "What's this all about, Mr. Michaels?" she asked.

"I am just wondering...this is a longshot, but do you have any recollection of a missing family member. Dating back to the 1940s?" Michaels asked.

A feeling of relief flushed through her consciousness and she smiled, "As a matter of fact there is. My mother's sister had a son that disappeared. The family never had any kind of explanation."

"Were you living in Chicago at the time?"

"Yes. In Bucktown. Story was Shaun went missing when he was, I think, twenty."

"Did your family file a missing person's report?"

"I am not certain but I assume they did because my mother said, 'the police never found out anything.' Why are you asking these questions?"

"Have you been watching the news about these gravesites that were recently discovered?"

"No. Please no. Is my cousin one of them?"

"Well, we recently got a DNA match from a Robert Burke. He..."

"That filthy bastard," she interrupted.

Michaels was not shocked at the sudden outburst but he did smile and continued, "His DNA was in CODIS. We identified similar DNA profiles with you and somebody named Brendan Burke."

"Yes, that's my first cousin on my mother's side. He died a horrible death from cancer a few years ago. He was such a nice man. Not like that pig father of his."

"So, Robert Burke was Brendan's father and also Shaun's?"

"Yes. God rest his soul."

"Well, I'll be doing a story about this tonight. Your distant cousin is the first person to be officially identified. Do you know when Shaun went missing?"

"I believe it was in the late 30s or early 40s. At least that's what I remember," she said, her mind searching for the information.

"Thanks, if you think of anything else please give me a call. Sorry to bother you, but I hope this gives you and your family a little closure. I am sure the police will be contacting you within the next 24 hours. Thanks, and again sorry for your loss and sorry to have bothered you."

Michaels said and hung up the phone saying to himself, "One down. Twenty more to go."

~~~~

Detective Tony Quag was clinging to life by a thin thread. He had a very weak pulse, but there was some minimum brain activity. He had a living will that ordered any life-prolonging procedures be withheld or withdrawn. His daughter Melissa was honoring his wishes reluctantly. She loved her father and vowed to be at his bedside at all times while he was alive.

~~~~

Peter Michaels was sitting next to detective Jack Warren in the Superintendent of Police's large conference room. Supt. Eddie Jackson sat at the head of the table. Chief of Detectives Jeff Kaczka, Lt. Tom Parker and FBI agent Lou Marinaccio sat to the right of the superintendent directly across from Michaels and Warren. The Federal Bureau of Investigations that often investigated corrupt cops was now offering their services to protect Warren and possibly Michaels.

Chief Kaczka had a trim muscular body and premature thick, gray hair, cut short on the sides, like Leroy Jethro Gibbs from the TV show, NCIS. "We have a safe house right around the corner from the police academy. We could house them there."

"Look Michaels and I live in the same building..."

A look of surprise emerged on the faces of everyone except Lt. Tom Parker. He lowered his head and covered his grin with his right hand.

"What." Warren exclaimed. "We live in the same building, so what. It will be easier to watch one building with two potential victims inside rather than two separate sites."

"Look," Michaels interrupted. "The station is providing me with a two man security team, 24-7. I am going to continue to work no matter what you guys decide to do. The only thing I agreed to do was to stop riding my motorcycle because I could be an easy target. I am absolutely sure some arrangements can be worked out, because I am told my detail is filled with retired federal agents and Chicago PD people."

Agent Lou Marinaccio was a New Jersey transfer who had worked on many protective details. He had a slight neck twitch that he nonchalantly adjusted by pushing his jaw with his right hand. His bicep muscles seemed to always be flexed, stretching the sleeves of his dark blue golf shirt. He said with a heavy accent, "Yeah. I tink we can work wit dat."

Lt. Parker suggested that everyone Warren worked with should be aware of the potential danger. "We have to make sure anyone around you Jack is notified and be comfortable with potentially being a target because of their proximity to you. Our work gets intense and when we are focused on a scene or the evidence, we sometimes are not aware of our surroundings. Everyone has to be careful here."

Supt. Jackson said, "Let's meet tomorrow. I want a plan in place in the next 24 hours, meanwhile detective Warren you are confined to desk duty until that plan is implemented. Is that understood, detective?"

"Yes sir," Warren mumbled.

Michaels stood up and handed Warren a piece of paper and said, "Your first victim is Shaun Burke. He was 20 when he went missing in the late 1930s or early 40s. A police report was filed back then but they never found the body. This is his cousin's name and phone number." Michaels could not suppress his smile. He knew the brass was thinking that he got a lot of his information from Warren. "Check it out. I'm doing a piece tonight on the ten."

CHAPTER 26

R yan O'Toole the fifth was on a recce of his 33rd victim's
behavioral patterns. Marcellious Baxter smoked a lot of
marijuana for a medical technician and that really pissed him
off. Baxter also broke the O'Toole family rules. He was 35 and black.
Number Five killed three other black males and two black females.
They also pissed him off for whatever reason he could think of at the
time.

Recreational marijuana was legal in Illinois. Baxter was leaving his
favorite store on Lincoln Avenue. He lived in a basement apartment in
the DePaul area. He always parked his blue Mini Cooper in the alley
along the fence. It fit perfectly and did not interfere with any traffic and
it was convenient for him to access his apartment. *That lazy son-of-
bitch.*

Baxter was getting out of his car when Five drove straight at him
with his high beam lights blinding him. Five was out of his van in a
split second, Baxter had his right hand up shielding his eyes. In one
swift motion the twelve inch knife went through his neck and carotid
artery severing his fifth and six vertebra. The pain never registered to
his brain. He was dead in an instant. Five had a towel on the wound
quickly and only a limited amount of blood splattered to the ground.

In approximately six seconds, he killed number 33, threw him in the van, shut the side door, and drove off.

It was a hot muggy night. The elderly people that populated the street were all in bed sound asleep. A midnight shower was predicted and the killer was sure the downpour would wash away any trace of blood.

Number Five congratulated himself for such a beautiful kill. He was thinking that soup was on the menu for dinner tomorrow night. He had plenty of trophies in the freezer. He was getting sexually aroused and he couldn't contain the satanic smile that covered his face.

~~~~

Peter Michaels was walking off the set with anchorman Ron Magers when two men dressed casually in golf shirts and light weight blue wind breakers approached him. He knew immediately that they were his security detail. They had that look: <u>Police.</u>

"I'm Tom Buettner. Like it or not we are your security detail," he said with a sly grin that immediately made you like the guy. Buettner was six-one. His shoulders were squared and straight. His gate was purposeful and authoritative. His brown hair was short and thinning. It always looked neat, even though he combed it with his fingers. Buettner's smile was constant, like his confidence.

"I'm John Kerbs. I'm with him. So that means I'm with you too," he said in a hoarse, raspy, smart ass tone. Kerbs was slightly taller than Buettner, but he was a little thinner. He looked like he could run forever. His silver rimmed glasses framed his brown eyes. His nose looked like it had been broken more than once. He walked with his shoulders squared away and his hands rolled up into fists. He never seemed happy, just determined.

Michaels shook their hands and introduced Magers to them and then he asked, "So, what happens now?"

"Nothing. You just go about your business and pretend we're not here. We will not interfere with whatever it is you do," Buettner said.

"Unless something happens of course that we need to take action," Kerbs interjected with a slight grin.

Michaels noticed that they seldom looked at him. Their eyes were always moving, searching, watching even in his workplace.

"What about if I'm with my girlfriend. You're not coming in my car."

"We'll see. It depends," Kerbs said.

"Fuck that," Michaels responded.

"We'll see." They both said in unison.

~~~~

The assassin was drinking a warm, stale bottle of Bud Lite while he watched the ten o'clock news. His basement apartment was dank and dark and dirty. His teeth were rotting from all the meth he used to do. His breath smelled like dead animals. He was not clean unlike the only two friends he ever had. They were germophobic. The assassin was a sociopathic killer like Cyril Dobonovich and Bing Lin An. He butchered his entire family with a thirty inch machete in their Humboldt Park home when he was sixteen. His mother and father and five siblings died instantly. He tried to hang himself but unfortunately for society it didn't work. It was because of his botched suicide attempt that he was admitted to the Madison Mental Health Center two years before his only friends were discharged.

He made his escape just three months ago. He began planning his revenge the day Dobonovich died trying to kill Peter Michaels. He vowed that he would finish what his brilliant friend had started. He added the two cops to his death list after they killed his other friend Lin An.

His hatred for Peter Michaels was flushing through his being like rushing river waters that carry rafters down a mountain side. "You smug fuck. I want to kill you right now but I need you to suffer first, looking over your shoulder every day for weeks, wondering when I'm coming for you. You fuck." That phrase became his mantra and every time he uttered it, his hatred multiplied.

He was anxious and upset because he had not heard a single word about the death of that police detective. He listened to all news radio all day. He was talking out loud to himself. "They called him Tony Quag. I got him good with that fentanyl spray. What the fuck," he yelled and threw his beer bottle down on the tile floor, shattering it into hundreds of pieces. Leaving the distinct odor of smelly old stale beer. "I killed him. I killed that motherfucker. I did kill him."

~~~~

Number Five had to turn down the air conditioner. He was sweating profusely. He took his trophies from Baxter's hand and foot and put them in the freezer just in case something came up and he couldn't make the family soup the next night.

He put Baxter's head under pounds of steaks in the garage freezer along with two others. He knew he had to dispose of them soon. He was severing Baxter's limbs while he watched the news. They had discovered nine more graves at Miller Meadows South. He recalled that Number Three buried five there. His father buried two there and he also buried two there. One black woman and one black male. *That will throw them off.* He was thinking how smart he was by breaking the long-standing family traditions.

He decided he was going to dump Baxter's remains at Bill's Creek on Ogden Avenue. The trees were tall and thick. The easement was very deep, and damp and dense. The crickets' cacophony that greeted him as he exited his van was loud but soothing to his ears. Number Five was sweating and smiling at the sounds as he gathered the packages containing Baxter's bones. It was a perfect spot to dispose of *the prick.* By the time winter came in a few months there would be very little left of Marcellious Baxter. *The natural environment would take care of that for me,* he thought and with a demonic grin he mouthed his newly thought of poem, "Bye. Bye…Baxter."

CHAPTER 27

Peter Michaels had another restless night. He was put to bed by his two new best friends Tom Buettner and John Kerbs which unnerved him. He invited them in for a bourbon or tequila but they declined. He had a double, Basil Hayden. He was thankful that his "Bug Man" nightmare didn't resurface. He woke up to the usual sounds of the city, police sirens, a beeping garbage truck and now two different best friends standing outside his door. David Mayo and Joe Lazzaroti.

Michaels wasn't surprised by the changing of the guard and he recognized Mayo immediately because he had interviewed him numerous times in the past about gang shootings in his district. He invited them in for coffee. They both said they already had theirs.

Mayo was six, two. His athletic body was toned and muscular. He was a star left fielder on the police department's baseball team. He retired from the CPD as a district commander several years ago. It was his security company that the station hired to protect Michaels. Mayo was quiet, sincere and all business. He acknowledged Michaels with a slight grin when they shook hands. "Good to see you. It's been a while."

Lazzaroti was a former DEA agent. He met him when his drug agency did a major heroin undercover sting operation in the commander's district. Lazz, as he liked to be called, was five-eleven. He too was athletic but very intense. He walked with his head slightly in front of his shoulders. He had a continuous look of determination on his face. He didn't smile much, not even when he shook Michaels' hand.

"I assume your routine will be the same as the Kerbs and Buettner team?" Michaels asked knowing the answer but he asked it anyway to break the ice.

Mayo answered for them, "Exactly the same."

Lazz didn't answer. He went to get the car.

"Mind if I join you?" Mayo asked but didn't wait for an answer he just got into Michaels' SUV with a smug grin.

~~~~

Investigative producer David Beedy filed a Freedom of Information request and put together a research program to send three student interns to the archives of the Chicago Police Department to examine missing person's reports starting in1969 and working backwards 40 or 50 years. All index crime reports from 1970 to the present time have been entered into the police department's computers. The search was narrowed down to males only between the ages of 18 to 22. Beedy gambled that the limited pattern would save endless hours of wasted time. There were tens of thousands of names to search through to find any connections for just 30 victims so far. It was a herculean task.

Beedy was taking them to a company van when Michaels walked into the office with his new detail. "How's it going?" Beedy asked looking at the new faces recognizing Mayo with a nod and a smile.

"It'll take some getting used to, but it'll be alright. Can't wait to see how Clare is going to react to all of the new stares," Michaels said and then asked. "You going to the warehouse on State Street?"

"Yeah I'm going with them for the morning to get them started. If you need me call."

Michaels nodded and then his cellphone pinged with a text message: **I c u got 2 new friends.**

Michaels showed his partner and then turned to his detail and held out the phone for them to read.

Mayo grabbed the phone and Lazz looked over his shoulder. Lazz asked, "Have you run a background on this phone?"

"Of course. It's a burner that the 'Bug Man' bought more than a year ago," Michaels said. Surprisingly, he was not surprised that his would-be-killer was contacting him.

Mayo noticed his reaction and quizzed, "You don't seem to be concerned about someone wanting to kill you?"

"Actually, I am not. He was probably trained or instructed by Dobonovich, that's why I think this Kevlar vest is a waste of time. If he tries to kill me, it'll be poison. It's going to be by a needle, not a bullet, of that I am pretty sure."

Mayo asked, "Do you have any idea who this person is?"

"Not yet, but we're working on it. Let's get some coffee."

~~~~

The sky was royal blue and cloudless. It was eleven o'clock in the morning and it was ten degrees less than it was yesterday, only 83, but the humidity was also 83 degrees. Vando's CSI team were just about finished clearing the last three gravesites at Miller Meadows South. "What have we here?" he whispered loud enough for the investigator next to him to look over.

"Whatta yah got Vando?" Officer John Wood asked, perspiration running down his red, Irish face, stinging his eyes.

Woody was a hard worker. He wanted to retire by the end of the year after 30 years on the job. He like many of his lifelong buddies were sick and tired of how the police were being treated in the city.

His fingers were thick and his hands were strong. He stood up carefully, winced in pain, reaching for his lower back, and walked over to Vando's site.

The skeletal remains that were totally exposed revealed a tall man over six foot. "Betcha a cup of coffee this is the first black man we've found," Vando said looking up at his CSI partner.

"Does he have a right thumb?" Woody asked pursing his lips and tasting salt.

"Nope!" he said abruptly.

"Left toe?"

"Ahhhh...Nope!"

"I got a woman over here," Mike Puskar announced after he examined her pelvic area. "She ain't got no thumb or no toe either."

Puskar became a crime scene investigator five years ago after he was shot in the hip during a drug raid in the Austin district. His hair turned totally gray while he was recuperating. He loved being the police until the last two years, but he didn't want to be sitting behind a desk. The Fraternal Order of Police fought to get him assigned to the Crime Scene Investigation unit. He never complained again about paying his union dues. He too was disgusted and was considering retiring earlier than expected.

All of a sudden the police radios erupted with the sounds of gunfire and screams about an officer down. A few seconds later it was officers down. Excited voices yelled "shots fired at the police. Officers down. Officers down." Four of the six patrol cars assigned to guard the crime scene rushed off to the 25th district where the gunfight was taking place.

Vando quickly dialed Jack Warren. He knew Warren was at police headquarters getting his protection detail assigned. His buddy responded quickly with a text. **Can't talk. 3 guys down in 25.**

The gravesites were on the boarder of the 25th district that's why all the radios were tuned into that frequency. Vando went back to work to extract the last three bodies from their resting places. He called Dr. Robert Crine to tell him about the possible change in the M.O. of the hitchhiker killer and then he started to wonder if they had a copycat killer.

CHAPTER 28

D eborah Duke was building family trees trying to identify the first 12 victims of the hitchhiker killer. Five of the trees were showing some distinctive relationships coming together. Victim #3 had a number of DNA matches to family members working in the medical field. Three other victims #7, #8 and #10 were showing some progress in common ancestries going back three or four generations: all sharing Irish heritage.

"How's it going?" Peter Michaels asked. "I haven't touched base with you in a while."

"It looks promising for about five of the victims so far. Interestingly, all of them are Irish," Duke said.

"I would think that is not uncommon in Chicago. These bones were buried, what? Back to 1920 or 1930?" Michaels inquired.

"That might be true for the first victims, but I am waiting for more DNA results from the others as well."

"This DNA stuff is fascinating and yet difficult for me to understand. I don't know how you do it." Michaels said.

"DNA is very reliable. It doesn't change. If I find any kind of match in current DNA, any kind, no matter how small…that begins the connection. Then I try to build backwards because half of a person's

DNA is from the mother and the other half is from the father. So, by going backwards, if I can match the shared genetic characteristics, known as 'alleles,' I can trace, let's say the grandchild to the child, to the mother and or the father. They all will follow their genetic network, but as that network goes backwards the familial DNA breaks down to half with each generation, we go back."

"So, is it reliable if it keeps breaking down by half?" Michaels asked quizzically.

"Oh, yes. It is very reliable. That's how I found my birth mother. I traced back my DNA to her DNA to my grandmother's DNA."

"I never realized that you were adopted. That's kind of cool," Michaels said with an acknowledging smile. "That's very cool."

"Peter, I thought you knew, that's how I got started in this DNA stuff in the first place. I found it fascinating."

"How did you find your mom?"

"Public records as well as medical records," she paused for a long moment and continued, "She became a nurse after she had me. Anyway, I now have access to almost anything, marriage records, death certificates, all of the public records stuff, and of course, I can also access CODIS, police records, prison records as well. DNA samples are required in a lot of workplaces now-a-days, where in the past they weren't. The DNA data base grows every day."

"How soon before you'll have some more victim's names?"

"I'll have a few for you in a day or two. I am developing genetic profiles as we speak. It is very time consuming, but sometimes we get lucky."

~~~~

Cook County medical examiner, Dr. Robert Crine finished washing all the excess dirt off the remains of the last skeletons that were displayed on three separate operating tables. He directed the high beam light to the right hand of the female, flipped down his magnifying optics, and picked up the hand gently, and asked, "Why did he choose you, my dear? Why you? You are not a typical victim of this killer."

FBI agent Tom Britten walked into the operating room and coughed to break the ME's concentration and to announce his presence.

"Agent Britten. How are you?" Crine asked not looking up but moving to the next table where the African American male's remains were glistening from the rinse water and the high beam surgical light. He picked up the right hand and examined it closely.

Britten's focused eyes followed the doctor intensely, "What do you think is going on?"

"I think we have three different killers from the remains that we have uncovered from Miller Meadows South. That's what I think," he said in a positive tone. "Come over here and look at this."

Britten approached slowly, reaching inside his coat pocket, taking out a pair of magnifying glasses that he used for close up work. "What do you have, Doc?"

"These two bodies have been in the ground less than ten years. No doubt. There is still some flesh in the pelvic area. They don't fit the M.O. of the other killings. First this one is female. She was stabbed in the throat and he took his trophies. She is black."

The forensic anthropologist was following Crine's logic with keen interest.

"This one also had some fleshy substance still in his pelvic region and around the chest cavity. He is also black, and the killer took his trophies from him as well."

The look on Britten's face intensified as he leaned over the remains and asked the ME to focus the light on the thumb area of the right hand. He examined it closely and then walked over to the female victim and did the same thing. "On the surface without our imaging equipment these marks look very similar," he suggested. "We will learn a lot more with the 3-D imagining spectrometers."

"My guess is that they were made by our left-handed killer." Crine flipped up his optics, folded his arms, and said, "I would like you to take the remains of another recent homicide victim to Quantico and examine it with the high-tech stuff and tell me if he was or was not killed by the same person who killed these two."

"How many more are we talking about?" Britten asked.

"Ten."

~~~~

CSI Tom Vander Aarde volunteered to be part of detective Jack Warren's protection detail on his days off. Sgt. Mike Garofalo, Sgt. Brian Alexander and Tact officer Frank Tedesco did the same. They wanted to protect their friend without pay, but they were refused. FBI agent Marinaccio wanted no part of personal friendships interfering with life and death situations. There were also complications with insurance and liability issues in case one of them got injured. All of them decided they would hang out with their buddy when he was off the clock.

The Superintendent of Police approved a two person protective team around the clock with supervision coming from the FBI, the U.S. Marshall's office, and the Secret Service Agency. He agreed that Warren didn't have to stay in a safe house, but he did have to check in with the assigned federal agencies at specific times with various changing code words.

The Superintendent also assigned detective Thomas Polston as Warren's new partner. Polston's six foot, four inch frame was surrounded with muscle. He did a minimum of 150 push-ups a day. He never drank or smoked. His blue eyes greeted everyone he liked with a smile, but if he didn't know you or disliked you or mistrusted you the same smiling eyes turned into probative sneers. Polston volunteered for the protection detail even though he knew the job was dangerous, demanding and possibly devastating. He loved being the police. He's been on the job for 18 years. During the first five years of his career, he never took a day off because he was afraid he'd miss something. The main reason he wanted to be on the detail; he liked Jack Warren from softball and he was committed and determined that no one was going to hurt him.

Warren was chomping at the bit to get off desk duty and back on the streets to find the hitchhiker killers and the person who wanted to kill him. He was relieved when he was released, but his joy didn't last long. His phone rang to the theme of the "William Tell Overture" and he knew it was Peter Michaels. He answered happily, "Hey what's up? I've been given the go ahead to get back on the streets."

"It's Tony." Michaels said in a tone that immediately took the wind out of both their sails.

"No. Please don't tell me."

"He's dead. His daughter just called me. He's gone…Jack."

Tears welled in both of their eyes and Jack Warren's voice cracked when he promised, "I'll find that motherfucker and I will kill him."

CHAPTER 29

I t took Peter Michaels 15 minutes to calm down Jack Warren after they agreed to meet later in the day. He called Tony Quag's daughter back. "Are you okay?"

"No. I'll never be okay," Melissa said trying to be brave, holding back tears. Her eyes already red from crying for the last two days.

"I am here for you, Melissa. You need anything at any time, you just call me. You have all my numbers."

"I will. I appreciate you being there for me and our family."

"Now I need you to do some things, so we can get to the bottom of all this."

"What do you want me to do?" Melissa asked, wiping her eyes with the back of her hand.

"Ask for all his medical records. You are his power of attorney and they are required to give them to you. We particularly need the tox screens to make sure we know what kind of poisonous agent was used to kill him. We'll compare them with what the ME finds."

"I have already asked for them. I knew you would want to see them. I can't believe this has happened," Melissa said in almost a whisper. She began to weep, her chest heaving, tears streaming down her cheeks.

"Melissa. I promise you; we will find out who this animal is. He will be brought to justice," Michaels said trying to reassure her. "I think you should also request that Dr. Crine do an autopsy. He will not sleep until we discover how this happened."

~~~~

Clare Claxton texted Michaels to call her. He hung up the phone with Melissa and immediately called her.

"I am so sorry. We just heard about Tony Quag. I know, you two were very close."

"He saved my life. I loved the guy," Michaels responded, tears welling in his eyes and a lump developing in his throat. "What's going on with you? Where are you?"

"I am at twenty-five," she responded.

"I thought you were at Miller Meadows."

"I was then half of the crime scene protective detail rushed over to twenty-five."

"What happened? Are you okay?" Michaels asked with concern in his voice.

"You are not going to believe this. You can't make this shit up."

"What? Talk to me."

"Our CSI guys were processing a carjacked Porsche over on Lake Street and the jacker comes back and tries to steal the same car again while they are dusting it for prints."

"You are kidding me, right?"

"No! Like I said, you can't make this shit up. So, they finally get him cuffed after a little scuffle. It's all on car cam and body cam footage. The bad guy goes on a rampage; I got asthma; my shoulder was injured. He wants to be cuffed with his hands in front of him. You know that is never gonna happen," Clare said excitement building her voice. "So, they search him, find no gun and call for transport."

"Don't tell me," Michaels exclaimed.

"No wait. So, Geoffrey Bentley comes and puts him in his squad to transport him to twenty-five."

"Yeah, he's a strong guy who can handle himself. What happened?"

"So, Bentley goes to get him out of the car and somehow, this fat fuck got his hands in front of him and he has a gun and he shoots Bentley right in the throat, through his voice box."

"Is Geoff dead?" Michaels asked concerned. "Where'd he get the gun?"

"The jag had the gun under his balls and halfway up his ass. I am not kidding you. Up his ass. That's why he wanted to be cuffed in front."

"What about Geoff? Is he going to make it? I don't need to hear about another cop dying today."

"He's going to make it but listen to this. The bad guy was out on parole. He has several unlawful gun violations, numerous assaults, and attempted murder. He gets out of the squad and shoots Bentley again in the chest and goes back in the car and starts shooting at the police responding to the call of 'shots fired at the police.'"

"Any more injuries?"

"Yeah. Two more guys get shot by this prick."

"Are they going to be okay?"

"We think so. In all, 60 rounds were fired in this gunfight, right in the garage area of twenty-five."

"Did they get the guy?"

"Yeah. He was shot three or four times. It was like the OK Corral. I saw the video."

"It's all crazy. Chicago has the toughest gun laws of any city in the country. The Chicago Police confiscate more guns off of the streets than any other department every year and the State's Attorney let's hardened criminals with gun violations out on the streets on I bonds every day and they wonder why 15 people on average a day are shot in Chicago. I don't understand it," Michaels said shaking his head.

"Listen, I have to go. Do you want to grab a pizza tonight?" Clare asked in anticipation.

"I'd love too. I want to see your reaction to my security detail. Where I go, they go. That's the deal."

"They won't be in the car with us, right?"

"I hope not. Hey, see if you can get some of that body cam video of the OK Corral."

Go to this video link to actually see this story:
https://vimeo.com/726476532/0cbc1cdcac

~~~~

The filthy assassin had been listening to all news radio for days trying to find out what happened to detective Tony Quagliaroli. At four o'clock in the afternoon his eyes lit up and a smile emerged on his unshaved face showing his rotten teeth when the newscaster announced, "Homicide detective Tony Quag, as he was known, died of unknown causes."

The killer knew it was fentanyl and he wondered *how long it would take those idiots to figure it out.* He was very happy that his butane spray invention to disperse the fatal concoction perfectly worked the night he surprised that murdering cop. He knew he was not as sophisticated as his two mentors and they always cautioned him to keep it simple. He had talked to Bing Lin An after he made his pipe bombs to dispense the ricin/anthrax mixture onto those fucking crazy football fans last year. *The news media did not give it much coverage. The only thing they reported was that those fucking cops killed his friend,* he mused mindlessly.

After he texted Peter Michaels to scare him and warn him to be looking over his shoulder, he decided that the young detective would be next. He hid in plain sight, dressed as a street person hawking cars in front of the television station and Michaels' condo on Michigan

Avenue. He was trying to figure out how he could get close to the cop to release the next fentanyl dose.

He knew he had to change his disguise and that meant he had to clean up his act so, he bought a head shaver and lather. It was time to look a little more normal. He also did something he hadn't done in a while. He took a shower.

CHAPTER 30

I t was like old home week when Peter Michaels and detective Jack Warren met at Mr. Taco's for lunch. Everyone knew one another in both of their protective details. They all played softball or basketball or hockey together over the years. Mr. Taco's has been on the corner of Ogden Avenue and Austin Boulevard for more than half a century. Weather and time had taken its toll on the one story building. It looked tired and dirty and scarred and orphaned. It was badly in need of a new tuckpointing job. Dirt and grime from the surrounding environment hid the need for the job that would never take place.

Hundreds of thousands of patrons shuffling their boots and shoes left the tile floor with a well-worn path from the front door to the rear door and the ATM machine by the restrooms. It was a cash only joint that offered some of the best tacos and burritos in Chicago. The walls were covered with a Mexican style tile with blue squared lines and coral-colored flowers. The once white menu board advertising the different types of tacos, quesadillas and enchiladas were now yellow from 55 years of grease and smoke wafting upwards clinging to anything it wanted to, adding to the ambience. The menu board was also missing a number of removable letters like the L in P ATE. The only thing fresh on the boards were the pictures of Pepsi products that announced: Coke was not sold here and that Pepsi was the drink of choice in Mr. Taco's.

It was the perfect meeting place for the security teams because it only had four booths with orange plastic pew like seats and worn laminated tables in the narrow rectangular dining area. Everyone could see everybody who walked in the door and everything that was going on in a single glance. All eyes turned to the cash register when a lone, short construction worker with long blonde hair and a yellow plastic helmet entered the restaurant. After giving him the once over, the security teams' conversation continued.

"Look, I don't think this guys is going to shoot at us. Melissa told me the doctors are sure Tony died from fentanyl. He was poisoned," Michaels offered.

"I can't believe Tony let anyone get that close to him that late at night," Warren interjected with concern curtaining his face.

"I don't think he did. I think the killer used some kind of delivery device. Tony was not that careless. The killer either threw a cannister or something and Tony inhaled the shit or there was some other sort of long-range method that was used. That is what we have to figure out," Michaels opined. "I think this person is connected to the 'Bug Man.' I'm telling you."

Detective Tom Polston's eyes sneered at the construction worker who slowly eased by the group turning sideways to slither past. After he exited, Polston's suspicions went on high alert, *Why wouldn't he leave by the door he came in from,* he thought. He jumped up and followed his gut feelings out the rear door. He was greeted by a bright burst of blinding sunlight that just emerged from behind a cloud and he temporarily lost his sight and that of his suspect. He glanced all around inquisitively and reentered Mr. Taco's.

"What's the matter Tom?" Warren asked.

"Did any of you think that short fuck was creepy?" Polston inquired.

The security people shook their heads in unison and then David Mayo, the head of security for Peter Michaels said, "Listen, I don't know if you guys know how bad this fentanyl stuff really is. It is very bad. It is very powerful and it only takes seconds for you to go down.

"Yeah, I saw a video the other day where a county sheriff in California got a foot away from some open fentanyl in a car and two seconds later she was down," Peter Michaels said.

"Fentanyl is 100 times stronger than morphine. The deputy was down in two seconds. They gave her five or six doses of Narcan and she was still overdosing in the ambulance taking her to the hospital. If something happens to anyone of us we have to act quickly."

"What is Narcan?" Lazzarotti asked.

"It's an opiate antagonist," Michaels informed.

"It comes in inhalers and epi-pens. We all should have at least two Narcan dispensers on our persons at all times during this security detail. It may take multiple doses to save a life. We have to be calm and decisive when we act," Mayo said and then added. "My company will buy each of us an EEBD half mask."

"What the fuck is that?" asked Sgt. Brian Alexander who was shifted to the CPD protective team because of his military background. The bosses no longer cared that Alexander was a close friend of Warren.

"It's an emergency escape breathing device. They are not that bulky but they are very effective for at least 15 minutes. If we are attacked like Tony Quag was, it will give us the time to get to our epi-pens if we need to use them. It will be a little pain in the ass to carry them but it could save our lives," Mayo suggested.

~~~~

The little blonde haired construction worker's dark, suspicious, beady eyes were squinting while he tried to hear every word spoken as he inched his way through the small group of cops. He spotted Peter

Michaels by chance leaving the TV station and decided to follow him, having no clue where he was going or what was happening. His curiosity just got the best of him and he wanted to see what he was up against.

He ordered his tacos, paid in cash, left a small tip in the plastic container that at one time was a milk carton and sat at the only remaining booth to eavesdrop while he waited for his order. *That big fucker looked at me suspiciously,* he ascertained but he also sat purposely with his back to them so they could not picture his face for any period of time.

Once he exited the building, he hurried to his truck, dove into the front seat just as the sun appeared from behind a cloud and cast a giant sun flare off his windshield blinding oncoming drivers and pedestrians alike. He stayed low for a couple of minutes, and when he felt comfortable that no one had noticed him he sat up, started the truck, took off his helmet and blonde wig and drove away. His curious eyes looked into the rearview mirror and observed the big cop walking back inside Mr. Tacos shaking his head negatively with a look of frustration painted on his face. The assassin smiled malevolently and thought, *I could have killed all of them at once if I brought my fentanyl canister.*

~~~~

Dr. Robert Crine prepared the body of Dr. Phillip Kaley for shipment to Quantico for a more detailed autopsy with the FBI's sophisticated forensic equipment. He was certain, however, that the same person who severed the trophies from the two black victims discovered at Miller Meadows South was Kaley's killer as well.

Sadness flushed his face as he pulled the body of detective Tony Quagliaroli out from refrigerator number "12" for his next autopsy. He gently slid the corpse from the gurney onto the operating table. Quag had what appeared to be a slight grin inched on his lips and that made Crine smile and reflect about his mother, who had often beat him as a child for no other reason than he didn't eat his peas for supper. A lot of his memories of her were macabre or nightmarish but the one he was thinking about now made him laugh out loud.

After the death of his favorite uncle, the family was making some of the funeral arrangements, his mother oddly announced to the room, "What's all the fuss about? When I die just put a ham bone up my ass and let the dog haul me away."

Dr. Crine mused for a while and then started talking to his friend as he fought the tears that started welling in his eyes, "How could this happen to you my dear and trusted friend? Who did this to you?" He whispered. "We will find the son of a bitch, I promise you that," he stated. He then started to make a "Y" incision into his friend's chest looking for information. "This won't hurt you now. I'll be delicate and thorough. If there are any clues you left behind, I will find them."

After an hour of intense work, he concluded that it was indeed fentanyl that caused his friend's untimely death, but he also had the tendrils of lung and liver cancer infiltrating his body, leaving shadows of Quag's imminent demise in less than two years. "I don't think I ever saw you take a drag on a cigarette or cigar in my life and I know you weren't a big drinker. Life isn't fair sometime, is it my friend?" He murmured.

Dr. Crine finished his dictation and put Quag's body back into refrigerator number 12. He walked to his desk, fell into his chair, started to think of how fucked up everything was, wiped the tears slowly filtering down his cheeks with the back of his hand and sighed, "My God, what is happening to us?"

CHAPTER 31

When Peter Michaels opened his eyes he was met with Clare Claxton's brilliant, happy go lucky blue eyes staring back at him. He smiled. She blinked and her eyes were no longer happy.

"What's wrong?" he asked. His smile was replaced with a *what's going on* look on his face.

"This security detail stuff can get old really, really fast. I am very concerned for you, baby. I couldn't stand looking over my shoulder every waking hour," she said leaning close to him nestling her head on his chest and shoulder. "You are very tense. It's not like you."

"We are working to find this guy and we will find him. I just hope sooner rather than later, but we will find him," Michaels tried to reassure the woman he was getting very close to.

"How can you be so sure?" She inquired.

"Dave's brother-in-law works in the mental health business. He helped us identify the 'Bug Man' Dobonovich. If this guy was at Madison Mental Health Center we will find him."

"And if he wasn't there?"

"Then we might be fucked."

She sighed heavily then pulled herself on top of him and kissed him full on the mouth.

He responded immediately. He groaned then rolled over and they made gentle, tender love for what seemed like an hour. It was the most relaxed he felt in over a week.

~~~~

Deborah Duke was sipping her hot black coffee smiling to herself as she snuggled one of her most prized possessions; a one hundred percent Siberian goose down pillow. She took the pillow with her everywhere she went because it offered her comfort while sleeping and thinking but it also served as an aphrodisiac whenever she got in the mood to make love.

She was feeling confident that she had developed five family tree names that would lead to positive identifications. She also had four others as very strong possibilities. Each of the first five victims shared a lot of DNA and she was able to put together a genetic network connecting family members with recent DNA that was available from criminal records, medical and military records. She suspected some of them were closely related because the DNA was very distinctive and it doesn't lie.

Her phone startled her and broke her chain of thought. It was a default tone that was not assigned to any of her known contacts. "Hello. Deborah Duke," she announced.

"Ms. Duke, this agent Tom Britten. I am going to forward you ten more DNA files that we have compiled from the latest victims."

"I was wondering when they would be coming over. I am close to nine genetic histories at this time."

"Wow. That was pretty fast. I am surprised," Britten said with a smile.

"I am pretty sure these first DNA trails come from the recent DNA files on record at workplaces and the military. I assume these victims are from middle class families. I only had one strong connection from CODIS," she informed.

"Well get them to us as soon as you can and we will get started with the gumshoe work," he said.

"I'll have at least five of them to you by the end of the day. I'm surprised to hear from you on a weekend," she said.

"I work any day of the week. Can't keep up with the workload. When you get everything together just call me. You have my number. You can reach me anytime, day or night," he said and they hung up.

Duke stood, walked over to the kitchenette area of her hotel room, poured herself another cup of coffee and dialed Peter Michaels.

The bell tone for Deborah Duke in Peter Michaels' phone was the old-fashioned telephone ring. He was sitting in his atrium room with Clare Claxton drinking coffee. He mouthed *I've got to take this* and said, "Hey Deborah you're up early on a Saturday morning."

"Peter, it's ten o'clock. I've been up since six. I have five for sure family tree names for you to look up, but agent Britten just called and caught me off guard. I told him I should have five names for him by the end of the day. So, you are not going to have a 24 hour lead."

"That's not a problem. We aren't working against each other, except the feds are not very willing to share a lot of information with guys like me even though they are working to keep me alive."

"How's that going?"

"It's new and right now it's a real pain in the ass, but it beats the hell out of the alternative of dying," he responded with a smile.

"It must be claustrophobic?" She asked quizzically.

"Yeah, I took Clare out for pizza last night and they wanted to drive in the car with us, but that is taking it a little too far. I told them to follow me, I wasn't trying to lose their tail or anything like that and they agreed. Plus, I am sure they have a tracker on my car."

"I guess that will take some getting used to."

"So, what have you got for me?" He asked reaching for his notebook as she started to give him the names of the first nine family trees she had uncovered.

~~~~

Lake Michigan was angry. Its waves were roaring loudly as they cartwheeled and crashed torturously and menacingly on the brown sandy beaches and splattered onto the cement embankments along Lake Shore Drive reminding everyone of the power Mother Nature has over all of us. The wind shifted from the north overnight bringing some relief from the extremely hot and humid July temperatures that plagued the city every day last week. The possibility of tornadoes in the surrounding six county areas were announced by all the television and radio weather forecasters.

Jack Warren didn't want to bother Peter Michaels. He knew that his buddy and his new girlfriend had a pizza date last night so he decided to walk to a well-known breakfast joint on Michigan Avenue just a few blocks south of his condo building. When he stepped outside he was greeted with a crisp chill in the air and an unexpected 20 mile an hour wind which blew his curly locks forward; distracting him. He pulled his jacket collar up, tucked his chin down into his chest and stuck his hands into his pockets. He was fingering two Narcan nasal pumps with his right hand.

His two bodyguards had taken a linear protective position, Sgt. Brain Alexander was in front and to the right of their charge and detective Tom Polston walked behind him favoring the left. They hardly paid attention to the short, stout woman in a black outfit wearing a protective blue medical mask pedaling her bicycle close to the buildings because of the heavy winds.

Sgt. Alexander barely heard the metallic clink of the tiny cannister that the woman dropped on the ground in front of Warren's feet as she quickly passed them by and turned right through an open gate of a half-filled parking lot. The killing move was well planned and precisely executed at the very moment the escape route was available to the would-be killer.

Alexander turned to look over his left shoulder when the fentanyl fumes first hit him. He staggered slightly within two seconds and fell down on the sidewalk. He was overdosing and passed out immediately. Warren and Polston reacted quickly putting on their EEBD protective masks. Warren kicked the cannister to the fence away from them. Its contents already spewed into the gusty cool air minimizing any other threat. Fortunately, there were just a few people out walking the streets because of the weather.

Alexander's eyes were rolled back into their sockets. They seemed lifeless but his moaning brought hope to Warren and Polston as each had their Narcan nasal spray units out and ready to insert into Alexander's nostrils. His breathing was shallow and weak. He was mumbling "I'm sorry. I'm sorry, I missed her," then he passed out again.

Polston inserted another nasal unit and plunged the fresh Narcan into his friend's nose. Warren depressed his radio button and screamed, "Officer down. Officer down. This is detective Jack Warren, 1432, requesting immediate assistance. Officer down at the ten hundred block of South Michigan Avenue. Send an ambo. NOW," he screamed.

Warren's focused eyes scanned the area looking for the suspect, whom he believed was now heading north on Wabash Avenue. "All units, a female suspect dressed in black is riding a bicycle north on Wabash. May be armed and dangerous."

~~~~

The CFD's EMTs were loading Alexander on a gurney after injecting him with another unit of Narcan. He was in and out of consciousness; the fentanyl appeared to be rushing through his body like rapidly moving flood waters flowing uncontrollably downstream but he was alive.

His eyes were trying to focus as he was coming back to the moment. "Where am I?" he asked drearily. "What's happening?"

"You are in a fire department ambulance. I am paramedic Joan Myers. You were poisoned with fentanyl but we got you. You are going to be okay. You're gonna be just fine," Myers tried to reassure him with a smile and constant medical attention.

She had been on the job for almost 20 years and she thought she had seen it all, until today. Fortunately for ambulance 63, all the paramedics just finished a three day training course on how to deal with this new killer that was plaguing the streets of Chicago.

Myers's green eyes never left Alexander's face as he went from O-D-ing to consciousness and back again into another world of dark cognizance. Her fingertips remained on his Carotid Artery feeling for a pulse and life.

The CPD's Narcotic's Unit seized enough fentanyl that could kill millions of people last week in a raid on a Chinatown warehouse. Police believed the synthetic opiate was manufactured in China with no restrictions and shipped here for distribution by Chicago's notorious street gangs, who could care less if people died. There seemed to be an unending need for this killing substance and unfortunately there also seemed to be an unending supply of fentanyl all over the city.

~~~~

Detective Tom Polston was totally focused as he watched over Brian Alexander while the medics were working on him in the Advance Life Support module of their ambulance. He slapped the rear doors twice after they got him comfortably situated for the ride to Rush Medical Center.

Jack Warren had his phone out calling Peter Michaels, who answered on the third ring.

"What's up brother?" Michaels answered with a big grin thinking his buddy wanted to know all the details of his date with Clare and what happened afterwards.

"That fucker just tried to kill me but Brian took the brunt of the fentanyl. The EMTs are taking him over to Rush right now."

"Is he okay?" Michaels asked in a panic.

"I hope so. We think so. It is amazing how quickly we acted with the Narcan, but we also lost track of the suspect, who was dressed like a woman, riding a bike of all things. It actually was a perfectly executed kill plan. Thank God it was windy," Warren explained.

"Well, that does tell us one thing," Michaels rationalized.

"Yeah, what's that?" Warren responded.

"That fucker is not as smart as he or she thinks he or she is to pull off a stunt like that on a windy day. That was not very smart at all."

"Whomever, the killer is, he is daring and resourceful."

"Yeah, but his carelessness will get him either caught or killed."

CHAPTER 32

The assassin dressed in black raced through the half full parking lot and turned north on Wabash Avenue pumping his bicycle hard. His head was down to reduce the friction that the north wind offered, sweat ran down his face irritating his eyes, his mouth was dry, the blue cloth medical face mask he wore to protect his identity was not helping him now because it filtered any fresh air that he could inhale into his burning lungs. He was cursing himself for dropping the fentanyl dispenser a second too late, missing his intended target.

"I will get that killer copper if it's the last thing I do," he declared as he skidded to a stop leaving a thin tire mark on the pavement. He jumped off his bike to stash it behind an empty, old worn out, gray wooden parking lot shed. He pulled a lightweight, blue windbreaker and running pants from his backpack, quickly changed into his new disguise, pulled off his brown wig, stuffed it into his backpack, put a Cubs baseball cap on his bald head and made his way to State Street, where he turned back south walking at a calm pace to avoid drawing any attention to himself.

Police cars were racing and weaving up and down the streets looking for a woman suspect dressed in black, riding a bike. He walked with his head held high trying to produce a curious look as the blue and whites searched the area for him.

A squad car stopped the killer as he approached Balboa and a female officer with her black hair in a French braid looked out her window and asked, "Hey, did you happen to see a woman dressed in black, riding a bicycle?"

"Sorry officer, I ain't seen no one," he lied. "What's going on?" He asked as quizzically as he could muster.

"Looking for a person of interest. That's all. Thanks," she said and pulled away with no further explanation.

"Sorry, I couldn't help," he offered as the officer left and then he muttered, "Fuck all you...fucking cops. Fuck you."

A young couple cuddled together walking against the wind, seemed to appear from nowhere; startled by the outburst. The killer just smiled at them exposing his rotting teeth and he tipped his hat saying, "A good morning, ain't it."

The woman was repulsed at the greeting. She gripped her husband's arm with a firm, tight squeeze and said, "Did you see that ugly fucker's teeth. Ugh!"

The assassin felt a cold blast of wind and when he reached up to touch his mouth, he realized that the medical mask that protected his identity was no longer there. His wicked smile was replaced with a look of fear and his eyes filled with hatred as he glanced over his shoulder searching for the blue mask. He instantly realized that it certainly contained his DNA.

He turned around to follow the young couple who saw his face and could possibly identify him. *I'm gonna have to kill em'.*

~~~~

Jack Warren got behind the wheel of the beat up, dark green Crown Vic squad and screeched down Wabash Avenue siren blaring, his eyes scanning every little corner, object, and buildings on his side of the car. Polston did the same from the passenger side window. He was not as familiar with the area as his new partner.

Warren slammed on the brakes and took a hard left into a half-filled parking lot between Wabash and State Street north of Balboa. He noticed a fraction of the bike's tire, jammed behind an empty parking lot attendant's shack. Polston immediately saw what was happening and keyed his mike, "This is detective Thomas Polston. I need a CSI team at the all-day parking lot at the corner of Wabash and Balboa. ASAP."

Warren was already out of the car, pulling on a pair of black latex gloves, slowly approaching the bike, eyes scanning everything in sight. He noticed a blue medical mask entangled on the bikes gear chain mechanism. The mask matched the kind the would-be killer was wearing when he attacked the trio walking down Michigan Avenue. "Tommy bring an evidence bag. They're in the back seat in the organizer," he yelled over his shoulder.

Warren picked up the mask and noticed some hair strands sticking to the inside of it. He placed his finger on it so the wind that just gusted couldn't blow it away. Polston handed him a clear plastic evidence bag and Warren placed the mask in it. "There should be some good DNA on this. That fucker may not be as smart as he thinks he is," Warren said looking at the mask, a hint of a grin surfacing on his lips.

"He was dressed like a she," Polston opined.

"He is a short little weasel and we are going to get him. Fuck him," Warren said.

The CSI team arrived and immediately went to work, carefully moving the bike out from behind the shed after taking dozens of pictures and began dusting it for prints even though the assassin wore gloves.

"There may be some sweat on the handlebars. He was pushing hard against this wind," Warren said and then turned to Polston,

"Tommy, maybe we'll get lucky with some DNA on that bike. I know we got some on the mask."

Warren handed the evidence bag over to the CSI team after he signed it to protect the chain of evidence. He took out his phone and called the number the EMT gave him.

Joan Myers answered on the third ring and without saying hello she said, "He's gonna be fine. He is fully conscious and his vitals are returning to normal. Thank God, you guys were on the scene to treat him right away. I don't know how much of that shit he inhaled, but with fentanyl it only takes five tiny granules; a sample the size of five little granules of salt is enough to kill you."

Warren closed his eyes, let out a sigh and prayed, "Thank you, Jesus."

~~~~

Ryan O'Toole the fifth was in his van following a red, chromed out Harley Davidson Fat Boy with the tall red headed bastard that beat him in a game of pool the night before and had the audacity to make fun of him in front of everyone around the table. The biker criticized him for missing a very easy eight ball embankment shot to win the game and fifty bucks. The winner smiled a big smile exposing his tobacco-stained teeth through his scruffy long red and gray beard the entire time of the insult.

Jack's Bar and Billiards on Ogden Avenue was one of those neighborhood taverns that attracted a lot of bikers and other derelicts who didn't care if anyone had a job or not, as long as they didn't have to wait too long for their next cold beer and the women had to have big tits and lots of colorful tattoos. The joint smelled of smoke, and marijuana, along with grease and bleach. It was dark and dank and dirty. It was the perfect place to find someone to kill. Someone who would never be noticed if they went missing.

Number Five was in one of those moods that would eventually end in someone's death and that someone was a six foot-two, redhead with a long beard and brown teeth riding a Harley Davidson Fat Boy. *You will soon be number 34, you fuck.*

CHAPTER 33

P eter Michaels was tired of looking over his shoulder for some nut bag he didn't know that wanted to kill him. He hated the feeling of not being in control of his surroundings. He just got off the phone with Deborah Duke, who gave him nine more names of potential family members of the first victims discovered. His phone rang as he fired up his computer. "Hey, what's up?"

Jack Warren was smiling, "We have some evidence that will lead us to Quag's killer."

"That's great. What did you find?"

"His mask and some hair samples,"

"Awesome. How's Brian?"

"He's going to be fine. They'll probably keep him in the hospital overnight. His vitals are back to normal but I am sure he will probably have to take a few days off. I'm going to check on him with Tommy right now."

"Okay, great, keep me posted. I got some more names I need to run down," he said than realized he may have said too much.

"What names?" Warren asked curiously.

"Just some research stuff that I am doing," he said shaking his head. He did not want to lie to his buddy.

"Hey, how's Clare?"

"She's great. She left this morning. She is going to visit her sister in Loyola Hospital. Not sure if we are going to go out tonight. She doesn't like having a posse following us around."

"Well, I tell you what, that posse saved Brian's life this morning and if that asshole comes after you, they'll save you as well," Warren said reassuringly.

~~~~

David Beedy got off the phone with his brother-in-law and an uncontrollable smile spread across his face. He called Peter Michaels immediately.

"I was just going to call you," Michaels said. "What's up?"

"We got him. We got the fucker," Beedy said.

"What? Who?"

"Ronald Carson."

"Your brother-in-law came through?" Michaels asked standing up from his atrium high top table as he started to walk around his condo with nervous energy.

"Yep. Old Ronald Carson escaped from Madison about three or four months ago. He was fascinated with Cyril Dobonovich. Hung around with him whenever he could."

"Probably a psychopath, right?"

"As sick as they get. He butchered his entire family with a machete, then tried to hang himself, but botched it, the rope gave way. Police got there and took him into custody. He was covered with blood at the time."

"So, he was committed not convicted."

"It was the botched hanging attempt that opened that door," Beedy conceded.

"And he wasn't discharged, he escaped?"

"Yep, almost killed a nurse who tried to stop him. Hit the guy in the head with some kind of pipe that he apparently smuggled in."

"Can we get a picture of him?"

"Billy is trying. He said there is an intake picture in his file. I told him we think he's the one threatening you and your buddy Jack Warren. He said he'll figure something out."

"Jack found Ronald's bike and his facial mask. He's sure they have DNA and some hair samples. What do we know about this psycho?"

"He's a short shit, only five, five. He is 31 years old. Brown oily hair, he apparently doesn't like to bathe. At Madison they referred to him as 'Stinky.' He's got brown eyes. He was a meth head and his teeth were starting to rot. He's got some acne scars on his left cheek."

"Any tats?"

"Don't know about that, but he had none when he was committed."

"I'll let Jack know. This info may save a lot of time for them. I am sure Carson has some DNA on file somewhere."

~~~~

Clare Claxton was driving south on First Avenue leaving Loyola Hospital where she just visited her older sister who had a kidney transplant operation several days before. She spoke with Peter Michaels and she was relieved to hear that Brian Alexander was out of the woods and would make a full recovery and that they identified the would be killer.

Clare brought Bullet with her because she felt that she had been neglecting him in her off time. Michaels told her she could bring the dog to the condo anytime she wanted.

It was not quite as windy in the western suburbs as it was in the city. As she passed some very dense forest, Bullet began to bark excitedly. The windows were down halfway, Clare didn't like her dog sticking his head out the window when she was driving.

"Hey settle down. What's with you buddy," she said, trying to calm him down. But Bullet continued to bark. Clare looked out the window and noticed vultures circling above a very wooded area to her left and curiosity got the best of her. She pulled over to the side of the road when she got the chance, got out of the car, took out her binoculars and scanned the area. A dozen big black birds were surrounding and swooping down into an area known as Zoo Woods. Bullet stopped barking once they were downwind from the original outburst. Clare noticed a road that seemed to disappear into the tall trees off of Cermak Road. She decided to investigate.

The one lane sun bleached and worn asphalt road gradually morphed into a gravel path that ended in a 20 by 20 square foot clearing. Clare surmised it was probably a maintenance road turnaround. Three paths were etched into the weeds and small brush that seemed to evaporate into the dense woods.

Clare was dressed in Bergdorf Goodman cigarette designer jeans, a short red Neiman Marcus LaMarque Kaia puff sleeved leather jacket, Salvatore Ferragamo black flats and a black, washed out "Grateful Dead" tee shirt with "Truckin" stenciled across the skyline of Chicago. She slipped out of her shoes, pulled on her heavy work boots, put on her police issued blue wind breaker jacket with CPD printed in yellow on the back. She decided to use a short leash for Bullet because the forest was thick and unpredictable. The pathway seemed to disappear with every step she took further into the trees. Tall limbs and branches reaching for the sun's rays were dancing to a slight breeze, swirling around, casting long, thin, kaleidoscope like shadows. There was a distinct smell of death in the air.

Bullet was pulling hard. "Take it easy boy. We have plenty of time," as soon as she said that Bullet stopped and sat. "Good boy," Clare murmured as she noticed what appeared to be an arm wrapped in a black plastic bag that was shredded from forest varmints and vultures looking for supper.

Clare slipped on some black latex gloves, took out her phone and took five or six pictures of the arm in the brush, then reached down to grab it and struggled trying to pull it free from its tangled resting place. She noticed maggots and ants and other strange looking bugs enjoying the lifeless environment. She quivered as a chill ran down her spine and goose bumps filled her jacket sleeves. She took off her latex gloves, pulled the cellphone out of her rear pocket, took some more pictures, sent them to Vando and then called him. He was the only CSI she really knew and she didn't want to disturb the crime scene any more than she already had.

"Hey what's up, kiddo?" Vando said with a smile on his lips that spread to his deep blue eyes.

"Hey, Vando thought I should call you. I just found an arm in some forest known as Zoo Woods."

"Oh yeah, over there off First Ave. I know where that is. My family used to have weekend picnics at the park there right across from Loyola."

"Well, I think you are going to be interested in this because I found a right arm with no thumb. It's freaking me out."

CHAPTER 34

P eter Michaels lost the argument of riding his Harley Davidson Street Bob over to the television station where he decided to make his phone calls to identify the nine victims from the research that Deborah Duke gave him. His security detail was on high alert after the attack on Sgt. Brian Alexander earlier that day.

Detective Tom Buettner drove, Michaels sat in the back seat along with Jon Kerbs. There was very little conversation until Peter Michaels broke the silence, "You guys really pissed off Clare last night."

"Tough shit," said Kerbs, "You are not getting out of our sight after Brian got hit today. This guy is nuts. You ain't dying on our watch."

"Yeah, I know. I know. I gotta tell you. I am tired of looking over my shoulder, but we know who this bastard is now, and we will find him," said Michaels trying to voice confidence. Just then his phone rang to the theme of "Rocky," he smiled and answered, "Hey Clare, what's up?"

"I'm with Vando. I discovered a crime scene."

"I thought you were visiting your sister."

"I did. She's doing remarkably well. She's waiting to be discharged later today."

"That's great news. So, what's happening now?"

"The hitchhiker has struck again. I found a right arm with no thumb attached to it in the Zoo Woods very close to the hospital. Vando is in a bunch of thicket and he found the chest cavity, a left leg and left arm so far," she said walking slowly around the clearing which was now filled with four other police cars.

"This is sounding to me like generational serial killers," Michaels stated and he didn't know why he said it.

"What makes you say that?" asked Clare, a questioning look curtained her face as she tried to keep her phone out of the wind's path.

"I really don't know. It just came to mind and I actually think it is a very good theory," Michaels said nodding his head affirmatively then he continued, "It certainly would explain the victims we have already found. I understand those deaths go back at least a hundred years."

"Vando just said, they are having a meeting with the superintendent first thing Monday morning trying to piece together all of what we have so far."

"You invited to that?" Michaels asked crossing his fingers hoping she would be.

"No. Garofalo and I are expanding our searches to other parks on Monday. It's going to be another long week."

"Hey, tell Vando we know who the killer is. I'm sure he'd love to know that."

~~~~

David Beedy was already at his desk talking on the phone when Peter Michaels entered the I-Unit's office. He motioned with a finger and thumb that he was talking to a family member of one of the victims then he mouthed "Coffee," and got back to his conversation. Buettner and Kerbs were waiting outside and perked up when Michaels walked by them and asked, "You want coffee?"

Buettner said, "I'd rather have tequila but coffee would be great." The security team followed Michaels into the almost vacant coffee shop.

"Tell me, Ms. Bolander. What was your missing great cousin's name?" Beedy asked.

"It was Christopher Bolander. He was my husband's distant great cousin and he's named after him. The family has been talking about it since the 1930s."

"The 1930s. Did they file a missing person's report? I can have our research team try to find it."

"I think so, but I am not totally sure. My husband doesn't know for certain either."

"Thank you for your time. If you think of anything else, please give me a call anytime, day or night." Beedy gave her his cellphone number and hung up just as Michaels walked back into the office.

"What was that all about?" Michaels asked as he handed his partner a cup of steaming hot black coffee.

"Christopher Bolander. That's the name of one of the first Edgebrook golf course victims. The Bolanders have been talking about the disappearance of their relative since the 1930s," Beedy offered.

"That goes along with my theory very nicely," Michaels responded.

"And what theory is that?"

"I think we are dealing with generational serial killers. Clare just found the right arm of a man apparently buried literally in pieces in the Zoo Woods. His right thumb has been severed. This can't be a copycat thing."

"I agree. We have not reported that the right thumbs of all the victims have been taken as trophies. We just reported certain body parts had been taken. This is getting really weird," Beedy said with a quizzical look.

"Actually, generational serial killers may not be as rare as you would think."

~~~~

Deborah Duke answered her cellphone with a smile looking at the caller ID, "You already made some identifications? I just gave you the information a few hours ago."

"Actually, Dave has already made three. That familial DNA stuff is fascinating," Michaels opined, "but listen, I've come up with a theory that we are dealing with generational serial killers. Does that sound too far-fetched to you?"

"It is certainly possible, but serial killers are not born. They can be made though, and there have been scientific studies trying to prove these genetic connections to violence and crime."

"So, is there a serial killer gene, so to speak?" Michaels asked.

"No, but there is something called the 'warrior gene,' and that has been the subject of many recent studies by neuroscientists. Listen, geneticist at one time did a study of prisoners in penitentiaries around the country and they discovered that a majority of the male inmates had a variant of a gene located on their X-chromosome, often referred to as the sex chromosome. At first they thought they found something connecting them to the violent crimes they were convicted of committing," Duke informed.

"Was there a connection?"

"No. They could make no scientific correlation between this gene variant and murder, along with other violent crimes, but forensic studies have been ongoing ever since and that's when we discovered the 'warrior gene.'"

"So, what is this 'warrior gene?'"

"It's called the Monoamine Oxidase A gene, or commonly referred to as the MAOA gene."

"And this MAOA gene does what?" Michaels asked excitedly but a little perplexed.

"This gene encodes for the Monoamine Oxidase A enzyme that breaks down neurotransmitters of crucial chemical compounds like serotonin, epinephrine, norepinephrine and dopamine," Duke explained.

"What does that mean in layman's terms?" Michaels asked now confused.

"We all have it. This MAOA gene; It helps the brain understand happiness, joy, normality, and saneness, but when our bodies don't have the optimal amount of it, when that amount decreases, it causes dire changes in one's behavior."

"What sort of behavior?" Michaels asked now totally engrossed.

"Behavior can be as nonthreatening as social awkwardness to psychopathic, leading to aggressive and sometimes deadly behavior. Throw into the mix, childhood abuse, loss, bullying and the disrespect of life…every so often…guess what?"

"You can create a serial killer," Michaels interjected.

"Exactly. In studies of serial killers, every single one of them had low levels of the MAOA enzyme. Scientists at Vasserdine's Molecular Genetics Laboratory examined 30 violent criminals, most of whom were murderers. They were looking for a variant of the 'warrior gene' and discovered that the combination of this gene variant and child abuse increased the inmate's chances of committing a violent offense by more than 400 percent."

"That's incredible," Michaels said enthralled by this revelation. "So, these combinations of the gene and the abuses don't necessarily produce serial killers, correct?"

"Yes, that's true but it's a dangerous mixture that can create the vulnerability of a violent adult; both male and female," Duke said and then asked, "Peter…are you alright?"

"Yeah, I'm great Deborah. I'm fine and now I am even more convinced that we are on the trail of generational serial killers. I've never heard of a story like this before. We don't know of any boundaries. Oh! By the way, we have identified the fucker who is trying to kill me."

CHAPTER 35

Ryan O'Toole the fifth was sitting in his van parked on Ogden Avenue across the street from Jack's Bar and Billiards looking for the tall red headed biker. His chromed out, red Harley Davidson Fat Boy was parked on the street out front with four other Harleys. The redhead had been inside for at least three hours. O'Toole decided that it would be a good time to take him down because he had been drinking for so long.

The biker lived in the Little Village neighborhood bordering the South Lawndale community. It's located east of Western Avenue, west of Cicero Avenue, North of Interstate 55 and south of the BNSF train line. It's a densely populated community that is 85 percent Latino. It has a relatively high crime rate with 71 shootings already this year alone.

Strangely, somehow this Irish, white, paled skinned redheaded biker seemed to blend into the heavily minority community without suspicion or concern. He lived alone off of Cicero Avenue in a small red brick bungalow with a two car garage that was in better shape than the house. The garage was also home for a spotless, shiny red 2005 Honda Accord, two other motorcycles, one red, the other black, and tons of tools along with an old, but very functional refrigerator with a poster taped to its door reading: **Born To Ride**. Its only purpose was to keep his Budweiser cold. That's where he drinks his last beer of the night, every night. That's where he parked his red bike. That's where Number Five decided to kill him.

Fuck Red, he thought. *Fuck him.*

~~~~

The bald, foul smelling, short assassin, Ronald Carson, followed the middle aged, blonde couple he bumped into while escaping during the police dragnet. They turned left on Polk Street in the Printer's Row neighborhood walking to their 18 story condo building still arm in arm even though the temperature started to warm up considerably. This community is considered very safe. There are a few local taverns but not a lot of high-end restaurants in the area, however just a few minutes away by UBER or public transportation there are restaurants that offer any food imaginable.

After they entered their building, Carson swore to himself realizing that killing them may be a little more difficult than he originally thought because it would be almost impossible to find out what unit they lived in and he didn't know their names.

Suddenly a young man turned the corner, ran up to the door to catch it before it closed and Carson stopped him, "Hey, sorry to bother you, but did you see that couple, the blonde couple that just entered your building?"

"Yeah, why?" he asked suspiciously.

Thinking quickly on his feet; "The man dropped his wallet and I was trying to catch up to them to return it," Carson lied enthusiastically, pulling out his wallet, showing it to the gullible young man.

"They're the Bradley's in 907," he blurted out and then realized he made a big mistake. "Here give it to me and I will return it to them."

"I'm afraid not. I don't know you. I'll get it back to them somehow," Carson said and turned around and abruptly walked off.

~~~~

The cicadas return after a 17 year hiatus was not welcomed in the Chicagoland area. Their screeching cacophony was loud, annoying, and causing CSI Tom Vander Aarde's hangover headache to amplify like the sounds of steel guitars and percussion drums pounding in his brain at the same time. His blue lagoon eyes were surrounded by tiny, thin streams of red blood. Vando was in bad shape, sweating profusely, cursing his buddies for the late-night poker game, and way too many fingers of Basil Hayden bourbon coupled with a few extra shots of 1800 Tequila.

By the time he found four other body parts: both legs, the left arm, and the torso with no head, he was drenched. The CSI's face was bleeding from a number of small razor like slits that managed to etch his face from low hanging branches and thorns hidden in the underbrush concealing the extremities he was trying to retrieve. He realized that the tips of each of the victim's fingers were cut off. *What a dumb fuck,* He thought to himself then he asked, "Hey Clare did you notice if the fingertips of the right hand were cut off?"

"Actually, I didn't want to foul the evidence. So, no. I didn't look that close. I thought I better just call you," she said shaking her head.

"Well, the asshole probably thought we couldn't ID the guy without fingerprints, but he forgot to take the palms which will be just as good for identification."

"Did you find the head?" She asked looking around the area disgusted by the thought of the head being buried somewhere else.

"No. I bet that's gonna be hidden or buried in another place. That's my guess."

"Yeah, I am sure you're right about that. Hey, I am going to get out of here. Thanks for coming over I hope I didn't hurt anything."

"You did great. Good job on relying on your gut instincts by the way. This could be a great lead to solve this thing," Vando said with a smile then added, "Hey, you going out with Peter tonight?"

"I don't think so. He might do a piece on the air tonight. They found out who killed Quag."

~~~~

"Hey, Jack, I am sending you a picture of Ronald Carson. Dave's brother-in-law just came through for us. Our artists are working their magic on it right now, making him bald, giving him a beard and hair. Different looks. I'm going to do the story tonight about Tony's death and the attempt on Brian today," Peter Michaels said pacing slowly around his desk, running his fingers through his hair, thinking.

"We should have DNA back no later than Monday night from the mask he dropped earlier today and this will help us cut right through the red tape bullshit," Warren said. "What do you know about him?"

"He's a short bastard. Strong. Crazy as they come. Killed his entire family with a machete. He escaped from Madison Mental Health Center about four months ago and almost killed a nurse during the process. He loved the 'Bug Man,' and Lin An. Oh, and all the employees called him 'Stinky,' because he hated to take showers and clean up."

"We are going to get this guy very soon. He's starting to make mistakes," Warren opined.

"It will be nice to get this posse out of the way and start spending more time on the hitchhiker," Michaels offered, "We have identified six victims today. Dave's been working his ass off."

"I like your theory about the generational stuff. I am going to bring that up at our Monday morning meeting," Warren said.

"Don't be giving away all my secrets, buddy. I've got a lot of time and energy invested into this story. I don't need anybody at headquarters leaking my information to other news outlets."

"Don't worry about it," Warren said smiling.

"Yeah, right, you know how this town works."

CHAPTER 36

After an hour-long discussion with station attorney Sam Phieffer on how to legally word his script that named Ronald Carson as the killer of detective Tony Quagliaroli and the attempted killer of Sgt. Brian Alexander, Peter Michaels was allotted three and a half minutes to tell the story on the ten o'clock weekend newscast. During the broadcast, Michaels showed four different pictures of how Carson could possibly look. Michaels also explained the connection and interregnum between Carson and the "Bug Man," and how they met and interacted together. He ended the story with Carson's sobriquet that the staff at the Madison Mental Health Center had given him: "Stinky."

The phones were ringing off the hook when Michaels walked off the set towards the assignment desk. A student intern yelled out, "Hey, Peter. You better take line three."

"News...Michaels."

"Mr. Michaels, my name is Jane Bradley. My husband and I saw this Carson guy this morning walking down State Street."

"When?" Michaels asks covering his ear with his left hand trying to block all the noise and commotion in the newsroom.

"It was after ten o'clock. We saw a police officer talking to him and she drove off."

"He said something to the effect of 'fuck the police' or something like that. I don't think he saw us until after he said that."

"You got a good look at him?" Michaels asked inquisitively.

"Let me ask you something. Does this maniac have rotten teeth?"

Michaels shot up from the chair he was sitting in with this revelation. "Yeah, we think so. He apparently was a meth head. Did he say anything to you?"

"Yes...something to the effect 'Have a nice day.' You know something stupid like that. Man, he was creepy."

"What was he dressed like?"

Jane Bradley described him and they hung up, but not before Michaels warned her to be "very careful."

~~~~

A light cool, steady drizzle began to peck and poke into the night's air. The day started off with brisk northerly winds that provided a welcomed relief from the long hot days of summer. The paved streets and concrete sidewalks released a mirage of steam and fog. For motorcyclists these types of wet conditions can produce some dangerous safety concerns because the streets can become very slick, very fast. Old, dry oil that settles in the porous asphalt is flushed to the surface, couple that with the friction that revolving tires can generate, you end up with slippery roads that make stopping, swerving, and sliding a clear and present danger, particularly for motorcyclists.

The tall redheaded biker was very cautious while driving home. He was proud that he limited his alcohol intake to a minimum that day particularly because of the unpredicted rain fall. He loved his beer but he loved life more.

He was a union carpenter. He spent the entire day at Jack's Bar and Billiards, not drinking, but fixing a long punch list of violations that his buddy and owner Jack Crow had been cited for from the city's health department. The four other bikers were electricians and plumbers. They helped fix numerous health and safety citations that were related to their trades. They were paid by Jack not with money, but with the promise of discounted beers for an entire year.

His friends called him Billy Bob. He spent six years in military service and did three tours in Afghanistan in an Army special forces unit. He did his share of killing and his share agonizing over it all. His long hair and his obstreperous beard were his private protest against the millennials that disrespect the American flag and service members in general.

His once muscular body was turning fubsy but the strength in his hands, fingers and forearms were entrenched from years of military calisthenics and commercial construction. He had few regrets: the hard work of hammering millions of nails into countless numbers of two by fours provided Billy Bob North with a good life. He was happy. He helped his friend today. He was tired and couldn't wait to get home, have a beer, and go to bed.

~~~~

Stinky was steaming. "You motherfucker. I am going to kill you," he screamed at the television set after watching Peter Michaels smirk, naming him "Stinky." He picked up one of his boots and threw it at the screen. It was a direct hit. "Fuck. Fuck." The thought of suddenly going out to buy a new TV flashed through his mind so, he picked up the other boot and in another fit of rage threw it at the TV again. It missed and knocked over a TV table along with a bottle of Old Style beer and a bowl of pretzels. "I'm going to kill that fucker, if it's the last thing I do."

Ronald Carson was stunned when he saw his face on television. He realized that he needed more disguises. He did not know that many people. He walked the streets with impunity in the past because he just seemed to blend into the environment that no one cared about street people. He had no concerns, but now that has all suddenly changed.

That prick Peter Michaels said he gave all the newspapers in the six county area the same pictures that he just put on television. How did he find me? He asked himself over and over. He promised he would kill that fucking reporter who killed his best friend within the next week.

~~~~

Ryan O'Toole sat in the alley three doors down from the red head's garage waiting and planning his attack. The van was running. The defroster was working hard to stop the windows from fogging up. It was a losing battle. The windshield wipers were used sparingly. He didn't want to draw attention to the foreign van in this neighborhood.

The big biker would be drunk, Number Five was sure of it. Shit, he'd been drinking all day. His sharp knife was on the passenger seat, waiting for his grasp. He wouldn't need the towel; the rain would take care of any blood. The body will be gone within seconds. He stretched his shoulders and rotated his neck in circles to loosen his tense muscles that were starting to cramp. He flexed his fingers. He was only two inches shorter than the biker. That was no big deal. The target was getting fat and out of shape. It should only take a few quick seconds. In and out like all the others.

That fucker should never have embarrassed me like that in that bar, he thought. His anger was building. He was getting furious. His anxiety was rising. He was ready to kill. A prescient smile etched its way to the edges of his thin lips when he heard the sounds of the screaming eagles approaching. His hand instinctively reached for the sharp, pointed knife. The smile spread. The adrenalin now surged like a torrent through his body.

Number 34 was coming home to die.

CHAPTER 37

P eter Michaels' cellphone began to vibrate in his pocket, he
smiled when he saw Clare's name. He had already fielded six
or seven other phone calls from viewers who had sightings of
the stinky assassin. The only one that was of real interest to him was a
neighbor who actually talked to the killer. He was upset because he
inadvertently gave the Bradley's name and their unit number to the
killer.

"You better let them know that you gave out their names. I am
going to call a police friend and let him know this information,"
Michaels warned and hung up the office phone. He finally got to his
cellphone, "Hey Clare, what's up?"

"I'm at your place and brought Bullet. Is that okay?" She said with
an erogenous smile, "and I brought a six pack of Corona Light."

"Perfect. I'm glad you called. I was going to invite my two new
security guys in for a drink. Now I won't."

"I'll be glad when this is over. It really can play on your nerves,"
she said. Her smile morphed into a look of concern.

"Well, after this story tonight, I have no doubt that 'Stinky' will
start to act more irrationally than ever. He'll make more mistakes.

Everybody will know what he looks like when the morning papers publish his picture all over the news."

"I've got something to show you when you get home. It's for protection," she announced in a stern voice.

Michaels' eyes widened, "I can't wait."

"It's not that. You dork. It's something I sort of made for protection. It's pretty cool actually," she announced.

"Hey, listen Jack's calling. I'll see you in a bit." He hit the accept button for his buddy's call. "Hey, what's up?"

"That hair fiber Carson left in the mask," detective Jack Warren insinuated.

"Yeah, what about it?" Michaels responded.

"It's not natural. It's from a wig," Warren informed.

"That's what I thought. You know this guy is going to move faster now on his timetable. If he saw my story tonight, he's going to be in a fit of rage. He's just like Bing Lin An. Fucking nuts," Michaels said warningly.

~~~~

The well-greased chain of the Genie garage door opener elevated the lightweight aluminum door effortlessly and soundlessly like a blue velvet performance curtain being hauled up to announce to the audience that the show was about to begin. This stage was a very clean, well maintained and completely organized mechanical shop, meticulously set up for protection in case of an unwanted intrusion from neighborhood gangbangers.

Billy Bob North was, if nothing else, prepared for action. He slid off his red Harley Fat Boy with ease, his back to the alley. His wet black leather jacket glistened from the rays of light that were produced from rows of overhead fluorescent bulbs that turned night into day. The rain grew heavier, silencing the footfalls of Number Five's approach from behind, but at the last moment North's military instincts alerted him to danger and he spun around only to be greeted by a sharp knife plunged in his lower abdomen.

"Motherfucker," North screamed and in an automatic instinctive defensive move, he crossed his forearms catching the wrist of his attacker shortening the killing thrust. He felt a searing sciatica type pain shoot down his legs.

O'Toole was taken by total surprise by this catlike maneuver. His prey was anything but drunk. He was alert, strong and ready for combat. In a counter move, O'Toole gave "34" a head butt which staggered him backwards for a moment but he did not go down.

Blood was dripping from the wound, but like any combat veteran North immediately applied pressure to stem the flow of his life source. "You Motherfucker, I'll kill you," he screamed trying to move forward but the pain was to debilitating. He staggered and looked directly into the eyes of his attacker and stopped, stunned as if tased. Those amber eyes suddenly brought about an instant cry of recognition, "You!"

The outburst caught Number Five by total surprise. He was never in Jack's Bar and Billiards before the night he played pool with those bikers. He never took off his sunglasses. The thought of *How did he know* flashed through his mind and he decided to retreat. He rationalized that he could return another time and shoot the fucker if he had too.

Billy Bob North was still on his feet, but barely. Unconsciousness was looming. His head was spinning. His eyes were blinking rapidly as if they were sucking in the oxygen he needed to prolong life. His mouth felt like liquid was forming at the back of his tongue. It took all the strength he could muster to hold his ground. His special forces' training repeating itself, screaming: **Never show your enemy any weakness**. So, he stood fast, holding onto the handlebars of his beloved red Harley Davidson Fat Boy. When he heard the sound of his attacker's vehicle exiting the alley, he took a deep breath, gasping for air and then everything went dark. He collapsed across his bike, knocking it down. Blood flowed over and around the engine block, puddling on the highly glossed shiny light gray painted floor like a scarlet letter. Ryan O'Toole's thin, sharp, twelve inch knife fell to the ground next to the crimson pool; an exclamation point announcing BIlly Bob North's death.

~~~~

Number Five was cursing himself, pounding the steering wheel of his van as he swerved onto Cicero Avenue with no regard for traffic. Blood from the cut on his forehead was inching down his face around his nose and onto his cheek. He reached for his towel and applied pressure to the area where he head bumped the redheaded biker.

"Fuck, where's my knife?" he screamed when he realized he must have left it at the scene. He frantically looked around the van's interior for his grandfather's treasured weapon of death and then a loud prolonged blare of another car's horn brought his attention back to reality and the wet slippery road and the parked car that he just side swiped. The van's wipers were swishing slowly and methodically, back, and forth, squeegeeing away the rain droplets that were popping and bursting like small bombs on his windshield. The glare from oncoming headlights exploded like bright yellow flares in front of his eyes, temporally blinding him, piercing his brain with lightning bolt precision, adding to his anxiety, excitement, frustration, and rage.

His mind was racing looking for answers. Blood. Knife. Fingerprints. Failure. He could not believe that he had been out maneuvered for the first time by a fucking old, fat biker. "I've got to think," he kept saying to himself out loud, over and over again, but the only thing that came to his sick, sociopathic, narcissistic mind was: NO TROPHIES.

CHAPTER 38

eter Michaels was halfheartedly arguing with his newly assigned security guard Jim Dorey even though they have known each other for years. Dorey's six-foot frame housed 195 pounds of muscle that was starting to soften from four Coors Lights every day. His brown hair was thinning but still neatly combed. He was disarming because his dark blue eyes were always smiling like his lips putting people he came in contact with at ease. His shoulders were slightly hunched and his gait was smooth but interrupted by a sore and tender left Achilles heel injury. He was always aware of his surroundings. He survived four shootings during his 25 year career. He was determined that Peter Michaels was not going to die on his watch.

"How many death threats do you get, Peter?" Dorey asked.

"I've had a few but last year there were a number of actual attempts. I'm not afraid to say that they unnerved me. I had some counseling over those," Michaels admitted, shaking his head.

"Hopefully we will find this character and we can put an end to this bullshit," Dorey said walking Michaels to his front door.

Just as he pulled out his key, the door opened, the surprised look on Michaels' face made Dorey draw his weapon. Clare's big smile was erased instantly and Bullet went into attack mode and growled ferociously. He bent down on his haunches and was ready to leap at Dorey when Clare commanded, "Bullet. Sit."

The dog immediately obeyed the order and put his head on Clare's left knee. He was rewarded with a gentle rub on his forehead and ears. "Good boy. Now what the fuck is this with the gun?"

"Sorry Clare. We didn't expect anyone to be home," Dorey declared.

"Shit. I am sorry. I was so engrossed in our conversation that I forgot to mention that you were here with Bullet," Michaels said as his stomach settled slightly.

"Remember, I wanted to show you that thing I made," she said not realizing that her hand was now trembling.

"Listen, Dorey, we'll be fine. I'll call or text you if I need anything," Michaels said trying to ease the tension that the incident caused.

"Hey, sorry. This whole thing has all of us on edge. Clare, I am so sorry but I really didn't know you were here," Dorey said apologetically.

"No problem," both Clare and Michaels said in harmony and shut the door.

~~~~

Tact Officer Frank Tedesco and his new partner, Kris Zimmerman, were returning to their district after interviewing a confidential informant about fentanyl distribution networks on the city's streets. Zimmerman was one of the first female officers assigned to a tact team. She was a gutsy cop, who had been shot twice in the line of duty in her ten years on the job. Her brown hair, sparsely streaked with blonde strands was pulled back in a ponytail. She was a sharpshooter with every weapon she touched. Her light blue eyes were alert, intelligent and constantly searching for the unknown. She noticed a dark blue van that swerved onto Cermak Avenue and then a motorcycle tipped over in a brightly lit garage with a man on top of it.

"Frank pull over, someone's down in that garage," she announced authoritatively.

Tedesco didn't hesitate a second. The Crown Vic answered with a sudden sharp left turn, fishtailing on the wet street. He threw the car in park while it was still sliding and they both jumped out drawing their Glocks ready for the unfamiliar.

Zimmerman noticed a pile of rags on the workbench, grabbed a handful and applied pressure to the dying biker's stomach wound. "Get an ambo," she hollered.

Tedesco keyed his mic, "This is officer Tedesco. 15435. We got a man down. He needs immediate medical care. Send an ambo to Cermak and Damen, forthwith."

"This guy has lost a lot of blood," Zimmerman said, concern filled her alert eyes. Blood was seeping out of the side of his mouth as he was trying to whisper something. Zimmerman, a combat veteran, was not afraid of blood, she saw plenty of it on two tours of duty in Afghanistan. She leaned in closer and put her ear to the victim's mouth. His malodorous breath made her wince.

"Amb…" was all she could make out as the biker with the red hair and gnarly, blood soaked beard went unconscious.

"I think he's asking for an ambulance," she said with a confused look then she felt for a pulse on his neck. One was there but hardly noticeable to her well trained fingertips. "I don't think this guy is going to make it, Frank. They gotta hurry," she proclaimed, shaking her head. Her eyes continuously scanning the garage and its contents.

"I'll get the crime guys here too," Tedesco said, "I thought I was going home to a nice visit with ma for a while and have a cold beer." When he activated his mic his voice became businesslike, "This is 15435. We need the crime scene guys here. I think this just turned into a murder scene." He stated, eying the twelve inch knife lying next to the pool of blood under the big, dead man. He rubbed his neatly trimmed goatee, "Hey Kris, this guy's a goner. Poor bastard."

~~~~

Ronald Carson, the assassin everyone called "Stinky," looked like an alien with his black protective mask clinging to his face; two bulging frosty glass eyes and a circular breathing apparatus covered his nose and mouth. He was sitting at the kitchen table that was covered with a plastic sheet, filling a little spray canister with fentanyl. He was wearing double latex gloves to safeguard his pores from the killing agent. It was a dank, damp feted room that smelled like it absorbed his body odor and urine; it was pungent and repulsive and caustic. The basement's single paned windows were curtained in a thin foggy layer of moisture with thin channels of water worming their way to the sills, spilling over and down the dirty wall, mingling into the existing mold infested once white floorboards. A cheap multicolored overhead light fixture appeared orange from the grease and cigar smoke that billowed up and penetrated its plastic panels and a single 100 watt light bulb that produced what appeared to be only 10 watts of glow. He could care less; he respected the killing agent more than he respected life itself.

Sweat was burning his eyes and inching down his spine. His filthy underwear was drenched and sticky. His gray hoody was cinched around his face creating a blood boiling, furnace like effect that overpowered his brain and his sanity and any sense of humanity. He was humming, "Here comes Santa Claus. Here comes Santa Claus," to himself, a twitch of an insane smile painted his graying lips. He was planning how he was going to kill the Bradleys in less than twelve hours. *How dare that bitch look at me that way. Fuck her!*

Stinky was in a very dark place that matched the darkness of his heart and the evil of his sinful, black soul. He was totally insane.

"Here comes Santa Claus. Here comes Santa Claus. Be ready to die bitch, because Here comes Santa Claus. Here comes Santa Claus right down Santa Claus Lane to your front door."

CHAPTER 39

"What do you think?" Clare asked with an efficacious grin and questioning eyes.

Bullet was laying on the floor next to her, sound asleep. Her fingers absentmindedly touching his ears.

Peter Michaels was rolling Clare's invention around in his fingers. It looked like a hand warmer but it was a purse with several small pockets for lipstick, a driver's license, a badge, a credit card and two Narcan nasal spray inhalers. The bigger pocket was like a holster for her new MP2, 380 pistol with two extra clips that held eight hollow point bullets in each.

"It's pretty cool. I just hope you never have to use it when you're with me. Do you have one in the chamber?" Michaels asked nervously. Until a few months ago, the last time he fired a weapon was when he was in the Army: That seemed like a hundred years ago. He did not particularly care for guns, but he obtained a concealed carry permit and relearned how to use handguns and shotguns after Cyril Dobonovich tried to kill him last year.

"Until we put this crazy guy in prison, or down, I'm not going anywhere with you without it. It will be like having a third security guard on your detail at all times," she said, and started tickling him with her toes. A nubile smile expressed itself as she toyed with him.

He was getting excited, aroused, so he stood up, took her hand, and they started walking to the bedroom in a slow steady stride, looking into each other's eyes with each step. Their passion started to percolate.

Bullet followed close behind them. "Bullet bed," Michaels commanded and surprisingly the dog got into his new doggie bed, curled his feet under, laid down, and sighed as if saying "Goodnight, but I'm watching."

"He must like you. No one has ever given him a command that he listened to and obeyed, except me," Clare said glancing over her shoulder with a look of admiration.

"Dogs love me," Michaels cooed. The flirtatious smile that started in his eyes, spread to his face. He squeezed her hand softly and started unbuttoning her blouse gently. She was pulling his shirt over his head. Their mouths were open, sensuous, and inviting. They exchanged hot breath...deeply. Desire building. Once their clothes hit the floor, they fell softly onto the California King size bed and kicked away the top sheet. Her blonde hair spread across the pillow like a silk scarf and her blue eyes reflected the soft flicker of a single electronic candle that sat atop the bed stand casting sensuous shadows that blended into the darkness. Clare's lips opened and invited him to come closer. He eagerly accepted her provocation and slowly caressed her skin and teased her with his tongue. Their passion was strong. Their lovemaking intense. Their beings blending uniquely together as if they absorbed each other into a single entity. They were both breathless.

An hour later they were sound asleep, their legs intertwined like a pretzel, their fingertips touching, their smiles satisfying.

~~~~

Ryan O'Toole, the fifth, nursed a pounding headache and painful muscles all night. He hardly slept a wink. He cursed the morning with a loud, ranting rage of foul language. His hatred spewed pushing him to the brink of despair and failure. Ice did little to help the swelling on his forehead but the butterfly bandage he applied managed to stop the bleeding and did its job of keeping the cut line in place. There would be no scar, he assured himself looking into the mirror while brushing his teeth. Both his eyes were black and blue and puffy. He made up his mind that he had to call in sick for work until his appearance improved. He pumped five more extra strength Tylenol pain relievers into his mouth and chewed them before he took a sip of water to wash them down.

He was listening to an all-news radio channel trying to find out if number 34 was alive or dead. He didn't care about the 27 shootings so far this weekend that left five gangbangers, and two innocent children dead, but he did smile when the newscaster announced that the police were investigating a homicide in the Little Village community of a well-liked, friendly biker identified as 49-year-old, Billy Bob North, a retired Army Ranger, and union electrician. Number Five was startled, however, when he heard: "Police were looking for a white male, driving a dark blue van in connection with the killing."

Shit. Fuck. Shit. He thought, *How'd they see me. Impossible.* He clenched his fist into a tight ball and was ready to slam it down on the radio when he heard; "Police were also investigating the deaths of James and Jane Bradley. The couple were apparently poisoned with fentanyl as they left their Printer's Row condo late this morning."

~~~~

Stinky slept for only four hours. His vituperative mood had him pacing around his basement apartment, throwing things at imaginary targets in every dirty room. The cold water he splashed on his face did nothing to shock him out of his groggy, angry condition. The cheap mint mouthwash that he gargled did not improve his offensive breath. He jumped in the mold scarred shower not so much to bathe but to shave his head with his little tractor like razor that left a rash on his skin but no cuts.

He dried himself with a mildewed, filthy, damp towel and dressed in the same foul-smelling hoody that he wore for the last month. He was oblivious to the odor that he left behind in his trail. He put what he needed into his backpack, slung it over his shoulder and slithered out the door, looking both ways to make sure no one was watching him leave.

He made his way to State Street and walked north towards Printer's Row. At Polk Street he turned west and waited in the empty playground area trying to act as inconspicuous as possible. He assumed the blonde couple would go out for breakfast after they did whatever they did on a Sunday morning to make each other happy. An hour and fifteen minutes later his assumption turned into reality as the gleaming couple exited their building and started walking towards a neighborhood breakfast place.

The assassin reached into his backpack and pulled out his protective ant mask, slipped it over his head and onto his face, loosening the tie strings of his hoody to help hide his appearance as he walked with his head down. He put the aerosol dispenser into his pouch pocket and started to quicken his stride, chasing the couple that walked arm in arm at a leisurely pace, looking warmly into each other's eyes, paying no attention to their surroundings. When Carson was almost directly behind them he shouted, "Hey."

The Bradleys were startled, and both turned around only to gasp in total surprise, looking at what appeared to be an alien from outer space. They instantly recognized the muffled voice of the assassin that the police told them to be on the lookout for, but they never thought in a million years that anything that sinister could happen to them a second time.

"Remember me, bitch," Ronald Carson said tetchily as he pulled the fentanyl container out of his pouch and sprayed it directly into their faces. They couldn't see him smiling behind the foggy glass lenses and the circular air filter covering his nose and mouth.

"No," they both screamed simultaneously, reaching for their mouths and noses helplessly to protect themselves as they buckled to the ground. Their breathing was short and wasted. They absorbed a direct hit of the fentanyl. Death was almost instantaneous. By the time their insane assassin, stepped over their falling bodies, they could no longer breathe.

The Bradleys were discovered by a neighbor who was on his way to church a few minutes later. Stinky was already a block away, heading east on Polk Street, walking at a brisk, unassuming pace. His mask was packed away. His bald head was shining in the morning sunlight. His evil eyes were shaded with dollar store, reflective sunglasses. The acerbic smile that spread across his face made several passersby step aside to avoid the dreadful expression that would contaminate the rest of their day or maybe the rest of their lives.

The verse, "There goes Santa Claus. There goes Santa Claus," repeated over and over again in his deranged mind, and the red and white painted face of "The Joker" from the *Batman* movie that was filmed in Chicago flashed in front of him making his caustic smile widen with every stride.

CHAPTER 40

P eter Michaels woke up to the smell of freshly brewed coffee and a blaring siren from a CFD engine truck roaring down Michigan Avenue responding to a probable heart attack in the building next door. Normally any movement would wake him from a sound sleep, but he was so exhausted from a crazy hard week, he never felt or heard Clare get up to take Bullet out for his morning relief walk.

She wore an award winning, perfectly beautiful smile and a body clinging, pair of white VAARA high-waisted ribbed biker shorts, along with a washed out blue CPD tee shirt. Her blonde hair was pulled back in a ponytail accentuating her high cheek bones, smooth skin, and deep blue eyes.

When Michaels saw her, he was ready for round two until Bullet came around from behind the kitchen island and pushed his head into Michaels' left leg looking for acknowledgement, and that quickly ended his coquettish thought. Bullet's tail was wagging back and forth and he seemed to be grunting his approval from Michaels' attention.

"Good boy. Good boy," Michaels said smiling and rubbing the dog's ears.

"I'm glad he likes you. He doesn't act that way around many people," Clare offered; her smile highlighted by bright red lipstick. "Coffee?"

"I'd love some. He is a good boy. He's a great dog," Michaels said. "You mind if I put on the news?"

"No problem. It's what you do," she said. Clare stopped pouring cream into his coffee when she heard the newscaster announce the breaking news story that police were on the scene of another fentanyl related death. A couple named Bradley from Printer's Row, less than two hours ago.

"That's the woman, who called me last night after my story about Brian being attacked. Her description of the person she and her husband ran into matched Ronald Carson's," Michaels declared, moving closer to the front of the TV.

"That bastard didn't waste any time," Clare responded, fully engrossed in the story.

Just then Michael's phone erupted to the theme of the "William Tell Overture," he answered, "What the fuck is going on, Jack?"

"My hunch, Stinky. Afraid the Bradleys could recognize him if we ever caught up to him," Jack Warren opined. "I warned them to be very careful."

"I warned her as well. He's coming after us next. I can feel it. You know that, right?"

"That's why I'm calling. The boss just reached out. He's adding an extra man to my detail. I guess we are all on the same page about that."

"Do you think Dave Mayo can get an extra EEBD mask for Clare. She doesn't want to leave my side, and I don't want her to be exposed."

"I'll reach out to Dave. That shouldn't be a problem. What is she going to do with the dog? There is no protection for him."

"I need to talk to her about that."

~~~~

Stinky noticed the white shorts and the incredible body before he noticed the regal looking 90 pound German Shepherd, the blonde was walking in the park. He didn't want to gawk but he couldn't help himself. She was a shockingly beautiful woman. Then he realized he had seen her before with that fucking, pest of an asshole, reporter from Channel 6 news and he turned his stare straight ahead and quickened his pace, clutching the fentanyl dispenser in his hoody's pouch with his latex gloved hand.

Bullet pulled suddenly on his eight foot leash but Clare had it securely wrapped around her wrist. He barked loudly. She calmed him with a single word, "easy."

A dog's sense of smell is 40 times greater than a human's. They have 200 million olfactory receptors in their noses. Although Bullet was trained as a cadaver dog, to find bones and dead human flesh, he could also sniff out bombs, drugs, and amazingly certain diseases, even emotions.

Stinky offered a combination of any number of offensive stenches, although he was totally immune to his personal hygiene and appearance. He never understood why people looked at him so weirdly.

Clare's eyes immediately began searching the surrounding area looking for the cause of this sudden abnormal outburst from her partner. By the time she caught a glimpse of the short guy in black jeans and a gray hoody, he was already turning the corner and out of sight at 11th Street.

"Here comes Santa Claus. Here comes Santa Claus," the insane assassin started to repeatedly sing again, as a new plan for his next target began to formulate in his deranged mind. He deposited the fentanyl dispenser he used to kill the Bradleys into an open garbage can at the corner of 11th and Wabash. "Here comes Santa Claus. Here comes Santa Claus."

~~~~

Deborah Duke was so excited to talk with Peter Michaels. She hadn't heard from him in days and she couldn't wait to tell him about all of her findings.

After only a few hours of sleep, each of the last three nights, she created genetic family trees for the last three victims that were buried at Edgebrook golf course, six of those buried at Shiller Woods along with two others from Miller Meadows South. She felt very confident that her genetic networks were powerful. She had a huge smile on her face when she dialed Michaels' number, but that was transformed into a grimace when he didn't answer.

When she got up to make another cup of strong black coffee, she realized how exhausted she really was. She yawned, stretched her arms out front and then behind her back, closed her eyes, rubbed her forehead, and sighed heavily. She had to steady herself and visualize her path back to the couch that she set up as her office in her hotel suite. Her braille notes were on the coffee table in front of her and she began to ease her fingertips smoothly and knowingly over the tiny protruding dots to read her notes.

The sound of "You ain't nothing but a hound dog," on her phone, broke her concentration and brought back that huge smile that she lost ten minutes earlier.

"Hey how ya' doing?" She asked.

"Good. You do know that someone is trying to kill me and stuff like that, but no big deal," Michaels mused with a look of delight.

"Yeah, what's going on with that?" She asked.

"He's coming after me and Jack next. He just killed someone earlier this morning. Fentanyl again," Michaels informed.

"Hey, how is your friend, what's his name? Brian."

"Brain Alexander, he's out of the hospital. He's got to take a few days off. He'll be fine. So, what's up?"

"Well, I have produced eleven more family trees for you. They are very distinct. I think they are cousins and they should produce lots of information for the case."

"What makes you so sure, they are that distinct and we shouldn't have any problems?" Michaels asked as he started to pace around his kitchen island area with his phone on speaker.

"Well, this may sound technical but try to follow me. Okay?" She said.

"Try me. You know how I am with this scientific sh...stuff?" He responded and rubbed his forehead, knowing he wouldn't be taking notes at this time.

"Ready. Each different family member share various levels of centiMorgans connecting them to someone in their family. The more centiMorgans you share with someone, the more closely you are related."

"Come on Duke." Michaels interrupted her, "Semi-mortant."

"No! Centi...Morgans or cM for short. It is a specific unit of measurement for the occurrence of a genetic recombination; in other words, it's a measurement of how often something occurs. Like, in the case of identifying a family member, the greater the distance between two genetic markers, the higher the number of physical opportunities for the exchange of DNA will occur during meiosis."

"Meiosis...like having sex?" Michaels asked a little confused.

"Not like that, but it's like when gametes are formed. There are cell divisions in sexually reproducing organisms that reduces the number of chromosomes in sex cells, or in the egg and sperm."

"So, you feel positive about all of this?"

"Peter, I am so positive. I developed genetic networks connecting a second and/or third cousins to each of the eleven victims' families. This common ancestral connection is strong evidence to family ties that stretch over generations."

"You're right that does sound very promising," Michaels said with a smile. "Anything else?" He inquired.

"If we could match up these genetic genealogies with geographic locations that would hit it out of the ballpark and my confidence level would skyrocket," she said in a flat low tone.

"You sound exhausted. You have probably been burning the candle on both ends, is that good for you...health wise?" Then he shook his head, hitting his forehead with the palm of his hand, hoping that he didn't offend her with that comment.

"No. No. I am fine but very tired that's for sure. I'll be fine. I spent a massive amount of time on social media research over the weekend that helped to match a number of family members. You know Peter, once something goes on the internet, it's there to stay. Forever. It's amazing how much personal information, users put out there on the cloud never to be erased." Duke affirmed.

"Yeah, it is amazing how much people put out there, just floating around for anyone to find and use and maybe fuck up your life." Michaels affirmed, and then asked, "Hey, how do you make those geographical location connections, you mentioned earlier?"

Deborah Duke smiled and said, "I also spent an enormous number of hours reading obituaries, birth certificates and birth announcements, along with marriage records and marriage announcements in the newspapers. There is something written about us from the time we're born to the time we die; from the time you started driving a car to any DUIs you may have accumulated on your record."

"Did you discover any interesting coincidences?" Michaels asked looking at his watch.

"Yeah, I think you'll be interested in this. A family member of victim number 14 is a Chicago police officer named Connie Neifert. She had a Facebook page where she posted that her grand, second cousin had gone missing in 1964 according to family history. Ms. Neifert revealed to her FB friends that; it was this missing cousin that helped her to decide on a career in law enforcement," Duke offered.

"I think I know her. She works out of the second district. Pretty woman if it's the one I am thinking about," Michaels said. "Anything else?"

"Let me just tell you. I am very satisfied that these matches are very, very strong."

"You said that. Sounds like you're loving this assignment," Michaels opined.

"I am loving it. I also examined the family trees upside down. I performed reverse genetic studies on each family member by looking at their same DNA samples from the opposite direction. I found proof positive DNA connections for each of the families. I will email you the information. It won't be hard to find out who these victims were," she opined.

"That's great news, Deborah. Do me a favor," Michaels said firmly.

"What's that?"

"Get some sleep."

CHAPTER 41

I t didn't take much convincing to lure Dr. Bruce Chambers to meet with Peter Michaels for dinner and conversation at Tufano's restaurant in Chicago's Little Italy.

Tufano's, also known as the Vernon Park Tap, is a favorite meeting place for sports fans to have a bite to eat and several cocktails before games. It's been around for more than 90 years. Chicagoans may have smiled when they saw Tufano's featured on the popular food channel show, Diners, Drive-Ins, and Dives, but for anyone who has ever eaten there, they already know the food is absolutely terrific. It's been owned and operated by the Di Buono family since 1930. The food is made from old Italian family recipes. Every bite melts in your mouth and brings a satisfying smile to your face. The menu offered on any given day is written on a huge old style black chalkboard displayed in the middle of the main dining room. Everything is delicious and very reasonably priced.

Michaels called his old friend Joe Di Buono to make sure he could get a seat in a quiet corner of the front dining room. He was sitting at the old wooden bar, drinking a vodka on the rocks, looking up at fan favorite Bobby Hull's Chicago Blackhawks jersey when Dr. Chambers walked in, precisely on time according to the antique, square wood framed, back lit, clock hanging on the wall right next to Hull's number 9 jersey.

"Hey, it's been a while," Dr. Chambers said extending his hand, and then bear hugging Peter Michaels.

Chambers always seemed to smile even when he wasn't. His aplomb personality shined through his blue reassuring eyes. His once thick brown hair was almost all gray. A smile emerged like a circle, spinning through a black hole in outer space, on his stubbled, full bearded face, revealing perfectly white teeth and self-confidence.

"One of these days we will have to meet without talking about work," Michaels said, offering the forensic psychologist the seat next to him. "Wanna drink?"

Billy already started pouring a glass of Chianti for the doctor. It never seemed to amaze Michaels how Tufano's bartenders knew what their patrons drank.

"Are you guys close to catching that crazy bastard who's trying to kill you?" Dr. Chambers inquired. The smile disappearing from his face.

"We are getting there. We know who he is. We will find him. He's starting to make mistakes." Michaels tried to reassure.

"He was friends with that insane Cyril Dobonovich wasn't he?" Chambers asked.

"Yeah, I am not as worried about Ronald Carson. That's his name by the way. He is a very dangerous person, but I am on the trail of what I believe to be a generational serial killer." Michaels stated, and continued, "that's what I want to talk to you about."

"Yeah, I thought that is what was on your mind. I did some quick research on serial killers after you called. You know the first identified serial killer was from Chicago?" Dr. Chambers offered.

"Yeah, I read 'The Devil in the White City,' his name was Henry Howard Holmes. He killed dozens of people and sold their body parts," Michaels recalled. "The guys we are investigating are Jeffery Dahmer types."

"What do you mean? Dahmer types?" Chambers asked totally engrossed in the conversation.

"They take trophies and I wouldn't be surprised if they were cannibalistic," Michaels said. "The stuff you see in the movies and on TV about serial killers is all bullshit, isn't it?"

"The entertainment industry doesn't really do law enforcement any great favors with their inaccurate depictions of psychopathic killers. Often psychopaths are featured as ghoulish predators or monsters that stand out in a crowd when in fact they can be anyone, a neighbor, a co-worker, lover, or homeless person. They are chameleons that rarely stand out and that characteristic makes them unobtrusive and, therefore, difficult to catch," Dr. Chambers said.

"Are serial killers born or made? I've read a number of studies. There is this thing called the 'warrior gene,'" Michaels suggested.

"Ah...I take it you are familiar with Monoamine Oxidase A or MAOA. It's the enzyme that breaks down neurotransmitters of crucial chemical compounds in the brain which, when associated with low activity form of the MAOA gene can influence violent behavior," Chambers affirmed.

"Yep, I know about them," Michaels said.

"Well, there is also a gene called CDH13 which is essential for cognitive flexibility and correct memory development. Deficiencies in this CDH13 gene can cause behavioral alterations associated with symptoms noted in neurodevelopment disorders like ADHD, including learning and memory deficits as well as extreme hyperactivity," Chambers said.

"So, are you saying, you can be born a serial killer, because of these genes?" Michaels asked.

"It's better to say, some people are 'natural-born potential killers.' Childhood environments, love or lack of it, violence, alcoholic parents, sexual abuse, or physical abuse all play a part.

"Here's what we know: 74% of all serial killers are from the United States, at least 84% are males, 82% are white, 15% are black and 3%

are Hispanic, and interestingly, Peter, 87% of all serial killers operate alone," Dr. Chambers offered.

Michaels pondered these statistics, sipped his vodka on the rocks, then said, "If my theory about generational serial killers is true, and 87% operate alone, then my guys would be in that other thirteen percentile, right?"

"I would think so because if they are passing down these violent behavior patterns, one would assume that they would have to work with one another at some time or another," Chambers concluded.

"This is some sick shit, doc," Michaels proclaimed.

"Yes, it is. Peter, keep in mind, profiling over the years has produced some specific traits about serial killers."

"Like what?" Michaels asked.

"Well, Ted Bundy was smooth talking but insincere, a common trait in serial killers. He had the perfect mask when he engaged his victims. John Wayne Gacy Jr. was egocentric and grandiose. He even played a clown at neighborhood parties where he probably targeted some of his next victims. Samuel Little is one of the most prolific serial killers in history. He's admitted to strangling dozens and dozens of women in multiple states. He had no remorse or guilt whatsoever for any of his actions just like most serial killers. They have no empathy. Their emotions are shallow. They're impulsive. They have poor behavior controls, and couple that with the need for excitement," Dr. Chambers said tilting his head to one side, shrugging his shoulders, and putting both his hands out in front of him, as if gesturing, "What can I tell you."

"It is amazing on how our childhood development affects the rest of our lives," Michaels said shaking his head sadly.

"It goes on and on Peter, but what I am saying here is, these negative traits developed over time, couple that with the 'warrior gene,' and whalla, you have a serial killer. I bet you that this so-called hitchhiker killer, you have identified, has many, if not, all of these traits," Dr. Chambers reaffirmed.

"Thanks, doc," Michaels said, standing, finishing off his drink.

Clare Claxton came in the door just as the informational interview ended. She was dressed in well-fitting jeans and a white blouse that emphasized her perfect breast. She smiled at Michaels with her blue eyes and her red lips but put her hand out to Dr. Chambers, "Hi. I'm Clare Claxton. I've heard a lot of good things about you, doctor."

"Well, Peter was just starting to talk about you. A pleasure to meet you, Clare," the doctor said returning her smile with one of his own filled with admiration.

The owner noticed the movement, smiled, nodded at Michaels, and led the party to their table. "Enjoy, your linguine aglio e oilo and shrimp, Peter. It's exceptional tonight," Joe Di Buono said to his old friend, winking, and bowing towards Clare.

Clare in return said to Joe, "It's always good to see you. Everything good?"

"Everything is fantastic," Di Buono said.

Michaels could eat aglio e olio and shrimp, three or four times a week and never tire of it, but he wondered with a puzzled look on his face, *how did Joe always know what I liked to eat?*

As they sat down Clare said, "I have to make this a short night. I'm going body hunting early tomorrow morning."

CHAPTER 42

D
r. Robert Crine was in a grumpy, crotchety mood when he started work on Monday morning at precisely six. The fact that his clean medical coats were not delivered on time and a new announcement of further county cutbacks, because of misappropriated funds, further added to his disgruntled behavior. Bodies were backlogged in his morgue because another bloody weekend in Chicago produced 31 shootings and sixteen deaths; six by bullets, one stabbing, one dismemberment and eight fentanyl deaths, two which were murder and six overdoses.

By the time he finished reading all the reports stacked on his desk, his hot coffee was tepid but he took a long sip, sighed, and leaned back in his comfortable desk chair that he brought with him 25 years ago when he started working as the Cook County's medical examiner. *Why don't I just retire from all this bullshit,* he tussled with himself but every time that thought crossed his mind, he had only to look at the crazy cases that kept him so busy and so enthralled.

Two cases caught his attention immediately. The dismemberment case was fascinating: six body parts but no head and strangely, no blood. Along with that, the limbs were filled with maggots and a number of other insects. The most important fact was that this mystery man had no right thumb and no left big toe. He was a victim of the hitchhiker killer, of that...Dr. Crine was sure.

Billy Bob North was an honored soldier who died a horrible untimely death at the hand of some maniacal idiot who probably burned the American flag. The ME was reading the police report filed by officer Kris Zimmerman. It was written in such a way that Crine instinctively thought this officer Zimmerman was a soldier at one time.

Crine leaned back in his chair, closed his eyes, and reminisced about his time in the Army. He was assigned to a mash unit at the end of the Vietnam war. Members of the military were always dear to him particularly because of the way people treated Vietnam veterans after that useless war. He joined the Army after his soccer days were over, but mainly because his mother said, "he was out of his mind to enlist in the service to fight in a no-win war."

Crine's mother was always very confrontational towards him, from physical abuse to arguments on any issues that surfaced; controversial or benign. He was always headstrong and very opinionated. Once he made up his mind, he went after the task at hand at full throttle. That's why people liked him; no one had to ever guess where he stood. If he liked you, you were on his good side and if he didn't, well that's a whole different story. When the phone rang and he saw the caller ID, he thought, *Why do I like this guy.*

"Hey, doc, it's Peter Michaels."

"I know. What the fuck do you want so early on a Monday morning?" Crine asked with an ironic smile.

"You have a couple, the Bradleys. They were murdered yesterday morning. We believe it was the same guy who tried to kill Brian Alexander on Saturday. We also think he is coming after me and detective Jack Warren very soon," Michaels warned.

Crine stood up when he heard this news, rubbing his forehead. "It's the same guy who assassinated Tony Quag."

"One in the same."

"That's the guy you had on the news Saturday night."

"Yep. That's the guy. Anything else interesting over the weekend?"

"Yeah, a dismembered body discovered Saturday morning. It's connected to the hitchhiker. Not a doubt in my mind," Dr. Crine informed.

"I thought I'd give you a heads up about the fentanyl case. I already knew about the hitchhiker discovery," Michaels said.

That comment startled Dr. Crine, "How'd you know about that?"

"My girlfriend is the one who found it. Her dog smelled it from the car when they were driving by," Michaels updated.

"You never cease to amaze me, Peter. How you find things out. Listen, I have got to get back to work."

He hung up the phone, called his staff into his office and he assigned the shootings and fentanyl overdoses to his three assistants. He took the Bradley cases, and the case he labeled Mr. Pieces. He liked to give names to the victims he operated on because he talked to them as he explored their remains seeking clues and information. He truly believed they answered him when he found something significant.

Mr. Pieces' death seemed draconian as he lay on Dr. Crine's operating table almost as if he were a crude jigsaw puzzle. "What an extremely harsh way to treat a body," Crine whispered as he pulled down his magnifying optics. He examined every body part meticulously, turning the limbs around, picking out the bugs and maggots, placing them in petri dishes to be examined more thoroughly under a microscope. He made palm prints because the fingertips had been cut off. He took samples for DNA testing. He summarized that Mr. Pieces had been dead about six or seven days from the condition of the tissue and muscles.

"This is very strange. There is no blood in your system. How could that be? Are you the victim of an embalmer?" Dr. Crine asked himself, trying to recall a case from a few years ago when he did an autopsy of an exhumed body. The remains had been embalmed and the corpse did have fluids. He dictated to make a note to retrieve that old case file.

As he made a "Y" incision in the upper torso he whispered, "You are the victim of a lefty, aren't you? The knife entered your right side with a hefty plunge. He cut through your intestines and nicked your floating ribs: number 11 and 12. Humm."

He washed off the ribs and took pictures of them. He noticed a certain similarity in the pattern from the knife's blade. All of this information was recorded contemporaneously. His secretary would transcribe it later for his formal report. It was almost noon and he had two more bodies to autopsy.

~~~~

Sergeant Conni Neifert was in charge of the Office of Community Policing program in the second police district. It was a job that fit her perfectly, working with the public and her outgoing personality. Neifert was a confident woman with an engaging smile that lit up her face. Her five foot nine inch frame was lean and toned. Her vocabulary voluminous and her life experiences bountiful. She rode a customized, V-twin engine, black Harley Davidson Shorttail that provided her with soul satisfying rides including twelve rallies at Sturgis. The community loved the fact that she was so accessible.

"This is Sgt. Neifert," she said, answering the call on the second ring.

"Connie Neifert? This is Peter Michaels. How are you?" Michaels announced.

"I am great. Haven't seen you in a long time. What's up? Am I in trouble?" She asked with a questioning look expressing itself.

"No...not at all. Listen, I have what I hope is interesting and good news for you. I am sure you know all about all these stories involving the killings that go back to the 1920s."

"You're calling to tell me about my great cousin, aren't you? He's one of them isn't he?" She inquired.

"Yes. Deborah Duke matched your DNA to a body recovered in one of the first graves at Shiller Woods," Michaels informed her.

"She got my DNA through the CPD, right?" She quizzed.

"You know Conni I am not sure how that all works, but I think so, and she found some of your postings on Facebook and made the connections that way as well."

A thousand questions were spinning in her mind. She leaned back in her chair, let out a deep breath, closed her eyes and tears began to well. She cleared her throat and asked, "So what now?"

"You know I don't have any official capacity in any of this and I am sure the department will be in contact with forms and reports and stuff like that," he answered.

"Yeah, it's like a victim notification process. I've done some similar stuff in the past," she added.

"Conni, I would like to do an interview. This is a very unique angle to these stories and I am sure there will be a lot of interest in what you have been through over the years," Michaels persuaded. "And you posted that this situation is what led you to become a police officer."

"I don't know Peter. I don't like cameras and all that exposure stuff."

"Come on, Conni. I have seen you dozens of times on that 'CrimeWatch' show that airs on the public access channel."

"Let me think about it," Seifert said and then asked, "Do I have to contact News Affairs?"

"I am not sure about that but here is my number." Michaels gave it to her and then added, "It will be a very good piece. I promise."

CHAPTER 43

C lare Claxton and Bullet spent the entire morning walking the pathways and tree lines of Ottawa Trail Woods Park. The sun was high and hot. The humidity was heavy and suffocating. Her blonde hair was in a ponytail and pulled through her baseball cap's adjustment strap. It was damp and thick. Her loose-fitting black combat pants were tucked into her boots and her long white sleeved fishing shirt was clinging to her tanned skin. Her badge was secured on her belt. She was tired, sweaty, and hungry.

Bullet was panting heavily and wagging his tail forcefully. He was anxious to find something so he could stop working and please his master. He looked up at her with sad, disappointed eyes, as they walked back to the parking lot.

Claxton dialed her supervisor, Sgt. Mike Garofalo, who answered on the third ring. "You having any luck?" he asked without saying hello.

"Nothing," Clare responded. "I've got to give Bullet a little time off. He's been working hard."

"Yeah, Nosey is tired as well," Garofalo said. "Let's meet for lunch at that taco place in Palatine then we can both go over to Deer Grove Park."

"You mean Tijuana Tacos off of Dundee?" Claxton asked with a disgusted look on her face. "Really Sarge?"

"Yeah. They're great," Garofalo said with a wide smile.

"They suck, and you know it, but you're the boss. I'm a half hour out," she said putting Bullet in the back of the K-9 SUV, pouring some water into a bowl for him to drink. While he lapped ferociously, she started the engine and turned on the AC. She sat back with cold air blasting her, taking deep breaths of relief, satisfaction filled her face. She took a long drink of cold water and rolled the bottle across her forehead. Her phone rang, as soon as she put the vehicle in gear to pull away, a gentle smile replaced the look of satisfaction when she heard Peter Michaels' voice.

"Hey baby, how's your day going?" He asked with an enthusiastic grin.

"Hot, long, and uneventful. How's yours?" She said trying to stay positive.

"Good, the interns have made contact with and have identified five family members of the first victims recovered," Michaels offered.

"That's great news. Did you talk to Conni?"

"Yeah. First thing this morning, well after I talked to Dr. Crine, that is. She is very glad to have some closure. I'm trying to get her to do an interview. She being the police and all, it would be a great angle to this enigmatic story."

"It would be...so, what did Crine say?"

"Those body parts you found were drained of all their blood. Vampire shit," he responded.

"That's weird," she countered. "I guess you're right. Now that you say that there wasn't a lot of blood on those limbs." She instinctively reached up to rub her forehead, her eyes searching for information and images buried in her thoughts.

"I think it's a very big lead. I'm heading out to Clinton City and the body farm."

"Why do you say big lead?" She asked putting both her hands back on the steering wheel.

"I am looking for a funeral home connection, you know if we find any bodies delivered by a funeral with the hitchhiker's signature. They have to have records of who dropped those bodies off. That could provide us with some way to identify the hitchhiker."

"You think he owns a funeral home?"

"Not sure. You never know, but once I find out...I'll know," Michaels said with a wide grin to his private inside joke.

"I'll see you tonight," Clare said with a smile, shaking her head, reminiscing how many times she had slugged him in the arm when he said that stupid apothegm.

~~~~

The hot, heavy air accentuated the malodorous stench of death as soon as Peter Michaels stepped outside of his car. His bodyguards, Jon Kerbs, and Tom Buettner, gagged at the smell.

"That surely is the smell of death," Buettner sighed as he reached into his coat pocket for a bottle of Vicks. He put a touch of the suave into each nostril, an old cop trick when they investigated a homicide and the victim had been dead for a long time. He handed it to Kerbs.

"I don't want any of that," Michaels said when offered the bottle. He approached forensic scientist Phil Thompson, who was making notes of a decomposing body. Thompson was five-ten, thin and bald. He was clean shaven. His blue eyes presented an academic look. His light green operating smock was stained with sweat.

"Hey, Mr. Michaels, the office said you were on your way. What can we do for you?" He asked inquisitively.

"I am curious. Do you have any bodies out here that are missing a right thumb, left toe and possibly a left ear?" Michaels asked intriguingly.

"Interesting," Thompson muttered.

"What?" Michaels responded.

"There is a crime scene investigator in the lab right now, looking for the same thing from the skeletal remains, we have on file," the scientist answered.

"Who?"

"A Tom Vander Aarde. I think is his name."

"Oh, yeah, he said he would be coming over here this week sometime," Michaels said. "How many bodies are outside here, doctor?"

"We currently have 24 at various stages of decomposition. You know the soil here is more alkaline, so it could take between eight to twelve years for a body to fully decompose. At Southeastern Illinois, on the other hand, the soil is more acidic and a body can fully decompose in five to six years," the forensic scientist informed.

"It never ceases to amaze me, how nature takes its course," Michaels said walking next to Dr. Thompson.

"Water extends the decomposition process; the body generally breaks down more slowly in water than in open air. It putrefies faster in warm, fresh, or stagnant water than in cold, salty, or running water."

"I assume bacteria also has an effect on decomposition," Michaels stated.

"See there, your biology class did teach you something," Dr. Thompson said with a smirk as he stopped in front a computer. He hit a few keystrokes and pulled up a registry and scrolled down. His eyes searching for noted anomalies or abnormalities.

Michaels was trying to read along with the scientist but he had a hard time focusing and following the blurry green lines that were swiftly rolling across the screen.

"Ah hah, here we go. Number 1567, Michael Chasen. Right thumb. Left toe. Left ear. Year 2019. Body donated by a will," Dr. Thompson said.

"How did the body get here?" Michaels inquired.

"Let's see." Thompson search a little further and said, "delivered by Killeen and Callawy Funeral Home."

"Got a name?" Michaels asked anxiously, adrenalin starting to rush through his veins like water thorough a fire hose.

"Yep. Stuart Blakley."

"Bingo" Michaels said with a fist pump. "Anymore?"

"Let's keep checking." The doctor said feeling the excitement.

~~~~

Ryan O'Toole was leaning into the bathroom mirror examining the butterfly bandage on his forehead. The cut looked perfect. There would be no scar. However, his eyes were slow to heal. The swollenness was in check from the constant application of ice packs. The once dark bruising was starting to turn yellow. He estimated at least another couple of days before he could be back to work. His boss was pissed off that he called in sick, using the excuse that he was in an auto accident.

I should kill that prick for his reaction to me taking my sick days. I was in a car accident for shit sake, He thought. That's when the reality of his O'Toole family lessons surfaced and calmed him down. **Never kill anyone you work with. That's too close to home.** You never ever want to talk to the police if you can help it. Never.

Number Five was getting antsy. He didn't get his trophies from that fucking biker. His craving for another bowl of soup was growing but he wanted more flesh and bones for the perfect flavor. *Maybe I should kill that reporter from Channel Six News.*

CHAPTER 44

Lieutenant Tom Parker sat at the front of the dark mahogany table in the superintendent's conference room conducting a meeting on any new security measures for detective Jack Warren. There was growing concern that Stinky was moving up his schedule to kill Warren and Peter Michaels.

When Sgt. Brain Alexander walked into the meeting uninvited, Parker's face flushed red. The lieutenant stood up, and his anger was silenced as Alexander put up his hand to calm him down and said, "I have a complete medical clearance to return to duty." He reached into his coat pocket and pulled out the doctor's report and handed it to Parker.

"The team's quick reaction saved my life," Alexander proclaimed getting a little teary eyed. "Boss, the Narcan did its miracle. Thank God the wind helped disperse the fentanyl. It hit me hard at first because I don't take any kind of medications but the doctor said because I am in such good shape my heart and lungs responded very positively. I want to be there when we catch this son of a bitch," Alexander pleaded.

Tom Polston raised his hand and said without waiting for permission to speak, "Listen boss, most opioid overdose patients can leave the ER one hour after receiving Naloxone, or Narcan. Me and

Jack took him home. The docs checked him thoroughly. He didn't have any of those side effects that fentanyl produces like nausea, vomiting, lightheadedness, dizziness, drowsiness, or headache. We need Brian on the team and on top of all that he saw the bastard."

Parker leaned back in the chair, his fingers formed into the proverbial temple, his middle fingers touched his upper lip, he sighed, leaned forward, and said, "So, what do we have on this stinky guy?"

Warren jumped at the opportunity, "His name is Ronald Carson. He escaped from Madison about four months ago, almost killed a nurse in doing so. He was an associate of those crazy bastards, Cyril Dobonovich and Lin An."

"Those are the guys who tried to kill Peter Michaels over a year ago. Right?"

"Yep, and now he's coming after me and Michaels next, and we think real soon. He killed Quag. He killed that couple yesterday in Printer's Row. Walked right up to them and sprayed fentanyl directly in their faces. Sick son of a bitch," Warren said. His face almost crimson with anger.

"Do we know where he lives?" Parker inquired.

"We got a lot of tips after Michaels put his face all over TV Saturday night," detective Warren responded. "I've got people standing by to prepare a warrant if we get lucky."

"All right, you guys know the plan. Let me know immediately if something pops on this maniac. Alexander over here. The rest of you guys are dismissed," Parker ordered.

Alexander approached shyly, "I'm sorry boss. I really want to be on this detail and get this guy. I know I should have called but seriously, I feel great. Everybody did a great job of taking care of me and now I gotta help out here."

"You ever pull a stunt like this again, I will write you up, now get out of here," Parker said.

Alexander did an about face, a big smile emerged and he silently mouthed "YES" with a fist pump hidden from the lieutenant.

Parker turned his face so Alexander couldn't see his smile and he mouthed, *We will get you, you dirty cop killing piece of shit.*

~~~~

The smell of the bones encased in their plastic containers was very unique but not anywhere near as repugnant as the bodies outside on the farm in the heat and humidity. CSI Tom Vander Aarde identified nine possible hitchhiker victims by the end of the day. There were 73 containers of bones neatly and systematically filed on three foot wide steel shelving that reached to the twelve foot ceilings in the lab's warehouse.

Fifteen of them had some anomalies that separated them from the others that had to be thoroughly investigated. Some had hands missing. Some had fingers missing. Some had feet missing. The angles of how the trophies were severed from the nine with the hitchhiker killer's trademarks all looked similar to the naked eye. Vando thought his work was over until his phone rang, "Hey what you got out there?"

"I have four bodies not fully decomposed out here. I'm trying to convince Doctor Thompson to let me look at the bodies more closely. He's not so sure that's a good idea to unearth them because disrupting the process can change the decomposition rate and perhaps contaminate their studies. I am working on him. He tells me you found nine more remains that look like the hitchhiker. Is that right?" Michaels asked.

"Yep...from what I can see, all the angles where he cut off the thumbs and toes look very similar. I am working on getting these bones to Crine and probably the FBI for further analysis," Vando informed. "We'll probably need a warrant."

"Yeah, I am sure. That's something I can't do, but listen, did you check the history? Where they came from and that stuff?" Michaels asked.

"Yeah, I already did that…they were all willed to the body farm for scientific research."

"So were mine, and they were all delivered from funeral homes," Michaels offered.

"I didn't check that but that's not hard to do. It will just take a few minutes. Their records are pretty thorough," Vando opined.

"See if you can get copies of the wills. I think it will be interesting to see how they compare to one another," Michaels suggested.

"Yeah, I can do that," Vando said in agreement. "Hey, how is your security detail handling everything out there?"

"Yeah, they are pissing and moaning about the smell. Man, it is really nasty," Michaels groaned, but managed to smile.

"Hey, maybe 'Stinky' lives out there with all the rest of those ghouls," Vando smirked.

"You are one sick puppy Vando. I've got to get back to work before they throw me out of here. We'll catch up later."

"Okay. I'll let you know when I leave. Beers later," Vando suggested.

"Vodker," Michaels retorted and smiled, using his nickname for Grey Goose.

~~~~

Stinky was anxious. Looking over his shoulder constantly. Ever since Peter Michaels put all of those picture of him on television two nights ago his thoughts became obstreperous. He hadn't slept well since then. He now hated his basement apartment. He hallucinated about living in a three flat like the one his friend Cyril described to him.

Paranoia replaced dreams of living in a world of fantasy with stygian thoughts of prison, straightjackets and infusions of psychotic medications rendering him motionless, helpless, and restrained. He felt he couldn't go home.

Perspiration gleaned on his forehead and as it drained down his temples and cheeks, it gathered in his embedded facial dirt and grime leaving mottled streaks of what appeared to be a network of thin wrinkles that invaded his skin, giving the appearance of dried, sun scorched earth craving water. "I'm being watched," he mumbled to himself over and over again. "I'm being watched." He swallowed two more Xanax pills and realized he only had three left. His filthy hand was shaking as he snapped the once white plastic cover back onto his filthy prescription bottle.

"How much money do I have?" He started asking himself in between his delusions of being watched. He began slapping his pockets, checking for his money. He pulled out $375 in dirty, wrinkled, damp bills of different denominations from his two front pockets.

Sweat was building up from the heat. He pulled his dark gray hoodie tightly around his face as if it provided a mask to hide from his neighbors. He was feeling very uncomfortable with his wet dirty tee shirt clinging to his chest and back. He turned into an alley to take a leak behind a dumpster when he noticed two squad cars turning down his street and then to his surprise a beat up blue Crown Vic passed with one person driving, and then another green Crown Vic with two detectives riding along.

Fuck, the cops found me. How? How the Fuck? Fuck. How?

CHAPTER 45

Deer grove is the oldest park in the Cook County Forest Preserve system, though it was not in the city of Chicago, the area was deemed part of the CPD's hitchhiker killer investigation. Deer Grove was filled with rolling upland forest interspersed with wooded ravines and wetlands. It had two trail systems. The paved trail was for pedestrians, cyclists, and cross-county skiers. The unpaved trail was longer. It is used by hikers, mountain bikers and equestrians. Deer Grove also offered a large open area for gatherings and picnics. It even had a model airplane flying field. There was also a newly renovated campground facility directly adjacent to the trail. That was where Clare Claxton and her boss, Sgt. Mike Garofalo set up their quasi-operational headquarters.

Claxton's stomach was grumbling, bloated, and churning. She cursed herself for eating a greasy taco and drinking a bottle of sweet orange pop. She was glad Garofalo assigned her to the northern portion of the undulating trails of the park. He took the south end and they were to meet in the middle unless one of them discovered any new graves. She was feeling gaseous, a little nauseous, and anxious. She wanted to be alone. Burping and passing gas relieved her distended upset stomach. She couldn't imagine the embarrassment of any prescient, uncontrolled bodily action while working next to Garofalo, particularly because he was one of Peter Michaels' best friends.

Bullet was pulling hard on his eight foot leash, anxious to work. He was breathing hard, panting heavily, his tail was swishing back and forth quickly and steadily. Forty-five minutes into their assignment, he barked and sat down proudly announcing that he discovered the newest gravesite. Claxton keyed her mic. The frequency was set at an informal setting. "Hey Sarge, Bullet has a hit."

"Where are you?" Garofalo inquired. His eyes reflecting excitement and pride.

"Probably a quarter mile from my starting pointing at the upper edge of the campground," she responded. "I've marked the site and I'm going to keep on looking."

"Copy that. I am on my way."

~~~~

Dr. Robert Crine was sitting at his office desk staring at the buzzing fluorescent lights on the ceiling above…in a quasi-trance. The smell of his half-eaten pastrami and corned beef sandwich lingered heavily in the air; its grease leached through the cracks of the wax paper it was wrapped in, staining his desktop calendar causing his handwritten notes to blur into undecipherable patches of blue and black ink and number-2 pencil. He was absent mindedly fingering and rolling a fresh, six inch long, crunchy, dill pickle, lost in deep thought; examining at how precisely it was quartered. He couldn't stop thinking about the cut marks on each of the bloodless limbs from the body he just autopsied and how they looked very similar to those of Dr. Phillip Kaley.

His assistant Dr. Donald O'Connell knocked on his door abruptly breaking his chain of thought, "Hey, Bob. You gotta come look at this."

Dr. O'Connell was six foot-two and overweight. His shoulders went up and down, right then left with every step he took. His brown hair was thinning. His green eyes were surrounded by brown horn-rimmed glasses that constantly slipped down his nose. His expressions were always enthusiastic. He never gave off a negative vibe and his demeanor was always positive. He didn't wait for his boss to acknowledge him. He just turned abruptly and headed back into the lab.

"What do you got, Don?" Crine said curtly. He jumped up and quickly followed O'Connell to his operating table.

"Take a look at this floating rib and vertebra. Notice anything familiar?" Dr. O'Connell asked looking over the top of his glasses, rubbing his chin with his right hand.

Crine flipped down his magnifying optics and studied the knife patterns on the two bone areas. He leaned in closer and in a voice a little louder than a whisper said, "I'll be a son of a bitch."

"You see it, don't you? Right?" O'Connell asked devoutly, now leaning forward trying to inch in next to his boss.

Crine almost hit him on the chin with his head as he straightened up snappishly, "This is that biker dude? Isn't it?" He asked rhetorically...knowing the answer.

"Yep...from Saturday night. We have the knife in evidence." The assistant ME responded eagerly.

"Let's get that over here and then to Quantico for a more detailed analysis. This is getting curiouser and curiouser all the time. Three totally unrelated killings possibly by the same person in a matter of weeks. We have a deranged serial killer on the loose and it appears he is amping up his time frame."

~~~~

The vulgar smelling fentanyl killer went around the block and snuck into an abandoned garage across the alley from his basement apartment. He was positive the police didn't see him enter. He pried opened a crack in the siding to get a better look at the police activity. There was one uniformed officer standing guard by his back door and another one was positioned at his garage and backyard gate. The detectives he assumed were inside tearing his apartment apart piece by piece.

Earlier that morning, however, Stinky removed all the remaining fentanyl and most of his possessions to the vacant garage that he was now occupying. Cyril Dobonovich told him to always trust his gut instincts and his gut instincts told him to get out of there quickly. He smiled and thought that his mentor was never wrong.

The cop killer was no longer concerned about his identity or his well-being. He knew the police knew exactly who he was because of that fucking Peter Michaels. He had enough provisions to last for a few more days, and he could care less that he didn't have a shower or a toilet. He had about 300 dollars left in his pockets and he didn't give a damn if he lived or died. His mind was thoroughly made up: Peter Michaels would die in the next 48 hours.

Panic filled his eyes as the officer stationed by the gate suddenly came to attention and started to walk over to his position. The stubble from his shaved head seemed to garb his hoodie like Velcro as he tried to pull it off. He reached into his pouch and fingered the fentanyl container that he had prepared to kill that pesty reporter just in case the cop got too close. The officer seemed to be repulsed by the odor of a dead rat or an animal or something fouler than he had ever smelled before as he approached the decaying, dilapidating garage.

"Shit," the young officer gasped and turned around coughing and gagging, then thinking; *nobody in their right mind could stand to be breathing that shit air.*

The small, dirty assassin breathed a sigh of relief, rubbing his filthy hand over his sweaty head, picturing spraying fentanyl into Peter Michaels face at the first opportunity that occurred. His smile revealed yellow, brown rotting teeth and his mind started singing; "Here comes Santa Claus. Here comes Santa Claus. I'm going to kill you Peter Michaels. Here comes Santa Claus."

CHAPTER 46

P   eter Michaels was trying to digest all the information he had
        uncovered at the Benjamin Franklin Institute of Technology's
        body farm. He was driving back to Chicago sitting next to his
cameraman Paul Nagaro who was speeding down the highway with
his security detail in tow. It was currently sunny and glorious on the
road but dark, ominous clouds were hovering over the horizon and
Lake Michigan was getting angry as thunder, lightning, and heavy rain
announced the late summer menacing storm.

Nagaro fortunately microwaved the video he shot at the body farm
back to the studio just before they left the Clinton City area. Producer
David Beedy was in an editing suite viewing the tape and taking notes.
Editor Ed Land was memorizing every frame of the video as it appeared
on the monitors. Beedy instinctively picked up the phone on its first
ring anticipating Michaels's call, "Talk to me."

"All thirteen of the bodies that Vando and I discovered had their
left toes and right thumbs cut off. Four of the bodies that were buried
outside were at various stages of decomposition, one was at its final
stage and would be transferred to the warehouse within the next two
weeks. It was very difficult to determine if the body that was
decomposing in the pond water had his left ear severed because it was

so bloated, but the other three left no doubt; the hitchhiker killed them," Michaels reported enthusiastically.

"When was the first one dumped there?" Beedy asked irreverently.

"A year after the farm opened...so in 1994." Michaels answered and continued, "but those were already decomposed and their bones were stored in containers at the lab's warehouse. Vando examined them. He told me, it was, 'eerie as shit,' being able to touch the bones and actually hold them."

"That's more than 20 years ago," Beedy responded after quickly doing the math.

"Hey buddy, I have no doubt that we have four or five generations of serial killers involved here that we are dealing with," Michaels informed.

"I'll bet none of the names are real."

"I am absolutely sure they aren't real, but listen to this, all of them had been delivered by some funeral home operator and I am positive his name is more bogus then the dead guys," Michaels offered.

"This is great news and incredible new leads," Beedy said smiling as he typed all the information into his meticulous note keeping system.

"Get this Dave, all of them were donated for the good of science. Every will was basically worded exactly the same with the exception of the donor's name."

"So, what's next?" Beedy asked.

"Well, let's report tonight that detectives are seeking warrants to have the bones and remains removed and analyzed at Quantico. There is still a lot of DNA work to be done. We have some 35 victims now."

"Maybe more than that," Beedy said rubbing his forehead.

"What do you mean by that?" Michaels asked quizzically.

"Your lady found more graves at Deer Creek this afternoon."

"How many?"

"They don't know, but at least seven or eight as of right now and still counting I think."

"These guys knew what they were doing. They were somewhat organized over the years. There is no doubt about that."

"Yeah, except for one thing," Beedy said.

"Yeah, they never thought they would be caught."

"Well guess what?" Beedy stated with a big smile.

Michaels answered the question before his partner could ask it, "We are getting closer and closer. There is no such thing as the perfect crime."

~~~~

"Pulmonary edema, that's how you died my dear," Dr. Crine said into the overhead dictation microphone as he expertly placed the heart of Jane Bradley into the weighing dish scale to his right. "I have never seen this much fentanyl in anyone's body. Nor have I seen this much clotting and clumping. My God you must have been dead before you hit the ground," he whispered, patting the woman's shoulder.

A lethal dose of fentanyl in humans is two milligrams. The Bradleys' bodies had at least twenty times that amount from the direct spray to their faces by their killer. Dr. Crine wanted to make sure that he wasn't exaggerating his conclusions because it had been more than 24 hours since the Bradleys were murdered and the autopsy began. The longer fentanyl remains in the body the more the drug infiltrates the body's organs. Recent studies have shown that postmortem redistribution of fentanyl in the blood continues and it can vary in heart blood and femoral blood giving some false readings because of the higher concentrations of the drug left in the remains. This in turn can affect the actual time of death and the decomposition process.

The ME stopped the autopsy and called Lt. Tom Parker not only to report his initial findings but to warn detective Jack Warren that no amount of Narcan will save him or Peter Michaels if they take a direct hit like the Bradleys did.

"Thanks, doc for the heads up," Lt Parker said, then continued, "The CFD and CPD have responded to over 11,000 opioid cases so far this year already. Overdoses have increased a thousand percent over the last five years."

"Tell me about it. I cannot believe what I am seeing and it keeps getting worse. You know 75% of all the overdoses belong to males, did you know that? It's so insidious," Dr. Crine said, shaking his head.

"I'm not surprised. They say more than 150 people a day die from overdoses related to synthetic opioids like fentanyl. Every day! Chicago is only getting worse and worse."

"Well, Quag wasn't as lucky as Sgt. Alexander. I'll tell you that," Dr. Crine reflected as sadness filled his eyes.

"Speaking of that, are you aware that more than 150 law enforcement officers in Chicago and Cook County have passed out since 2017 from inhaling fentanyl while doing their routine daily jobs," Lt. Parker informed with a glum look on his face.

"How many died?"

"At least a dozen."

"It all makes me sick to my stomach," Crine interjected. "Anyway, I gotta get back to work. I just wanted you to know that this crazy son of a bitch is crazier than I ever imagined and I wanted to warn you about it," Crine said as he laid the phone back in its cradle not waiting for a response.

~~~~

Clare Claxton forgot about her queasy stomach after she and Bullet found the first grave. Lots of water and then the adrenalin rushing through her veins brought her back into full focus and out of her lunchtime funk. After she initially called Sgt. Garofalo, she continued to push forward down the serpentine trail and soon discovered another gravesite, five or six feet from the first one.

"Hey sarge how far away are you? I just discovered another one. These graves are not as close to one another as the other ones we found at Shiller and I don't think they are as deep either," she proclaimed into her radio mic.

"Nosey just came to a stop. I am about halfway to you, and I just gotta hit," he responded as sweat starting to drip down his neck and spine. "I gotta call the lieutenant," Garofalo responded. "We need to get the CSI guys over here."

"This is crazy. It might be bigger than all of them, if you're finding bodies a half mile away from me," Clare opined.

"I know. This is insane," Garofalo said, shaking his head knowing the gravity of the situation that was developing in front of his eyes. He didn't think it could get worse until he looked up at the foreboding skies and thought, *SHIT!*

The irritating cacophony from the grasshoppers rubbing their legs together came to a sudden halt and the weather changed in an instant. The hot, heavy, muggy air quickly turned chilly and wet and unfriendly. Lightning struck a huge Sequoiadendron Giganteum tree near the campground where Claxton started her new assignment. Bullet's ears drew back when the giant Sequoia split and he squatted at the crack of thunder that rumbled and shook the ground under their feet. Claxton unleashed her dog and commanded "Come." They both ran full speed toward their SUV, and the shelter it provided, and the cold water it offered in the cooler and the rain gear that was now inevitable. Their day was not over; it was just beginning.

CHAPTER 47

D etectives Jack Warren and Tom Polston had to put Vicks in their nostrils. The smell of Ronald Carson's basement apartment was so overwhelming and obnoxious it caused the two veteran detectives to gag. Their mag lights brought the dank, dreary, dark environment to life. They walked a wide circle around the dining room table that apparently was Carson's fentanyl work lab. A pair of blue latex gloves turned inside out laid on top of a trace amount of a white substance that was clinging to the sticky table like talcum powder adheres to a baby's skin.

Warren unconsciously fingered the Narcan inhaler in his coat pocket. "I'll tell the CSI guys to wear oxygen filters when they process this filthy piece of shit...hole," the detective said with disgust.

Polston nodded his approval without speaking and kept slowly moving his light around the room, shaking his head. "This prick only has the clothes on his back," he observed.

The dresser drawers were basically empty. Two filthy, dark stained, smelly tee shirts were balled up in a corner of the top drawer, a whitish layer of a thin grass like scab appeared to be growing in their crevices. Nothing hung in the closet except several bent, black, and white wire hangers. An assortment of food encrusted the dishes that were left in the sink. The slow dripping faucet water allowed pockets of mold to form and cling to the sides of the top three plates. The once white stove was mottled with a viscous coffee colored substance that was gooey. The condition of the gas burners was just the opposite; dry, rusted, and flakey. The garbage can under the sink was filled with chili cans, beef stew containers and mac and cheese remnants. The malodorous smell of rotting meat wafted upwards filling the air with the unbearable stench of death. Damp, empty rolls from paper towels discarded on the moist floor acted like petri dishes overcome by a cyanotic, slippery membrane that scientists haven't identified yet.

"This is the kind of shit that fascinates Vando," Warren proclaimed. "He loves finding clues in this stuff."

"He's at that body farm today. I talked to him this morning," Polston said.

The two detectives walked up the half stairs. Polston had to duck his head. They were met by the security detail of detectives David Mayo and Joe Lazzarotti in the backyard.

"Phew. You better change your clothes. You find anything down there?" Mayo asked with a look of repugnance.

"Yeah, shit, garbage and fentanyl," responded Polston.

"Let's call Vando. He'd love to go through this place," Warren said with a smile.

"He may not get a chance. Sgt. Garofalo and Claxton found more graves out at Deer Grove," Lazzarotti said.

"How many people did these guys kill?" Warren asked as he slipped into the driver's seat of his beat-up green Crown Vic trying to add up the number of victims they knew about. "These maniacs have killed, what…forty people that we know about so far?"

~~~~

Deborah Duke was rolling an evidence bag containing the DNA of the only victim that didn't have her thumb and toe cut off that was discovered at the Edgebrook burial site. She identified her as "Jane Doe Young." She read the FBI summary report of the analysis and began to put together a family tree.

Duke was fascinated with her findings of serial killers. Over 90 percent of them are male and they tend to be intelligent with higher-than-normal IQ's. They also tend to come from markedly unstable families. So, she wondered *WHY was this young girl's body buried with these other victims. Was she from an unstable family or is she even connected to it all?*

She was frustrated because there were absolutely no matches to any of the information currently available that she had tried. She could not triangulate anything from anyone that was connected. She could not create a genetic network from all the known samples they had uncovered. She picked up her phone.

"Dr. Britten, I can't make any connection for a family tree of 'Jane Doe Young.'"

"No genetic network. Any thoughts?" Duke asked the forensic anthropologist and federal agent Tom Britten.

"Many serial killers spend time in institutions as children and have records of early psychiatric problems. I'll check if there are any data bases at Quantico and get you access," Britten said then another idea came to him. "You know many serial killers are fascinated with starting fires. I'll check if we have any DNA information on or about arsonists in our files as well."

"I already ran all the information through CODIS," she explained.

"Yeah, it's just a hunch. Sometimes information may be filed in different ways by different investigators with different interests and I may be full of bologna, but it's worth a try," agent Britten offered.

"You know serial killers also have high rates of suicide. Do you know of any databases for suicide victims?" Duke asked.

"You might check with Dr. Crine's office. The locals may keep records like that and he may be able to help you there," he said.

"Thanks Dr. Britten."

"Please, just call me Tom and your welcome. Let's see if we can start building that tree," he said with a smile and hung up.

"I will identify you 'Jane Doe Young' if it's the last thing I do," Duke said aloud with a look of determination. "I will find out who you are."

~~~~

Dr. Robert Crine was exhausted but determined to find some answers. He was sitting in his office with a single desk lamp on and the fluorescent overhead lights off. Their constant buzzing was giving him a headache. His eyes were heavy and bloodshot. His red reading glasses were perched on the end of his nose. He was leaning on his left hand supporting his chin and cheek. His right hand was busy with a number 2 pencil making progress notes on a yellow legal pad. He had scribbles and lines on three pages trying to make connections to Terry Peterson to Billy Bob North. Why dump bodies instead of burying them. Were there copycat killers. Most victims were young men until recently. WTF???? Why????

Dr. Crine dropped his pencil and stretched out his arms over his head, yawned and pinched the bridge of his nose with his writing hand. He had been thinking for more than an hour. There was still something gnawing at the back of his mind.

I am forgetting something. What is it? He kept asking himself.

The desk phone rang and brought him back to the moment. He picked up on the third ring and answered to the soft voice of Deborah Duke.

"Hey, Deborah. How are you? Everything okay?"

"Oh, yes. I am fine. I'm just a little frustrated. Maybe you can help me," she said.

He picked up his pencil as he listened to the genetic detective asking about arson deaths and suicides, he wrote two more notes:

STINKY IS CRAZY, CRAZY, CRAZY...CRAZIER THAN WE EVER IMAGINED???

CALL PETER AND JACK!!!!!

CHAPTER 48

P eter Michaels was relaxing with his car seat set all the way back enjoying the hum of the tires on the wet road that was putting him into some sort of Zen state of consciousness with his eyes closed. A smile was painted on his face as his ear pods delivered peaceful gospel music from Elvis Presley on Sirius XM radio.

Cameraman Paul Nagaro was behind the wheel driving below the speed limit in a hypnotic state from the windshield wipers methodically swishing from side to side rhythmically removing the nickel sized raindrops pinging off the front windshield.

Nagaro almost swerved off the road when Michaels was jolted to full awareness after he grabbed his heart thinking it had just exploded to the loud ring tone of the "William Tell Overture" that blasted on his phone interrupting Elvis' 1967 classic, "How Great Thou Art."

"Shit," he yelled, gripping his chest, looking down at the caller ID, taking a deep breath and exhaling. "Hey, Jack? You just scared the shit out of me. What's up?" he exclaimed.

"You should touch base with Dr. Crine. Stinky killed the Bradleys with a direct spray to the face with fentanyl. He's never seen that much of it in anybody's system before. He's worried about us because if we are attacked the same way there will be no survival."

"No surprise. We figured as much after Quag was killed, and the Bradleys went down outside in the fresh air."

"He must have some kind of homemade dispersing device. We found fentanyl residue in his shit hole apartment. We're waiting for the CSI guys to confirm, but I have no doubt, he's coming for us," Warren warned.

"I know...I can feel it in my bones. On the brighter side, we got some great information today at the body farm. I'll share it with you later. I am heading back to do a piece on the ten," Michaels informed.

"Yeah, I talked to Vando. We are preparing a warrant as we speak to collect the bones and anything else we can take away from the body farm to send to the FBI for further analysis."

"I am going to Southeastern Illinois's body farm tomorrow and do the same thing. I have no doubt they have bodies there that we can tie to the hitchhiker as well," Michaels opined.

"I'm heading out to Deer Grove. Your lady and Garofalo found a lot more bodies."

~~~~

The rain presented itself like a tropical storm driven by 55 mph winds for almost an hour at Deer Grove. When Clare Claxton got back to the gravesites she discovered earlier, she could not find a single one. The yellow plastic demarcation flags were nowhere to be seen; they were all blown away. Even though the ground was soaked and puddles blanketed the search area, Bullet barked and sat down announcing another find.

"Good boy," she said rubbing his ears but then a quizzical look curtained her face as she thought, *this has to be a third grave site.* "Sarge, I have lost my earlier two graves because of the wind and rain but I am pretty sure Bullet just hit on another which is further away from my first two," she reported to Garofalo.

"Copy that. I have lost my original finds also," he informed her.

"I am going to work my way back to where I started. This could be significant," she said as she planted a new yellow flag this time pushing the wire stem deeper into the muddy ground. Within three steps, Bullet barked and sat again. By the time Claxton got back to her original location, she ran out of evidence flags.

"Hey, Sarge, I've got seven new graves. I need more flags. You got anything?" she asked.

"I've got three. You notice anything different over there, Claxton?"

"Yeah, now that you ask. These sites are further apart than the earlier locations. Not so structured or planned out," she responded.

"I've called a supervisor. He should be here shortly. This rain ain't helping."

"Copy that. I need to get some more flags. I've got a big stick I can use to mark number seven."

"Holy shit!"

"What?"

"Nosey just found another one."

"How many you got now?"

"That makes four so far."

"This is gonna be huge, Sarge. That's eleven more and we're not finished yet."

~~~~

Ryan O'Toole burped and the foul smell of death filled the air. He was smiling as he started to clean up the dishes after he finished his meal of the family's soup. He was soaking the thumb and toe bones that were left over in a bowl filled with bleach. Eight pieces in all. There was no flesh left on the digits. The two gallon glass jar sitting on the sink was half full. It was the fourth jar that had been handed down by the O'Toole family. More than two hundred trophy bones glistened in the light. There were also two jars of ears sitting on the kitchen table that looked like a lava lamp filled with white pieces of sinew floating in a crimson liquid. Six jars in all.

He could not bring himself to destroy the incriminating evidence, but he planned to move them to his second house that had more hiding spots in the dark cellar. The trophies have been around for a hundred years and Number Five planned to add more.

He was invigorated and intrigued with the thought of who would be his next victim because he had used the last of his trophies for dinner. He was going to work in the morning and knew he could not kill another patient. There could be no patterns. No trail to follow, yet there was a male nurse that worked in the lab next to his that he hated. A complainer like that fat fuck.

He looked at the bruising under his eyes in the mirror. A little makeup would cover up the last of the yellowish green still staining his skin and glasses would aid in the camouflage. He smiled at his image and poured himself a glass of scotch.

~~~~

Stinky was rolling the last of his fentanyl cannisters around in his fingers in between bites of Spam that he was eating with a filthy spoon he stole from a diner in Bucktown. He was convinced that his move to the garage saved his ass from capture and he was confident that nobody knew he was there. He hadn't taken a shower or bathed in days. The stench from the bucket in the corner of the abandoned garage filled with feces and piss didn't faze him at all, neither did the flies buzzing over the rusting container.

He planned to kill Peter Michaels the very next time he and his blonde, arm candy, girlfriend walked that dog in the park across the street from his condo. His recce proved invaluable. The trees offered him perfect cover for the attack. They would never see him coming. Their behavior pattern proved to be the same; whenever they were home they took that stupid dog out so he wouldn't shit in the house.

He would have plenty of fentanyl left over to use on that arrogant cop. He too was predictable because he generally left the condo no later than 7:30 every morning. He parked his car in the same spot every day in the lot adjacent to his building. It was like clockwork. Those security guys are getting laxer and laxer. They no longer stayed around throughout the night and that cocky detective doesn't wait for them anyway to show up when he leaves. *Dumb bastard,* he thought.

The assassin planned to hide under the car next to the old, beat-up Crown Vic. One quick spray and the job will be over. *Here comes Santa Claus. Here comes Santa Claus. Right down Michigan Avenue. Fuck you...detective what's your name?*

CHAPTER 49

R on Magers was sitting at his desk in deep thought with his feet up next to his computer screen. The script, he just printed for the lead story on the ten o'clock news announcing the findings of 12 new graves at Deer Grove, was laying on his lap when Peter Michaels walked in unannounced.

"What are you thinking about?" Michaels asked curiously.

"Oh...just how crazy this world is. I never imagined a story like this in all the years, I have been doing this. Did you?" he asked reflectively.

"We both know fact is stranger than fiction. Once I learned about the warrior gene, this doesn't surprise me one iota. Natta."

"Pretty productive day at the body farm?"

"Yep, lots of work to do. Hey...how long do fingerprints last on paper?"

Magers sat up and started a google search. "It states here: 'Fingerprints have been developed on porous surfaces (papers, etc.) **forty years and later after they were placed there**. They can also last a very long time on non-porous surfaces.'"

"That's very interesting. Thanks. I've got to call Jack Warren and tell him to subpoena the original intake papers from the body farms. We may get lucky," Michaels said as he stood up to leave.

"Where's your detail?" Magers asked.

"I don't even see them anymore. They just seem to blend into my surroundings. They're here. They're watching. They're on high alert. I think Stinky, that sick son of a bitch is going to strike soon. I can feel it," Michaels opined. The smile leaving his lips.

"See you on the set. I've got a lot to think about and I'm going to Southern Illinois tomorrow and check out their body farm. I just thought of something that will confirm that these killings have been going on for over a hundred years."

~~~~

Deborah Duke was mulling over the family tree she constructed for "Jane Doe Young." She checked for suicide registrations, missing persons reports, mental health institutions, arsonists, prison records. Days of searching. Nothing; then it dawned on her that she didn't cross reference anything from medical workers who have to register their fingerprints and DNA once a license is issued for them to practice in the state of Illinois.

She knew it would take hours, maybe days to link the information if it was in the data base. She found the search engine, pressed enter and leaned back into her chair and imagined the green lines filled with information flashing across her screen and thought, *Let's see if your hiding in there.*

~~~~

Dr. Robert Crine spent that last two hours of his working day examining the 12 inch knife that was used to kill Billy Bob North. He was sure that the killer had submerged the blade in bleach numerous times to wash away any evidence. He flipped down his magnifiers determined to find some residual blood that may have been absorbed in the wooden handle or deeper into the crevices of the tang where the blade meets the wood. He picked up a periodontal probe and meticulously started pecking at the old wood. To his surprise after just 15 minutes some dark flecks of wood or detritus dropped onto the sterile white paper on his worktable. A smile creased his lips as he started to talk to his findings. "What do we have here? Did you make another mistake you dirty son of a bitch? We will find you."

He cautiously collected all of the trace samples and placed them into an evidence bag and reached for his phone to call FBI Agent/Forensic Anthropologist Thomas Britten.

"I just found what I think is blood on a knife that was used in a recent homicide. I need your best guys to analyze it."

"Can't your people do that?" Britten asked.

"I think this could be multiple blood samples and your people are the best to determine that, and time is of the essence," Crine said staring intently at the evidence that he was holding up to the light.

Another phone call materialized on his screen and he said, "Gotta go." He hung up on the FBI agent and answered, "I'm glad to see you're still alive."

"Yeah…me too. Jack said you wanted to talk to me. I don't have a lot of time I have a spot on the ten. What's up?" Michaels asked.

Dr. Crine filled him in on the latest developments and told him to be very careful because Stinky had a way of spraying a large amount of fentanyl in a very short period of time. "Be very careful, Peter. This guy is crazy," Crine warned.

~~~~

Peter Michaels hung up the phone and immediately started making notes in no particular order but whatever came to mind he wrote down.

He was confident everything was coming together after what they discovered at the body farm.

He was so deep in thought that he lost track of time. A show producer came running into the office yelling, "Hey, Peter you're on in less than a minute. Get your ass to the studio and comb your hair. You look like shit."

Michaels jumped up, threw his notes on his desk, and ran out the door combing his hair with his fingers. He forgot his tie. Thankfully Tina the makeup artist was waiting for him and managed to make him look presentable when the red tally light went on.

~~~~

Michaels' notes outlined what they knew so far about the generational serial killers:

#1 Terry Peterson, dismembered, bloodless limbs with both thumbs and toes cut off????? Why both toes and thumbs??? Certain it was same knife and angle.

#2 Why Zoo park and not buried like the others??? Killed approximately 7-10 days ago.

#3 Peterson was a commercial real estate agent. Identified by a palm print from his real estate license. No one noticed he was missing because he was supposed to be on vacation. Did the killer know this or did he give a damn????

#4 Is there a connection to an embalmer???? NO BLOOD????
BUT bodies at Ben Frank body farm were delivered by funeral homes???
No doubt the same will be true from SEI body farm???

#5 Preliminary…No question the 12 inch knife used to kill Billy Bob North was also used to kill Dr. Phillip Kaley.
<u>NEW</u> Dr. Crine may have found new blood evidence on knife.
Send to Quantico to verify??? POSITIVE.

#6 That knife or one exactly like it, most certainly was used to kill at least dozens of other victims found at Edgebrook, Shiller (Woods) and M M (Miller Meadows) and the Zoo??? Quantico????? NO QUESTION IN MY MIND.

#7 At least two killers are left-handed and perhaps two others were right-handed???? Are they related???? I AM SURE THEY ARE.

#8 There are no such things as coincidences!

#9 How many killers are there in total????

#10 How many are currently active?????

#11 We now have a total of 53 deaths at four massive grave sites and BF body farm. How many more?????

#12 Probably more at SEI BF???? Without doubt????

#13 Is it possible that these killings go back to the 1920s and 30s????
YES…YES…YES????

~~~~

Officer Felicia Fleming just finished watching the ten o'clock news. She was giddy with excitement. She was scheduled to meet with CSI

Tom Vander Aarde, the guy they all called Vando, at the new gravesites at Deer Creek Park in the morning. She had been accepted as a new crime scene investigator. She could not be happier. The job she had been working towards was going to become a reality.

She changed into a pair of light weight nylon shorts and CPD tee shirt to get ready for bed. She took her strawberry blond hair out of the pony tail it is normally in when she works and brushed her beautiful straight white teeth. She blinked her eyes, looked into the mirror, and took out her green tinted contact lenses. She hated the amber eyes she was born with. She never knew her father and if he was the one who passed on the prolific gene. She was bullied and ridiculed at school because of them. They drew too much awareness to her five foot, nine, muscular toned body, and her high cheek bones. She hated the attention. She just wanted to blend in. Nothing more. Nothing less.

She loved being the police and the opportunities that it offered to her, and now she would be in the perfect position to fulfill the new desires that were suddenly appearing in her dreams and thoughts and consciousness. She didn't understand them but they were stirring her curiosity and making her sexually aroused.

A smile inched across her lips as she checked her alarm and she reached up to turn off the night light. She just touched herself slightly and moaned loudly as an unexpected orgasm exploded and all of her tensions were released with the pleasure of it all. Then she fell into a deep peaceful sleep.

CHAPTER 50

C hicago's Grant Park is perhaps the largest of the last bastions of protected American Elm trees. Dutch Elm disease ravaged millions of the trees planted throughout the Midwest starting in the 1960s. Chicago Conservatory volunteers have planted more than three thousand new hybrid elms along the Michigan Avenue corridor trying to bring back the biological luster of the past. These beautiful trees provide shade in the summer, shields from blustery winds in the winter and they absorb tons of carbon monoxide daily from the trucks, cars, and buses offering forgiveness for their emissions as the vehicles freely travel the city's streets unaware of their sins.

Stinky was waiting in the shadows of one of the big, tall trees whose veiny, six-inch leaves were waving at the stars, glistening like far off diamonds in the half moon lit sky. For the past two nights, the assassin was hiding in plain sight across the street from Peter Michaels condo. He blended into the ethereal environment wearing his filthy hoodie and black jeans. A dog couldn't see him but without question it would be able pick up his scent.

Ronald Carson lost all sense of reality. He was totally insane with only two thoughts that poked and prodded his demented mind: Kill Peter Michaels and kill detective Jack Warren; NOW. Nothing else mattered. He had rehearsed his attacks dozens of times since he avoided capture and moved out of his basement apartment and into the dilapidated garage just days ago.

He was seated with his back leaning against the grand old elm tree, eating the last morsel of his Spam with a black plastic fork that only had two prongs left on it when the lights in Michaels' condo flicked on. He must have dozed off because he didn't see Michaels arrive. He had a clear angle of the front door and the entrance to the garage from his recce position.

"Here comes Santa Claus. Here comes Santa Claus," he started singing to himself. The rage building inside his manic mind. "I'm going to kill you tonight," but then the lights went out and Peter Michaels seemed to disappear, Stinky stopped singing. He covered his ears and screamed at the top his lungs like a werewolf howling at the midnight moon. The sound so piercing that dogs in nearby condos began to bark and yowl and wail from being awakened from a deep sleep by this disturbing shriek of death. Stinky slithered into the shadows and then the alleys trying to make his way back to Bucktown and the safety of his garage, and loneliness, and hunger, and his raging thoughts of killing himself.

~~~~

Clare Claxton picked Michaels up in front of the studio after he finished his four minute report summarizing their newest findings of the generational serial killers on the ten o'clock news. Clare was watching the story on her phone app while waiting for him to finish, she smiled when he walked up to her Lexus coupe and tapped on the window.

"You really think these guys have killed more than fifty people?" she asked as he got into her car. He kissed her lightly on the lips, reached into the back seat and gave Bullet a hearty rub on his ears.

"By tomorrow night I am sure it will be more than 60," he replied, smiling giving Bullet one last rub.

"Why? What are you doing tomorrow?"

"I'm going to Southeastern Illinois' body farm. I guarantee there will be more there. Dave has already confirmed some of that with his old journalism professor who has been doing some legwork for us," Michaels said.

"That's awesome. Can you trust their work?"

"Oh, we'll double check everything but I have worked with J-students in the past and they pour their hearts and souls into projects like this. I have no doubt it will all be spot on."

"Are you driving there? It's a five hour trip."

"Believe it or not...Dave's mentor and friend...professor Scott Byers is a pilot. He has his own plane and he's here and he is going back to Carbondale in the morning. I'm jumping on. I hope it is okay for me to spend the night by you we are leaving at 6:30 in the morning."

"No problem. I'm just exhausted. I had a very busy day. I couldn't believe we found that many more graves at Deer Grove. What a yucky day with that downpour," she said sighing.

"Yeah, I know. I talked with Jack apparently they are going to hit that site with a lot of CSI manpower tomorrow and excavate the entire area in a single day."

~~~~

Deborah Duke's computer dinged. A person with just average hearing would not have heard it from that far away, but Duke's hearing was not average, it was extra acute. She was in the kitchenette of her hotel room brewing some green tea when the alarm went off. To her it was like a classic distress signal of a jail break piercing the quiet, gentle peace of sleep. LOUD AND OBNOXIOUS.

A smile lit her face with the certainty of a positive acknowledgement: An identification. The system was blinking, green. A connection had been made. She had finally found someone related to "Jane Doe Young."

Her printer was already punching out a brail report as she entered the room. It was pitch black. The curtains were drawn. She was in her environment. At peace with herself. Calm. Confident. She took a sip of her tea waiting for the final page. She neatly stacked the papers, squared them off and sat down at her desk. Her fingers began to sense the findings; methodically and slowly revealing the results. Her mind immediately started to calculate the DNA analysis. A smile of true self-assurance etched in the corner of her lips. Deborah Duke had no doubts of her abilities.

Each person shares various levels of centiMorgans connecting them to someone in their family. The more centiMorgans you share with someone, the more closely you are related. "Jane Doe Young" possessed about 6800 centiMorgans, 3400 from each parent. *Definitely Irish* she thought.

The further you go back into your family tree, the number of centiMorgans gets cut in half. For example, you share about 1700 centiMorgans with your Grandparents, and 850 with your Great Grandparents, so 425 with your Great, Great Grandparents.

So, who are you...425? And where did we find you? She thought to herself. Her fingers read the name Ryan O'Toole; a medical technician licensed to practice in the state of Illinois over twenty years ago.

What can you tell us Ryan O'Toole? Who was your great, great grandma? Why was she buried with12 other victims of at least two serial killers? Who are you Mr. O'Toole? Who are you?

CHAPTER 51

T he six passenger, white and maroon Cessna Turbo Station HD
high wing aircraft was fueled and ready for takeoff when Peter
Michaels arrived on the tarmac at 6:25. Professor Scott Byers
looked like a smaller version of Indiana Jones with the exception of a
neatly trimmed white mustache. Byers was five foot-nine and 135
pounds soaking wet without an ounce of fat. His muscles were strong
but lean. His grip was firm but his touch was soft. His white, wavey
hair was stylishly cut over his ears. His blue eyes complimented his
warm smile. His old, worn, brown leather aviator jacket molded to his
shoulders as if he was born in it. His voice was commanding but gentle.
Byers was a man of confidence and preparation. Michaels liked him
immediately and would not have been surprised if he pulled out a
brown leather aviator cap and goggles when he sat in the pilot's seat.

"I'm Peter Michaels," he said extending his hand.

"I know who you are. I have been following your work for years,
ever since my prize pupil David Beedy started working with you,"
Byers acknowledged.

"Nice plane."

"Yeah. I worked out a great deal with the university. I have been
flying most of my life. They pay for the upkeep and storage and fuel

when they use it. They pay my fuel when I fly for school business. It's been a win-win for both of us over the years."

"Dave told me about it. Thanks for your help."

"Here you can look at this stuff when we take off. My students have identified nine corpses that fit your criteria. Two of them are still in the ground. Seven in boxes. I don't think you'll be there long. It's very thorough research," the professor said looking over his glasses handing Michaels the folder.

"I'm sure it is," Michaels said with a smile. "I'm sure it is."

~~~~

Dr. Robert Crine was standing on the paved hiking path assessing his new crime scene. Twelve red plastic flags on eighteen inch wire stems identified the new graves in an irregular pattern. The markers pointed to the low clouds lingering in the east that appeared bright orange with flaring red streaks painted by the morning sun's rays. It was a rare, almost prophetic tapestry announcing the new day with temperatures in the high 80s along with heavy, sticky humidity.

Crine assigned one crime scene investigator to each of the 12 new burial sites discovered at Deer Creek. His instructions were very clear: As soon as the remains could be unearthed and moved he wanted them transported to the offices of the medical examiners from the six surrounding counties. They volunteered their services that afternoon to not only help with the backlog of autopsies but to move this unprecedented generational serial killer investigation forward.

"Get them to the MEs as quickly as possible," he told CSI Tom Vander Aarde. "I don't care if there is dirt, clay, pinecones, or any other kind of shit in their rib cages. We can flush their cavities out on the table."

"I agree," Vando said. "Hopefully, one of the biggest things we are going to find from these sites is the number of killers we are dealing with."

"How many newbies do you have here...working, Vando?" Crine inquired.

"Just two. Felicia Fleming and Conrad Hilton," Vando said raising his eyebrow as he looked at his boss with a cattish grin.

"You're kidding right? Conrad Hilton?" Crine asked incredulously, eyeing his lead investigator over his reading glasses perched on his nose with a similar grin.

"Who is this Fleming?"

"Number one in her class. Loves forensics I'm told. I have never seen anyone this excited about digging up bodies," Vando said. "She's at site seven, over there."

~~~~

Felicia Fleming's strawberry blonde hair was pulled back in a ponytail. Her sports bra and tee shirt were already drenched in sweat. Her white protective suit not only made her feel very uncomfortable because it created a steam bath effect causing her to perspire more profusely but more importantly it drew attention to her and her deep green eyes. She hated people staring at her. Her wraparound aviator sunglasses were a permanent fixture on her face. They were a mask to shield her amber eyes from the outside world.

Her hands were moving quickly but cautiously. She calculated that she had 18 to 20 inches of dirt to move before she reached the critical point of touching the remains and then she would slow down. One might conclude that she was reckless but Machiavellian would be more accurate. She was very precise and knew exactly what she was doing. She created a rectangle 24 inches wide and six feet long. Her military digging tool was sharp and pointed. Her movements were steady, consistent, and smooth. She wanted to be the first investigator to unearth a victim and take it to the ME's office personally.

She was driven to learn as much as she could about forensic investigations and evidence gathering techniques, but she had no idea why that compulsion was so great. She just knew it was there and she didn't care.

~~~~

Detectives Jack Warren and Tom Polston went back to Ronald Carson's basement apartment to take a second look. The dank, dark unit now had two very distinctive odors: Mold and rotting meat. The Vicks salve they put in their nostrils could not overcome the stench. Warren was gagging. Polston was swearing.

"Son of a bitch...and why did you want to come back here?"

"Look. He's coming after me and Michaels today, tomorrow...soon. Something is eating at me. I don't know what but I have to look one more time," Warren explained as he pointed his mag light at the kitchen sink.

"The CSI people took all this shit away days ago. What do you expect to find?" Polston asked frustrated.

Warren got down on his hands and knees and opened the cabinet doors under the sink. He took a deep breath, held it, and plunged his head into the open area and there in the very corner was a piece of paper, crumbled and soiled. He picked it up and withdrew, exhaling, "What do we have here?" he said, releasing his breath.

"What is that?" Polston asked curiously.

Michaels stood up and unfolded the paper and examined it. "It looks like an expired CTA train pass." Michaels observed.

"Well...if we're lucky we may be able to find where he boards the train. There is no telling where he gets off but we can get some uniforms to be on the lookout for the next few days," Polston opined.

CHAPTER 52

T he flight from Chicago to southern Illinois was pleasant, peaceful, and relaxing.

Peter Michaels took two ginger chews to settle his stomach and minimize his headache from motion sickness while he read the findings of Professor Scott Byers' student investigators as soon as the Cessna Turbo plane took off. It was a perfect day to fly and at 18,000 feet, there was no turbulence, just the gentle hum of the engine propelling the aircraft at 150 miles an hour. They were in the air a little more than two hours.

"Your students' work is pretty impressive," Michaels said looking out over the horizon, wishing he had a baseball cap to help shield his eyes from the bright morning sun's rays.

"Yes, they are very excited that you trusted them enough to get involved," Byers cooed.

"Dave speaks very highly of you as a teacher and mentor. I am not surprised that the work was so thorough," he said, as they began their decent then Michaels asked in awe, "What is that?"

"That is the Shawnee National Forest."

"It is beautiful. Looks like it goes on forever," Michaels said in wonderment.

"More than 280,000 acres of God's incredible creation. It's the only national forest in Illinois," Byers said softly. "I never get tired of seeing it when I fly."

"Are those horses on that narrow path? That looks scary," Michaels said pointing at four people on horseback.

"Everyday occurrence in the warm months. They're mainly quarter horses. They're pretty sure footed," Byers replied. "There are hiking paths, ATV paths, and believe it or not, there are roads winding throughout these majestic, dense trees and you can barely see them."

"Is that a mountain region?"

"That's the Garden of the Gods. Incredible rock formations for as far as you can see. Stunningly beautiful. Isn't it?" Byers said in a low respectful voice.

"Unbelievable. What's that over there?" Michaels asked excitedly.

"Those are vineyards. Miles and miles of grape vines. Southern Illinois produces some very lovely wines. The wineries are becoming very popular and they are helping the area with tourism and economic growth," Byers opined.

"I should come back here and spend some personal time. It's absolutely gorgeous," Michaels said looking out over the breathtaking vistas.

"If you do, make sure you visit in the fall. The colors of the trees are magnificent. You can't believe the brilliance and the beauty," Byers said and then warned, "Here we go. We'll be on the ground in a few minutes." The plane went into a wide looping left turn, heading for a landing strip in an open field next to the university's body farm.

Adrenalin began to flush through Peter Michaels. He had no doubt the hitchhiker killers disposed of at least nine bodies on the grounds not a mile from where they landed.

~~~~

Ryan O'Toole was watching the ass of a nurse pushing his patient out
of the operating room on a gurney. An evil smile etched its way to the
corners of his mouth. He was getting aroused, not in a sexual way, but
in a killing way. He decided Teresa Marserovich was going to die very
soon. He never liked her because she was always indifferent towards
him and that made him feel inferior. He didn't know where those
feelings came from; they were just there all the time from the first time
they met at the hospital. He hated her and at that moment he knew he
was going to kill her before the weekend was over. Once he made up
his mind, he started planning when and where. He knew where she
lived.

His phone vibrated in his pocket, startling him. It was very unusual
for his phone to ring at all. He had very few friends. He looked
curiously at the ID number that appeared on his screen. "What the
fuck," he said to himself. Then he thought *What would anyone from
Channel Six News want with me?* He sent the call to voicemail and
looked over his shoulder, feeling as if everyone in the lab was staring
at him. Worried lines of anxiety seemed to plow their way across his
forehead. He instinctively pushed his tinted glasses up his nose to hide
his squinting amber eyes. His paranoia was unfounded; no one was
paying any attention to him.

As he began to retrieve the call, he was startled when his phone
vibrated again. This time the call was coming from the Chicago Police
Department. "What the fuck," he mumbled as he sent the call to
voicemail. He turned pale and felt like he was going to throw up.

"Hey, Ryan are you okay, man?" A nurse asked when she noticed
the worried look that curtained his face.

"Yeah, I'm fine. I might have to leave. Family problems," he
retorted as he rushed out of the lab and down the hall searching for a
vacant room. Sweat was running down his back and his armpits were
already stained. He put his ear plugs in and found the voicemail from
Channel Six.

"Mr. O'Toole, this is Dave Beedy. I work with Peter Michaels. We happened to find a very distant relative of yours that was buried at the gravesite at the Edgebrook golf course. I'm sure you heard about it on the news. If you get a chance, please give me or Peter a call." He then gave him their numbers.

O'Toole was looking out of the window searching the roof tops of the nearby buildings that were reaching up trying to poke the gray, storm clouds that were forming in the east. The second voicemail was similar but from a cop named Jack Warren.

"Mr. O'Toole, this is detective Jack Warren. We discovered the remains of a distant relative and would like to talk to you about it and hopefully give you some closure. Call me please," he said and left his call back number.

"Fuck, fuck, fuck. What do they know." Great grandpa warned never get involved with the police.

~~~~

Stinky was starving. His last empty can of Spam was sitting next to him as he huddled in the corner of his new house. The dilapidated garage behind his old basement apartment. He watched the two detectives enter his place. The shorter, curly haired blond one he recognized immediately. The tall muscular one with the flat top haircut made him shutter. "What the fuck are they looking for?" he asked himself.

"I don't know. Those other guys were there for hours," he answered himself.

"You didn't leave anything around that could identify you or incriminate you, did you?" He asked as the internal conversation continued.

"I don't think so."

"Well how did they find you. If you are so smart?"

"It's that Peter Michaels, prick."

"What are you going to do about that prick?"

"I'm going to kill him."

"When, loser?"

"In the next 48 hours. I am going to kill him even if it kills me. Here comes Santa Claus. Here comes Santa Claus. I am going to kill you, you son of bitch. Here comes Santa Claus." He stopped singing and began talking to himself again. "You ruined my life when you killed my friends. You are going to die," he promised.

He was sitting on the filthy garage floor, rocking back and forth, holding his knees to his chest. His insane mind was running rampant. His headache intensified. His anger building. "I'm going to kill you, Peter Michaels if it's the last fucking thing I do."

CHAPTER 53

FBI Agent Thomas Britten was on a conference call with Dr. Robert Crine and detective Jack Warren after he received the blood analysis report from the knife used to kill Billy Bob North and Dr. Philip Kaley. Even though it had been thoroughly rinsed and sprayed with bleach not all the trace evidence was washed away.

"The bureau's blood spectrometer discovered four different blood types hidden in the knife's crevices," Britten explained.

"Let me guess, Billy Bob North and Doctor Kaley for sure, right?" Dr. Crine interrupted with a sly grin, satisfactorily confirming his earlier suspicions that the knife was used in both recent murders.

"Do you know who the other two victims are?" Warren asked.

"At least, one more," Britten informed. "Scientists were able to identify an Alex Birchman. Apparently, he served on some Illinois state legislative committee investigating real estate fraud in the Chicago area and his DNA was on file."

"I'll start looking into him. Somebody has to know about him if he was on that committee," Warren said.

"The fourth sample has yet to be identified. We could not match any DNA to that victim but the scientists did conclude that his blood was the oldest of the samples. Not sure if that means anything yet," Britten conceded.

"It means one thing for certain," Dr. Crine interjected.

"What's that?" Jack Warren asked.

"These people have been killing for a long time," agent Britten said in a voice just above a whisper.

~~~~

The forensic lab and storage facility at Southeastern Illinois University's outdoor decomposition research facility (body farm) is a nondescript gray cinderblock building, but once inside a sophisticated, elaborate working laboratory is revealed. Stainless steel tables with high definition microscopes and futuristic forensic equipment filled the room. The yellow walls brighten the entire space helping to morph the gloomy subject matter into a friendly, energetic but studious working environment.

The skeletal bones of 53 men, women and children are stored on green metal shelves that reach to the 12 foot ceiling in a designated area at the back of the room. No names are used to identify the remains; only numbers that are codified, starting off with the year, month, and day each body was accepted for study.

There were six containers set aside on two folding tables near the entrance door for easy access. Each of them had a yellow envelope taped to it. Journalism students were excitedly talking with other criminal science and anthropology students working in the lab. They were anxiously awaiting the arrival of a notable visitor from Chicago to answer any questions the investigative reporter may have about their research assignments.

Dr. William "Billy" Moors walked over to them and announced that Peter Michaels would be there shortly, he had just landed at the airstrip on the edge of the farm. Dr. Moors had an interesting medical career. He spent 25 years as an obstetrician and gynecologist. He brought thousands of children into the world as the most sought-after baby doctor in Southern Illinois.

He developed a love for forensic science however as a pharmacy student at University of Pennsylvania decades before. He was a soft spoken and a gentle man. His five foot three inch frame was never threatening, always soothing. He loved bringing children into the world but he was absolutely fascinated and intrigued with the study of death and what took people out of this world. He was particularly interested in crime related deaths and how forensic science could help solve those crimes. So, for the last 15 years he studied and taught forensics at the University's body farm and he is now its director.

A five gallon pot of water, with a bleach like cleaning solution, and a skull was boiling on a laboratory stove. Graduate student, Joe Rocco was stirring the pot. The skull belonged to a victim who spent eleven months buried in the acidic soil near a copse of trees on the three acre body farm. Rocco was preparing it for further study, research, and storage. The student looked totally different than he did weeks ago on that sleepy, hungover morning when he signed in and accepted the corpse of Walter Sullivan.

There were 18 other bodies in various stages of decomposition on site and victim #220723, identified as Walter Sullivan, was one of them. His naked remains were placed in a thick wire cage, sitting on a cement slab in the outdoor environment totally exposed to the weather conditions. The body was missing a right thumb and left big toe. Its flesh was melting away like a hot candle. The head was tilted down making it impossible to see if the left ear was severed.

Dr. Billy Moors was still not certain if he would move body #220723 to check on the ear as Peter Michaels had requested. He was a stickler for protocol and protocol was to never move a body once it was placed and documented because that would interfere with the decomposition process and the factual results.

When the journalism students came to the lab and started asking questions about the nine similar cases, Rocco became very curious and immersed himself into the investigation. His whole attitude about working at the body farm changed instantly and the graduate student became reenergized about his career in the forensic sciences.

He suddenly remembered that intake day several weeks before because the person who delivered the remains signed a different name from the last time Rocco recalled seeing the same man the year before when he first went to work at the lab as an undergraduate. He was certain it was the same man because of his eyes: They were cat like.

Rocco was a track star at the university; he ran the hundred yard dash and the low hurdles. His six-foot frame was muscular, toned and tan. His dark brown eyes shared the ever-presen smile on his face, those eyes were now more focused than ever before. He became very excited when he discovered that the bodies in question were delivered by four men with different names, working for three different funeral homes. He felt confident that the man who signed his name as Stuart Blakely from the Logan and Logan Funeral Home and the man who signed his name as Phillip Stuart from Killeen and Callaway Funeral Home were one and the same. He was no handwriting expert but he knew the "Stuart" signatures looked very similar. He could not wait to talk with Peter Michaels.

~~~~

David Beedy was getting ready to call another victim's family identified by Deborah Duke when an intern knocked on the door and said, "Hey Mr. Beedy, this was delivered by a currier about fifteen minutes ago. Its addressed to Mr. Michaels."

"Thanks," Beedy said, and walked over to the 16 inch square box and immediately became suspicious. It was sealed with clear plastic tape and the address was written in black block letters, probably with a Sharpie fine point marker on a standard sheet of white paper. There was no return address and that sent out a warning sign that Beedy ignored and picked up the box which felt like it weighed ten pounds.

He shook it, and whatever was inside seemed to move slightly. Beedy instantly put it on a desk and cleared the office.

He called Peter Michaels who picked up on the third ring. "Hey what's up?"

"Someone just delivered a box addressed to you. I picked it up and something moved inside. So, I cleared the office hoping it's not going to fucking explode," Beedy explained.

"Well, if you think you should call the police, call Jack, and ask for help, or open it. I just landed and I'm heading over to the body farm and lab."

"I'll think about it and I will call Jack no matter what."

"Call me if it's important. I should be back there later this afternoon," Michaels informed and hung up.

Fifteen minutes later after Beedy called detective Jack Warren, and there was no explosion, he went back into the office and decided to open the box. Warren was on his way over to the newsroom. Beedy took out a boxcutter and gently inserted the razor blade and slowly began to cut his way around the edge of the box. His hands were shaking and perspiration beaded on his entire forehead, armpits and back. He said to himself, "Are you fucking crazy, Beedy? Do you want to die over this fucking job?"

There was no one else in the room. If he was going to die he didn't want anyone else to suffer his humiliation. He slowly opened the flaps and stepped back. Nothing happened. He took a deep breath and noticed bubble wrap surrounding what looked like black fur.

Just then the same intern, who brought the box into the office in the first place, escorted detective Jack Warren into the room. "What are you doing? Are you nuts Dave?" Warren exclaimed excitedly.

"Probably, but it didn't blow up so, I'm sure we are safe," Beedy said, then yelled at the intern, "get a cameraman in here now."

"I don't know if that's a good idea," Warren warned.

"Fuck it. It's our property and you never know."

A camerawoman was in the newsroom and in less than a minute she burst into the office, not thinking about her personal safety but only of getting video for a possible I-Team story. "I'm rolling," she proclaimed.

Beedy reached into the box and gently removed what he immediately knew was a head. A reddish liquid was pooled at the bottom of the package. Beedy's hands were now almost shaking uncontrollably as he started to unwrap it.

"Son of a bitch!" Beedy said astonished. He was no longer shaking as he stood there in shocked disbelief staring at the head of the disgraced detective known as "The Closer." Lorenzo Garcia.

"Street justice," Jack Warren whispered. A slight grin etching in the corner of his mouth. "Street justice."

CHAPTER 54

CSI Tom Vander Aarde coordinated the exhumation of the last twelve corpses found at the Deer Creek crime scene. It was the first time since the serial killers' graves were discovered weeks ago that he didn't personally participate in the extracting process of any of the bodies. He was a hands on, take control, type-A personality, who loved being in charge of this new investigation.

He was also supervising two new crime scene investigators. Conrad Hilton needed a lot of supervision and Vando had his doubts that he would cut it. He already threw up twice.

He thought Felecia Fleming was a little too reckless at first because she was working at a feverish pace for a rookie and he was concerned she may damage some of the evidence they were trying to preserve.

"Hey Fleming…what's your hurry? You gotta be careful that you don't scar the bones in that gravesite."

"I got it boss. I tested the middle portion of the dig to check the depth. I read in one of the supplemental reports that most of the victims were all less than six feet tall. I made my perimeter six-six in height. I got this."

Just then her shovel blade hit something solid. Probably a rib.

"Hey slow down. You've got plenty of time. Do it right! Slow down or I'll take you off the site," Vando yelled.

Her cheeks flushed crimson immediately and something inside of her psyche just exploded. *You motherfucker, I might have to kill you for embarrassing me like that...out here in front of my cohorts.* She shook her head as if to clear it and wondered where that notion had come from and she immediately realized she could be a killer. She gathered her thoughts, calmed herself and said, "Sorry boss. I'll take my time."

"It's not how fast we clear the area. We need to be precise. You'll get there," Vando tried to reassure.

If I didn't have so much to learn from you...you might be my first one, she contemplated.

~~~~

The Cook County Morgue was bursting at the seams with dead bodies. The coroner had to utilize a refrigerated truck to handle the overflow. A Chicago gang shoot out resulted in five deaths last night, coupled with eight other deaths from the weekend and now twelve new hitchhiker skeletons would soon be added; the workload was overwhelming. Dr. Robert Crine welcomed the help from six other medical examiners from the surrounding counties but he did not like the idea of not having control over autopsies in his own facility. The urgency to solve the serial killings was mounting and left him with no other choice so, he sent two bodies each to his colleagues.

Magnified pictures of the severed areas around the thumbs and toes of the earlier victims were emailed to each ME. Crine was certain that all the victims were murdered by the same serial killers so, with specific instructions and chain of evidence protocols he released the victims.

Now the waiting game was afoot.

~~~~

Ronald Carson was awakened by the sounds of heavy equipment being set up at the end of the alley. There was a bulldozer, a front loader and two dump trucks lined up waiting instructions from the crew chief.

Stinky looked through the boards and watched as a black cloud of smoke burped from the exhaust pipe of a yellow bulldozer as the operator started up the leveling machine. The metallic sounds from the grousers or steel tracks was deafening to him as the machine approached down the asphalt alley to the dilapidated garage he called home for the last two weeks. It came to a stop ten feet away from where he was standing. His astonished eyes bulged. He put his hands over his ears, started running in little circles and then he began to silently yell at himself.

The operator hollered back to the foreman, "Dis the one?" Then he said, "Son of a bitch! Sumthin' dead in dare. Damn man."

The crew chief came running to the garage and gagged at the smell of death. He looked inside and saw a man in a dirty gray hoodie and black pants running around seemingly screaming but no sound was coming out of his mouth. "There's some crazy son of a bitch runnin around in there. Call the cops. We ain't knocking dis down til they git him outta dare."

The filthy assassin was running around in circles.

"How'd they find me?"

"I don't know."

"What are you gonna do?"

"I gotta get away. I gotta kill that guy."

"What guy?"

"You know that reporter."

"What about the cop?"

"Him too."

"You better go. They just called the cops. Run."

With that Stinky knocked down the door and started to run down the gangway.

"Wait...you forgot your juice."

"Fuck."

He stopped, turned, and ran in a few circles as if he didn't remember where he just came from and returned to the garage. Panic exploded in his eyes. His forehead creased in a frown of four rows of stringy flesh as he started to search for his fentanyl dispenser. He found it laying on a rotting two by four in the corner, grabbed it and fled as fast as his legs would carry him.

~~~~

Ryan O'Toole was in the corner of an empty visiting room when he decided to call that reporter Peter Michaels. He pushed the thoughts of killing Teresa Marserovich to the back of his mind. He could deal with that later.

His hands were shaking as he pulled out his cellphone and dialed the reporter's private number. After several rings he heard the familiar voice.

"This is Peter Michaels. I can't take your call right now, but if you leave your name and number, I will get back to you as soon as I am able."

"Fuck you...you exact prick...'as soon as I am able,'" he whispered to himself in anger and stuffed the phone back in his pocket.

He left the visiting room and went back to the operating lab looking for his boss.

When he found him, he announced, "I've got a splitting headache. I've got to get out of here."

"Sure. We are not too busy this afternoon. Go ahead...get well. We have a full schedule tomorrow," the supervisor related sympathetically.

O'Toole thought that this might be his last day of work. He decided he had to move to his second house in the suburbs. He had enough money stashed away and he had done well in the stock market He thought, *It might be time to blow this town.*

~~~~

Detective Tom Polston was in the car waiting for Jack Warren to return when his alert alarm sounded. He turned his radio to dispatch and heard the call that a Streets and Sanitation crew found some crazy person running around in a garage on the 2100 block of West Cortland Street. He knew immediately that was in the exact area where they searched Ron Carson's basement apartment. He called his partner, "Hey Jack something's going at Stinky's place. A streets and san crew just found him and he's on the run."

"You go. I gotta wait for a supervisor. Peter just had the head of Lorenzo Garcia sent to him anonymously in a cardboard box."

"You're kidding right?"

"I'm looking at it right now. The Latino gangs made sure that 'The Closer' will never fuck with another Hispanic again."

CHAPTER 55

J ust as Peter Michaels began his session with the students in the body farm lab, he received a text from his partner David Beedy. **U won't believe this but we just received the head of det Lorenzo Garcia in a box.**

Michaels didn't want to be rude to the students but he was stunned by the text. "I'm sorry but I just got a shocking text and I have to deal with this immediately," he told the students and professors waiting for him.

He called Beedy on speed dial. "What is going on? Garcia's head? Poetic street justice." He said in disbelief.

"I can't believe it either, but yes. It's awful. Jack is here. I took video of it when I opened it. I'll write a piece for the ten. You'll be back right?" Beedy asked.

"I should be for sure. Scottie is ready to fly me back as soon as I finish. Tell Jack he better get a warrant ready. These kids have done an outstanding job of research. I read the info packets on the flight down here. I'll be in touch. There's lots to do."

"The police are on their way over to take this into their possession. Crine wants to see it right away, as if he doesn't have enough on his plate. Stay in touch. See you tonight."

Michaels hung up and apologized to everyone telling them the Cliff notes version of the "head" story. Everyone was fascinated and then he started to shake all of their hands as they welcomed him on campus, excited to share their information.

Dr. Billy Moors suggested they go outside to the farm before it got too hot, "We have two remains in varying stages of decomposition that fit your criteria. Walter Sullivan, Number 220723, is in a cage and I am afraid we can't move his head because the flesh is like jelly. If we attempt to adjust him it will spoil the study but you can clearly see that his right thumb and left big toe are cut off."

"I am sure the police will get a warrant for all the remains once the final decomposition stages are complete," Michaels informed the doctor.

The farm had the distinct smell of death but it was not overwhelming because a cool southernly breeze was blowing. Sullivan's body was starting to look like a melting wax candle from the scorching heat and he had only been there for a month.

"Hmmm," Billy Moors mused. "That's funny?"

"What's that?" Michaels asked.

"Sullivan's intake report states that part of his scrotum sack was severed off but not an ear."

"That's interesting. It breaks the pattern for sure," Michaels wondered out loud.

"Yes. It is interesting because by the measurements, it could possibly be the size of an ear," Moors pronounced.

"Coincidence, you think doc?"

"Forensic science doesn't believe in coincidence, Mr. Michaels," he replied. "You of all people should know better than that."

"Do you have the original intake paperwork?" Michaels inquired.

"I'm certain we do."

"I am sorry to say the police will probably get a warrant for all the original paperwork. They'll send it to the FBI lab in Quantico for fingerprint analysis."

"I figured that and the students have gathered all of what you will need. I'd give you all the paperwork if it were up to me but you know…protocol," he said with a shrug.

"I appreciate that. I really do. The warrants may have been already emailed by now anyway. I hope the students wore latex gloves when they handled the forms."

"Oh…they did for sure. I told them not to manhandle anything without protection. Not sure what you will find, we have no idea how many people touched that paperwork over the years," Dr. Moors informed.

"The FBI can do some amazing things with their superpowered computers, Hey, by the way, how long does it take for a body to decompose?" Michaels asked as they walked up a slight incline towards a wide, swiftly flowing, cold stream that runs through a heavily forested area of the farm.

"That's what's interesting about #210813, a Mr. James Kirk."

"You mean like the Star Trek, James Kirk?" Michaels asked with a hint of a smile. "What's so interesting?"

"His remains will probably be removed in a few days. His stage three decomp was delayed significantly because of the atypical extreme cold winter we had last year. Kirk's underwater and typically remains can last from ten months to years under water. He's lasted almost a year, because of the intense freezing weather. If he was in this earth, he'd be a box of bones by now."

"From what I read in the summary report of the students, Sullivan and Kirk were brought here in 2021 and 2022…before that the last corpse of interest was brought here in 2009."

"That's right. After you talk to the students, you should spend a little time with my graduate student, Joe Rocco. He has something very interesting to share with you."

"Yeah, what's that?" Michaels asked with a quizzical look.

"He took in both bodies. Sullivan and Kirk. He swears it was the same man that delivered them. And guess what?"

"What's that?" Michaels asked his interest totally peaked.

"Same guy. Two different names. He thinks he can prove it."

"Yeah. How's that?"

"I don't want to spoil his big moment, but he's right."

~~~~

Stinky was moving as fast as his legs would carry him, but without running. He was heading south on Damen Avenue. He could not afford the fare for the bus or a train. His destination Grant Park. His determination: Kill Peter Michaels or detective Jack Warren or both.

People on the sidewalk paid little or no attention to him as he meandered his way through the crowded street but when he passed them, his obnoxious odor instantly made his presence known. Fortunately for him, the blue and white squads with sirens blaring were heading to his garage in the opposite direction.

Ronald Carson appeared to be lost within himself when suddenly he sensed he was being watched. He instinctively looked over his left shoulder, somehow in that moment in time, he caught the glance of detective Tom Polston who was racing hot, northbound down Damen Avenue.

Polston had the same sense. He jerked his head to the left. His eyes were operating like the lens of a camera capturing images and objects on the flash drive of his brain. He spotted Stinky in that same second and looked out his rearview mirror searching for the first opportunity to safely make a U-turn. The seconds seemed like hours. He was too late.

Carson slithered into an alley and wedged himself behind two trash bins and the dark red brick wall of a pizza parlor. He was a chameleon blending into the dirt, grime, garbage, and filth of a Chicago alley.

He was now totally insane. The conversation he was having within himself was pushing him further over the edge. Nothing was going to stop him. He had nowhere else to go. He gripped the fentanyl dispenser in his hoodie's pouch. He clinched his teeth. The exchange in his head was loud and troubling, but not a single sound came from his mouth as the bitter argument began.

"How did they find you?"

"I don't know. I left no clues."

"Are you sure?"

"Quit asking me questions. I am ready to die."

"You can't die. You have to kill that bastard, Peter Michaels."

"I know. I know and I will. Leave me alone."

When the conversation finally ended that soothing song that calmed him down started to play: "Here comes Santa Claus. Here comes Santa Claus. Peter Michaels is going to die today. Here comes Santa Claus right down Santa Claus Lane."

CHAPTER 56

T he Journalism Students were sitting at their specific stations when Peter Michaels was escorted back into the laboratory. Each one had a packet of victim information placed in front of them, along with a container of the victims' bones.

Dr. Billy Moors introduced graduate student, Joe Rocco, to Michaels who smiled broadly when they shook hands. "Dr. Moors tells me you may have met the killer on two occasions."

There was a sudden gasp in the room with the announcement of this new information. All eyes turned towards Rocco at once, and more respect and admiration for him surfaced immediately. Rocco had helped each of the students gather their information and he guided them through all the protocols of the lab's chain of evidence procedures.

He had two packets in his hands. Beads of perspiration gleaned on his forehead, a nervous twitch expressed itself in his brown eyes after Michaels said, "Let's start with numbers 220723 and 210813. The last two victims, whose remains are still outside."

Rocco's hands were trembling slightly as he put down the packets and pulled on a pair of latex gloves before he opened the folders. He nervously coughed to relieve his tension, took a drink out of a water bottle then he started with a raspy voice.

"Victim 220723 was delivered to the University on July 7, 2022. Walter Sullivan was a white 60-year-old, male. He donated his body for forensic research by will. That will, however, is now suspect," Rocco said with an air of confidence.

"Why is that?" Michaels asked.

"We have found that all nine of these bodies were willed to Southeastern Illinois University. The wills are basically all exactly the same almost word for word. I think that Stuart Bradley who signed in Mr. Sullivan is the same person as Phillip Stuart who signed in Mr. Kirk, number 210813. I am no handwriting expert but I examined the script of Stuart's signatures and they look very, very similar. You can tell that by the slant of the handwriting. It's from a left-handed person. The 'S' is very distinctive.

"I was a little out of it when I signed in Mr. Sullivan but since we started this research project with you, I am 99 percent certain that they were both delivered by the same man but from different funeral homes. I remember distinctly that he was left-handed."

"What do you mean you were a little out of it?"

"Well...we had a fraternity kegger the night before and I was a little hungover," Rocco confessed. His cheeks flushed with embarrassment.

All of the students burst out laughing. A wide grin appeared on Michaels' face as well, and he said, "I know that feeling. Mr. Rocco. Go ahead."

Rocco grinned and continued confidently. "I find another thing very interesting Mr. Michaels."

"What's that?"

"I asked each of the students in this project to check the intake dates of all of these bodies from Chicago area funeral homes. Guess what?" Rocco asked but didn't wait for a response to his rhetorical question. "Every single one of them were brought here on a Friday afternoon."

"Why do think that is?"

"Simple. It's no coincidence at all. It's party time. These guys knew that Friday afternoon was the perfect time to deliver the bodies because there would probably be very little scrutiny given to these drop offs right before the weekend parties were about to begin."

All the students once again nodded in agreement.

Peter Michaels told the students to take a quick break, he needed to call to get warrants for the two body farms in Illinois asking for as much of the original paperwork as possible. The FBI was going to be inundated with these findings. Not only more DNA samples to test, but handwriting analysis, and comparisons of similar cut patterns in the bones where the thumbs and toes that were severed.

Two hours later Michaels had finished with the students. He was pleased with the quality of their detailed work. There were nine victims from 1996 through 2022. Interestingly five bodies were delivered from 1996 until 1999. The next body came in 2006 and not another one until 2009. There was a lag of almost 12 years between 2009 and 2021. One thing was certain though, all the victims were delivered by three different Chicago funeral homes. The same three funeral homes were used to deliver the 12 victims at the Benjamin Franklin Institute of Technology's body farm less than an hour from Chicago.

Michaels gathered the students and thanked them for their great work, then he concluded, "There are a total of 21 bodies used in forensic science studies by the two universities, all right under the noses of authorities for the last 26 years. Never forget…fact is stranger than fiction. These serial killers were bold. They operated with impunity in clear sight, and they had the audacity to have the taxpayers foot the bill for the coverup of their murders."

~~~~

Ryan O'Toole, the fifth's, 27th victim was defrosting on the floor of his living room for almost 24 hours. A counterfeit Persian rug, purchased at a discount warehouse franchise, was absorbing the water seeping out of the body. He was embalmed and cut in half. His head was severed but resting on the corpse's chest. That's the only way O'Toole could fit the dead man in the freezer after he killed him more than three years ago. Henry Rudishman's frozen remains in the house didn't bother his killer for a single second. He was just another piece of meat that would one day have a definite purpose.

Number Five started the thawing process shortly after Peter Michaels called to question him about his great, great grandmother's body being found by the police at the Edgebrook golf course.

Henry Rudishman was a white male who worked at a neighborhood hardware store. He was a friendly guy, who everyone liked including Ryan O'Toole. He was the exact same size as O'Toole, along with the same age, height, weight, hair, and that was precisely why and the only reason why Henry Rudishman was dead. If he had amber eyes he would have made the perfect substitute.

Number Five never played by the family rules. He killed more than any of the other O'Tooles, male, female, it didn't matter, his only criteria for death was that the victim had to be at least 18-years old. He killed Rudishman as an afterthought because one day, a few years ago, it occurred to him that, if he ever got caught by the police, having a look alike would help buy him some time to make a cleaner getaway. He never thought he would get caught, but he knew he should have an exit plan just in case. Henry Rudishman was part of that strategy.

O'Toole had not slept very well since he botched the killing of that biker Billy Bob North weeks ago. The phone call from Peter Michaels sent him over the edge. He was always thinking; trying to figure out what clues he left behind, besides the knife that is. He could think of nothing.

He convinced himself not to panic. He had a second home in another county, under another name. He could hide in plain sight if necessary. All he had to do was grow a beard, shave his head, and lose a few pounds. The hard part would be to stop killing for a while.

He just finished packing all of his clothes into his SUV when his cellphone vibrated in his pocket. He looked at the caller ID. *What the fuck do he want? That Peter Michaels is pissing me off.* He put the phone back in his pocket and waited for it to go to voicemail.

He started to wipe down his house to get rid of any fingerprints on the high gloss white door frames and then said, "Fuck it. I don't need to work that hard." He knew that he could never get rid of all the prints. He lived here too long. He saw on "48 Hours" or was it "Dateline" that a lot of killers burned houses down to get rid of any trace evidence. It's a simple solution. That's what he would do, and that's when he decided to defrost Henry Rudishman.

He went into the cellar to collect the six glass jars with all of his families' trophies. Bones and ears...more than a hundred kills...an average of one kill a year for the last hundred years and he had the most of any O'Toole. He felt proud. He smiled as he began to pack the jars in boxes, carefully stuffing bubble wrap around them.

He went to his work bench and took out an old space heater, shaved some wiring so that they would overheat to ignite the gasoline. He would be long gone by the time the fire started. His cellphone vibrated to remind him he had a voicemail.

"Mr. O'Toole, this is Peter Michaels, I see you tried to call me back. I just got back from an out-of-town trip. Would like to talk to you about a distant relative the police discovered in one of those makeshift graves at the Edgebrook golf course. When you get a chance can you give me a call at 312..."

"I'll give you a call alright to find out where you live. You might just become number 38. You prick," O'Toole said to himself out loud. Then he took one final walk through of his house to make sure that he left no personal items that could be traced back to him. He did not want to leave his leather recliner but he had no choice. If any neighbors did see him leave, it would be as though he went to the grocery store.

The faulty space heater would take at least an hour to overheat. He ran an exposed wire into a five gallon container filled with gasoline. He then doused the body of Henry Rudishman with two more gallons of gasoline, and pushed the two body parts together as close as he could possibly connect them. The thawing body no longer smelled of formaldehyde. He put Henry's head in a pillowcase and slung it over his left shoulder.

He stood in the middle of the room with a huge grin, and then he plugged in the space heater and said, "Hast-ta la-vista motherfucker," then he left without looking back.

CHAPTER 57

C lare Claxton and Peter Michaels' relationship was getting stronger and stronger. While holding each other close, the last time they were together the "L" word surfaced. They both said, "I love you" at precisely the same moment, and of course that lead to a night of intense tender love making and the next morning, it was more of the same. They were both very happy.

In the last four days, however, they barely saw one another or talked to each other. Their schedules just seemed to conflict. Clare had early morning calls to search for more gravesites and she worked until dark. By the time she took care of Bullet and showered, she was totally exhausted, went to bed, and started all over again the following morning. Their conversations lasted less than a half hour in those four days. Clare made up her mind that she was going to see Michaels tonight. She packed an overnight bag and food for Bullet then she drove downtown to Michaels' place. She was hungry and horny.

Peter Michaels was working nonstop trying to piece together the growing amount of information of the generational serial killers' case that he had uncovered so far. He and his partner suggested that they produce an hour-long documentary, adding more to his workload.

He could account for 64 bodies so far. The skeletons from the Edgebrook golf course dated back to the 1920s. Everyone was convinced there were more bodies buried somewhere.

Michaels' flight back from the Southern Illinois body farm was smooth, a tail wind made it almost a half hour shorter than the trip down but by the time they got clearance to land at Midway Airport, it ended up being 20 minutes longer. He was worried that he would not make his live shot on the six o'clock news, so he recorded a voice track before he left downstate as a precaution. Even though the story of disgraced detective Lorenzo Garcia's head being delivered to his office was a good one, Michaels could not stop thinking about this once in a lifetime serial killer story. He didn't care if he was on the set or not.

During the ride back to the studio, Michaels called Ryan O'Toole, twice. Deborah Duke was 100 percent positive that O'Toole was genetically connected to the lone female that was buried at Edgebrook. He was a medical technician and it was required by law that his DNA be on record to get licensed and certified. Michaels was anxious to talk to this O'Toole guy, his voicemail greeting was a metallic sounding, female voice that announced a number, but nothing personal. It gnawed at the back of his mind why O'Toole was not that interested in finding out if he was in fact related to the female discovered at the hidden gravesite. That just seemed a little odd to him, and he lived by a number of mantras like; *if something was a little odd...something was a little off.* Another mantra he lived by, *it's not because I am so smart, it's because they're so stupid.*

~~~~

Ronald Carson emerged from lower Michigan Avenue's homeless community along the Chicago River. He blinked at the bright sunlight. He had been underground for several hours searching for food, water, and acceptance. He found none of them. He was not well received by the homeless people living in their encampment where there was little hope for the future and the constant reminder of misery from the past. It would take time and a constant presence to be welcomed and Carson, even in his crazy state of mind, knew that time was one thing he was running out of.

These people protect their own and their property with their lives. He was not one of them. Everyone thought that the little man in the dirty gray hoodie and black jeans was weird even by their vacant standards. Stinky never had a lot of friends from grade school to high school to the Madison Mental Health Center.

His internal conversations had now verbally surfaced. His ramblings and bantering going from asking questions to answering them annoyed everyone, who heard him yelling at himself. He was making his way down Michigan Avenue to Grant Park. His stomach ached from lack of food. He grabbed a hamburger wrapper in a garbage can and ate the remnants of moldy onions, a slimy pickle, and a ketchup-soaked bun. When he finished it, he just threw the paper on the ground and kept walking south.

Once he saw Peter Michaels building he made his way into the trees and found an area where he could watch the lights in the condo. They were on and someone was moving around. He smiled and his internal conversation began again.

"Do you want to sit down?"

"I'm getting a little cold."

"Then you should rest. Tonight, could be the night."

"I'm ready for that bastard. Tonight, is the night."

"Finally. Good. Rest."

"Yes. Tonight. Here comes Santa Claus."

~~~~

Ryan O'Toole, the fifth, was stuck in heavy traffic on the Eisenhower Expressway driving to the western suburbs. His second home was in Villa Park. He bought it years ago under a name of Jack O'Brien and rented it to a schoolteacher for almost eleven years. The teacher developed some heart issues and moved back to Morris, Illinois almost two years earlier. O'Toole started visiting the house shortly after that so his neighbors would not get suspicious if he ever had to move there. It was now that time.

The house was in a quiet middle class community about 20 miles west of downtown Chicago in DuPage County. The yellow brick, ranch style house with a two and a half car garage was set back on a sizeable, tree filled lot that offered shade in the summer, colorful leaves in the fall and firewood in the winter. It butted up to a municipal golf course. He could dig graves in the backyard if he wanted to and he would never be noticed. It was a perfect hiding spot. He never met any of his neighbors and he hoped to continue that form of solitude.

The house itself was plain, simple, vapid, just regular. A local lawn service maintained the property at a reasonable price. They cut the grass in the summer and shoveled the snow in the winter. He paid his monthly bill by a direct deposit to the company's business account. He never talked to any representative, once his renter left, he just transferred the automatic payments from a new checking account he set up on the internet.

The inside of the house was drab, with beige walls, white ceilings, and trim. There was a single cheap picture of a cowboy roping a steer on the wall over a nondescript tan couch. There was not one single personal item on display in any of the rooms. It felt lifeless.

O'Toole exited on St. Charles Road when his phone rang. It was that Peter Michaels again. He had no intention of answering it. *That fucker never gives up,* he thought. The only O'Toole rule that Number Five truly believed in was authored by his great, great grandfather; At all costs, stay away from the police and those nosey newspaper people. Avoid attention as much as possible. Attention is trouble.

~~~~

The powerful explosion sounded like a bomb. It shattered the windows on both of the houses on either side of Ryan O'Toole's Logan Square home. Within a minute the entire structure was engulfed in fire, spreading flames from the center of the house to the outer walls in less than 30 seconds. Seven minutes after the Chicago Fire Department received the call they were on the scene.

Battalion Chief, Arthur Norman, responded to hundreds of fires during his 30 years of service to the city. He had absolutely no doubt that the one he was now watching...was arson. Nothing burns that quickly without an accelerant. He had no concern for the burning building itself, his main objective was to save the houses on each side of the fire. He needed to protect the entire block. The homes were old and dry and potentially combustible. The winds were shifting. Norman's concerns were mounting. He started screaming orders and his firefighters responded immediately to flush as much water as they could pump on the surviving homes.

He was not going to send any of his firefighters into that house to investigate until it had time to cool down. His past experience and his gut told him that the fire was set to conceal or coverup something. He queued his radio and asked the dispatcher to get an arson team to his location and to notify the police.

"Let's find out who owns this place," Norman said. "This feels very suspicious."

CHAPTER 58

P eter Michaels just got off the set after finishing his on camera report. He convinced the ten o'clock producers to let him do a voiceover package for the later newscast. He wrapped his standup close outside the studio on the riverside. As he gave the hand mike to his cameraman, his cellphone vibrated in his pocket. He was hoping that it was O'Toole but when he looked at the number a smile spread across his lips and eyes.

"Hey baby, how ya doing? Are you there yet?"

"I should be there soon. Traffic is very heavy. Roosevelt Road is all backed up," Clare informed him with a smile. Her eyes sparkled with anticipation.

"Want me to stop and pick up anything for supper?"

"I don't care if we have a frozen pizza. I took tomorrow off. I'll open a bottle of wine to let it breathe."

"I can't wait to see you," he purred.

"Me either, hurry home."

Michaels liked the sound of that. He had been thinking about asking Clare to move in with him. He missed not seeing her for four days. That's what prompted the thought of living together. He had not felt this good about a relationship for a long, long time.

~~~~

The moon was full and bright and magnificent. It lit the chilly night's air. The northerly wind made the leaves dance to a steady rhythm casting gentle shadows on the street and flowerbeds separating North and South Michigan Avenue below. The coolness was a welcomed relief from the stifling summer heat that had smothered the city for weeks. Even the grass smiled, the moisture glistened on each blade as if it was a morning dew. Ronald Carson's ass was wet from sitting on the ground next to a tree. He never took his eyes off Peter Michaels' condo.

His inconsequential internal conversation ceased the moment the kitchen light appeared. He was on his feet in one steady motion. He pulled on his wet ass instinctively and then pissed himself. He felt the warm sensation and he adjusted his pants. His insane mind went on full alert and his right hand made its way into the hoodie's pouch. He fingered his fentanyl dispenser gently like he was holding a rosary in his childhood. That was a long time before he massacred his parents and siblings.

Stinky could not see Peter Michaels motorcycle but he could hear it. Those Screaming Eagles pipes had a very distinct sound. The assassin could never forget that loud calling card. He smiled for the first time in weeks.

"Tonight, you die. You cocksucker. Tonight, you die. Here comes Santa Claus. Here comes Santa Claus."

~~~~

Deborah Duke left a voicemail message for Peter Michaels earlier that day. She wanted to get back to Southwest Florida. She was mentally drained and physically exhausted. Any work that she had left to do, she could do from home. For almost six weeks she compiled more than

60 genetic profiles. She had reams of information packed in banker boxes and felt confident that she could access all the files she needed from anywhere. She also missed her husband.

"Hey, Peter, I appreciate the opportunity to work with you again. I am out of here on a late afternoon flight. I am surprised that this Ryan O'Toole hasn't called you back. I think he may be someone of interest. Find him. Be careful of him. Hmmmm. Be safe. Call me when you can."

~~~~

Detective Jack Warren sent all the original paperwork from the Benjamin Franklin Institute of Technology that they collected to FBI agent Tom Britten earlier that morning in a special police pouch. The intake times for the 12 victims coincided with the timeline that Peter Michaels had suggested. Only two were signed in during the late 90s, the others in between 2000 and 2020. All of them on a Friday afternoon. All of them from the same three funeral homes. All of them willed their bodies for forensic scientific research.

Peter Michaels delivered the Southeastern Illinois paperwork to Warren when he arrived at the studio. The weekend was fast approaching and everyone was hoping that they would have at least some preliminary results before Monday. Things were starting to pick up momentum and moving quickly.

~~~~

Dr. Robert Crine was wrapping up a zoom call with his colleagues from the six surrounding counties who performed the autopsies on the remains collected at Deer Grove. Their conclusions were very interesting. After they all compared notes, they surmised that the victims were killed by four different people according to the blade tessellations used to sever the left big toes and the right thumbs.

"So, what you are saying is seven of the patterns were an exact match to the earlier kills that we discovered at Edgebrook?" Dr. Crine asked.

"Positively! Without a doubt," Dr. David Schotts, the ME from DuPage County stated firmly.

"That means they could date back to the 20s and 30s," Dr. Crine offered.

"DNA and Carbon testing will confirm these findings without a doubt," Dr. Deanna Stone, the ME from Kane County said. "There is absolutely no doubt about that. None."

"And the five others?" Crine asked looking through the autopsy reports.

"Those matched perfectly to the bones found at Schiller Woods and Miller Meadows," Dr. Roberta Herrman, the ME from Lake County said, and then offered, "Three of them were left-handed, one was right-handed."

Dr. Crine leaned back in his chair, rubbed his chin, and said, "Wait a second let me show you guys another pattern." He pulled out a different picture and put it up on the screen. "What do you think?"

"That bone was not buried. It looks fairly fresh," Dr. Stone said.

"Can you zoom in a little?" Dr. Herrman asked.

Dr. Crine filled the whole screen with the blade's pattern.

All of his colleagues said at once, "Left-handed."

"That pattern matches two of those recovered from...let me see here," Dr. Schotts said pulling up his pictures, making a comparison. "That matches two of the victims from Schiller Woods."

"That's my conclusion as well," Dr. Crine confirmed.

"Is that a recent case?" Dr. Stone asked.

"Remember reading about Dr. Phillip Kaley?" Crine asked.

"Yes, the surgeon from the University of Chicago. A month or so ago," Dr. Herrman said.

"Yep, one and the same," Crine said.

"That means?" All of them asked almost in unison.

"That means, at least one of these serial killers is still active right now," Dr. Crine confirmed.

~~~~

The elevator ride up to the tenth floor seemed like it took ten minutes. Michaels was generally always aware of his surroundings, but when the doors opened, he burst into a run. The only thing he wanted was Clare. He was sexually excited like an 18-year-old kid. His hands were shaking as a Freudian sensation aroused him more than he already was when he inserted the key into the lock. As soon as he opened the door, Clare rushed to greet him smiling broadly. Bullet followed but the dog must have sensed something special was about to happen because he stopped as soon as Michaels grabbed his master and picked her up. Bullet turned around and went to his bed.

They fell against the wall and kissed hard and passionately. Their skin felt like it was on fire. Perspiration formed on their foreheads, upper lips and down their backs. She was ripping at his shirt. He was pulling down her black leggings. He almost lost it right there. She was wet with anticipation. He cupped her firm buttocks in his hands and carried her to the kitchen island. He swept papers off the countertop in one swift motion. His shirt fell to the floor. His pants were down. He was sexually aroused and panting heavily. When he finally entered her, she gasped erotically, and dug her nails into his back fervidly, he winced enthusiastically, the pain only adding to the pleasure of the moment and within seconds they climaxed together. After the sensual explosion they held each tightly but gently. They were both out of breath and simultaneously said, "I love you."

CHAPTER 59

The stinky assassin was agitated. His wet pants were chaffing his ass. His patience was nonexistent. He was pacing in circles. His face was a tapestry of odium and rage. His eyes were a reflection of hate and despair. His internal argument was fulminating with the voices in his brain screaming at each other. His pace quickened as he put his hands to his ears trying to stop the thundering rant.

"Are you ready?"

"I am so ready. Why doesn't he get here?"

"He'll be here shortly."

"What happens if he doesn't come?"

"He'll come."

"Are you sure?"

"Well, if he doesn't just kill her."

"I have to kill him. He killed my friends. He's fucking mine."

"Well, looky, looky, look who's coming?"

Stinky suddenly stopped and glided in the shadows behind a tree. He reached into his pouch and fingered the fentanyl dispenser.

The beautiful blonde, the dog and the cocksucker were walking directly at him. Smiling at each other. Laughing as if they didn't have a care in the world. They looked so happy, he thought. Adrenalin started to percolate as he began to focus. He gripped the fentanyl tightly…"It's time to die."

~~~~

Michaels and Clare took a quick shower to cool off and refresh. Their love making didn't stop at the kitchen island. It carried over into the bedroom. They were spent but eager to caress one another again and again. They couldn't stop kissing. They were getting ready to fall back into bed when Clare said, "Stop. I've got to take Bullet for a walk. He hasn't been out in hours."

They both got up and dressed in shorts and tee shirts. Neither put on underwear. They knew it wouldn't be long before they started making love again.

Michaels took a deep breath, exhaled, and said with a dramatic sigh, "I'll go with you. Let me take out a pizza and put it in the oven on low."

She took a sip of wine, a hint of a gloating, appreciative, gratifying smile appeared on her lips. She felt totally in love. She wanted to spend the rest of her life with this man. Bullet nudged her leg as if he knew what she was thinking. She reached down and rubbed the top of his head. She purred, "Good boy. Good boy. Where's your leash?"

Bullet gave a happy jump and started turning in excited circles at the word "leash." He knew he was going for a walk. Clare put his collar on and hitched him up. "Settle down, Bullet. It's okay were going."

Michaels put the oven on bake at 200 degrees. Slipped the pizza in. He took a sip of wine and said, "Ready?"

They started walking to the door when Clare remembered her purse. The one she made. The protective detail was all but disbanded after weeks of surveillance and protecting Michaels with not even a hint of danger; he dismissed them for the night.

"Do you really need that?"

"Probably not, but you never know, do you?" Clare said smiling and then reaching up on her tip toes gave him another kiss.

~~~~

Stinky became alert when he noticed the revolving door starting to move. He waited until he saw the order in which they were walking. They were so happy. *Fuck you; you prick,* he thought as he watched and stalked in anticipation of his charge.

They crossed Michigan Avenue with the light on ninth street. Clare had Bullet on his leash with her left hand. The dog was eagerly pulling her forward. Her right hand was in some pink, fluffy thing. Peter Michaels was on her left so Stinky slithered around a big tree for a direct attack on his friend's killer.

"Hey, Bullet calm down," Clare said softly. As soon as the dog's paws touched the grass, he instinctively lifted his leg and began to drain his bladder. They walked a little further into the park and Bullet found a tree.

That's when Stinky made his move. In his insane way, he figured they were paying more attention to the dog relieving himself then they were to anything else around them. The would be killer started his charge...running fast. When he was ten feet away, Bullet instantly smelled his foul odor and immediately went into protective mode.

Just as Stinky reached the couple he extended his right hand holding the fentanyl dispenser...spraying, he screamed, "I'll kill you, you motherfucker."

Bullet launched at his wrist and he caught a direct spray of fentanyl. The dog's jaw was strong and his teeth broke the flesh. Bullet's weight pulled the assassin's hand down but then his grip was gone and he dropped straight to the ground. Twitching, withering, dying.

The killer was so outraged, he could feel no pain; only anger and hatred and revenge as he reached Michaels. Clare instinctively moved her finger to the trigger of her MP2-380 and squeezed. The sound of the gunshot reverberated in the calm night air, reminiscent of the bells of Notre Dame announcing evening vespers. The bullet entered Ronald Carson's right eye and waltzed through his brain. The last memory he had was not about a bright angelic light welcoming him to heaven but of the scorching fires of hell melting his flesh from his bones before everything went black. Death didn't immediately register as Carson's momentum carried him forward into the arms of his target. Peter Michaels was knocked backwards but somehow maintained his balance. The stench of his assassin was foul and ugly and disgusting. It felt as if Carson was covered in a gritty Vaseline like substance when Michaels grabbed him and threw him to the ground.

Clare came over to him and put another bullet in his forehead igniting the end of her pink furry purse for a second time. She dropped the purse, turned, and ran to Bullet. She got down on her knees and picked her partner up into her arms, wailing, "No. No. Bullet. Please God. No. No."

She was ready to give him mouth to nose resuscitation when Michaels stopped her, "Clare, honey. You can't. It will kill you. That fentanyl will go directly into your blood stream. You can't. I'm sorry baby. I'm so sorry."

She didn't want to listen. She ignored the warning and she tried again but Michaels restrained her. He said, "I have Narcan." He reached into his pocket and pulled out a dispenser and shot it directly into Bullet's nostrils. Clare was holding his head up in total disbelief, in total shock. Tears continued to flow down her cheeks uncontrollably. She was rocking, looking up at the stars, pleading with God, tightening her grasp of her beloved Bullet. Her lips were quivering, she kept repeating, "Why. Why," but no sounds came out of her mouth.

Michaels grabbed his cellphone and called Jack Warren, who answered on the second ring. "Where are you? Were those gunshots I heard?" Warren asked worriedly.

"Yeah, we are downstairs in front of the building. Carson tried to kill me and Clare. Bullet stopped him and saved our lives and now he's dead. Call 911 and get down here."

Michaels put the phone in his back pocket and sat down next to Clare and wrapped his arms around her and Bullet. Tears filled his eyes and then rolled down his cheeks in a steady stream. He tightened his grip with Clare and Bullet. Both of their shoulders were heaving up and down in unison. In agony. In despair. In anguish.

The sounds of sirens from first responders pierced the evening air. People began to gather. Some with their cellphones out taking pictures adding more sorrow to the disturbing scene of death and hatred and grief.

Clare was whispering, "Why. Why. He was just a dog. He never hurt anyone. Why. Why, God. What did he do to you?"

"I am so sorry honey." Michaels whispered in her ear. "He saved my life and yours from that maniac."

Clare continued to cry but there were no more tears to shed. She lost her partner. She lost her best friend and companion. She was losing interest in everything she held dear to herself as she slid further and further into a dark abyss of nothingness.

CHAPTER 60

Within 90 seconds, three squad cars and two CFD ambulances arrived on the scene. EMT Joan Meyers was holding Clare Claxton's hand trying to comfort her. She gave Clare a sedative to calm her down. Her eyes were puffy and red and tired. Her nerves were shattered along with her heart. Her skin color was pasty. She started to drift into an uneasy unconsciousness.

Peter Michaels was talking to detective Jack Warren when Lieutenant John Haskin walked up to them.

"Mr. Michaels, I am Lt. John Haskins."

"Hey, John. I know who you are. You're Clare's boss."

Haskins was a big man. His six foot-four, 225 pound frame was muscular. He was the commander of the mounted patrol division. His hands were thick. His grip was strong and powerful. His fist looked like it could punch through a brick wall with ease. His deep blue eyes were engaging but soft; they were sorrowful at the moment.

"How is she?"

"Not that well. I think she should go to the hospital for observation. She was pretty traumatized by all this," Michaels said with sad eyes.

"I can't even imagine. I know she loved that dog," Haskin said sympathetically.

"What happens to Bullet?" Michaels asked.

"I'll take him to our vet. He'll be pronounced DOA. We'll put together a burial service plan in a few days," Haskins informed.

"I've never seen a burial service for a police dog," Michaels said.

"You'll never forget it. We honor our horses and canines just like we do an officer who was killed or catastrophically injured in the line of duty. We are even dedicating a section for them at the Police Memorial Garden."

"That's awesome. Thanks for your help Lieutenant. I've got to go check on Clare," Michaels said. They shook hands and Michaels walked over to the ambulance that was getting ready to transport Clare to the hospital.

Her breathing was shallow. Her eyes were closed but twitching. Her dream or nightmare was apparently threatening her subconsciousness. Her muscles were convulsing. Tears trickled out of the corners of her eyes.

Haskins covered Bullet in a blue police blanket and picked him up as if the one hundred pound dog was a puppy. He reverently placed him in the back of his K-9 SUV, saluted him and closed the hatch. His eyes welled with tears and his throat swelled with sadness.

Bullet was six years old.

~~~~

The body of Ronald Carson was unceremoniously carted away by an ambulance to the county morgue. Dr. Robert Crine would do an autopsy in just a few hours but everyone knew the cause of death. Insanity and two bullets to the brain.

The scene in front of 880 South Michigan was chaotic. Television crews, reporters, photographers, producers and 15 squad cars along with three ambulances surrounded the crime scene. Reporters were yelling questions at Peter Michaels. He hated being the center of a story. It was the fifth attempt on his life in 18 months. He walked over to the microphones for an impromptu presser.

"Listen. My girlfriend and I were attacked by a lunatic earlier tonight. She was not the target. I was. Her dog, Bullet, gave up his life to save ours. This has been very traumatic and draining. I will give you all more later but I still have a debriefing with the police. That's it for now."

He finished and walked away from the crowd and cameras to the homicide detectives who were waiting to debrief him. When he finished he and Jack Warren went up to his condo.

He knew Clare was sound asleep at the hospital because Joan Myers, the EMT, left him a text message. She was also worried that Clare was going into a state of depression. Michaels feared the same.

The condo's fire alarm was just about to erupt. Smoke was wafting out of the oven, filling the kitchen area. Michaels opened the oven door and pulled out the dried up, burned pizza that was cooking for more than two hours.

Warren opened the windows and turned on the fan.

"Son of a bitch. I forgot all about that fucking pizza. Want a bourbon?" Michaels asked.

"Make it a double," Warren responded.

Michaels poured them each a double Basil Hayden. "I am worried about Clare. She really loved that dog," he said rubbing his forehead slowly and thoughtfully with his hand.

"I hate to say this buddy, but some guys become suicidal when they lose their partner. I'm not saying that is going to happen to Clare but be prepared for some behavioral changes," Warren opined.

"Yeah, Joan said she was also worried about depression. So am I. I'm madly in love with her. We were really getting close, then all this shit happens."

"Give it some time, my friend. Give it some time."

~~~~

Ryan O'Toole stored the head of Henry Rudishman in the basement freezer and began to panic slightly. He was thinking about how many other heads he had stored away at the funeral homes and he couldn't recall if it was three or four or more.

He also stowed the trophy jars in a hidden corner of the root cellar. The old-fashioned cellar was the main reason he bought the Villa Park house. It offered great hiding places. He decided to go upstairs and watch the news…wondering if they discovered the body of Rudishman at his Chicago home.

He was sitting back in the recliner watching the ten o'clock news clicking his remote back and forth through the stations when the story of Peter Michaels' attack came up on Channel Six. He was trying to forget about that pesty reporter, but the news story piqued his interest. Peter Michaels just told the reporters that he was the main target of the assassin.

A malicious smile etched its way into the corner of Number Five's lips as the thought of killing Teresa Marserovich was replaced with the illusion of killing Peter Michaels. He was beginning to obsess with the image of serving up Peter Michaels thumbs and toes in the O'Toole family soup.

He picked up his phone and started to scroll through his pervious numbers and then hit redial.

CHAPTER 61

B attalion Chief Arthur Norman returned to the Logan Square house fire from the day before. He met with his arson investigators and two homicide detectives. The smell of filthy ashes, smoke, gasoline, and death hung in the air like the smog that smothers the mountains in Southern California.

Detective Chuck Ruoff was poking at the midsection of the charred remains with the eraser of a number 2 pencil. The skeletal rib bones were virtually disintegrated by the severe heat and they looked like badly burnt Australian lamb chops that were overcooked on a very hot barbecue grill. Ruoff's face was covered with a mask of suspicion. He didn't need his instincts to tell him this was a murder scene. The first big clue; the body didn't have a head. The second; the body seemed to be cut in two.

"This guy was cut in half. The killer tried to burn the evidence with an intense fire to cover it up…no doubt about it. I'll bet my life that he was murdered probably long before the fire was set," Ruoff theorized.

"Why do you say that?" Norman asked.

"Even though most of the bones are burned beyond recognition, here look at the separation of the spine above what's remaining of the pelvic region. The killer thought the intense fire would disguise the area but the heat just further separated the spine." Ruoff pointed out.

"Trying to identify this guy through DNA. It ain't gonna happen," suggested detective James O'Toole shaking his head. "Trying to amplify DNA genetic markers from bone fragments this highly degraded will probably be impossible."

Ruoff then said, "Not to mention that badly burned bones are prone to contamination with external DNA. We may never ID this poor bastard."

The two arson investigators shook their heads in agreement then the Battalion Chief offered, "We may not need DNA. My secretary just texted me. The owner of this house is a man named Ryan O'Toole."

"Any relation to you, partner?" Ruoff asked.

"I've got a lot of relatives, but I have never heard of any one named Ryan, and certainly not from around here," James O'Toole stated emphatically.

~~~~

Peter Michaels brought a clean set of clothes for Clare Claxton to change into the next morning. Her eyes were puffy and tumid. Her voice was raspy and sad. She was subdued and tired even though she slept through the tormented night. The sedatives did their job physically but the nightmares of Bullet's death minimized their effectiveness for her mental health. Clare was upset and demoralized.

"Hey," she murmured as Michaels walked into the room.

"Hey." Michaels almost whispered back. After a pause that seemed like ten minutes, he asked guardedly, "How are you feeling? Did you sleep well?"

"How do you think I feel, Peter? Like I want to go out and party. What a stupid question. How do I feel? I feel like shit."

The room went silent. The air conditioner's sound seemed to burst out like the torrents of a giant waterfall surging down the side of a mountain. Tears started to trickle down Clare's cheeks. Michaels turned and looked out the window and was greeted with pellets of rain dinging off of the glass pane. It was a gloomy morning only to be made worse by the thoughts of what loomed ahead. His shoulders seemed to slump. The incredible feeling of love that surfaced just 24 hours earlier, now seemed destined to depression and rejection.

"Why don't you change and I'll take you home."

"I want to go to my house. I don't know if I can ever go back to yours and be reminded of what happened last night."

Michaels felt like he was just stabbed in the heart. "I understand. Let's just take this one day at a time. I am so sorry, Clare. I really am."

~~~~

FBI forensic scientists at Quantico determined that the 22 bodies that were dropped off at the two Illinois body farms over a 23 year period were killed by two separate killers, and both were left-handed. A detailed computer analysis of the cut line patterns, particularly from the area where the right thumbs were removed, confirmed everyone's suspicions.

FBI agent Tom Britten was on conference call with Dr. Robert Crine and detective Jack Warren. "We have some interesting findings."

"You have two left-handed killers, right?" Dr. Crine interrupted.

"Yes. Your theory is correct. The same person killed the first four victims from 1994 through 2000 that were disposed of at the Benjamin Franklin Institute of Technology's body farm. The nine other victims at the Franklin farm were all killed by another left-handed killer."

"The patterns of these dumps are also interesting to me," Warren interjected. "Why do you think there were no bodies dropped off in southern Illinois between 1999 and 2020?"

"Our profilers think that the killers may have taken some time off or weather conditions during those years between 2000 and 2020 may have prohibited the killer to take the drive that far away. There are any number of theories that they are tossing around, right now."

"Of course, they buried dozens of other bodies in the forest preserves around Chicago," Warren suggested.

"There was just one overlapping kill from the Southeastern Illinois campus," Britten offered.

"I think it is safe to assume that these killers were related or at the very least, they knew each other," Dr. Crine suggested.

"The profilers think that is a very safe assumption. They're leaning to related. There is too much coincidence in these kills," Britten said.

"So, what about the overlap in Southern Illinois?" Warren asked.

"Four of the five bodies disposed of there were killed by the same person between 1996 and 1999. One of those killed in 1999, was killed by the same person who killed the other four that were left there between 2020 until the present day," Britten informed.

"You don't have to be a profiler to draw the conclusion that these killers are related. I think Peter Michaels' theory that these are generational serial killers is no longer that far-fetched," Crine said.

"I believe our profilers are about to come to that conclusion," Britten said.

"What about the fingerprint and handwriting analysis. How soon will that be completed?" Warren asked.

"Soon. Very soon," Britten concluded.

CHAPTER 62

T he 35 minute ride from the hospital to Clare's house seemed like it took three and a half hours. Her eyes were sad and her lips quivered, revealing sorrow and anguish, deep within her soul. The only thing she said during the drive home in almost a whisper was, "I'm sorry."

She was in a silent world, devoid of any thoughts, drained of all emotion. She was fixated on the horizon, staring out at an angry gray sky that was producing rain droplets. The only sound came from the windshield wipers; magnified by the methodical and rhythmical swishing of the blades clearing the drizzle every few seconds.

Peter Michaels was speechless. His stomach was churning, the acid belching up his esophagus burned his throat. He was the happiest man in Chicago 24 hours earlier, thinking about asking Clare to marry him. He had announced his love for the first time in as long as he could remember. He was now smothered in remorse, desolation took over his thought process and woe pierced his heart that just yesterday was filled with the hope, happiness, and more joy than he had ever dreamed possible.

He stopped in front of her house, turned off the ignition, put his hands in the ten and two o'clock position of the steering wheel and sat there silently, tears slowly cascading down his cheeks. He whispered, "You ready?"

Clare didn't say a word. She just nodded slightly. Her trembling hand reached for the door handle, but the door seemed to open miraculously as Peter Michaels reached down to help her up and out of the car. He put his arm around her shoulder as they walked up the steps. There was a stiff reaction to the tender touch but not a total rejection. He unlocked the front door and Clare walked into the house, dropped her purse on the living room chair and went directly into her bedroom and shut the door, not saying a word. Not looking back. No affirmation.

Peter Michaels was in as much shock as Clare. He found a piece of paper and wrote a note: "My Dearest Clare, I am so sorry. Please call when you are ready. I'll be waiting. I love you, Peter." He left the message on the dining room table. Tears slowly seeped down his cheeks and he wondered if he would ever hear from or see her again as he closed and locked her door.

~~~~

David Beedy was in the investigative unit's office with his three person team of student interns. They were plowing through their missing persons paperwork and had now identified 49 of the 63 victims that were killed by the hitchhiker. It was an operose task.

"Dave, how many victims do you really think are out there murdered by these crazy guys?" asked Judy O'Connell, a senior journalism student from Michigan State University.

"Your guess is as good as mine. I don't know if we will ever find all of them," Beedy offered.

"Well from the lists you gave us; here is what we know: Edgebrook golf course had 12 victims and the female non-victim, Shiller Woods had eight, Miller Meadows had eight, there were 12 at Deer Grove, thirteen were left at the Benjamin Franklin body farm and nine were disposed of at Southeastern Illinois's body farm," Chuck Cornelli, a junior at Northern Illinois University offered.

"And don't forget that one guy that was dismembered and dumped in the Zoo Woods over by Loyola Hospital," offered John Toti, a senior from Northwestern's Medill School of Journalism.

"I can't help thinking we just know of a fraction of these victims," Judy O'Connell said.

"We may never know the true number. We don't even know how many victims were actually buried in graves. Some could have been cremated for example. There could be twice as many as we have found," Beedy said.

"Why do you say that Dave?" Toti asked.

"As journalism students, future reporters, why do you think I would say that?"

"Because we know that the 22 victims that were delivered to the body farms, were delivered by someone disguising himself as a funeral home employee," Cornelli said.

"Exactly. I have calls out right now to all the funeral homes that delivered bodies to the farms. This may have been their fatal mistake. Thinking that no one would ever connect the dots, and figure out that angle," Beedy said.

"Man, that Deborah Duke is really something. I don't know how she does it, building those family trees, tracing that DNA from at least a hundred years ago," Judy O'Connell opined shaking her head.

"Now there is a person that you have to totally admire. Never letting blindness interfere with her goals. I can't believe how brilliant she is. It was an honor to work with her," Toti said.

"No question. She is just a wonderful person. Peter and she go back years. She helped us find a missing person for one of our sources some 12 years ago. She is incredible," Beedy said.

"Hey Dave, line one for you. It's Peter."

~~~~

FBI agent Tom Britten was putting together his report from the analysis of all the paperwork from the body farms by the appropriate experts. The fingerprint guys pulled dozens and dozens of prints from the wills and the intake forms. Surprisingly they were able to identify two very distinct left thumb prints.

One of the prints from the intake papers from both the Benjamin Franklin Institute of Technology and Southeastern Illinois University that appeared several times that went back to the early 90s and then never appeared again after 2000. Interestingly another print then surfaced several more times from the same body farms after 2001. The experts reported that there is no doubt two separate males were responsible for dropping off all of those bodies.

The bad news was neither of the prints matched anything in CODIS or any other law enforcement data bank.

All the signatures on the 22 wills that were used to donate the bodies for scientific research came from just two different people FBI handwriting specialists concluded. They were left-handed. They had a distinctive slant. The experts also agreed that the wills were all fraudulent.

Graduate student Joe Rocco was correct; the signature of Stuart Bradley and Phillip Stuart were the same person who was left-handed with a very Idiosyncratic "S" that stood out even to a nonexpert.

FBI profilers came to a consensus that the two killers were closely related, probably father and son.

FBI agent Tom Britten was waiting for the stenographer to finish the report before he called Dr. Robert Crine and the detectives leading the investigation.

He did however call Deborah Duke and gave her the shortened version of the analysis. He also wanted to thank her for all her work and see if she would be interested in working with the FBI in the future.

CHAPTER 63

Peter Michaels was sitting in the cockpit of his cherished Dr. Detroit, a Beneteau 411, sailboat, trying to relax and find comfort from another one of the loves of his life: sailing. The lines were banging and clanging inside the mast. It was a metallic cacophony that brought him pleasure most of the time but at the moment it felt like he was at a funeral and the sounds he loved seemed like a dirge. The yacht was bobbing from port to starboard from the oversized wakes of the power boats traversing the waterway making their way out to Lake Michigan.

The dock was covered with bird shit, reflecting his mood. He had not been on his boat in over a week. He would normally grab the hose and wash the poop away because he couldn't stand the thought of a filthy dock and then stepping up onto his meticulously clean boat but today was not a normal day. His heart was heavy. His mind was numb. The grace from the sun on his face and the slight southerly breeze that usually brought him peace and tranquility did little to comfort him at the moment. He was sad and clutching a glass of Basil Hayden, beer was not going to cut it, but bourbon was not a drink he preferred in the early afternoon. He was deciding if he wanted to ease the pain of losing Clare by getting drunk and stupid or if he should bury his sorrow in his work to pull him out of his funk. It was the first time in weeks that he wasn't totally consumed by thoughts of serial killers or by being stalked and murdered by some insane stinky son of a bitch. He was on that slippery slope of reality and the edge of despair.

The blare of the "William Tell Overture" broke his gloomy feelings and even brought a slight grin to the corners of his mouth. "Hey Jack, what's up?"

"Hey…how ya doing buddy? Where are you?" Jack Warren asked but knew his friend was on his boat from the sounds produced by the orchestra inside the main mast.

"I'm sitting on the Doctor, deciding to work or drink," Michaels responded sounding despondent.

"Give her time. It's pretty traumatic to lose your partner. She might need some therapy for a while," Warren said softly.

"I know that. I will give her all the time in the world, but I think she is leaving town," Michaels said sadly.

"What do you mean leaving town? Where would she go?"

"She was talking in her sleep at the hospital. She's thinking about resigning or at least taking a leave of absence from the job and moving to Arizona to be with her sister who had a kidney transplant," Michaels said.

"You guys will figure it all out but, in the meantime, don't get drunk, get busy. We are getting close to identifying this guy."

"What do you mean? What don't I know?" Michaels asked now fully alert and back into reporter mode.

Jack Warren filled him in on the fingerprints from all the documents examined by the FBI.

Michaels smelled the Basil Hayden, closed his eyes, sighed heavily then he poured the bourbon overboard, locked up the boat and called his partner.

~~~~

Ryan O'Toole, the fifth, opened the freezer door and stared at the head of Henry Rudishman. His hair, mustache, and eyebrows were covered with an icy frosty film. It reminded O'Toole of the old Star Wars movie, "The Empire Strikes Back" when Luke Skywalker was riding his Tauntaun across the wind-swept snow plains of Echo and he was attacked by a Wampa. The snow lizard was killed and Luke was taken to a cave and hung upside down. The Wampa creature's long white hair was laced with an icy frosty film and tiny snowballs.

"Too bad you had to die, Henry. You were actually a very nice guy. I hope you give me enough time to get the hell out of here," O'Toole said to the propped head with his dead eyes staring back at his killer.

Number Five was struggling with whether or not he should go back and collect all the heads he had stored at the funeral homes or just forget about them. He was trying to remember how many he actually left behind. *Was it four or five. Fuck I can't remember.*

In the end, he figured if the cops found the heads he would be long gone.

His phone rang and he recognized the number. It was that fucking pesty Peter Michaels calling again. He hesitated to answer it then hit end. His next call was to AAA, He asked for all the information they had for Alaska.

~~~~

Dr. Robert Crine shot up from his chair. He finally realized what was gnawing away at him. The small blood sample that he took from Dr. Phillip Kaley's elbow weeks ago was still in the lab's refrigerator.

"You idiot. You should have had that tested long ago," he yelled at himself internally. He found the sample just as he left it. He was not worried about the chain of evidence because he was the only one who had touched it. He packed it in another evidence bag, signed it and sent it over to the lab.

If it didn't match Dr. Kaley's blood he would also send it to Quantico and have the FBI do a more thorough examination. Dr. Crine was convinced they were dealing with four or five serial killers.

~~~~

Adrenalin started to trickle into Peter Michaels's veins when he dialed Ryan O'Toole's number but when the phone finally began to ring, it exploded within, and flushed out his melancholic memories as if he were born again. "Come on pick up. Pick up you prick," Michaels begged.

His next call was to his partner, "What's up?"

"The interns did a great job. We have identified 49 victims and have talked to 41 family members. They were all relieved to get some closure," David Beedy said, then changed the subject. "How are you, Buddy?"

"I'll be fine. I just have to absorb this craziness. I am devastated that Bullet died saving my life but you know with murder comes tragedy and grief. I knew that son of a bitch was coming for me but so did she. I just never thought Bullet would be a victim. He was a great dog."

"Yeah, he was. Listen I started calling the funeral homes."

"Are they fighting us?"

"No, actually George Killeen Jr. wants you to call him."

"Okay, I'm just pulling in right now. I'll be there in a few."

CHAPTER 64

C ook County survey engineer, Ralph Sieja, was looking
        through his laser leveling camera mounted on a yellow tripod
        checking the topography on Ogden Avenue to widen the
road when something caught his attention in the corner of his eye. He
walked over to check it out when he suddenly stopped in his tracks.

"I'll be a son of a bitch," he said as he bent over to examine what
looked like a leg and a foot with a missing big toe. He pulled out his
cellphone and dialed a number.

"News, Michaels. Hey what's up, Ralph? Long time no see."
Sieja's name popped up on Michaels ID screen. Once he had a source,
he never erased a number because you never know when something
strange will happen. Today was one of those days.

Sieja was the source, who a few years back tipped off Michaels to
a large number of ghost payrollers and dozens of lazy laborers at the
Cook County Forest Preserve. The laborers came to work, slept all day,
never picked up a shovel to dig a hole and checked out. The ghost
payrollers just picked up their checks on payday but never showed
their faces at their assigned jobs. All on the taxpayer's dime. The
Chicago Way.

"Hey, I have been watching your stories on all those bodies and stuff."

"Yeah, what do you have?" Michaels asked, knowing there had to be a connection.

"I'm out here on Ogden Avenue near Joliet Road surveying a new road project and I just discovered a leg that was washed up or drug up somehow from a deep ravine running along the roadway. It's weird."

"What's weird?"

"It looks like the big toe was cut off or chewed off," he said.

"Don't touch a thing. It could be an active crime scene. Where exactly are you?"

Sieja told him his location and they hung up. Michaels did what any good reporter would do; he called for a cameraman and then he called the police.

~~~~

Detective Jack Warren told Michaels that he would go out to the scene after he finished with his call to Dr. Robert Crine.

"What's up with Crine?"

"He wants me to pick up a blood sample that he thinks may belong to the killer of that Dr. Kaley and personally deliver it to the crime lab."

"That happened more than a month ago."

"Yeah. He put the sample in the fridge and then all those bodies started coming in and he forgot about it. Let's hope it helps."

"I think we are getting really close to identifying this guy," Michaels said.

"I think so too." Warren affirmed.

~~~~

Sergeant Mike Garofalo got to the new crime scene shortly after Paul Nagaro did. Nagaro recognized Garofalo immediately and started

shooting video of his dog "Nosey," going right to work searching for
more bodies. The cadaver dog slowly went down the steep incline, his
nose sniffing and his tail looked happy.

It was a fairly cool day for late July because the sun was hiding
behind bright white clouds but every now and then its rays peeked out
bringing warmth to the air. The humidity was mild but everyone at the
work site or crime scene was perspiring. The work became intense and
anxiety was rising with the temperature.

Nagaro remembered Sieja from the lazy laborer's story that he shot
with Michaels almost two years ago. He said hello, put a wireless mic
on him and asked him to describe what he had found. The interview
was short and to the point, just like the producers wanted. As soon as
the interview was over, Nosey started to bark; he found the other leg.

"Good boy," Garofalo said rubbing the dog's ears.

Jack Warren arrived on the scene and yelled down at Garofalo,
"Whatta you got?"

"More body parts but they're really in bad shape. You'd better get
Vando over here. This is the kinda shit he loves."

Warren called the crime scene guys and then put on a pair of latex
gloves to examine the leg that Sieja had found. It smelled of death and
decay. It was putrid. Insects and maggots had penetrated the limb.
Within a matter of seconds, Warren knew the toe was cut off, not
chewed off. "Number 64," he said to himself and then he called Dr.
Crine.

~~~~

George Killeen Jr. was pissed off after Peter Michaels told him that
someone used his funeral home's name and hearse to drop off at least
fourteen bodies at both of the Illinois body farms. "Do you have a
Phillip Stewart or Stuart Blakely that works for you?"

"Never heard of him," Killeen responded.

Michaels went down the list of eleven more names all aliases that were discovered on the intake forms. Killeen responded negatively to all of them.

Michaels then read the funeral director the names of all the victims that were dropped off at the body farms starting with Walter Sullivan and James Kirk which were the last two. He didn't recognize a single one.

"They were probably all aliases anyway," Michaels offered, then he asked, "The victim identified as Walter Sullivan was really a big-time real estate mogul named Alex Birchman. Does that name ring a bell?"

Killeen was looking at a ledger of clients and said, "Never heard of him either. What other funeral homes were used?" He asked.

"Yours, McMurry and Macintosh, Logan and Logan and Wiezechiezick."

"This is crazy. Absolutely crazy." Killeen reacted.

"Can you think of anyone who would do something like this?"

"I can't. I can't believe this. How long has this been going on?"

"Since the body farms began back in the 90s, up until a few months ago."

"God, that's more than 30 years," Killeen said pensively.

"Look I am going to be breaking this story on the ten. We believe that these are the victims of generational serial killers and that they were related somehow or they knew each other through family connections. Even the FBI profilers have come over to my way of thinking that these guys may be from the same family," Michaels offered.

"Same family. Wait a minute. Ryan O'Toole. The O'Tooles," Killeen said excitedly.

The hair on Michaels arms and neck rose immediately. "What did you say? O'Toole? What about the O'Tooles?" Michaels asked jumping out of his chair surprising David Beedy, who rushed over to hear the conversation. Michaels put the phone call on speaker.

"The O'Tooles. Father and son. Both of their first names were Ryan. They had been working for us for at least 30 years if not longer. The son Ryan just quit here about a month ago. Just up and left."

"Did you talk to him at all?"

"Nope. No explanation. No thank you for letting me work here on my own schedule. No kiss my ass. Nothing. Notta. He just quit."

"What about the father?"

"His father, I think he was the fourth. Yeah, Ryan O'Toole the fourth, he died a horrible death of cancer. Colon cancer, I think. It was around Christmas or Thanksgiving time in 2000 or 2001 as I remember," Killeen said thoughtfully.

"What can you tell us about them?" Michaels asked curiously.

"They were both good workers...kept to themselves most of the time. The old man, he was an embalmer. Damn good one I might say. Never missed a day."

"Did he work full time?"

"He never worked full time for us per se. As a matter of fact, he worked for all the funeral homes you mentioned. He was a great embalmer. He was always in demand. He was fabulous with makeup. He could make a person who died an awful death of cancer look like he or she was never sick a day in their life."

"Did the son do any embalming?"

"Not that I am aware of. Don't know if the father taught him how to do it. He was a smart kid. I know that."

"Did he work there a lot?"

"He was part time. He was some kind of nurse or a medical technician of some sort, I think."

"Mr. Killeen will do an interview for us. I can be over there in thirty minutes. Believe it or not, you may have just helped solve about 50 or 60 murders."

Killeen agreed to the interview. He turned a ghostly pale color. He started to tremble and then he threw up in the waste basket under his desk.

CHAPTER 65

Peter Michaels drove separately from his cameraman to Killeen and Callaway Funeral Home for the exclusive interview with the only person who had spoken to and knew two of the generational serial killers. Michaels needed some privacy because he wanted to talk with Clare Claxton. It had been days since he dropped her off at her house and they hadn't spoken since. Her number went straight to voicemail, and his mood went straight downhill and his heart followed.

"Hey Clare, it's me. I'm really worried about you, baby. I haven't heard a word. Are you okay? Please just give me a call and let me know that you're alright. I miss you lots."

He debated whether or not if he should say that he loved her, but decided not too because he didn't want to add any more stress to her life right now. All he knew was that work was the only thing that kept his mind off of their relationship and kept him sane. Things were moving quickly in the serial killer investigation and his gut told him Ryan O'Toole and his father were in fact serial killers. He was sure of it.

~~~~

Michaels notified everyone that he definitely connected the dots between the O'Tooles and the funeral homes. He also told them that he was totally convinced that Ryan O'Toole, the fifth, was the last of the serial killers. He suggested that they should no longer waste time with things like facial recognition. DNA tracing could be cut shorter. CODIS didn't list O'Toole, but the Illinois Department of Licensing and Regulation had his fingerprints and his DNA on file. They also had a picture of him that was only a few years old.

~~~~

Detective Chuck Ruoff contacted Jack Warren and reported that the fire at O'Toole's house in Logan Square was arson and that a body was found inside matching O'Toole's description.

"Anything suspicious about the body?" Warren asked.

"It was burnt beyond any form of recognition. I am sure that it will be impossible to get any usable DNA." Ruoff said.

"Anything else?"

"Yeah, it had no head and his body was cut in half."

"Well, whoever that victim was he isn't O'Toole. Did you search for the head in the house?"

"Yeah, but Notta."

"Okay. Let me know if by any chance we get lucky on the DNA. I guarantee the dead guy isn't our guy."

Detective Ruoff and James O'Toole never told Warren about the embalming table that was discovered in the basement because they had no idea what it really was.

~~~~

FBI agent Tom Britten's scientists immediately identified Number Five's fingerprint on eight of the intake documents and the fraudulent wills.

With that finding the FBI profilers all agreed that the other significant print was that of Number Four.

They still could not, however, identify the fourth blood sample that was discovered on the 12 inch knife left at the scene of Billy Bob North's murder, but they started looking at medical information from Illinois on the chance that it may have come from someone in the medical field.

Dr. Robert Crine sent over the information to the crime lab analyzing the blood sample found on Dr. Phillip Kaley's elbow. He left instructions to expedite everything and to contact him immediately if they had a match to O'Toole.

~~~~

During the entire time Peter Michaels conducted his interview with George Killeen Junior, his phone was vibrating. He had to stop the interview and shut it off because it was so distracting.

Videographer Paul Nagaro had ample time to set up some dramatic lighting which added to the funeral director's total credibility. It was the first time the audience had heard from anyone who actually knew the killers. He described both of the O'Tooles personalities and certain traits that fit the profile of a serial killer.

The Killeen interview was spellbinding and when it was over, Michaels had the sudden thought of searching the funeral home for any possible evidence that the O'Tooles may have left behind. Killeen had no objections and showed him around the inner working area from the embalming room, the supply room, and the storage area.

"Do you use freezers or refrigeration lockers? Can I see them?" Michaels asked.

"Sure, right this way," Killeen said walking to the refrigerator where they stored bodies until they were embalmed.

They found nothing but Michaels had a feeling that there had to be something else. "Do you have any other areas or equipment they may have used?" he asked.

"There's an old freezer off of the garage but I am not even sure if it's working or not," Killeen offered.

"Let's just take a look," Michaels said.

As they approached the old freezer Killeen said, "That's odd."

"What's odd?"

"I haven't been in this area in years. I am surprised the freezer is turned on," Killeen said and then opened the door. The overhead light was out.

"Do you have a flashlight?"

"We should have one somewhere. Give me a minute," Killeen said.

It took several minutes to find a flashlight and he had to hit it in the palm of his hand to get it to brighten up.

"Let me have that if you don't mind," Michaels said as he took the flashlight and began moving systematically around the freezer. He spotted two boxes tucked in the far corners almost out of sight. "What do we have here?" he said in almost a whisper.

"This is very strange," Killeen said as he reached for one of the boxes. His hands trembling. He grunted when he picked it up. "This must weigh 30 pounds," he said as he put it down on a workbench.

The top of the box was folded and tucked in at the corners but not taped. Killeen opened it; a look of shock and disbelief curtained his face. "Oh, my God in heaven," he exclaimed. Horror in his voice.

For some reason, Michaels already knew what they had uncovered, "It's a head, isn't it?" Michaels said calmly. He was not surprised.

The head was that of a young white male and it was frozen solid; the eyelids were closed, his lips were opened and appeared in agony, his hair was apparently brown and fell over the ears and his left ear was cut off. "Son of a bitch. Ryan O'Toole is the killer."

Michaels retrieved the second box and this time he was surprised when he opened it and pulled out another head. This one was an older black male. His eyes were wide open, expressing fright, his lips were tight exposing pain and probably surprise and his left ear was removed with surgical precision.

Nagaro took video of all the action and reaction of the funeral home director. Michaels did a standup close in case he couldn't appear live on the news set for the ten o'clock.

"I'm going to get this back to Dave and Ed Land. I wouldn't doubt if they gave you the time for the entire newscast tonight. This is unbelievable," Nagaro said.

Michaels called Jack Warren and told him what he had discovered and he also told him, "You better get over here ASAP, my friend. There is no doubt Ryan O'Toole is our guy."

CHAPTER 66

P eter Michaels called the other funeral homes that delivered
bodies from Chicago to the Illinois body farms and asked
permission to come over and look at their refrigerators and
freezers. No one objected so, David Beedy set up schedules to video
all of the searches. On his way to Logan and Logan Funeral Home,
Michaels once again called Ryan O'Toole.

"Come on pick up, you son of a bitch." Michaels droned. The call
went straight to voicemail. "Mr. O'Toole, this is Peter Michaels. I have
been trying to reach you for several days. Why are you avoiding my
calls? I suggest you watch the ten o'clock news tonight. You are going
to find it very, very interesting."

Michaels hit the end call button ferociously. *Not a question in my
mind that you're the killer,* he thought.

~~~~

Chester Logan's face looked like a caricature drawing of Red Skelton
with a reddish toupee that looked like a bad rug tilting off the center of
his head toward his left ear. Peter Michaels had to bite hard on his
lower lip in order to squelch the grin that was forcing itself on his lips

when they shook hands. There was no question Logan had money; his blue Armani suit fit like a glove; his red tie seemed to jump off his heavily starched tailor-made white shirt; his black wingtips were highly shined reflecting the bright LED ceiling lights on the toes.

"Nice to meet you, Mr. Logan," Michaels said.

"I am not sure what this is all about," Logan said questioningly.

"Ryan O'Toole and his son worked for you for years, is that correct?"

"Yes. The father was a great embalmer and did a lot of work for us and others. He kept to himself pretty much. The kid only worked part time. He cleaned up in the operating room and sales office. He also drove the hearse from here to the churches and to the cemeteries, stuff like that you know what I'm saying. He was also very quiet most of the time."

"Yeah, that's what Mr. Killeen said too. Can we look in your freezer?"

"I'm not sure. What is this about?"

"I'm surprised the police haven't contacted you yet. They may be getting a search warrant."

"Now you are scaring me. Come on Peter, I've known you a long time. What's going on?" Logan asked. Perspiration started to percolate on his forehead and trickle down his spine.

"I hate to tell you this but we believe that the O'Tooles are serial killers and I'm guessing they used your vehicles to transport some of their victims to various burial sites around the city and state," Michaels informed.

Chester Logan fell into his oversized office chair, the color drained from his face, his hands started to tremble and he felt the sudden urge to urinate. "Fuck!"

"We found two frozen heads at Killeen's. I'm not saying there are any here but we have to find out. If it's okay, I'd like to check for our story on the ten o'clock news tonight and if we find anything I am sure the police will be here immediately," Michaels said. "Can we look?"

Logan got up, took a deep breath, and exhaled slowly. "Follow me."

They walked downstairs to the embalming room. A huge state of the art stainless steel refrigerator/freezer was positioned on the far wall. As they approached Paul Nagaro immediately started taking video. It took less than a minute to search the area. The shelves were almost empty, Logan and Logan had every viewing room upstairs occupied with the bereaved.

"Do you have an extra freezer that is operational?" Michaels asked.

Chester Logan guided them to an old double sized, standup freezer that seemed to be running on its last leg. "I don't know the last time this was used. I am actually surprised its turned on," Logan said.

Michaels glanced at Nagaro who immediately turned on his camera and light. Logan opened the double doors in one sweeping motion and took a deep breath. The freezer only had a few items in it but in the back there was what appeared to be an object shaped like a head wrapped in white cheesecloth. "What have we here?" Michaels asked as he reached into the far left lower corner and extracted the bundle.

"Don't tell me that's a head?" Chester Logan said, closing his eyes and turning pale again.

Michaels placed it on the embalming table and walked around it giving his cameraman a chance to zoom in and out and pan from Michaels to the head and back again. "Do you have a hair dryer?" Michaels asked.

Logan went to the makeup room, collected one and started to blow warm air on the frozen head. A few minutes later they both looked at each other and Michaels said, "Here let me try this." He began to unravel the mummy like head. When he removed the cloth, Chester Logan almost fainted.

"Oh my God. Oh no!" Logan said holding onto the operating table to maintain his balance.

"Do you know her?" Michaels inquired.

"Yes. She used to work here twenty years ago. That's Mildred Wesinovich. She disappeared decades ago."

"So, that was when Ryan O'Toole, the fourth, worked here, right?" Michaels asked.

"Yes. That's right. I think Mr. O'Toole died shortly after Mildred disappeared."

"What kind of person was she?" Michaels asked.

"Oh...She was a complainer, alright. She complained about everything. She had a tough life but nobody cared and I don't think Mr. O'Toole liked her very much. Like I said he generally kept to himself but he did say, 'she was a bitch,' all the time." Logan offered.

"How long ago was that?" Michaels asked.

"I think it was the late 90s. One day she just disappeared from the face of the earth. It was sad. She had very few friends if any and she had no family that I'm aware of. She sort of vanished and no one bothered to call or be concerned about her. It's a shame really. One day she was here and the next she was gone and nobody gave a shit," Logan opined.

"Son of a bitch," Michaels said. "Now, we can match murders to both of them."

~~~~

Dr. Robert Crine was examining the head of the black victim discovered at the Killeen Callaway funeral home. He was preparing to take some DNA samples to help identify the victim. "Let's see here," he whispered. "You were killed by a lefty that's for sure."

"Hey doc, it's detective Jack Warren, on line two," an intern yelled.

"What's up Jack. I'm just examining the John Doe head from Killeen's and collecting some DNA samples."

"No need. Facial recognition just came back. He's Tyrone Jamemason. He had an extensive juvenile record and one run in with the law as an adult. He qualified for the second chance program and reportedly cleaned up his life," Warren reported.

"Well. Well. How did he come in contact with O'Toole?"

"Why do you say that?" Warren asked.

"There is no doubt he was killed by a left-handed person. The blade pattern is a perfect match to an O'Toole. He can't be 25 years old. So, it has to be O'Toole…what the fifth?" Crine said.

"I bet they worked together at Saint James hospital on the near westside. He was a janitor there and O'Toole was some sort of technician."

"The evidence is mounting big time. Why in the world would the killer leave a head around to be discovered?" Crine asked.

"They probably never ever thought they'd get caught. Remember Peter's mantra. 'It's not because I'm so smart. It's because they're so stupid. The father and the son didn't think in a hundred years they would be caught," Warren said.

"Hey doc, crime lab on line three," the intern yelled.

"I'll have all these reports together in the morning. I gotta go. Crime lab is holding."

"Yeah, I have to call the state's attorney. This is a solid case."

CHAPTER 67

R yan O'Toole, the fifth's anger was building and he was about
to explode as he listened to Peter Michaels' voicemail. "That
cocky, arrogant fuck can't talk to me like that and give me
orders or ultimatums. Who the fuck does he think he is?" he screamed
at the top of his lungs at nothing or anyone in particular.

O'Toole threw his phone into his fake red leather recliner. He
clenched his fists as he paced around the ranch style house...steaming.
His face was flush. Red. Burning. He thought his skin would blister.
His blood pressure was rising. His mind was racing. His heart was
pounding. He had never been this upset. He never wanted to kill
anyone more than he wanted to kill Peter Michaels at this very
moment. His world was collapsing around him.

*What the fuck does he know? Where did I fuck up? How did he
find me?* His thoughts were running rampant. His tremulous hands
were out of control. He had never felt the feeling he was experiencing
at the moment...FEAR.

His eyes were stinging. Irritated by the sweat seeping off of his
forehead blurring his vision as he picked up his phone and blindly
dialed the number that Peter Michaels had left him over a week ago.

~~~~

The fifth and last head that Peter Michaels discovered was at Wiezchiezick's Funeral Home. He was in awe that the killers would leave that kind of physical evidence behind, basically in plain sight and not get caught over the years. He had no doubt that two of the heads belong to the father and the other three belonged to the son. Michaels believed that scientific analysis would bear out the time differential.

Other news crews were showing up at the funeral homes. It was after six o'clock.

David Beedy was already writing and editing their ten o'clock news script as Michaels exited the rear door of the funeral home. He had the assurances of Stanislaus Wiezechiezick that he would not let any other news people in his funeral home to take pictures.

The other stations would get video of the CSI guys arriving at the funeral homes to gather the evidence that Michaels had discovered. He hoped that Vando would be the lead crime scene investigator because he knew Vando would say only two words to reporters…"No Comment."

Peter Michaels left Paul Nagaro at the scene as a safety precaution to get the same pictures everyone else would get just in case something unexpected happened. His phone rang but he didn't recognize the number. "News Michaels."

The fury in the caller's voice was unmistakable. "Who the fuck do you think you are…threatening me to watch your narcissistic, sorry ass on the ten o'clock news, you cocksucker."

"Well, hello to you, Mr. O'Toole. Sounds like you're having a very bad day," Michaels responded with a flare. "You know I am going to record this conversation."

"Fuck you."

"Would you like to do an interview and tell me how many people you have killed, Mr. O'Toole?"

"Fuck you."

"Fuck me. Fuck you. I got you. I can tie you to at least a dozen murders right now, Mr. O'Toole."

"Is that all. You don't know the half of it, you fuck. You don't know shit."

"Well, I would love for you to tell me more. Will you do that?"

"Here is what I am going to do. I am going to kill you. Leave town, and never to be found. Do you hear me you arrogant bastard. I am going to kill you."

"Well, you know where I work," Michaels said defiantly.

"I also know where you live too you arrogant prick and I know where your cop girlfriend, lives too. So, fuck you. I'm coming for both of you," he screamed and then the phone went silent.

Michaels was strong and alert until he mentioned Clare. That unnerved him and then his hands began to quiver just like his upper lip.

~~~~

"Why do you have to aggravate people who want to kill you?" Jack Warren asked, as a grim look loomed across his face. "Tell me everything he said."

"I can do better than that. As soon as I knew it was O'Toole, I hit record; you can hear every word."

"It's illegal to record someone in Illinois unless you told them you are recording them."

"I told him I was recording him. He didn't say not too. Even so, do you think I am going to worry about recording him when he threatened to kill me numerous times?"

"What do you want to do?"

"I'm coming back to the station, talk to Sam and the power's to be and then I am going to do a story tonight that is going to send shock waves through the city."

"What are you going to do about your safety, you idiot?"

"I am not worried about me. I am worried about Clare. I haven't heard from her in over a week. I don't know what's going on. I am nervous about that. What do you think?"

"I'll call Garofalo. He may have some ideas."

"Okay, thanks. Let me know as soon as you hear anything."

"I will. Be careful. I am going to send some units over to the station. Be careful you hear me?"

"Yeah, thanks."

~~~~

Sergeant Mike Garofalo did not break his promise to Clare Claxton not to tell anyone about her leaving town indefinitely. He took her to the airport two days earlier. She took an undetermined leave of absence from the department and moved to Scottsdale, Arizona to visit her sister and to sort out her life. She never loved anyone more than Peter Michaels and she hated him at the same time. She was struggling with those feelings. They were debilitating. Deep. Destructive. Heartbreaking.

She knew from the beginning that being with him could be dangerous because of his relentless efforts to get to the bottom of any story he was working on with no regard for his safety. She also knew it was dangerous to be a cop in a city like Chicago. She never thought she would lose one of the closest friends she had ever had because of love. Bullet loved her and apparently Peter Michaels as well. He loved them more than life itself and he paid the ultimate price for saving their lives with his.

She was lost. Now estranged and psychologically troubled. When Garofalo told her about the new threat on her life she released him of his promise and allowed him to tell everyone that she had left the city. The new promise however was to tell no one where she went.

Although Garofalo knew how much it hurt Peter Michaels not to know; he would not break his promise. He told no one. It hurt him immensely, but he was a man of his word and everyone respected him for it.

Clare Claxton changed her phone number and thought that she may never talk to Peter Michaels again. She had never felt this lost.

CHAPTER 68

D r. Robert Crine was leaning back in his chair with his feet crossed on his desk, his eyes were wide open but unfocused, blank, as if staring into the black hole of a faraway galaxy that extended beyond any known scientific discovery or universe. He was at total peace. A providential smile was evident on his lips. He was in a meditative state of consciousness as if looking down at his present form of existence. His head was slowly swaying to Beethoven's piano concerto number five that was playing in the background just above a whisper.

The knock on the door was so slight, it did not interrupt his demure demeanor. He was awaiting a lab report on the analysis of the blood sample he took off of Dr. Phillip Kaley's elbow. From the sound of the technician's voice earlier in the day Crine knew he was right.

His assistant Donald O'Connell tiptoed into the office and silently laid the report on his boss's desk as if an imaginary "Do Not Disturb" sign hung from the ceiling. He didn't utter a sound.

When the piano concerto ended and the applause started, Dr. Crine came back to the reality of the deaths that they were dealing with. He opened his eyes, blinked, put his feet on the floor, pulled himself closer to his desk, spread the report out in front of him, read it and then a rewarding smile that started in his eyes. spread to his lips.

He reached for the phone robotically and called Jack Warren, who answered on the second ring. "Hey what's up doc?"

"Ryan O'Toole killed Dr. Phillip Kaley," Crine announced. "We got him. It's irrefutable. A direct link. That bastard killed that young, brilliant surgeon for no apparent reason."

"I am sure Kaley just happened to be in the wrong place at the wrong time," Warren opined.

"Let's just find that bastard and put him away."

"Did you know that Peter talked to him earlier today. He threatened to kill him," Warren informed.

"Hey, are you going to see Peter soon?"

"Yeah, I am not going to leave his side until we find O'Toole. Why?"

"Come over here. I have an idea that might help protect him."

"I will see you in a few. I'm just around the corner."

~~~~

The new blood evidence gave Peter Michaels that last nail in the coffin that he needed to convince station attorney Sam Phieffer that it was legally permissible to name Ryan O'Toole as a serial killer.

There are all types of governmental reports that give investigative reporters incredible latitude to write incriminating stories about their targets' involvement in any sort of wrongdoing including both violent and white-collar crimes, corruption, fraud, illegal medical procedures, conspiracies, and/or any type of scams imaginable. These documents include lab reports, to and from memos, emails, autopsy reports, FBI 501 files, secret government reports, supplementary police files, justice department informational analysis reports, wiretap transcripts, official law enforcement investigative files and other state and federal agency's reports such as income tax filings, Security and Exchange Commission charges of insider trading, etc.

These types of investigative files are sacrosanct for a reporter's defense in cases of libel, slander, defamation, and invasion of privacy.

Peter Michaels had dozens of official reports that tied Ryan O'Toole and his father to at least twelve murders and 54 others that were tied to the O'Toole family over the last 100 years.

Phieffer generally helped make scripts even stronger because he knew how far his reporters could push the legal line. Peter Michaels was given seven and a half minutes to tell his story that named the O'Toole family as generational serials killers. It was captivating, clear-cut, and compelling. Everyone in the studio from the floor manager to the director in the control booth were spellbound. When Peter Michaels played the sound bite of Number Five that he recorded on his cellphone threatening to kill him and that he didn't know the half of it, all eyes were focused on the reporter. You could hear a pin drop.

When the story ended, Peter Michaels asked if any viewers had any information about Ryan O'Toole the fifth, or any member of the O'Toole family to call police or him. The phones immediately started ringing off the hook in the newsroom. Show producers, assignment editors, interns, and other reporters were inundated with calls.

David Beedy took a call and yelled out to Peter Michaels, "Hey, Peter, you better take this one. The lady says you know her son and it's important."

"News...Michaels."

"Peter, this is Mrs. Grillo. Ted's mother."

"Hey, Mrs. 'G,' I haven't heard from you in ages. Is everything okay? Is Teddy okay?"

"Yes. Yes. Everything is fine with us, but I may have some disturbing news for you."

"Mrs. 'G,' what are you talking about?"

"This O'Toole man you had on TV tonight. I know that man...but his name isn't Ryan O'Toole."

"What do you mean, it's Ryan O'Toole. He's a serial killer and he's a very dangerous man. He kills because he likes it."

"At the clinic, we knew him as Reginald Sampson."

"What clinic? What are you saying?"

"Do you remember, I took that part time job at the Northwestern Sperm Bank Clinic working on weekends to make ends meet?"

"Please don't tell me he is a sperm donor?"

"I believe he was the highest paid sperm donor at the clinic. He had very high-quality sperm. Donor sperm is always in demand and when you have high quality sperm like he had, he was in demand. I think, the clinic has paid him tens of thousands of dollars over the years," she informed.

"How does that work?"

"Well...they pay, let's say $70.00 when the sperm is collected and another $30.00 to $50.00 once the sperm is released to be used. Now that doesn't mean that each sperm insemination is successful to produce an embryo and ultimately a baby."

Peter Michaels fell into a chair in total disbelief. "Isn't there a specific number," he stumbled, "A limited number of times you can donate in a single week?"

"Yes, for the average donor, it's twice a week. For a high-quality donor that this Sampson guy was...he could donate at least three times a week and he was also allowed to bring the sample from home and that's what he did week after week for years. At least that is what I was told. Almost every Saturday that I worked at the clinic, we collected a donor jar from him."

"How is that possible?" Michaels asked shaking his head.

"Not only was he a high-quality donor, but he also apparently worked at a hospital as a medical technician of some sort and that gave him carte blanche; it opened the door to him for total access. It was basically no questions asked."

Every year, 30,000 to 60,000 donor babies are born. In the United States the laws with sperm donors are somewhat lax. Families wanting children will go to any lengths and expense to accomplish their dreams. Limits often fall through cracks and blind eyes are turned.

"It's big business, Peter."

"Mrs. 'G' is there any way you can get me some proof of what this Reginald Sampson did? I know the 'HIPPA' laws, and all that but if there is any way you can help me, I would be eternally grateful." Michaels said, crossing his fingers.

"I can't promise you anything, Peter. I have been retired for over a year. I know some people who still work there, I can't promise you anything, but I'll try."

CHAPTER 69

F   BI Agent and Forensic Anthropologist Tom Britten was sitting
    in a lab studying ten high definition pictures of bones that were
    projected on a 12 foot by 12 foot screen. He focused on the
areas where the right thumbs and left toes had been severed. He could
manipulate the pictures to be side by side for exact comparisons or he
could put four pictures on the screen at one time. He could magnify
each knife pattern. He could rotate the specific areas of interest and
examine them with three dimensional accuracy.

Britten totally agreed with his colleagues. They categorized fifty-
seven of the victims that were discovered in Chicago and came to the
conclusion: They were dealing with five very distinct serial killers
dating back to the nineteen hundreds, starting about 1920 to the
present day. Three of them were left-handed and two were right-
handed. The scientists theorized that all of the killers passed down their
grotesque techniques through the generations because of the exactness
of the dismembering patterns. They reported that "it had to be taught."

All twenty-two victims from the body farms in Illinois were killed
by left-handed males. One of them, scientists labeled killer "A." They
determined that "A" killed ten of the victims and the other twelve were
killed by a person, they labeled killer "B."

They also determined beyond a shadow of doubt that "B" killed Doctor Phillip Kaley because the very distinctive knife pattern in his death matched twelve of the victims from the body farms. Their theory was further confirmed that day after agent Britten received the results of the blood sample discovered on Dr. Kaley's elbow and it belonged to a person identified as Ryan O'Toole.

~~~~

Number Five sat in absolute amazement at the accuracy and the amount of information Peter Michaels put into his story. O'Toole could not believe that he had forgotten about some of the heads he and his father had left behind at the funeral homes, but he then realized that he had three more heads in his basement freezer. *I'll dump those off one at time when I leave town,* he thought.

He started planning his exit and packing his belongings days ago right after his phone call with Peter Michaels. He decided to take just summer clothes. Any other stuff that he needed he could just buy when he got to wherever it was that he was going to go. Florida or Georgia. Maybe South Carolina. He was not sure but he knew it had to be a warm place. This all came up so suddenly. He never thought he'd live anywhere other than Chicago. He knew the city like the back of his hand. It was where he learned to kill. He knew the streets and the alleys. He knew where all the bodies were buried.

That smart ass, prick Peter Michaels doesn't know the half of it.

O'Toole didn't realize how badly he was sweating until a drop of perspiration dripped on the light pink shirt he was folding to put into a cardboard box. His hands were also trembling. *Son of a bitch,* he thought as he collapsed on the edge of the bed. *Settle down. You'll have time to kill that fucker and get out of town. Just slow down and think!*

He would not. He could not leave the trophy jars filled with the family's treasures. He already had them packed in bubble wrap from his move to his suburban getaway house. The one registered to Jack O'Brien. His car was registered to Reginald Sampson. *I'm smarter than all of them.*

He also closed all of his bank accounts registered in the name of Ryan O'Toole.

He had over a hundred thousand dollars in cash. His biggest concern was how to close out his investment accounts. With all the money he made from selling his sperm over the last 25 years he bought Apple and Google stock at very low prices and the stocks had split so many times it made the killer a very rich man. The millions he had tucked away from his investments have become a nightmare because he didn't know if he would be able to retrieve any of the money. The feds would surely be all over everything they could trace back to him. His anger was raging. Blood rushed through his carotid arteries like rushing water flushing through and filling a collapsible garden hose. He felt like he was going to explode and pressure started building in his chest.

"I'LL KILL THAT MOTHER FUCKER, SO HELP ME. I'LL KILL HIM."

~~~~

Peter Michaels, Jack Warren, Brian Alexander and Vando were drinking Basil Hayden and Tom Polston was drinking a Coke at Michaels' condo after the ten o'clock news.

"He is going to come for you, Peter. You know that, right?" Jack Warren said putting his empty glass down on the kitchen countertop, reaching for the bottle of bourbon.

"One of us will always be with you. We will not leave your side," Alexander said. "No matter what."

"I appreciate all of your help and concern. I really do you guys, but I am not sure he even knows where I live. I assume he does but I am not sure," Michaels said unconvincingly.

"You're not that hard to find, Peter," Polston interjected. "Everybody knows something about you since that crazy bastard, Cyril Dobonovich, tried to kill you, last year."

"Every enemy you ever made knows where you live," Vando said sarcastically. "I know you are a stickler for accuracy Peter, but you should not have done those stories about the attempts on your life with your condo in the background."

Michaels was starting to feel depressed, thinking about the enemies he had made over the years. He was never afraid of the Mafia boys, but he was afraid of the corrupt attorneys and doctors that he had exposed.

"Do you have a protective vest?" Alexander asked.

"Yeah. I have one and I have this stainless steel medical instrument tray that Dr. Crine gave me," Michaels offered.

"What's that for?" Polston asked.

"Crine thought it was a good idea, in case this guy tries to stab him. Serial killers are creatures of habit. O'Toole either stabs his victims in the stomach or he goes for the juggler, at least that's what Crine says and he knows a lot about these sick bastards," Warren said.

"It just feels so weird, putting this down the front of my pants," Michaels said.

"Weird or not when you are walking outside, you wear that stupid thing. It just might save your life," Warren said affirmatively.

CHAPTER 70

T he day after Ryan O'Toole killed Billy Bob North when he heard on the news that the police had a description of his van, he painted a two inch wide, white line on the vehicle's side to disguise it. The authorities surely would have reported such a distinctive mark if they put out an APB (All Points Bulletin). He also stole a set of license plates from a car in the hospital's parking lot and put them on the van. More importantly he basically took the van out of circulation by hiding it in his garage and only used it when he absolutely needed too. He bought a new midsize white KIA SUV with a cashier's check.

He had three coolers packed with dry ice and the remaining heads that he had in his basement freezer. He sealed the coolers with Gorilla Tape to stifle any smell of death that may seep out of the coolers. He put them in the van with the white stripe and drove it to the parking structure at O'Hare Airport's International terminal and left the van in a spot on the third floor in the middle of the crowded garage. Hiding in plain sight.

He spent almost an hour expertly wiping the van of any fingerprints before he left his suburban house. He called for an UBER for a ride back to Villa Park and was dropped off at the Walgreen's at the edge of downtown. He walked home with a White Sox baseball cap on his head and aviator sunglasses covering his eyes. His new beard was filling in nicely and his shaved head was starting to tan.

He knew where Peter Michaels lived and as usual he had reconned the area at various times for three days and nights. He knew that Michaels didn't keep a strict schedule. He pretty much came home an hour after he did a story on the ten o'clock news. It depended on if he had a few beers with his buddies after the show. Sometimes he rode his black Harley Davidson motorcycle but most of the time he drove his black Ford SUV.

Ryan O'Toole decided he was going to kill Peter Michaels in his condo's parking garage after he finally snuck into the building and discovered that the prick parked his car and motorcycle in a corner spot. The area was not very bright. The passenger side door was up against a wall and a three foot wide cement, weight bearing column protected the other side of the SUV and left room for him to park his Harley next to his SUV.

It was a perfect kill zone.

~~~~

Hegewisch is one of the 77 ethnic communities in Chicago. It is located on the southernmost side of the city. It has the most vacant land of any community in the city and it is also home to the only trailer parks in Chicago. The incredible success and popularity of the Harborside International Golf Center and its 36 holes of golf attracts a lot of people to the area. Real estate developers wanted to take advantage of this renewed interest and redevelopment plans resurfaced to build at least 200 new homes.

Hegewisch is bordered on the north by 128th Street, the Illinois/Indiana state line on the east, Brainard Avenue or 138th Street on the south and West Burley Avenue, Torrence Avenue and the

Bishop Ford expressway make up the western border. There is very little crime in this community of blue-collar workers which consist mostly of police officers, firefighters, and city workers.

Heavy earth moving equipment was plowing dirt for the proposed housing project some thirty yards off of West Burley Avenue. Several old wooden telephone poles provided a little obstacle course for the bulldozers. One operator came to a sudden stop when he noticed that he had unearthed what appeared to be the chest bones of a human skeleton.

"Holy shit," he exclaimed and grabbed his cellphone to call his supervisor.

It took less than ten minutes for a police squad car to arrive at the scene. Officer Jack Porter leaned over the bones, put on a pair of latex gloves, and examined the remains barely moving it. Porter went to the academy with detective Tom Polston and decided to call him before he called his supervisor.

"Hey Tommy, it's Porter. I think I have something that is going to be very interesting to you."

"Yeah, haven't heard from you in a while. What's up?" Polston asked with a smile etched in the corner of his lips.

"A bulldozer operator just turned over a human skeleton out here in Hegewisch. I know you are working on that case now with Jack."

"Can you see any arms or legs?"

"Nope! Just the chest, the rib cage. It's still intact. You know what I'm saying?" Porter responded.

"I'll contact Vando, see what he thinks. You better close that site down for now and declare it a crime scene. Don't let anyone near those bones. There could be more bodies," Polston said.

"Copy that."

~~~~

Detective Jack Warren took a furlough day and was sitting next to Peter Michaels in his office. He told his friend immediately about the new find that his partner just told him about.

"Do you think it's going to be another massive grave site?" Michaels asked.

"Not even sure if it is connected to these serial killings. We won't know anything until Vando and his guys get out there and investigate," Warren opined.

"What about Garofalo and the K-9 units?" Michaels asked.

"I am sure they'll call him out there to check. They'll want to clear it." Warren said.

"Let's grab some lunch."

~~~~

Ryan O'Toole never saw the tall blonde woman parking her Mercedes Benz C-300 near the elevators on the third floor. Sandy Isaacson was a retired executive assistant at Chanel 6 News. She knew everything that ever went on at the station and she also knew everyone who ever worked there or visited her boss, the general manager. She was one of those people who had the gift: everyone liked to talk to her. Little went on that she didn't know about.

Isaacson was on her way to Italy with a couple of girlfriends for a twelve day vacation that was planned more than a year ago. She was always very aware of her surroundings because she spent a lot of time talking with Peter Michaels about safety and the crimes he investigated. That's probably the reason she thought it more than a little odd that the man with the beard and reflective aviator sunglasses, who was walking quickly, kept looking over his shoulder at the van he just parked.

She looked at her watch and felt the panic of not getting through security on time for her trip. *It's probably nothing,* she thought and put the incident in the back of her mind.

CHAPTER 71

R yan O'Toole was dressed like a ninja warrior, black field pants, black shoes, a long black sleeve tee shirt and a black baseball cap. He unobtrusively blended into the evening as dusk faded into darkness. It was hot and humid. The moon and the stars were curtained with dark, slow moving, storm clouds allowing only slivers of light to peak out every now and then. Loud thunder roared in the distance signaling a summer squall. The swirly light winds changed the peaceful sounds of wisping tree leaves into an unsympathetic rhapsody of despondency. The streetlight on the corner of Tenth and Wabash was shot out by Number Five's high powered pellet gun shortly after his arrival. He parked his car in an illegal spot without concern of a ticket: he would disappear in a couple of hours after he killed his 38th victim never to be seen again in Chicago. His plan was in motion. He was hanging out near Peter Michaels' condo waiting for his opportunity to sneak into the garage which came at 9:05 pm.

The heavy gray metal garage door groaned as it's motor began the work of lifting its load. O'Toole quickly moved to the condo's rear wall for cover. A black SUV with heavily tinted windows exited the garage and turned left. Number Five hugged the dark bricks, remained still, and waited until the car moved away. He knew he had approximately 18 seconds to make his entrance. He dove under the closing door, moved hunched over to the grimy wall, stood, and started his trek up the ramp. The smell of exhaust smoke and gasoline hung in the humid air confined in a tunnel of concrete and metal. O'Toole's senses were on high alert anticipating another car coming down the ramp, exposing his presence before he could get up to the first floor parking area.

Sweat was flowing down his back, around his neck and into his armpits as he quickly made his way up the ramp. His amber eyes began to sting. He immediately turned to his right, embraced the wall, and slithered to the far dark corner of the garage and the additional protection of a black van. He quieted himself, took some deep breaths and a long drink of water from the bottle that he had in his backpack.

The killer had at least an hour and forty-five minutes to wait before Michaels would get home from the television station. He started to rehearse the kill in his mind. He closed his eyes and smiled, a very evil smile.

~~~~

Peter Michaels couldn't help grinning. He and his partner David Beedy convinced the ten o'clock show producer to give them a minute and a half to report what might be one of the first kills of the O'Toole family. It was no small feat because changing the story lineup on a newscast less than an hour before show time is critical. Michaels didn't get all the information until 9:15.

Sgt. Mike Garofalo and his dog Nosey found the remainder of the bones in the Hegewisch redevelopment area scattered because the bulldozer's blade showed no mercy as it plowed through the hardened earth. It took CSI Tom Vander Aarde several hours to process the scene. There was only one body: the right thumb and the left toe were cut off. Dr. Crine would confirm that the remains were indeed one of the generational serial killer's victims: Perhaps the first one. He would compare the knife's pattern to those of the earlier victims.

Vando had no doubt it was another hitchhiker victim. He told detective Jack Warren, who in turn called Peter Michaels. It was that phone call that convinced the show producer to change the newscast's story line up that late in the night.

It was the lead story. Michaels reported the new findings and then announced that the total number of victims they had discovered so far was 65 and that the remains dated back to the 1920s.

~~~~

Ryan O'Toole was surprised that Michaels' car was parked in its spot and that he must be riding his Harley. This at first perturbed him because he thought number 38 would probably be driven home by one of his friends and all of his preparation and waiting would have been in vain. He broke the overhead light nearest Michaels' parking spot on his recce. His killing plan was set.

The sound of the garage door lifting followed by the sounds of the Harley's Screaming Eagles exhaust pipes dismissed any concern that Michaels got a ride home. O'Toole smiled and moved one row over to the parked cars adjacent to Michaels' spot. He crouched and waited. Perspiration percolated on his forehead; anxiety built. He took deep breaths through his nose and long exhales through his mouth to relax. He fingered the handle of his new 12 inch knife; a reassuring smile creased his lips. His left knee began to ache. *Fuck*, he thought. *Not now.*

Michaels turned left at the top of the ramp and then right, down his parking lane. He stopped his bike and became suspicious; something was wrong, it looked way too dark. He took off his goggles and noticed glass on the floor, looked up and saw the broken light, and he knew immediately that was not right. He took out his cellphone and hit his emergency preprogramed 911 code to alert Jack Warren that there was a problem. He then fingered the small pistol in his pocket. He was glad he wore his leather jacket, but his leather backpack now felt a little heavy.

He put his bike back in gear and slowly drove over the glass pieces on the floor crunching them as he made a wide turn into his parking spot. He killed the ignition and easily slid off his seat and saw some sudden movement in his right rearview mirror. His mind suddenly went into defensive mode, then he heard the crushing sound of glass under the foot falls of his killer moving quickly at Peter Michaels screaming, "Number 38, you cocksucker. You're mine."

Michaels was holding his bike up with his left hand on the handlebar when he turned to meet his attacker head on. He was stunned at the satanic look on Number Five's face and those stunning, wicked yellow eyes. His killer had a knife in his left hand, when he was a few feet away, Michaels pulled his bike down crashing it to the ground. It was an offensive move he discussed with Jack Warren and Brian Alexander last night. O'Toole slammed into the rear wheel causing him to trip, stumble and fall forward with his momentum flinging him into the air. He stretched out with his left hand gripping his knife, reaching forward to stab his target.

In that split second, Michaels turned his body to the right and ducked trying to make himself a slimmer target. He dove to the ground and felt O'Toole's knife go into his leather backpack, torquing his body in the opposite direction. He instantly felt a piercing, lightening like flash of agony in his left shoulder as if it were ripped off of his body. He yelped in pain.

Ryan O'Toole landed on top of the downed motorcycle and winced when his ribs and back hit the handlebars and gas tank. "Fuck. I'll kill you, you son of a bitch," he screamed at the top of his lungs. He was in an awkward position as the bike slid forward like a winter sled slamming into a guardrail of the parking lanes. O'Toole saw stars at the moment his head slammed into the metal rail; blood began to flow down his face. The taste of blood in his mouth reenergized him.

His anger mounted and his desire to kill exploded as he scrambled to get on his feet, fumbling around trying to find level ground to steady himself and continue his attack.

Peter Michaels never experienced excoriating, ripping pain like he now felt in his left shoulder. Tears filled his eyes; he loosened the grip on his revolver and he grabbed his shoulder with his right hand. He put both his feet on the floor, leaned his back against a black Lexus and pushed himself up, using the sedan as leverage to help him stand. He took a deep breath, cleared his head, grit his teeth, reached back into his pocket, and pulled out his MP2, 380.

Both men now stood facing each other. One with a knife. The other with a handgun. Ryan O'Toole's wild rage overtook any sense of doom. He rushed at Peter Michaels with his knife in his left hand raised, screaming, "I'll kill you. You motherfucker."

Peter Michaels was surprised at his internal calm. "Don't do it, O'Toole. Don't do it."

"Fuck you," Number Five yelled and lunged at his prey.

The deafening sounds of the gun shots echoed throughout the garage, ricocheting off the metal vehicles and the cinderblock walls and the concrete floor. The first bullet hit O'Toole in his pubic area slightly above his penis and testicles, stopping him in his tracks momentarily as the impact of the bullet registered some sort of burning sensation in his brain. His wrath so furious that he continued his onslaught like a wild animal moving in for the kill. The second shot entered through his larynx and severed his fourth and fifth cervical vertebra. He collapsed instantly like a marionette puppet as if the puppeteer dropped the stringed control bar. O'Toole's knees buckled to the left, his left hand was over his head, his right hand bent at the elbow next to his chest. The last words that Number Five would ever speak were, "I'll kill y...."

CHAPTER 72

D etective Jack Warren took the stairs two at a time and burst through the parking garage's door. The distinct odor of spent gun powder drifted into the humid air invading the ever present smell of exhaust and gasoline; instant panic flashed through his psyche. "Peter...Peter. Are you alright? Where are you?" He screamed. Perspiration rushed his skin like a rash. His eyes scanning the area searching for his friend.

"Over here, by my spot," Michaels said, breathing heavily, looking down at the body on the ground at his feet. "I think he's still alive. He has a pulse," Michaels said in the voice just above a whisper.

"You okay?"

"I might have a broken shoulder. It hurts. Bad. His knife hit my backpack and spun me around. My shoulder is probably out of its socket. Fuck, it hurts. That move you taught me last night was perfect, although my bike is fucked up."

"Forget the bike. Thank God, you're not dead," Warren said as he knelt down and put his fingertips on O'Toole's carotid artery searching for a pulse. He found one, but blood was barley pumping into his motionless body. He looked at the dying man's wide-opened, motionless amber eyes then O'Toole blinked and Warren jerked his hand back. "Fuck, he's one scary son of a bitch and he is alive."

The assassin's face was covered in blood from the cut on the top of his head. His amber eyes were searching for anything that made sense; the ceiling, right then left, then empty and hopeless. O'Toole was trying to figure out his situation. He could not speak. He could not move his legs or arms. Tears escaped from the corners of his eyes and trickled down the sides of his face making small, thin tracks that disappeared into his beard.

The entrance wound in his throat looked like a spot of blood the size of a dime. Warren pulled out his radio, "This is detective Jack Warren. Badge number 1437. I need an ambo at 880 South Michigan Avenue in the parking garage, forthwith. Use the back garage door off Tenth to gain entrance. It will be open."

~~~~

EMT Joan Myers arrived on the scene a few minutes later. She applied pressure on the killer's wounds, cleaned up the blood, and applied bandages. She wrapped his neck in a soft cloth collar to stabilize him. She put an oxygen mask over his nose and mouth. O'Toole's breathing was shallow and slow. His face was ashen. His amber eyes on the verge of lifelessness.

Ryan O'Toole, the fifth, felt no pain. He was paralyzed from the neck down. He apparently could hear what was being said around him, but he could utter no words, the bullet shattered his larynx. When his eyes were open they searched, darting from one side to the other. His amber eyes also painted a tapestry of despair on his black soul; scared, panicky, terrified, timorous, fearful.

The conversations between the EMTs working heroically to save him left no doubt in Number Five's foggy mind that he would be paralyzed for the rest of his life: Alive but helpless. The only thing left in his future was insanity: haunted by everything he ever did in his life.

A dead man breathing. He wanted to kill himself but couldn't. There was absolutely no one in his life that cared about him. No one that he knew at least.

~~~~

Dr. Robert Crine confirmed in less than five minutes that the newly discovered body in Hegewisch was killed by the same person that killed four of the people discovered at the Edgebrook golf course. He took samples for DNA analysis and sent them to the FBI in Quantico.

He called Deborah Duke and told her to expect the samples to develop another family tree for what may well be one of the very first victims of the O'Tooles.

~~~~

There were more than 30 parking tickets on the windshield of a White KIA SUV illegally parked on Tenth Street and Wabash Avenue. It dawned on detective Jack Warren that the car may belong to Ryan O'Toole because they never figured out how he got to Peter Michaels' condo on the night of the attack. Warren got out of his car and found the VIN number (Vehicle Identification Number) and ran it through the Secretary of State's office and discovered it belonged to a Reginald Sampson, the new alias of Ryan O'Toole, discovered by Peter Michaels.

Warren got a search warrant the following day and found the trophy jars filled with thumbs, toes, and ears. Everyone was totally shocked when they discovered that the O'Tooles killed 121 people over the last 100 years.

Peter Michaels finally figured out what O'Toole meant when he started running at him that night. He told Warren, "Remember me telling you that O'Toole hollered 38 when charged toward me. I bet that it meant I was his 38th victim."

"I bet you're right. This is some very sick shit. They have already shipped those trophies for further analysis."

~~~~

The day Sandy Isaacson got back from Italy she was exhausted but determined to call Peter Michaels and tell him about the suspicious man and the dark van with the white stripe that was parked at O'Hare. It drove her crazy for her entire vacation.

"I don't know if it's anything or not Peter but you always told me to trust my gut. My gut tells me it ain't right. So there, I told you."

"Thanks, Sandy that shouldn't be hard to check out. I'll pass it on," Michaels said.

It turned out to be a great tip and another incredible story. The van was filthy with dirt, dust, and detritus. There was the distinct smell of death escaping from the vehicle when the police arrived. Officers popped the door lock and discovered three coolers that contained three heads.

Closure finally came to the families of Henry Rudishman, Terry Peterson and another young man named Christopher Strackler that was reported missing twelve years ago. All of them had Ryan O'Toole the fifth's signature knife pattern marks on their necks.

~~~~

Peter Michaels was in physical therapy. His fingers climbing up a peg board on the wall exercising his left shoulder to avoid surgery when his phone rang. He looked at the caller ID. "Hey Deborah how are you doing? Haven't heard from you in a while. What's up?"

"First of all, How are you?"

"I'm good actually. Trying to avoid an operation. That son of a bitch really messed up my shoulder but the doctor says this therapy should help. It's feeling better every day, but that's not why you called."

"You're right. I wanted to be the first to tell before I call the authorities. That young man they just found. He was the easiest victim we have ever identified."

"Yeah, why is that?" Michaels asked forgetting the pain in his left shoulder.

"His name was Vincent Carey. He was reported missing in September of 1921. His family's DNA is on file with the Chicago Police Department." Duke informed.

"He was a cop?" Michaels asked, his attention fully focused.

"No. He wasn't a cop but someone from his family since the time he disappeared back then has become a police officer. There have been fourteen Careys on the job since 1924."

"Wait. Don't tell me, Chief of Patrol, William Carey, is related?" Michaels asked incredulously.

"Yep, one in the same. I wanted to tell you so you could get an exclusive with him. He'll be notified within the hour," Duke said.

"Thanks for the heads up. I owe you," Michaels said.

"You don't owe me anything. Peter thanks for bringing me in on this investigation. I have never worked on anything so challenging," Duke said in a soft voice. "Good luck. Take care of yourself."

"Thanks, you too. I'll be in touch," Michaels said and hung up. He stood and was about to put his phone in his pocket when it vibrated again. He didn't recognize the 480 area code but he always answered his phone.

"Hello, this is Peter Michaels."

"Peter. It's Clare."

Tears immediately filled his eyes and began to filter down his cheeks. He involuntarily fell into the orange plastic chair next to his locker stunned, his lips quivered, his mouth was scorched, his heart felt like it was in A-fib. He could not speak. His head tilted between his shoulders. He never felt this vulnerable in his life and then it hit him; He really was so lucky to be alive. He smiled and said, "Hey."

BOOKS BY PETER KARL

You Can't Win…Unless
(An Investigative look at the game of blackjack)

Why is a Simple Game So Hard?
(A. Duffer)

<u>Peter Michaels Thriller Series</u>

On the Night of a Blood Moon

Bug Man

Amber Eyes

<u>Coming Soon</u>

Lifting Waites
A Political Thriller

Copy That
A Peter Michaels Thriller

ABOUT THE AUTHOR

Peter Karl is a retired award-winning television investigative reporter who has been inducted into the prestigious Silver Circle of the National Television Society of Arts and Sciences for his work that spanned over 40 years. Karl is the recipient of 11 Chicago Regional Emmy Awards, the esteemed George Foster Peabody Award, two DuPont-Columbia Awards, the Robert F. Kennedy Award for journalism excellence and he was once named the national Sigma Delta Chi Investigative Reporter of the year. Karl has also been the recipient of death threats during his career as he reported on police scandals, corrupt politicians, mafia kingpins, drug dealers and some of Chicago's most ruthless street gangs.

Made in the USA
Monee, IL
07 August 2023

40603884R00215